EXCRUCIATING BLISS

EXCRUCIATING BLISS

A NOVEL BY
JON DAVIS

Published by FRENCH PRESS
281 112th Avenue SE
Suite 5
Bellevue, WA 98004
USA

2012 Paperback, Second Edition

www.AuthorJonDavis.com

Twitter: @authorjondavis
Facebook: www.facebook.com/authorjondavis

Library of Congress Cataloging-In-Publication Data
LC Control No.: 2011922889
Excruciating Bliss / Jon Davis
2012 Paperback Edition
Bellevue, WA: French Press, 2011
1105
p. cm
978-0615652955

Printed In the United States of America

ALSO BY JON DAVIS

Thieves, Whores & Dinosaurs

January

According to the gauntlet of intellectuals I'd been subjected to those last three years in college, an artist can only create a masterpiece if he is starving. While I didn't disagree with them as they were all well-paid geniuses, I questioned the statement in one way: can an artist be malnourished on a psychological level and not simply on a physiological one? As countless academics and their students leisurely pondered this same thing, I found I had to answer the question, as it wasn't my stomach craving fulfillment, it was my soul. Unable to recall the last time my thirst for something innovative and avant-garde had been doused, it appeared both my generation and nation were undergoing a cultural famine. The New American Youth was staring at blankness waiting for a revelation.

I emerged from my adolescence in the Age of Terror just after the turn of the millennium. I recall those years as the epoch of ignorant excess, borrowed fortune, widespread conspicuous consumption, drunken frivolity and celebrated greed. The youth were empowered and entitled, the elderly were over-medicated and made voiceless, and subsequently incarcerated. Degenerates were imprisoned, and everyone else confined to the jobs they hated but were too infirm and afraid to seek a change.

At the age of 22 I found myself living in Seattle. At the time I deplored the city, having only moved there to attend college. Today I have the wisdom of knowing there were far worse cities to become an adult in. I suppose the misery I felt in those years was the manifestation of yearning for something new. Oh to be awestruck by unfamiliarity! The Pacific Northwest could feel dreadfully isolated sometimes, especially in wintry January. I'd lived in Washington State all my life and traveled very little in my youth. As a teen I'd always dreamed of moving someplace chic like Manhattan or London. Somewhere I would start a fabulous life just like on television where the only thing I did at my high-paying white-collar job was mingle with fashionable friends while simultaneously epitomizing the utmost in style. It was the kind of fantasy where at the end of the day I'd giddily bounce home to a plush and expansive apartment filled with witty, nostalgic knickknacks and conversation pieces only an interior designer could conjure up. In this delusion I'd make love to my model of a mate multiple times nightly. It was the kind of vision where everything appeared perfect, and now in retrospect, was an illusion I held out in front of myself in order to summon the motivation to escape a place devoid of anything greater than mediocrity.

In September I was to return for my fourth year at the University of Washington. Even though the school was marvelous and most of my professors capable intellects, no matter what subject I studied I couldn't help but feel like I was on an assembly line. In giant stadium-like auditoriums I'd sit with thousands of fellow students for hours in the dark, listening to my instructors showcase their infinite knowledge.

The most liberating experience in my life up to that point was to drop out of college. At the time I told my parents I was taking a hiatus from college, informing them via email: "I need to take a year off for individual study." I did this in order to maintain my weekly allowance of $50, which in those days felt like a lot of money. To have lost that would have meant having to move back home, something neither party wanted.

Growing up I was under the impression that college was supposed to be the guaranteed free ride and that those who graduated were to effortlessly obtain rich and fabulous lives. The power of the college degree seemed like yet another myth to me. Everyone had a degree: the guy selling cigarettes at the gas station (a Bachelor's from Notre Dame in marketing); the busty tattooed redhead striping for dollars at the Lucky Lady on First Avenue (a MBA from UCLA). And I, a lonely accounting clerk, had 75% of a Bachelors of Arts degree with a major in photography. No matter how much I tried to convince myself to finish the program, I couldn't help but dread how inconsequential an education was. I didn't know at the time that twenty years later I'd long to return to those halls to hear those scholars debate and to witness formerly dormant young minds coming alive with contemplation and imagination. In my later years I'd think about returning to college, only to pass on the idea, not wanting to be mistaken for the professor by the young students.

What I don't regret about departing university life was having my parents drop $25,000 a year whilst I loathe the whole experience. I felt bad not having qualified for any scholarships or grants. But as an upper-middle-class male with only moderately good grades, the only organization that was willing to give me a free education was the U.S. military. Regretfully, I could have applied for a scholarship for gay students but that would have included telling my parents I was a homosexual, something I wasn't ready to do.

Teens today use college as an excuse to leave home and start a life of independence and decisions. For me the only thing exciting about going to college was the potential to freely engage in sex and drink all sorts of booze. It's embarrassing to admit the reason I went to college was for the sex, but when you're a closeted homosexual living with two conservative parents, the chance to live without their conformist ideas and mere presence can be almost as enticing as seeing a hot guy. Not to say I don't love my parents, they were just hicks who didn't understand what it was like to be fundamentally and secretly different than the majority of society.

I was born, raised, and oppressed in La Conner, a very small but lovely seaside town on the pebbly banks of the Upper Puget Sound, 55 miles north of Seattle. Today the town is considered a suburb of the ever-sprawling Seattle metro but when I was a kid our town couldn't have felt farther from civilization. Before it was the diminutive tourist enclave and picturesque artist's colony it is today, La Conner was a fishing village, home to more boats than people and a culture dedicated to this one industry. Men worked from before sunrise and well after dawn and did very little else with their lives. Women raised babies and maintained the house — they had no further expectations than this. Somehow the social paradigm of the 1950s had been preserved in that fishing village, where the only thing narrower than the gravel country roads were the minds of the people who lived there. It was the kind of community where you could either be a man or a woman, your role predetermined by what you had between your legs. There were no options, no pathways to eccentricity, and nothing extraordinary about anyone was embraced. People lived to live, and that was all. Occasions were celebrated with vanilla cake, weekends spent cleaning the house or tending the yard, and nobody questioned anything. People travelled rarely, and when they did it was almost always to visit a sick relative or attend a funeral. It was all just the way it was. Still and unadorned, without purpose or meaning, as those two things were never comprehended, let alone questioned in public. If you had a crisis of spirituality you went to church and asked a man named Jesus for some insight. If you were excluded or felt alienated from the church because of a secret you had, such as a sexual identity that was unappreciated in such locales, then you were on your own. Jesus couldn't help someone who chose "sin" without shame or guilt.

My peers at high school had the same conservative beliefs as my parents. I can remember many times in class any mention of Seattle would result with someone making a comment about the "freaks," "liberals," "fags" or "snobs" who lived there. At the same time any mention of Seattle would stir my own voracious curiosity. To me, Seattle was the capital of cool, the mythical graveyard of grunge and the prosperous playground of some of the world's richest and most industrious people. And it was the one place it was okay to be a freak. In bucolic La Conner I certainly felt like one.

Regardless of societal isolation, through television and magazines I decided early on I would have an enviable, stylish, metropolitan life. At the age of 18 I saved everything I had earned from a summer of bagging groceries and moved into my dorm at the University of Washington. The excitement of living in a giant city overwhelmed me. Unlike La Conner, where after six o'clock at night you could walk down the middle of the street with a blindfold on and not worry about getting hit by a car, the streets of Seattle were always packed, millions of people going everywhere all the time, the pace never ceasing. The excitement I felt just from being near chaos pulsated within me. It was then I knew I was what those farmers back home called a "city boy" and Seattle was the gateway to my cosmopolitan dream. To think there were cities ten times larger in population (New York!) intensified my desire to see, explore, devour and just live the world.

· · ·

Riding the bus to work made me uncomfortably aware of society's absolute lack of personal discretion. In the crowded, steamy bus people would feel at ease discussing anything. I could have been sitting there reading the Help Wanted Ads and I'd hear a cell phone ring, a moment later, "Hello… hi… no I haven't got my results yet, I'm on the way to the doctor right now… No, if it's positive I told him I was going to abort it… I don't care, the man's a loser… I'm not having any of his kids!"

Sex, divorce, STDs, ex-lovers, politics, and especially religion… if it was taboo, it was discussed at full volume on the bus. A relief it was to get off the bus and arrive at work. For a moment anyway.

Despite a moderate paying job that stressed me endlessly, I considered things could be worse. I worked in accounting at OmniCare Northwest, a large group of 95 idiotic specialist physicians. Prior to working for doctors I was under the impression you had to have a brain to be one. That's not the case. You wouldn't believe how stupid they are. I realized how humanly foolish doctors are at the company Christmas party. OmniCare rented a shitty Elks Club-style banquet hall in some Seattle suburb (did I mention doctors are cheap too?). Anyway, every single doctor brought their entire goddamn family while employees were limited one guest (needless to say I brought zero). There was dancing and feasting by the doctors while their employees were subtlety herded off the dance floor. All night the doctors failed to acknowledge us. Not one of them asked me what my name was or what I did. The closest thing I got to conversing with one was when an Endocrinologist handed me his car keys and asked me to park his Land Rover.

My first and only acquaintance at the company was Cara Jacobs, who I met at the above referenced Christmas party. Unlike the majority of my co-workers (a herd of fat, sassy, hormonally imbalanced middle-aged women lacking any refinement, and who all seem to be transplants from Atlanta or Chicago), Cara was friendly and had much of the same tasteful nature I had. The best part of knowing Cara was her gossip. She always filled me in on the current social standings and hearsay of everyone in the office. She knew who was gay, who was a curious, who beat their kids, and which managers to avoid. It was the only source of titillation in that dreadful office.

Cara was sensational, bawdy, 29, and an unforgiving slut who'd tell me all about the men she slept with, usually a new one every weekend. I fantasized what it must've been like to be her, having casual sex with men who were undoubtedly hot. Up to that point Cara was the most attractive woman I'd ever become friends with. She typified a certain female archetype I'd seen on television. It was exhilarating to see one living and breathing right before my eyes. She was into handbags and designer clothes, even though she couldn't afford them. In a way I wanted to be her. Not because she had a vagina but because she was confident. I almost envied her for being a tramp, something I would've been if I wasn't so cursedly reserved.

What I liked most about Cara was she didn't care about anyone other than herself. I don't know if it's from being raised on a farm, but one of my most maddening attributes was my inability *not* to dislike people. I got along with everyone I worked with. It drove me insane not having the ability to speak my mind.

Once upon a monotonous afternoon I was copying a billing manual in the basement of our building when a young man by the name of Thomas Jennings introduced himself to me as he entered the Xerox dungeon. Thomas had a corporate hunk vibe about him, always dressing with a tie even though our office was business casual and did not require one. I had never wore I tie to work so when I saw someone wearing one I assumed they had some sort of leadership position. I'm not the first to note that power is an aphrodisiac.

Thomas explained he worked in Human Resources and their copier had broken down. He asked if I would mind him using my department's machine. Considering the reputation of our copiers I figured it wouldn't be long before I'd be asking to borrow his. I also thought doing him a favor might result in a new friendship, dreaming he'd ask me out on a date and we'd become passionate lovers.

"Go right a*head*" I jested, Freudianly emphasizing "head." I'm not sure he noticed the inflection.

Thomas was a bit taller than me, probably six-foot-three. His ass looked firm and his arms thick, his waste absent of love handles and legs proportionate to the rest of his athletic body. He was a diamond in the very rough. Most of the other men at OmniCare were over 40, fat, bald, knew not of deodorant and liked to eat onions at lunch. The pessimist in me concluded Thomas might just be a temp, or worse, straight.

As Thomas made several copies I stood behind him arranging the papers I planned to copy, making sure to check him out liberally. I could tell he was older than me, probably a hair past 30. No big deal, an older man could educate me on the ways of the world, and bedroom.

"So you're new here, right?" he asked turning around just as my eyes went from inspecting the front of his trousers to carefully reading whatever the hell it was I was copying.

"Six months. I've been here since June," I replied distractedly, as if the documents I held in front of me were both captivating and important.

"Six months," he pondered, "I can't believe I haven't noticed you before."

"I'm easy to miss," I sulked.

"What position?" he asked. I don't need to explain what my first thought was.

"Accounting... I'm the second assistant to the associate supervisor," I chirped as if my title were prestigious. It basically meant entry level.

"So you're on the *bottom?*" he simplified, emphasizing the word "bottom," which I picked up on immediately. I thought to myself that my reaction to this blatant come-on should be timely and business appropriate. Then a moment passed; I didn't know what to say. Thoughts of exclaiming in porn video style "fuck me now" filled my mind and then I tried to think of something else but I couldn't. I just smiled at him and snickered. Images of us going at it on top of the copy machine filled my head. These images were graphic and even included the idea of genitalia being pressed on to the copy machine's glass, creating strange and wonderful collated documents for the whole office to enjoy. As Thomas walked away I conjured another image of the Xerox repair man contemplating how a sticky white substance got inside the duplex mechanism.

Did someone just flirt with me? Who was this guy? How in the hell did I get in such an exciting situation? I had so many questions I knew I must pay a visit to Cara. Whenever I had a question about anyone's personal life at the company, Cara was the one to consult. She didn't know a thing about business, but when it came to who was fucking who, if Cara didn't know then nobody did.

"Thomas Jennings? The name sounds familiar," Cara implored as she shuffled through the annals of her brain while arranging papers on her desk, an attempt to appear as if she were multi-tasking. "Oh yes, Tommy. He's been spotted at the mix bars."

"Mix bars?" I questioned, unfamiliar with the term.

"Yeah, the clubs where it's gay and straight. Mostly dance music but the crowd gets along. Haven't you ever been to a mix club?" she inquired. I was embarrassed to tell her the truth.

"Club! I've never even been to a bar, let alone a club."

Cara gasped so widely I could see she still had her molars. "No wonder you're lonely. You need to put a little nightlife into your life."

I huffed at her suggestion. The idea seemed simple. I didn't know what was keeping me from going out at night. Maybe it was my lack of friends. Who wanted to go clubbing alone? Then I imagined how appealing a stranger who is confident enough in his tough, loner status could be. Certainly people went out by themselves sometimes. Why hadn't I ever gone alone?

"You're right. But what *life*?" I began to pout. "I'm pathetic. I'm 22, I have a shitty job, no boyfriend, no savings. According to society, at 22 I'm supposed to be engaged, have a kid on the way, be mid-to-lower management while actively clawing my way to the top of some glamorous company like Nordstrom or Microsoft."

"Shut the hell up," Cara countered in a whisper. "Maybe at 42. At 22 our generation hasn't moved out of the house, let alone discovered the exhilarating liberty of having what is called a career."

Cara was right. But I still felt like a failure in the making. When I was younger I always imagined my twenties being filled with endless pleasure... parties, concerts, art society... where was it all? The life I craved was either waiting to be initiated or was just a fantasy.

"I remember a man once came into the office and took Tom out for lunch," Cara burst in recollection. "Rumors were swirling."

"Probably just his brother," I replied, always clinging to the most cynical of likely circumstances.

"I know how we can invade his privacy and potentially break the law doing so," Cara quipped. "When all else fails, MediWeb!"

MediWeb was a giant network of medical information that insurance companies, physicians and pharmacies used to track their patients' medical records. For some reason everyone in the office, whether their job required it or not, had unlimited use of this potentially disastrous little tool. The most common abuse of MediWeb was looking up celebrities in the system and selling their most intimate and federally protected medical information to tabloids. The software's ability to invade one's privacy was truly notable. In searching for a patient's records, parameters such as sex, hair color, weight, city of residence, employer and age could be used to locate their profile. This was meant to locate patient information for unconscious people in the hospital who had no identifying information on them. In turn, from just a casual knowledge of a person you could find their complete medical history, some of which included photos of their various health conditions, like herpes lesions. It was wonderful!

"Here it is, I found him," Cara delicately announced as she pulled up the account.

"Don't you feel dirty?" I nagged. Cara made a wild grin leading me to believe she loved to snoop.

Cara clicked on PHYSICIAN CLAIMS HISTORY and watched as several doctor visits appeared on the computer screen. She clicked on the most recent with a Dr. Frank Malloy, an Internal Medicine specialist. Once the visit opened the physician's dictation appeared on screen. Cara quietly read aloud some of the notes from Tom's visit.

"...patient complains of irregular diarrhea, along with abdominal cramps, denies blood in stool. Patient is possible candidate for Irritable Bowel Syndrome drug study..."

"What's irritable bowel syndrome?" I asked.

"It means his boyfriend has a really big dick," Cara laughed. I was disgusted but couldn't help but giggle a tiny bit.

Suddenly, Cara's telephone rang. To both Cara and my surprise, OmniCare Northwest had in recent months implemented a new Information Technologies Securities Manager whose job it was to ensure all patient information was being used for legitimate purposes. In the previous weeks Cara's computer had been flagged by the system as a suspicious user, causing an investigation into why she was using the MediWeb function on her user account. When she accessed a colleague's account her supervisor was alerted. Cara's ass was booted out the door that afternoon. She even received a fine of $500 from the Washington State Department of Health for illegal use of confidential medical documents. I was in no way implicated by her wrongdoings, which I heartily condemn. Her firing nonetheless intensified my resentment for OmniCare.

. . .

Less than a full month into the New Year I discovered my job was killing me. It wasn't the actual work I found torturous, it was the office itself. I could feel the abundance of fluorescent lights poisoning me. If it weren't for Thomas Jennings, the glimmering and beautiful young opportunity for romance just down the hall, I probably would have found a new job just after Cara was canned.

Being one of only five men in an office of 45 women was maddening. Every one of the ladies in the office seemed to be at that age in life where she was either pregnant, just had a kid, or was in the deep dark hot-flashing midst of menopause. Their desks were covered in photos of babies and kids, all of which looked identical to me. I was all for personalizing one's environ, as I had done by decorating my cubicle with art postcards from the Museum of Modern Art. What was so tedious about working with these women was that no matter what a conversation was about, it would always end up being about their kids. Nonstop, all day I unintentionally overheard conversations such as: "…the doctor was worried because I was only dilated to seven centimeters when little Madison started her descent. I just wanted to say 'hold on honey, mommy's not ready yet. You don't want to rip me open now do ya?'" Then the mother would laugh and ask her coworker "isn't that just hilarious?" to which they'd insist it was, although it was probably the third or fourth time they'd heard that story.

I was always fascinated how one of these Office Mommies could be asked a perfectly non-family question, like "Sally, do you know where the printer cartridges are kept?" and they'd reply with something like "Last night my husband came home and Jefferson had wet his diaper. My husband, being the darling he is, volunteered to change him and when he did Jefferson peed on his hand. Isn't that the funniest thing you've heard in your entire life?" No matter the circumstance they could turn a conversation in to an anecdote about their kids. I dreamed of replying: "No, it's sedate and boring. You must really have a pathetic life if your son pissing on your husband is the highlight of your evening. Now where's the fucking toner bitch!?!"

At the time I assumed something happened to a woman when she had a baby; a sort of hormonal or psychological change that reprioritized everything. Giving birth seemed to compel women to give up their own lives in order to care for a newborn. At that age, in that office, I couldn't think of anything I'd want less than a child. I was in to feeding only my wants and desires. I was still trying to raise myself and to bring a new person in to the world and having to care for it would have meant sacrificing a life's journey yet to be embarked upon. I suppose my negative view of the women in the office could have been borne from jealousy. They were able to do something I would never be able to: produce a child. And because of that I decided I would somehow get to do things they would never have the pleasure of doing. Things like seeing the world and learning more about life than could ever be taught in a classroom or from checking out books in a library. If I couldn't have what they did, I was going to get my hands on something they couldn't. I just didn't know what that was.

The repetition of the Monday to Friday, 9-to-5 grind began tearing me up. Fed up with the bus, I opted to walk to work. Every morning was hell trying to find the energy inside my still sleeping body to crawl up the street to the office on top of First Hill, and every afternoon lazily drifting back down the hill, mysteriously tired from sitting on my ass all day. I couldn't count the number of times I'd schlepped down the hill, got to my apartment, and without warning just fell asleep, most of the time right on the floor in front of the TV. Once I even fell asleep in a chair in the lobby while waiting for the elevator. This sort of incident got me worried. What if it had been the street I'd fallen asleep on? I could have been man-raped. So embarrassing it was waking up in the chair, door key in hand, waiting for the elevator that had come and gone. I didn't know how much time had elapsed while I was asleep, but in a building the size of the one I lived, a 20-minute nap could have meant a dozen people coming through the lobby.

I've always found it ironic and amusing that I worked for a company that prescribed anti-depressants by the truck load, yet I was the most depressed person I knew. I couldn't remember the last time I felt good about being myself, or when the last time I said "I like me!" I dreaded my life for many reasons, mostly due to the lack of friends. And the ambition to do great things with my life was gone. The job I once found tolerable, if not slightly enjoyable, had turned sour. There was seemingly no light at the end of the sewer tunnel I was living in.

But I was determined to get help, even without the aid of an expensive therapist. Using the Internet (caution!) and the enormous resources of the Seattle Public Library, I treated myself for depression. Through self-help books and psycho-analysis studies I found the simplest of cures: do whatever makes you happy (if it's legal). In the past I recognized my tendency to be more calm and cheerful when in the midst of art. A sporadic journey to the nearest museum could often eliminate my sulking. But like many treatments, the effectiveness of the museum soon wore off and I began a search for a new remedy.

Other times when I'd felt dejected, merely reminding myself of how fortunate I was had been a successful means of elevating my spirits. So, I said to myself, "Jimmy, your apartment is deluxe and fairly large. You have great furniture." The statement was affirmative and I believed it to be true until another, more apprehensive voice inside me cried, "The apartment is average and unquestionably overpriced. You purchased all the furniture with credit cards and now struggle to find the money to pay the minimum payment each month." Shocked I might have a multiple personality or just a self-abusive one, I decided right then I had to answer the question I'd been putting off since I first comprehended it at the age of 17: *When will I be happy?*

The answer had to be out there, I just didn't know it yet. I tried again to be an optimist, to list all the great attributes I had (thick hair, nice eyes, caring personality, straight teeth). But no matter how many I noted all I could think was *it's not enough*!

Maybe it's because I'm an American, or a male, or just the precarious combination, but when I declared "I want more" the request startled me. How dare I want more? I already lived in the richest, fattest, and most pampered nation in existence. How could I possibly be unsatisfied? Suddenly another question came to mind: when is I *deserve* more warranted when we have so much to be thankful for? I conceded there may not be a god, no reason to live, only debt and questions. At the end of a life the only thing in abundance might just be discontent.

FEBRUARY

I was a wee-bit hung over when I stumbled into the office 45 minutes late having celebrated the Chinese New Year the previous night by myself. I sat down at my desk to find work had piled up (I'd called in sick on Thursday because I had a cough and again on Friday to see a movie… again, by myself). A set of pamphlets with account numbers and corresponding passwords had been due for distribution on Friday. I was horrified to discover I'd yet to copy the 200-page manuals.

Upon entering the copy room I was delighted to find my favorite guy from H/R using one of the machines. He looked stunned when I entered, as if I'd caught him copying his dick.

"Hi there," he said, nervously accompanied with a twinge of a smile. As he attempted to remove what he was copying he accidentally dropped a bright green sheet of paper at my feet. As I leaned down to pick it up I read: "LIVE! FEB 7th – GREASY FECES @ THE MOORE." It was a promotional flyer for a concert.

"Going into advertising?" I said smiling, comforting his apparent fear I would relay word of his inappropriate use of the copy machine to his boss.

"Yeah, my band is playing The Moore and I didn't want to go to Kinkos. It's so expensive."

"I know what you mean," I agreed and said something that most certainly was the gin from the previous evening talking: "I'll be honest and admit I've copied a few questionable items down here in my day." When the phrase was in my head it sounded timid and fun. But out loud it sounded lewd. He laughed anyway.

"Thanks. I mean, anyone else probably would've told their supervisor I was using this thing for personal use."

"*Please!*" I said, rolling my eyes flirtatiously. "Do you know how many people take home boxes of tissue and coffee creamer packets? Everyone steals! I saw one lady in data entry take home a printer. Nobody said anything."

There was a sudden, precarious silence. I may have sounded like I was advocating theft, which I wasn't. As I loaded my masters into the copier he stood there as if he wanted to ask me something. Tired of the constant innuendo between us I nervously asked, "Can I have one of those flyers? I've been looking for a reason to go out." Once again, the sentence sounded innocent in my head but out loud sounded as if I was implying I wanted to go out to see him.

"The Moore? That's a gay bar isn't it?" I blurted without consideration. How is it that alcohol can give a person so much confidence but so little acumen?

"No," he replied sternly. At first I feared he'd taken offense to my assumption. But then came something so unexpected I knew romance between us was inevitable, "We were playing the whole gay scene but pretty much every queer bar in town got sick of us. So we're playing for the straight kids too." Tom and I were now at a timeless crossroads of who would ask the age old question, "Are you gay or do you just *look* like a homosexual?"

Thomas suddenly excused himself from the room, citing an H/R emergency. I was left with the bright green flyer, which I viewed as my key to discovering Thomas's true personality. His coy demeanor seemed a cover for his inner queer, or so I imagined.

That entire week I anticipated Greasy Feces' show at the Moore. Counting down the days to see Tom and his band in rock star regalia only made the wait seem lengthier. But eventually Friday night came around and I was one of the first in line to see the show. The Moore was one of those giant, old, dirty theatre-turned-music venues where the floors were covered in at least three layers of sticky mystery fluid you'd get an STD from if you were so unfortunate enough to fall down. The place was surely not my scene but if a boyfriend resulted, the exposure was worth the disgust. Advertisements for various festivities were plastered all about the theater. Thomas Jennings, H/R office pretty boy by day turned into Tommy Knockers at night, lead singer of Greasy Feces, a Brit-pop wannabe post-grunge troop of two drag queens playing guitar, a drummer dressed as Ronald Reagan, and himself, a dark vinyl-clad Maybelline wearing cyber punk. The look was stunning and provocative but not nearly as sexy as Tom's dayside attire of shirt and tie.

The crowd of Goth girls and biker boys were uproariously rowdy. Fortunately the drinks were cheap and strong. I was on my third cocktail just before the show was to start. The thought of Tom doing naughty and shocking things to his band mates in order to entice the crowd thrilled me. The band, all wearing skimpy black women's lingerie came out to a roaring mass as the music began. Well, I guess you could call it music. It was a cacophony of screaming and what sounded like the vicious torture of a four piece band mixed with some synthetic pre-recorded pulsing sounds. Honestly, the music was tripe and I lost interest forty seconds into their set. But it wasn't just the show I came for, it was the backstage antics afterward.

As Greasy Feces played into their final song, an ode to Ziggy Stardust, I made my way to the restroom. Unable to walk upright without assistance, I gently held on to anything and anyone I could on the way to the urinal. As I peed for what seemed like hours I heard the music stop and the crowd roar as another band took over the stage. The cheering and screaming made my mind spin and just as I was zipping up and attempting to wash my hands I had the overwhelming urge to sit down. I clawed my way into a stall and sat down on the toilet.

In the stall everything was spinning. I puked on the floor and then had the wisdom to launch the forthcoming round of vomit into the toilet. I must have continued randomly puking for ten minutes until I heard some mischievous giggling from the stall next to mine. Drunk and curious, I peeked through a glory hole cut in the stall wall. In my spinning daze I witnessed Tom Jennings standing in the other stall as his erect penis was suckled by two college-age groupies, one of them wearing a Hello Kitty T-Shirt, the other wearing a vinyl tube top with claw marks in it.

I puked again.

As Thomas began to squeal and come in the neighboring stall I began to crawl out of the bathroom.

I felt a lot more sober on the walk home thanks to the vomiting. The city was quiet compared to the club, which was comforting. When I got home the image of Thomas having his dick sucked by the two women sickened me and I couldn't fall asleep as it was the only thing I saw when I closed my eyes.

On Monday as I sat at my desk updating the general ledger in between glances at a fabulous new Pottery Barn catalog, Thomas stopped by.

"What'd you think of the show Friday?" he eagerly baited. His questioning startled me as I was busy adoring some silk drapes.

"The show," I said at once, uncertain of how to tell him I hated it. "It blew me away." The wrong choice of words, but he wouldn't catch the reference.

Thomas explained Greasy Feces was playing at a bar in Tacoma the following Saturday and I could get in half price if I mentioned his name.

As he gushed about how great their music was all I could think of was how badly I wanted him to leave my desk. The sight of him in any circumstance tormented me. I had done to Tom what I'd been doing to many straight men before him, and that was to fall in love with him before I even knew him. My imagination, too furtive for its own good, generated fanciful romantic ideas of him and I, so much so I'd began believing what I was dreaming.

Tom seemed overtly friendly toward me for another week. He probably misconstrued my politeness as the behavior of an admiring fan. I'm sure he genuinely wanted to be my friend. But the agony of having him come by my desk multiple times daily began wearing on me and I eventually told him, in so many words, I had no interest in his music.

• • •

It was one of those shitty, shitty, shitty February afternoons on a Sunday that I chose to go grocery shopping. It was a very stupid idea as it was raining, and it was certainly not one of those typical Seattle rainstorms that is misty and indecisive. This was full-blown cyclone rain. The kind of precipitation that New Yorkers who'd moved to Seattle called "East Coast rain."

I was dragging in probably twelve grocery bags in to the lobby of my apartment building. Every bag was bulging they were so full. As I reached to press for the elevator button, one of the bags, of course, burst open. Cans and jars went rolling every which way, and wouldn't you know it, the elevator door opened just then.

As I stooped to retrieve my spilled cans I instantly felt a wave of embarrassment take me, noticing someone exiting the elevator. I glanced up to see a towering blonde girl who looked my age, maybe younger. I immediately noticed how well dressed she was. From the tailoring of her jacket and the subtle, exotic fragrance that wafted about her I presumed she was rich. She was extraordinarily beautiful, but not in that pedestrian sort of way. Her body was lean and graceful, her muscles covered in movie star skin. The little makeup she wore was tasteful and restrained, only a hint to accent her amazing eyes and lips. She reminded me of Cara Jacobs, the girl from work who'd spend all her money on designer clothes even though she was months behind on the rent.

This mysterious girl immediately paused when she saw I'd blown a bag. Without hesitation she helped me collect the cans and find room for them in the other bags.

"Same thing happened to me yesterday," she said, chasing after a can of pinto beans rolling toward the lobby door.

"Oh don't bother, I can get these," I said, trying to find a bag I could use to carry the beans in. "But thank you."

"I'm Loren," she said handing me the can of pintos along with a finely manicured hand to shake. "You're the first neighbor I've met."

"Jimmy." We shook hands and as we did she picked up some of the grocery bags I'd set down. My first thought was that she planned to run off with them when I turned my back. But then I noticed her Christian Dior high heels. She could neither run in those, and had no need to. Shoes like that cost ten times the amount I'd spent on groceries that day.

"What apartment do you live in?" Loren asked, boarding the elevator with me in tow.

"Twenty-nine C," I replied. She pressed the button for my floor. "You are certainly a *neighborly* neighbor."

"Thanks," she shrugged and smiled.

"You know as I think about it," I contemplated, "you're the first neighbor *I've* met too. Usually when I see people in the hall they've got their eyes to the floor or the ceiling."

"Or they're busy talking on the phone," she joked, having experienced the very same neighbors. These were the types who would do anything not to associate with people they didn't already know.

"How long have you lived here?" she asked.

"Almost a year."

"Yes, there are a lot of out-of-towners in this building," she explained, "not just this building, this whole goddamn city."

"How do you know *I'm* not an out-of-towner?" I asked, trying to be playful.

"I can tell a Washingtonian boy when I see one." She said smugly, it was so sexy. I was convinced she was flirting with me, but what a whore if she was! "You are, aren't you?"

"Yes. I'm from La Conner," I imparted.

"Oh, I *love* La Conner," she gasped, "I go up there every year for the tulip festival."

"Oh really, my dad is a tulip farmer."

"What a splendid occupation," she said romantically as the elevator came to my floor.

Never in my life had I made a friend from a complete stranger on the street, or the lobby for that matter. That afternoon I felt it long overdue I accomplish such a task. Accordingly, as we made our way out of the elevator and down the hall toward my apartment, I asked her if she would like to come in for a glass of wine. She welcomed the idea and I felt giddy from head to toe.

If there was one thing in my paltry life I took great pride in, it was my apartment. On the 29th floor of the Market Plaza Tower at Pike Street and Second Avenue, the cusp of the tourism district, I lived in a studio-plus-den. The neighborhood is very expensive now, but when I moved there the Seattle economy had tanked, sending lease prices plummeting. The tower was originally built to house luxury condominiums but flipped to rental units when the downtown housing market began to take a turn. I was living in what was supposed to be a $500,000 condo for just $995 a month (plus utilities). So what if that was over half my monthly wage?

Inside my apartment I quickly poured each of us a glass of Marilyn Merlot and turned on NPR knowing my favorite Swing music program was on. It truly set a mood of sophistication, or at least I thought it did.

"I can't believe this," Loren confessed, "I thought everyone in this building was an elitist ex-Californian who was pissed off at the world and decided to move to Seattle in order to isolate themselves from a society they hated… and here I find you, an obviously charming young man with the most handsome little apartment."

I laughed as she flattered me. As the music roared and I put the groceries away, she toured my apartment examining the décor. It must have been the collection of *Hedwig And The Angry Inch* figurines on my coffee table that alluded to her I was undoubtedly gay. The slight discomfort in her I detected, probably from being in a strange man's apartment, turned to ease at once. It was always so charming when women found gay men to be a kind of safe haven.

As I finished unloading the groceries, Loren announced her affinity for my apartment, calling it "avant-garde" and "creative." I took it as a compliment considering the paintings were all strange, self-made abstracts and the shabby, reclaimed furniture was desperate to appear chic. I figured she was just being polite until she began asking where I got what and how much I paid for it. I was smart enough not to divulge where I purchased anything, only stating that they were acquired through friends and that everything was "one of a kind." This left open the possibility she might want to buy something I had made or refurbished.

We sat down in the living room and began talking about our careers and desires. Loren told me that she was an aspiring model who had just dropped out of Stanford and had moved back to Seattle to "find herself." By the look of Loren, a tall waif with flawless skin, spry breasts, a minute waist and enormous, yet curious eyes, I doubted she would be aspiring for long. Her look was *the* look of the day.

I confided to Loren that I too had dropped out of college. As we laughed over the coincidence we discovered we'd both fled college within two weeks of each other. It was little happenstances like this that both got us to wondering if our paths had crossed simply by chance, or by the inescapable pull of fate.

After moving past my collection of film posters she studied my photography exhibit of portraits I took while in college. These photos were all intangible monochromes of random models standing in front of landmark buildings and bodies of water. Some were posed in pornographic states of undress and stance but could still be considered arty because of the blurry lens.

"These are great Beaton!" She said, "I've never seen this set."

"Beaton?" I asked.

"Cecil Beaton, he took these," she insisted. I scoffed thinking she was joking.

"No. I took these a couple years ago," I replied, joyful. Being mistaken for Beaton is possibly the greatest compliment a wannabe photographer can receive.

"You did? I recognize them. Where were they published?" she asked as if it were some sort of interrogation. Initially I felt a bit threatened and didn't want to tell her that they hadn't been published anywhere. By the way she consumed each photo, staring at each for a prolonged moment, studying every shape and shadow, I realized her enthusiasm came from an authentic interest in the work.

"These were just for a class," I disclosed. "I got a B for the project. The instructor was generous. I turned it in late."

Loren continued to study the photographs in a state of absolute absorption. Not even my art instructors in college scrutinized my work like she did. I had a hunch my photographs were good. I wouldn't have kept them if they weren't. But for them to be able to enthrall a photography connoisseur such as Loren was exciting.

"I'm guessing you like them?" I asked.

"I do, I really do. So much of the time black and white is a cliché, but your contrasts are so subtle. It's refreshing. Every photographer out there right now is a god damn shock artist. But these are a return to elegance, almost early *Harper's Bazaar*. Have you seen *Bazaar* from the thirties and forties? That's glamour!"

It was immediately clear Loren and I were meant to be friends as I then presented to her my collection of early *Harper's Bazaar* magazines. It was the one and only thing I collected.

"Now this is bizarre," she punned. We both laughed at her cornball humor. I opened a bottle white wine and we sat on the floor giggling at each other and drinking. I contemplated how such a random meeting between two strangers could result in what I hoped would become a lasting friendship.

Loren stayed until after midnight discussing photographers and fashion. I asked her whether or not models really were obligated to sleep with the fashion designers whose runways they paraded down (her answer: "no, they're all gay!"). In this vein of chatter we discussed Loren's hunger for success in fashion. She declared she was on the verge of breaking through to the upper echelon of the modeling industry, a statement I viewed at the time as a grandiose fantasy.

Unfortunately, the conversation reverted to me when Loren queried about my career.

"Did you drop out of college for a job?" She asked, her assumption embarrassing me. While I longed to work in the media, my day job was far from anything I studied in college.

"No. I work for OmniCare up on First Hill. Not anything nearly as glamorous and rewarding as being a paid photographer."

"What are you waiting for?" she questioned bluntly. The question was an unforeseen kick in the conscious. *What was I waiting for?*

"I don't know…" I said, then added, "I feel exhausted."

"I know what you mean," Loren soothed. "College is a drain, but it's no excuse to give up. If photography is your passion you have to find it in yourself to pursue it. So many people give up on their ambitions before they've even really made a go at them."

I didn't know what to say and it was obvious to her. Nervous, I took a long drink of wine and contemplated why I'd given up on photography. Had college really sucked the ambition out of me or was I the one to blame for losing the passion to create?

"I'm sorry," Loren recanted. "We just met and I'm already grilling you on something I'm sure is much more complex than I'm aware."

"No. You're absolutely right," I allowed, "your honesty… it's refreshing."

"I tend to speak my mind. It usually gets me in trouble."

In a blatant effort to take all examination off me and my life, I changed the topic back to her. "What makes you think you'll make it as a model?" I asked. This question couldn't have been more inept as the answer was blatant. Loren was one of the most stunning young women I'd ever seen, not only in real life, but in the fashion magazines I was always getting lost in.

"I love design and photography. If I had any visualization skills and could take pictures like you do I'd be behind the camera. But I can't so I figure why not stand in front of it?" Her answer seemed sharp, maybe a little rehearsed.

"I thought you were going to tell me," I teased, "the reason you wanted to be a model is because you were the most beautiful person you know."

"Yeah, that too!" she chuckled.

We had a couple more drinks. I became completely drunk but Loren remained poised and eloquent, even after we finished eating the vegetarian Thai food I had delivered. We talked for hours about everything. She was the smartest and most energetic young woman I had ever met. Around two AM we called it a night and I walked her to the elevator.

"If this isn't too forward," Loren said with a bit of a tremble in her voice, "would you like to go out to dinner sometime?"

"I would love to," I instantly replied. It was the first time anyone had asked me out.

"Fantastic," she said smiling. "Are you busy Friday?" She had the kind of excitement in her voice I assumed girls reserved for the men in their lives.

"Nope," I replied without having to think. "But just to make something clear. I'm-"

"Gay, I know. I would never ask a straight guy to dinner. That's *his* job!"

She took a piece of paper out of the tiny little purse she carried and we exchanged email addresses and phone numbers.

"What apartment do you live in?" I questioned, not knowing to press the up or down button at the elevator panel.

"Forty-A," she said. I knew immediately what apartment was hers because it took up the entire top floor of the building.

"That's the penthouse?" I speculated. I questioned how a 22-year-old aspiring model could afford such accommodations. "Do you live with your parents?" I naively asked.

"No. I own the building," she replied plainly, as if it were ordinary for a girl her age to own a residential skyscraper in downtown Seattle. Bells suddenly went off in my head. How could I be so stupid? Loren was not just a girl, she was Loren *Anders*!

"You own the building?" I asked, wanting to see how she'd explain who she was.

"Yes. It was part of an inheritance I received a couple years ago." She provided no further details of her personal finances. "Anyway, I had a great time tonight Jimmy. And thank you for dinner. It feels like we just met in the lobby two seconds ago but any minute the sun is going to come up." As she spoke my mind struggled to comprehend what she was saying. I was fascinated how she brushed the fact that she was a billionaire off like it was a piece of lint on her shoulder. She was Loren Anders, a famous heiress and tycoon in her own right. How I accidentally befriended this woman of vast notoriety was beyond me.

As the elevator arrived she gave me a little kiss on the cheek just like we were in a movie or something. At that moment I felt more glamorous than I had my entire life. As I walked back to my apartment I recalled everything I could about Loren's family, gathering that the Anders were to Seattle what the Rockefellers were to New York. They were the closest thing Seattle had to a monarchy. The would-be King was William Charles Anders, inventor and engineer who started work at IBM in the 1970s and would eventually be credited with inventing and patenting, of all things, the mouse pad. His experience in deriving profit from the invention led him to found his now legendary company, AndersGroup, a consulting and investment firm. The company's forte was licensing patents and other intellectual properties to other companies – a "clearinghouse of ideas," as one historian put it. In the 1990s they branched out in to a half dozen other industries, their most profitable venture being cellular telephones. William Anders became part of Seattle's burgeoning population of billionaires, occasionally ascending to one of the richest men in the world when stocks were acting bullish.

William Anders's wife, Cathryn, became Seattle's utmost socialite, best known for organizing the family's generous contributions, such as the Anders Symphony Hall, home to the Seattle Philharmonic, and donating millions in cancer research to the Fred Hutchinson Institute. Her biggest gift, a $300-million dollar expansion project for the Seattle Art Museum, immediately made the Anders name supersede the Getty's and the Guggenheim's as America's most extravagant philanthropists of modern art. The family's goodwill was felt by the public. Anywhere they went in Seattle crowds would gather to give thanks and to praise them for their commitment to civic improvement.

The entire region wept the day that William and Cathryn were killed when their helicopter crashed into Lake Washington as they returned home from a meeting in Bellevue. Loren, 17 at the time, heard the news via television as she toured Italy with her tutors. *The Wall Street Journal* compared Loren's immediate return home to that of Queen Elizabeth's when her father died as she toured Africa. "She is a young woman primed to take hold of an empire she must now call her own," the paper declared. Loren would inherit the entire Anders estate, comprised of $4-billion in stock of AndersGroup Inc., $2 billion cash, and another $6 billion in the family's miscellaneous assets, comprised of real estate, bonds, and other investments. The details of the inheritance, mostly the giant numbers associated with it, were the substance of many newspaper articles at the time. While many felt sad for Loren's lose, few could honestly admit they didn't dream of being her.

Although both investors and passive spectators expected Loren Anders to eventually play a role in managing AndersGroup, no one predicted she would be appointed president of the company at the age of 18. A highly figurative role, the president of AndersGroup had no active day-to-day function at the company. The CEO of AndersGroup, who was nominated by the board of directors and then elected by shareholders, appointed Loren to the role of president. It was the president's role to act as the company's main spokesperson and to embody everything the organization stood for. With 30% of the company's stock now in her possession she had an overwhelming say in who became CEO of the company. It was common knowledge that she voted for a CEO that would appoint her president.

Barron's quickly printed a scolding editorial, proclaiming her tactic as "a potentially fatal mistake in a historically great company." An outlandish statement really, figuring that most all major decisions were done by the new CEO of the company, Hubert Redding. When questioned about the outrage she'd caused while appearing live on CNBC, Loren joked, "I had to keep the Anders name on the company stationery somehow." Stocks would rise seven percent the same day. It was as if investors were more concerned with continuity than qualifications. An 18-year-old serving in any such role at that large of a company, no matter how ceremonial, was unheard of.

Further media speculation would suggest that Loren Anders wanted the name and image of a leader without proving to be one. Many investors, confident she was "her father's daughter," would profitably learn Loren *was* a leader. She'd been by her father's side since she was 15 years old, observing carefully how the company functioned. The Board of Directors often made jokes to William Anders about whether or not he'd approved several major decisions with "Little Loren," as her inevitable control of the company was no secret. No one ever predicted her reign would occur so early and so suddenly.

Within the first year of Loren's presidency profit margins had risen 15%. She would lead the company through the dot-com disaster of 2001 with finesse, quickly acquiring everything she felt had been undervalued, a move that would later pay off many times over. By the time Loren Anders took a leave of absence from the company to attend college, assets had grown substantially and new subsidiaries and acquisitions had begun making profits earlier than anticipated. Her drive to innovate the company, consolidate operations, and make efficient departments that lagged behind their corporate rivals would drive the company's stock to an all-time high. When she moved in to her dorm room at Stanford, Loren held the title of World's Richest Woman, World's Youngest Billionaire and according to *Playboy*, World's Sexiest Freshman.

As I sat in bed that night recalling what I could about Loren Anders, I was in disbelief I'd hit it off with such an icon. Even though I'd never previously acknowledged what it must be like to be her, she seemed very sensible and untarnished by extreme wealth. I questioned how she could be fascinated by a boring minion like me. Loren Anders truly had the ability to acquire anything in the world she wanted. She had met royalty, pop stars, and every U.S. President elected since she was born. What could she find in me that was so fascinating?

As I thought about the complete absurdity of my situation, I also pondered what Loren Anders was doing living at the Market Plaza Tower. The place was certainly no dump but I've seen pictures of the penthouse, and while it's nice, I couldn't imagine it being nice enough for *the* Loren Anders. Its paltry 5,500 square-feet must have been a cozy departure from the 23,000 square-foot Lake Washington waterfront villa her family used when they stayed in the city. I'd later find out it was a home Loren abandoned not long after the death of her parents.

I leapt out of bed as curiosity plagued my mind. I went to my computer and typed 'Loren Anders' into the search engine. I found countless articles and biographies on her, mostly documenting her perilous rise to the top of America's wealthy. The most informative article I found of fairly recent publication was from *Seattle Lifestyles* magazine. Titled "Movin' Way Up," the article used Loren Anders recent acquisition of the historic Smith Tower as proof that Seattle's housing boom was becoming more outrageous than ever thought possible (before crashing with equally historical significance). It described, in sensational tabloid fashion, the rumor that Loren's intention with the Smith Tower was to turn the top floors into one giant residence. This same article also claimed Loren had intended to live on the 101st floor of the recently completed AndersCenter but decided against it as the tower was already too much of a target for terrorism.

I went back to bed and fell asleep immediately, dreaming of being in a marathon where I had finished the race but kept on running just because I could. I'd had this dream before and as the familiar events began to play out I could predict the end: I would not stop running until I got hit by a car.

The next day I awoke as if I'd won the lottery. I was full of joy having a new friend who was so worldly. Loren was the type of person I wanted to have shape me into their most cherished confidant. As I floated to work everything seemed perfect. Listening to the city that morning made me feel more alive each moment. The buses, cars, people chatting and laughing, the bums jingling their change cups, the amateur musicians on Pine Street, and the occasional whistling espresso machine made the city sound as alive as I felt. The city and I in unison for once!

As synchronistic as the city and I had become, the work day seemed to last forever. Each agonizing minute dragged along as I worked and tried not to think about what time it was. When the day finally did conclude I rushed home expecting to find a message from Loren on my voicemail. But there was no message. I tried not to think too much of it, figuring she was a tremendously busy woman. I would give her the rest of the day and if she didn't email me then I'd email her.

A very long day passed, so I wrote to her:

Hi Loren,
Just wanted to say I can't wait to go out to dinner with you this Friday. Call me. I don't know what to wear, etc. Stop by any time if you'd like!

Three more days passed with no response. So I wrote to her again:

Loren, I called you. You weren't there. I'm sad. Call me back.

Another four days passed and I grew weary and angry. Trying to be composed and polite I wrote:

Loren...Maybe I just dreamed I'd met you and we hit it off talking art and society. Oh well, looks like I'll never get to be friends with the great Loren Anders. I guess I'll just continue being the pathetic and lonely me I am so used to being.

* * *

There must be a god. Who else could be a bigger son-of-a-bitch by fooling me in to thinking I'd snagged a debonair billionaire as a friend? Only a vengeful, homophobic god would suddenly rip her out of my world. It was so painful to be so close to an extraordinary person, only to have them disappear as mysteriously and as suddenly as they had arrived. The familiar, tiresome, resentful days at work would continue. I'd loathe myself sitting in my cubicle staring at the carpeted wall. There I was again, miserable and unable to work up the will to do anything about it. In Loren Anders I saw a hint of intrigue and glamour. In myself I felt the utmost pity. There in that cell I wondered what Loren was doing. I assumed she was in some exotic locale spending exorbitant amounts of cash on things she'd never need or use, while I was in my familiar crater of desperation. That night over a bottle of sparkling wine

I bought for $3.99, I declared to myself and to the bums in the alley below my balcony, "I will not be a loser!" Those same bums screeched drunkenly back, "you go girl!" I felt like throwing the bottle at them but there was at least $0.75 worth of liquor yet to be drunk, and I wasn't about to waste good liquor.

In that moment, with no prospect or hope on my horizon, I became determined to make some sort of change, if only emotionally. I wasn't going to let the world get me down! Desperation had become so passé and I longed for something new, even if it was borne from a lonely, tipsy evening spent yelling things off the balcony.

I went inside and turned on the Jazz radio station and began spouting off as I always did when I drank alone. I protested my shitty job, my lackluster finances, and the romance drought I'd encountered my entire adult life. The radio became a bore so I turned on the television to a cable station playing that show about those fabulous city people who have everything. You know *that* show, the one where they sit at the café and talk about their so-called "problems," like a boyfriend's penis being too large or not knowing how to spend a million-dollar inheritance. If only they knew real problems, like not having enough money to pay the water bill or buy groceries. Tonight's episode was about not getting enough sex, of course, those greedy fictional urbanites got to have their cake and fuck it too! The show made me as depressed as the main character, a Barbie Doll looking blonde, who was complaining that three times a week was not enough for her. I would have settled for three times a year.

I took a seat in the kitchen to go through the mail. Because so many of the bills were past due I'd let things build up for a few weeks. After sorting through ads for new luxury condos in Belltown and South Lake Union, I came across countless requests for payment to all the magazines I'd subscribed to but failed to actually pay for. Then, something made my day: I observed a very plain envelope in the pile of mail sent from a town in Delaware. I'm always cautious of envelopes without a return address on them because they tend to be collection notices. But this envelope felt stiff like there was something good inside. Eagerly I tore it open to discover inside perhaps the best present I'd received in years: A brand new credit card!

"Whoa," is all I could say as I held the shimmering silver card in my hand. To be the recipient of a credit card was confounding as I had a terrible credit score. Unsure if it was actually mine, I checked the name on the card to see if it had possibly been put in to the wrong mailbox. But no, JAMES L MINOR was printed right on it.

This was by no means my first credit card. I had applied for it in order to get 10% off an Amazon.com order, never expecting to actually qualify. The card's design was elegant, like a piece of jewelry and looked glorious and powerful in my hand. It made me feel the same way and I couldn't wait to buy something with it.

In retrospect, I know being approved for a credit card shouldn't make a person feel accomplished. But it did. I activated the card at once and ordered a pizza. I then recalled what I told myself I would do if I got the card: go to New York City!

On the Internet I found a great five day travel package in April for $999, including round-trip airfare, 3-star hotel with a Broadway show of my choice. I just prayed OmniCare would let me have the time off. They were assholes like that, forbidding vacation days from being used consecutively, so even though I got two weeks off a year most employees were lucky if they could get more than two back-to-back days off at a time. I stumbled to bed, drunk as a wino and happy as could be. I was going to New York soon.

The next day at work was a complete fucking blur. I was still drunk (I got to bed around 4 am) and excited about my trip to New York. In the fantasyland that was my mind I imagined I'd arrive in New York, find the place marvelous, and in those five short days find an extravagant socialite to hire me as their butler and ditch my plane ride back to dinky Seattle (after becoming a New Yorker I would brush off any reference to Seattle as *Seattle Who?*). I'd be an arrogant, eccentric Manhattanite just like the ones I'd seen on TV. It would be easy because it was my perceived destiny.

After sobering up around lunchtime I decided it imperative to ask for the time off in April. Guinevere, my boss, was a frumpy 47-year old divorcée with three twenty-something kids and a colon polyp. She was always on a mood swing so I hoped this morning she'd be amiable towards my Manhattan ambitions. In her office I calmly asked for the three days off. I had utilized the weekend in order to reduce any conflict in getting the time off. She said no, asserting the company was already down two accounting clerks and until we filled those positions no one was going on vacation. She reminded me, "with Seattle's current unemployment rate of 0.0000017% it's extremely hard to find decent employees." It was this same reason I had my job.

I left the office as if Guinevere's declination were no big deal. But on the walk home I decided I would quit my job in order to get some culture and see the grand dame of all cities. If OmniCare wouldn't let me have three little days off then I would tell those bastards to "fuck off, I'm going to New York!"

On the way home from work I stopped by the library and checked out *The Fabulous Traveler's Guide To Manhattan*, a fat, glossy, glib literary masterwork depicting what a tourist with a million-or-so dollars to spend on a vacation might do if he were in The Big Apple. It was fantasy reading and it was perfect for me. I'd always found books portraying reality to be tedious.

After examining the pages of *The Fabulous Traveler's Guide* I decided to cook myself dinner and watch the news. As I ate my formerly frozen eggplant parmesan and let the TV squawk in the background, I found myself unable to stop reading this wonderful guide in which I discovered Bergdorf Goodman ("Bergi's"), Henri Bendel ("Bendi's"), and Saks Fifth Avenue ("Saks"). I fantasized about staying at the Plaza or the Waldorf, and what it would be like to stroll through glorious Central Park, not to mention all the other enthralling bedlam that resided on the island of Manhattan.

It was not until the TV news began a piece on a giant earthquake in Lima that killed scores of Peruvian's was my attention diverted from my new bible. What caught my eye and ear was a woman's voice who sounded faintly similar to that of Loren Anders. Then I gazed at the TV screen to see a gruff, dirty woman in a yellow hard hat that looked just like a homeless version of her being interviewed. On her hard hat I could make out the faint logo of AndersCare, a global humanitarian organization. I was so obsessed with my fantasy guide to New York it took me another 15 seconds before I realized the tattered woman on the TV *was* Loren.

In my oblivious, self-obsessed isolation where I'd swore off the news, all political assessments, and any knowledge of contemporary world events, I was entirely unaware of a devastating earthquake that struck Peru. Loren Anders and her cavalry of emergency disaster relief, operating as the non-profit humanitarian relief organization AndersCare, was actively restoring humanity to the traumatized region right beside local and international governments.

No wonder she hadn't replied to my email.

· · ·

A week after discovering Loren was helping earthquake victims, I received an email from her. When I saw it sitting in my inbox I was afraid to open it, positive it would contain text in the vein of "you ignorant idiot, if you'd get your head out of your ass and began caring about people you'd realize that feeding thousands of suddenly homeless disaster victims is a lot more important than lunching with you!"

Luckily it said no such thing. The email was an apology from Loren, stating she'd heard about the earthquake in the middle of the night and before sunrise her and a convoy of airborne aid was in route to Lima. She also said she would've called but was just too busy. The email ended "PS: I'll be back in Seattle tomorrow. Meet me at L'Anders at Fifth and Pike around noon. Wear something nice. This fag hag likes her pretty boys looking pretty."

Social catastrophe averted!

Loren Anders was perfectly unaware of the fact that I, a real person, had a job. Lunch with her would mean sneaking in and out of the office, an act that would require me to return to my desk and somehow make it look as though I hadn't been at lunch for several hours. Despite the danger in doing that, the risk of losing my job somehow seemed worth having lunch with her.

L'Anders, a gourmet vegan culinary nucleus, located in the Retail District on the 44th floor of a bank skyscraper, was Seattle's shining beacon of restaurant eclecticism. Loren's helicopter was parked on top of the building so I knew she'd already arrived. When I saw it I checked the time and hoped I hadn't kept her waiting. As the President of a billion-dollar multi-national finance firm, I suspected she could throw one hell of a tantrum if someone kept her waiting. As I entered the lobby of the restaurant I was horrified to find it empty. Its lavish cotemporary-meets-Beaux Arts dining quarters were a mess, some of the tables didn't even have chairs or tablecloths. *Was Loren foolish enough to assume this place was open for lunch?* I wondered this just as I heard a delightful beckoning from Loren.

"Honey!" she decreed, flowing elegantly across the room in a floral silk skirt and top. I suspected she'd looted several designer boutiques while in Lima.

"The place is a mess, but don't worry, we still get to eat," Loren cheered.

"So if you pay extra they'll open it for lunch?" I queried, naïve to the truth.

"Absolutely not," she snapped. "The only person who eats lunch here is the owner… and her friends." Loren's bold haughtiness reminded me of a young Donatella Versace.

"You own the place?" I foolishly asked having failed to recognize her name in the name of the restaurant.

"Yes. We open next week, I couldn't be more terrified. Rumor has it that *Saveur* is flying some critic out from New York just to tear the place apart."

Because the menu of L'Anders was still a few days from perfection, Loren had the chefs serve us a foray of dishes, each a marvelous celebration of decadence and imagination. The first item I gorged myself on was a beet & pear salad with lavender-walnut vinaigrette, followed by parsnip gnocchi on rapini. It was the kind of food you'd only see on television. The only thing better than the way it looked was the way it tasted. The range of flavors, not just on the various plates but in each bite, turned on taste buds I'd never used before.

"You don't think it's *too* vegan do you?" Loren asked, elegantly slurping on a chanterelle mushroom truffle crème soup.

"No such thing!" I applauded over my cantaloupe soufflé accented by several small cranberry tarts. "An adventurous foodie wouldn't care that it's vegan. It's just too delicious to resist."

"You know I wouldn't have to open this place if Seattle had a goddamn respectable vegan restaurant." At this point her persona switched from delicate to unruly.

"I know. They're non-existent here," I said as if I were an authority on such establishments.

"Everywhere in fact," Loren relinquished, "not even New York has a good vegan place."

"Really?" I mulled. I couldn't believe New York wouldn't have the best of everything. "I guess that means there's room for expansion."

"I like the way you think!" she rasped laughingly.

"I'm going to New York in April," I mentioned, feeling admirable.

"Is it your first time?" Loren mused. She was probably baffled to hear that someone she knew hadn't ever been to New York City.

"Yes. I couldn't be more excited."

"It's been said that 'you haven't been anywhere until you've been to New York,'" she said. "And it's *so* true... Are you going alone?"

"Yes," my eyes unintentionally widening.

"Good. It's the best way to go. I remember my first trip to Manhattan. I was seven. I went alone... well just me and my staff." By 'staff' she meant bodyguards. "I compare it to losing one's virginity!"

"*Really?*" I was so turned on to hear her speak of Manhattan. To know she possessed the same passion for what I assumed was the world's greatest city was all the more delightful.

"So why don't you live there?" I asked.

"*Live* in New York City!" she erupted. "Are you kidding me?" Her sudden distaste for the town confused me.

"Why wouldn't you?" I endured.

"I can *visit* anytime. If you can visit New York City whenever you want there's no point in *living* there. I much prefer Puget Sound, thank you very much." My only response was the hint of a chuckle. "Here the cabs will at least slow down just a bit before compacting you into the asphalt. In New York, watching someone get pummeled by a taxi is a vile form of curbside entertainment. They consider it survival of the fittest or something. Dog-eat-dog, if you will."

The Seattle pace, while still upbeat and enviable in contrast to other cities, was becoming too slow for me. I craved a breakneck, 24-hour pace. What she described, while gruesome, enthralled me.

"You know they hate me in New York," Loren laughed as she poured me a glass of wine that was so expensive the restaurant made diners prepay for it a week before their reservation.

"Why?" I asked, wondering how an entire city could hate such a beautiful and alluring creature. Her flamboyance, charm, and bravado all seemed very much in line with Manhattan values.

"They hate every billionaire that doesn't live in New York City. Shit, they hate *everyone* that doesn't live there, period. Billionaire or not." Her statement was one she'd made famous previously in the publications of *Time* and *USA Today*. It was Loren's claim that several generations of Wall Street millionaires were unwilling to fathom how a man like her father, who had a work force of less than 1,000 men and women, who did business not in the commerce capital of Manhattan but in a suburb of Seattle, surrounded by a forest of towering virgin evergreen trees (and not skyscrapers), could surpass all their fortunes combined. Further outraging the Manhattan power stratum was the increasingly repetitive tradition of Seattle and San Francisco producing a new technology tycoon every two or three years. Suddenly the glitter of New York's rich were quickly losing their luster to a West Coast group who were exponentially wealthier.

"That can't be true," I blurted. I wasn't going to let Loren tear down my vision of New York City.

"Seriously, they're boycotting the construction of the AndersBank Plaza because I don't live there," Loren explained. I was certain there had to be other factors involved. After all, the AndersGroup commercial properties division had a reputation for bullying.

As we continued to eat we began discussing everything, including each other.

Every aspect of my life that I considered pathetic, from my farm boy childhood to my big city poverty, Loren found to be extraordinary and fascinating. She rejoiced in my "humble-hood" and "bohemia," attempting to flatter me and convince me that my lifestyle was, in a way, simple and therefore desirable.

"You get up, go to work, and go home," Loren explained. "It's fantastic. Nothing looms over your head. How would you like to report daily to two million shareholders? If the price of their stock goes down even a single percentage point they threaten to fire me, not because I'm the Chairperson but because my name is the brand," she said, illustrating what I considered a frightening reality for her. Every connotation about her being a stereotypical dimwit fashion model she proved fallacious. Loren was dynamic, powerful, and according to her, my new best friend.

As we left L'Anders, Loren pleaded for me to tell her what I thought of the food.

"If my mouth could orgasm, it would have just now."

"It can, I'll show you how," Loren joked, displaying a handsome wit. "I'm glad you liked it."

Despite being one of the most protected private citizens in the country, I found Loren Anders to be, surprisingly, one of the most sensible and clever. Just like me, she loved to read, worshipped jazz and couldn't get enough of art. She almost fainted the day it was announced there would be a Jasper Johns retrospective at the Seattle Art Museum. Beyond art, we shared a fascination for magazines and films from the 1940s and 1950s.

One of Loren's favorite and most used quotes was: "Extraordinary people live extraordinary lives." I felt that knowing her enhanced my extraordinariness at least a million percent. But what enchanted me most about Loren was how analogous her life was to mine. Nights I once spent alone at the library gazing at giant art books by Avedon or Beaton were now spent with her doing the same thing. It fascinated me that she, a billionaire who could afford her own library, spent it at the Seattle Public Library just as I did. If the two of us hadn't collided in the lobby of my apartment building we would likely have done so in the stacks at the library. To Loren, the library represented unending knowledge, a predatory virtue she venerated. Whereas I frequented it for artistic amusement, she scoured its contents for greater knowledge of all things. One of her greatest fears was complacency. Often she'd justify her unending research by illustrating the downfall of other tycoons. As amusing at their stories were, they were sources of great inner tumult for Loren. A day did not pass without the names of Hearst or Hughes being invoked to warn of behavior that could result in her losing her empire.

After dropping out of college and returning to AndersGroup, Loren found she was returning to a company in dismay. The stodgy crew that made up the Board of Directors, her figurative grandparents, were troubled by her abandonment of college and weren't about to let her have any responsibility at the company she didn't work hard to earn. Never one to back down from a challenge, Loren saw to it that the company regained its footing and became a well-oiled profit machine. Within months of her return revenue was on the ascent again and the company was completing the crown jewel of its property developments, The AndersCenter. The mixed use campus of nine city blocks was Seattle's largest structure, incorporating five office towers, a 175-store designer shopping arcade, a 20 screen cinema, 16 restaurants, four Starbucks, and the palatial office of the world's most powerful 22-year-old.

AndersCenter was still approaching completion and closed to the public, so you can imagine my wonder and excitement when Loren said "Want to come up and see my new office?"

Loren's office incorporated the entire 101st floor, the absolute pinnacle of the tower, so high that when you gazed out the window you could see only sky. You had to look down to see hills or water. The office was so ridiculous in size and design I immediately compared it to that of a comic book villain's lair.

"It's the tallest building on the coast," Loren prided as she led me out on to her giant balcony circumventing the entire office. "We were going to make it the tallest in the world."

"Why didn't you?" I asked. The thought of Seattle having the world's tallest building rapt me.

"The city council wouldn't approve it. They still see this town as a little backwater just pretending to do business on a global scale. They're from another era."

"Maybe someday, eh?"

"Maybe. They're even making me remove my name from the top spire," Loren cried. She took me out to her giant wraparound deck to show me what she was talking about. Atop the office was a giant antenna with ANDERS emblazed in platinum silver down its shaft, lit with dazzling emerald lights. Advertisements and corporate logos, no matter how tasteful, were illegal on skyscrapers in Seattle. "They're just a bunch of granola-fed asses. If I didn't love this town more than life itself I'd pack it all up and head to Dubai."

"Undoubtedly," I said, the words stammering out of my mouth as I clung to the railing. I'd never been in such a tall structure before. Wearily I looked over the edge of the building. I was able to spot the Space Needle, a little white dot that appeared as though it were miles below us.

Loren confessed to me her job as President of AndersGroup was highly symbolic and ultimately boring. She would joke "a giant office like this was constructed for me so I can flip through magazines in all day." I'm sure the cost of her office alone could have fed several small countries for several decades, but Loren didn't mind, explaining, "You can only give to people so much, you know. They've got to get off their ass sooner or later." I loved her sensibility at the time, even if it was slighted.

That afternoon I completely forgot to go back to work. I didn't care. Being in the presence of Loren was much more important. And who cared if I got fired and couldn't pay the rent? Loren owned my apartment building. Certainly we could have worked something out.

We sat in her office eating the customized dessert the chef from L'Anders had sent us off with. We read every fashion and home décor magazine in existence, all the while watching old movies on her cinema sized television. The TV was a gift from the married 51-year-old President of Sony who'd proposed a certain type of merger between them.

"This is the life. I really admire you," she said, her statement bewildering me.

"WHY?" I asked thinking she'd gone mad.

"You've completely seduced me," she said, laughing and shaking her head. It was apparent she really was smitten with me. I thought it funny how I could have seduced her. I was just an ordinary young man with many similar interests. How was that at all appealing? When I considered Loren Anders was a highly protected young woman, her thrill of the ordinary seemed explainable. It had likely been years since she'd seen or spoken to a commoner like me, who had a job, tiny little bills to pay, and insignificant worries such as planning for retirement. She was fascinated by me because I was an oddity in her realm of the super-privileged.

A person of wealth will find it easy to obtain acquaintances, as was the case with Loren. She belonged to many clubs, such as the Billionaire's Club, the Young Woman's Business Association, the Sotheby's Exclusive Buyers Council, and the Barnes & Noble Reader's Advantage Club. But it was a very secretive Seattle society Loren belonged to that would change my social standing forever. She was part of an exclusive crowd of five friends, each one a particularly influential person in the community, and each a paragon of our generation's growing control on modern global commerce. Loren told me in two weeks they would be having their monthly dinner and asked if I would like to attend, possibly replacing a regular attendee by the name of Roger Davies.

Allegedly Roger had begun talking of marriage and meeting "the right girl." The group had identified Roger as an undistinguished playboy who didn't fit in with their group for several reasons, the biggest being he didn't care about art, held no regard for the fundamentals of fashion, and complained whenever they discussed foreign films because he was one of those types who couldn't stand to read subtitles. The group celebrated individualism, career, and solidarity. Roger Davies had turned 30 with no career, no standing in the Seattle social hierarchy, and no potential as a valuable friend.

Loren explained to me one tawdry revelation on how someone as undesirable as Roger had ever been admitted into such an exclusive assembly: he was willing to perform without fee or limitation cunnilingus on several of the group's female members (Loren excluded). His oral performance was so revered and "widespread" he began entertaining clients for the small fee of $200 per 30-minute session. He quickly developed a cult following and word of his amazing talents spread like herpes. His services were billed as a religious experience on Seattle's ritzy eastside where e-commerce billionaire wives sat at home with nothing between their legs to play with. Once news of his burgeoning clientele reached the group his exile was inevitable. Post-exile, his technique would be documented in his book, *Giving Women Head: True Tales Of Satisfying With Your Mouth*, a bestseller among women who would buy it as an instruction manual for the man (or woman) in their life.

Once my invitation to the group was complete I felt an overwhelming need to impress these five people. Compared to Roger my talents were non-existent. I'd never even seen a vagina in real life, let alone revolutionized the method in which they were stimulated.

"I feel like such a loser," I whimpered to Loren. "You make it sound like you guys are the cream of the social crop."

"You're not a loser," she coaxed. "You don't have to be anything special to join the club. We're just friends. Besides, look at me. I'm an unemployed model. How embarrassing is that?"

"You have style and fashion knowledge," I explained. "You know famous people. You're exactly what a compendium of our generation's social elite would want. At the other end of this style spectrum is me. As of a month ago I had no friends. I am the epitome of pathetic."

"You're right," she said falsely. "I'm calling everyone up and announcing you will be absent from our dinner because you're a *fucking loser*!" She grinned, mocking my own words. "C'mon! You're perfect for us. We're all loners and outcasts, not one of us was popular in prep school or college. In essence we are a group of the rehabilitated. You will be our latest conspirator."

My unyielding determination gave way to Loren's pleading. Any self-doubt and personal pity I had turned to gibberish, and Loren's strong persuasion to make me feel admirable succeeded.

Loren's cajoling did little to help later that night when I discovered my anticipation to be accepted by her friends would lead me into yet another spell of sleeplessness. I could barely doze off. And at work I couldn't stop thinking about the strange and eccentric friends she must've known. I worried endlessly about how they would perceive me. Would they think I was boring or divinely simple? Simply cute or downright mollycoddle-ish? Of all the things worrying me, the most taxing deliberation was about what I would wear.

MARCH

I'd found in life that managing and maintaining friendships were often a lot of work. Wanting so much to be admired I've continually tried to impress friends with wit and humor, attempting to secure their camaraderie. At the age of 22 I had yet to make a good, honest, close companion of anyone in a plethora of acquaintances. It was sad really. So when a girl like Loren Anders came into my life I made it my utmost priority to assure our fledgling friendship would not be squandered. If only one friendship had ever truly mattered to me, it was this one.

One night while packing up Loren's belongings for the big move to her new penthouse at the Smith Tower, we watched *Some Like It Hot* while discussing what we'd learned in life from Hollywood.

"Are you Tony Curtis or Jack Lemon?" she persisted. Loren had asked me this question three times but each time I ignored her not knowing a single difference between the two.

"Jack Lemon," I finally said. "Tony Curtis is just a little *too* good at playing a woman. He's bossy too."

"You can't be Jack Lemon, I'm Jack Lemon," Loren fought.

"Have you noticed," I began, "that in all of Jack Lemon's movies he's just an ordinary great guy who does crazy things in order for people to like him when in reality if he were just himself and not his latest creation, people would probably like him just as much?"

"I know the feeling. No matter what he ends up alone," Loren replied. Her answer dismayed me. I was reluctant to believe that Loren knew what it was like to truly be lonely. She had a team of people around her constantly. Butlers, maids, executives, bodyguards, secretaries and assistants, all of them striving to make her life as enjoyable as possible. *How could someone so fawned over be lonely?*

I knew then Loren and I were meant for each other. We may not have been lovers but we were destined partners. She was lost, and I was too. I felt I'd lost my parents, she really had lost hers.

From then on, Loren Anders and I, ragtag Jimmy Minor, would spend every minute of free time we had together. We started spending the night in each other's apartments. When I got off work I would rush over to the AndersCenter just to hang out in her glamorous corporate lair, watching her make phone calls and teleconference with other famous tycoons. Strangely, they never talked business, only inquired to see how so-and-so's wife was doing or sending condolences because what's-his-face's mom had passed away. I would brag about my new friendship at work, certain none of the office herd believed me. Most of the people I told didn't even know who Loren Anders was. These same people thought JC Penney was a luxury department store.

Since the moment Loren Anders took me into her world of excess, time had flown by. So fast in fact I'd almost forgotten the most important social event of my life was about to commence. Loren had invited me to meet a group of her friends at the Space Needle for dinner and hopefully initiate me into what she billed as the town's "young social elite."

My insignificant wardrobe consisted entirely of designer knock-offs, end-of-season throw-outs and "buy 'em or we'll burn 'em" clearance specials. Upon closer examination of my clothing I discovered I only had five complete outfits, one for each day of the work week, none of them splendid enough to impress important movers and shakers. Motivated by my shiny new credit card, I decided it was time for a wardrobe expansion.

Alone, I walked over to my favorite haunt, J. Crew. They were having one of their famous all-year-long sales. That's where they mark up the goods and then put sales stickers on everything, making you think you got a herringbone sweater for 10% off when in truth no one ever paid the original price. I found some nice corduroy pants and a Pacific Northwest-meets-Burberry sweater. As I stood in the mile-long cashier line contemplating my choice of clothing, my cell phone rang. It was Loren.

"Hi, what are you doing?" she asked in the same way someone does if you've stood them up. I began to panic.

"I'm shopping," I said innocently. This excuse is always justifiable whenever one has failed to meet prior engagements. Other excuses such as "my father died, I'm at the hospital" can also suffice.

"Are you downtown?"

"Yeah, I'm at J. Crew."

"Eeew!" she screeched.

"What!?! What's wrong with J. Crew?" I quarreled, offended she had dismissed one of my favorite stores.

"It's so, I don't know, last century."

"Okay new millennium girl, where do you suppose I shop with my budget?" This was supposed to really throw her. I wasn't sure she even knew what the word 'budget' meant.

"About three blocks south. I'm standing outside of it right now," Loren proposed. Her curious tone and nature made me question if she had some sort of devious plan. I couldn't be more enthralled.

"The only cool store three blocks south of here is..." I paused, realizing the only respectable place to shop south of Pacific Place was "Mario's! I can't afford Mario's."

"Get over here. They just got the Spring Marc Jacobs menswear line in, the girl is still putting it on the rack," she announced and hung up.

I was inexplicably dumbfounded at that moment. I dropped the suddenly tacky pants and the horrid sweater I'd been clinging to and ran out the door like a shoplifter who's about to be apprehended. The brisk sprint three blocks seemed to take forever. For every moment I had to wait as cars filed past on Pike Street I thought to myself, "There's probably a line of gay men and metrosexual dot-comers just waiting for the Marc Jacobs line to hit the racks. Will I get there too late? Could it all be gone and I'll have to wait until next fall until I got my first piece of MJ?"

Stepping through the double doors of Mario's was like stepping into heaven, except it smelled a lot better. Now I was not intimidated in the least by the snooty staff for I was now among the league of their consumers. As *The Thieving Magpie* plaid softly in the milieu I found Miss Loren Anders strutting her runway caliber body through the store in a black satin Givenchy femme fatale dress and stilettos. The staff had apparently begged her to give it a lap around the store.

"Hi honey!" Loren proclaimed, spotting me as I came in. "How do you like it? It was just flown in. It's got jet lag. I think I have to buy it."

"It's evil looking," I raved. "Very corporate ball buster chic."

"Enormous!" she cried. This was the word she occasionally used instead of 'awesome' or 'cool.'

Loren paraded past the array of mirrors and kissed me on each cheek just like she'd seen socialites do on the BBC. The double-smooch was now our standard greeting.

I was introduced to Todd, my new personal shopping assistant. Prior to my arrival, Todd had received strict instructions on what to tailor me with. "Nothing trendy, just the classics. Lot's of black. Think minimalism, sleek, Prada, Comme Des Garcons, Helmut Lang. Don't fuck this up Toddy!"

The new Marc Jacobs Spring Collection was a behemoth in style and event appropriateness. From dinner jackets and pinstripe pants to punk inspired sweatshirts with mischievous phrases spray-painted across the shoulders, Mr. Jacobs had issued a collection to fit the modern man's diverse and chameleon-like taste. Before Loren could change from a Givenchy into a Roberto Cavalli, my evening attire had been chosen. There wasn't a thing in Mario's I didn't like, or an item Loren wouldn't buy for me.

Loren Anders must have really liked me. Or she was just in the shopping mood that day as her purchases were not exclusive to my wardrobe. For every item she bought me she would purchase three for herself. That day we injected some serious cash into Seattle's elite boutiques. After we hit Mario's it was on to Barney's, Hugo Boss, Nordstrom, Louis Vuitton, and Butch Blum. While I was being fitted for a suit, my first, Loren was busy ransacking the wares of Escada, Eileen Fisher, Chanel, Yves Saint Laurent, Gucci and Furla. I'd always dreamt of coming in to these stores and raiding their inventories. For it to really be happening was a delirious shock. These places were so sophisticated they never even asked for payment, they just smiled and said "Have a glorious day," as if the clothes were free. Not until our third round of shopping did I notice one of Loren's shadowy assistants tailing us everywhere we went, paying for all the lavish merchandise upon our exit. To think it was some little mousy red head's job to slink around, paying for everything she wanted. Oh the dirt that girl must have had!

When the shopping trip ended, Loren and I skipped over to a salon named Grrr! on First Avenue in super-hip Belltown. By the look of the salon's splatter painted walls and obscene window mannequins, it would have been fair to assume the place had been founded by a pack of punks. Because of this it seemed like the most avant-garde of all the places we visited. After a half-hour of contemplation, my loose brown sugar head of hair was trimmed and accented with subtle sandy blonde highlights. After demanding she look more "trampy," the hairdressers gave Loren some dark streaks in her platinum hair.

Tchaikovsky's first piano concerto roared in Loren's armored limousine as we made our way back to our apartments at Second and Pike. In the car I exposed my sudden arrogance to Loren.

"I feel so glamorous right now." After saying it I expected her to grill me on how spending money and being a flagrant consumer shouldn't make anyone feel good.

"Me too!" she unexpectedly wailed.

"But it makes me feel bad. All the money we…" I had to correct myself, "*you* spent could have fed thousands of little starving children in villages all over…" I paused, unable to think of a locale dotted with villages of starving children. "Malawi," finally came to mind.

"I'm sure much of the sales tax I paid will go to help the starving," she said, trying not only to rationalize our conspicuous consumption, but to convince herself she wasn't contributing to 'all the things that were wrong with America.'

I really did feel glamorous, like a well-paid gigolo strutting his hot shit down Hollywood Boulevard. I decided a gentle and friendly speech on economic tolerance would be well received. "It's not like you spent that much. And anyway, you're going to donate last season's wears to the Salvation Army, right? It's a good cause."

"Are you fucking kidding me?" she aggressed. "I'm auctioning it all off. I'm not going to pay five hundred dollars for a skirt, wear it once, and then donate it to some socialist militia who'll unknowingly pawn it off on some chubby suburban housewife that'll stretch the seams. I'll do the smart thing, auction it, and donate *some* of the proceeds to the poor and starving," she proposed, carefully inflecting the "some."

As Loren's limousine pulled to a stop and we began to unload the metric ton of goods we'd hedonistically acquired, I noticed the doorman (a boy really, I think he was maybe 17) standing by a couple of well-dressed moving men. The doorman pointed the movers our way.

"Excuse me, Miss Anders?" asked a burly, unshaven, rustically attractive moving man with a bright toothy smile. He wore a striped construction worker-style shirt with the top two buttons open making him the sexiest moving man I'd ever seen.

"Yes," she said, as if she'd been recognized from one of the ten dozen fashion magazine spreads she'd hardly been featured in.

"I'm from Vanguard. We're here to pick up some boxes for transport to," he looked at his clipboard, "506 Second Avenue."

"Oh yes. I'll show you upstairs," she piped, quickly jaunting towards the elevators. Had the man not been wildly handsome she would have pawned him off on one of her dozen or so assistants. I assumed she had been just as interested in his good looks as I was.

As Loren supervised her team of moving men I unloaded the limousine and laid out all the clothing she'd bought me on my bed. I couldn't begin to calculate how much she'd spent. After a quick inventory of my items I found she'd bought me 12 T-shirts, nine dress shirts, seven sweaters, 11 pairs of pants, nine pairs of shoes, six belts, 36 pairs of socks, 24 undershirts, six jackets, two hats, four wallets, and three man-bags. The pile of expensive clothing amassed on my bed was the most ridiculous sight I'd seen to date. Never before had I encountered so many splendid choices. Picking something to wear suddenly became an unbearable task.

* * *

Following three hours of contemplation, and trying on all my new clothes, mixing and matching and re-matching (and even considering a mid-dinner costume change), I finally decided on an outfit for the night's affair: Missoni Sweater, Stone Island jacket, D&G Belt, and Hugo Boss pants.

Without the aid of Loren, who was busy closely monitoring her squad of sexy moving men at Smith Tower, it wasn't until 7:42 - eighteen minutes before dinner – did I realize my wardrobe adventure had become such a time consuming blunder. I scuttled out the door and ran to the monorail station, intermittently glancing at my new Tiffany watch with pride. A moment later I was in a train and on my way up to the Seattle Center with six minutes to spare.

At the Center station I sprinted for the fountain in front of the Space Needle, my planned rendezvous point with Loren. I began to panic when I didn't find her there. My gorgeous watch told me it was 8:01. I assumed she went up the Needle without me.

I frantically dialed Loren.

"Yes honey?" she answered.

"I'm sorry I'm late," I sulked.

"So am I. We just left the tower. I'll be there in two seconds," she said. I figured she was joking, all of downtown was submerged in Friday night gridlock and I couldn't imagine Loren riding the monorail. "Make that one second," she reiterated.

As I stood at the fountain I took notice of several dozen of the hundreds of tourists pointing towards the top of the Space Needle. I thought they must have all decided to gawk at the building in synchronicity - until I heard the roar of a helicopter. I peered up to see Loren's silver helicopter descending the height of the Needle, carefully landing in a patch of lawn at the base near the Imax dome. A bevy of Loren's security and handlers met her at exit from the helicopter. Tourists began approaching her, only to be deflected by her wall of armed guards, the whole mass moving its way toward me as I waited by the fountain.

The girl certainly knew how to make an entrance.

"Good evening," I hailed to the starlet. Tourists snapped pictures as Loren hugged me. She wore a sparkling white Versace mini-gown. "That was incredible!" I shouted as her helicopter roared off up in to the night sky.

"I didn't want to be late. What time is it?"

"You're right on time."

"Are you nervous?" she asked, observing my stiffened stride.

"A little bit," I mutedly replied eyeing the crowd of onlookers staring at us.

"I was nervous too," she exposed. "It's extremely intimidating to be introduced to a group of people touted as the premiere social influences of our city. Don't you think?"

"Yes, definitely," I said. My eyelids twitched nervously as I forced myself to smile cutely. Her brief estimation of the group made me all the more anxious.

"You really shouldn't be nervous. Once you see how arrogant and self-involved these people are you'll either think they're ridiculous and find everything they say to be contrite, or..." she paused, having had a mid-sentence realization.

"Or what?" I inquired. She hesitated to respond. She must have been working out her new idea, or even trying to dispel it.

"...Or you'll become exactly like they are and love yourself endlessly," she said this as if her breath was being pulled out of her.

"Love myself?" I asked, her choice of words questionable. I tried to make a joke and said, "You know they say ninety-percent of men and sixty-percent of women love themselves on a daily basis."

Loren didn't find any humor in my response. She'd become unexplainably languid. Self-conscious, I began to question if Loren was having second thoughts about introducing me to her friends.

As we walked through the thick Friday night crowd and toward the looming Space Needle, Loren gently pulled me aside. At first she didn't say anything. Sensing she was trying to say something important and heartfelt I dropped all attempts at humor.

"Please don't change," Loren pleaded. Then came the exposition: "It seems every time the group inducts a new member they somehow mold this person into what they think will be a great accessory to our crowd. I know I've changed drastically since they accepted me, but I needed it. You, you're so, I don't know... *real*."

"I'm *real?*" I questioned. Someone telling you you're "real" can often mean "less than extraordinary," just as the term "pedestrian" or "commonplace" can describe someone who's ugly and boring.

"*Real*, as in original," she began to elaborate. "You have such an imagination. There's a certain virtue about you Jimmy. A sort of innocence. And you're always honest with me. I don't think you've ever told me a lie. You've just got a fresh look on life." I had to interject. Her explanation was starting to sound like a tampon commercial.

"Thank you. I've never been called fresh before," I said smiling at her. She returned a feeble grin.

"I'm just saying I don't want them to corrupt you. I've already turned you into a designer-label-loving fashionista. God knows what they'll do to you."

"I won't change for anybody," I said. The truth was I wanted to change radically and in any way I could.

During the elevator ride up Loren explained: "They're really not important, you know. It's not like Seattle is the hippest city in America anymore. Maybe if this was New York or Los Angeles, then you'd have a right to be on edge. They're just my friends, they're all rather nice and they just *happen* to be *the* social elite of our entire generation. It's no big deal, really." What she said sounded unbelievable. I passed her words off as a kind of bragging or social dementia, until I met everyone.

As the doors to the elevator split open every eye in the Space Needle's restaurant turned to Loren and her handsome beau, me. Loren took my hand and led me past the concierge, who smiled at her, obviously out of recognition. We sat at an empty table for seven overlooking Lake Union. A waiter immediately filled our water glasses as Loren ordered the two of us a pair of cocktails. As we waited for our dining companions to arrive, late of course, Loren quickly tried to give me a short profile on everyone who'd be attending the informal ceremony.

"Here's the deal," she began to dish. "The outspoken leader of the group is Blaine Fredricks. All you need to know about him is he's 29, some sort of tech-exec at Microsoft and extremely into trendy electronic gadgets, you know all that Japanese shit that is way too complicated for its own good. Oh, and he's rich. But not as rich as me, of course." She giggled. I loved how she loosely alluded to her wealth.

"Is he hot?" I asked. I anticipated all her friends were good looking. She seemed to exist in a separate world where the beautiful frolicked and the ugly were absent.

"Definitely, but not your cup of tea," Loren said. "He likes girls. And he's freaking out about turning 30, so he's in that gotta-get-the-fucking-out-of-my-system mode. Don't hit on him. He hates it when guys hit on him. He's not a homophobe, he just doesn't like gay people." Her last statement was completely ridiculous and we both chucked when she said it. "You know what I mean," she amended.

"I think so," I nodded.

"The other four members are harmless, very friendly. Let's see, there's Chelsea, Sonya, Walter, and Nina. I think you'll like Chelsea, she works at *The Sound*."

"Really," I chirped identifying the career potential. *The Sound* was Seattle's hottest weekly Arts & Lifestyle publication, and the only one I could stand to read. *The Sounds'* two competitors, *The Stranger* and *The Seattle Weekly,* both read like juvenile rant pieces with a tone similar to a high school newspaper. *The Sound,* however, was a gem, celebrating the arts and the city without the endless criticism and derision. *The Sound* was a soapbox for new ideas, not old complaints, and everything it covered it coveted. Every young journalist in Seattle dreamt of working for a paper like *The Sound*, and now I found myself with the prospect of making a very valuable connection with Chelsea Hudson, the editor-in-chief.

"Give me some dirt on these people," I insisted, "I'll be less nervous if I know something naughty about each one."

With a smirk, Loren deliberated for a moment, placing her palms flat against each other likely she was praying for a juicy morsel of hearsay. "I'll start with Chelsea. She's a workaholic if there ever was one. When she walks in here she's going to have a cell phone in one hand, a cigarette in the other, and likely one of the waiters pouring a drink down her throat. Ever since she got promoted she hasn't taken one goddamn day off. Not a moment goes by she's not editing copy, conceptualizing the next issue's cover, *something*! Chelsea's one of those girls who'll have a heart attack at forty. You know the type," Loren said with a lovely, tragic wave of the hand.

"What about the other one, Sonya?" I begged.

"Oh yes," she recollected. "Sonya is a darling. The most wonderful person you could ever meet and probably the most fashionable in the group. She has one of those cosmopolitan dream jobs as Women's Fashion Director at Nordstrom. She makes well past six-figures. It's going to be sad to kick her out of the group."

"If she's so successful why would you guys kick her out?" I asked. Loren gave me a glare as if I was the most naive person she'd ever seen.

"Because next month she turns 31-and-a-half. In October it's thirty for her."

"Ah," I nodded. "The malevolence of aging."

"Listen, when I joined the little club here it was considered graceful to bow out when you reached 28. Now, it's like you have to be forcibly removed. For Buddha's sake, Sonya joined seven years ago! It is time for her to move on."

"Seven years," I repeated, underscoring Loren's remark. "What exactly is the point of this group? Why have these people come together?"

Our drinks arrived and I was growing ever impatient of the faceless guests. Loren began to answer my question just after she downed her first glass of champagne. This was before I'd even had the chance to dab the celery salt rim of my bloody Mary.

"The point is to network," Loren explained. "Groups of the social elite are established simply to help each other achieve one another's aspirations. Just look at the range of industries we're in. I'm in fashion and global finance. Blaine Fredicks is in computer technology. Chelsea Hudson's a member of the media. Sonya Klein is in retail. Walter Dennison, banking and finance. And Nina Kensington, entertainment."

"Entertainment? What's she do?"

"Nina is A&R Manager for the Seattle office of the Universal Music Group. *Very* well paid. Knows a lot of Seattle's finest rock stars."

"All of Seattle's finest rock stars are dead," I said. My first slurp of bloody Mary was like untying a verbal corset. I felt so much more at ease with just a dash of vodka in me. "Or they've moved to Los Angeles."

"I know, she has a dream job. The grey hairs at UMG still think Seattle has a viable music scene."

Loren described the group's fifth member as Walter Dennison, whose job title was Brand Strategist at Washington Mutual – at the time the largest savings and loan in the United States. At age 28, "Walty" had been credited with the bank's youth market supremacy, having designed campaigns that lead twenty-somethings to recognize "WaMu" as their favorite place to keep their money. Walty's marketing had worked so well nationally that the bank's name was as favorably revered and recognized as that of Coca-Cola and Sony.

"Walty is my favorite," Loren admitted, "he's like my grandpa, except he's young. And alive."

"How is he like your grandpa?" Loren's greatest contradiction always seemed to be herself.

"Very wise, filled with knowledge, like he was born in the 1950s or something. His perspective on any topic, no matter how remote, is always thought out. His intellect has been tempered like that of someone with a lot of first-hand experience. He lacks the impetuousness that is engrained in our generation. In contrast to the others Walty sticks out like a Christmas tree in the desert."

Blaine Fredricks was the first to arrive. I was intimidated initially by his imposing height and toned stature, not what I expected from a tech-exec. His hair was cut short and died bright red, like the color of cherry soda. Blaine was dressed in all black with matching thick-black-frame glasses. He was the epitome of the dot-com chic, and a little reminiscent of a vampire, except his skin was tan. He entered the restaurant like he owned the place, which in this type of crowd, could have been possible.

Loren stood and greeted Blaine with a smile, hug, and her trademark euro-kiss on each cheek. I shook his hand and he smiled warmly at me. The duration of the handshake went past "nice to meet you, stranger," to "I can't wait to blow you," or so I thought.

Blaine apologized for being late but then noticed the four other empty chairs at the table and realized he wasn't the only one running behind.

Loren and Blaine oozed chemistry. He sat right next to her and as he spoke she leaned over close to capture every word he emitted. Be it in regard to Microsoft's foray in to the satellite software market or whether or not he thought his gardener was a legal resident. When I heard Blaine begin talking passionately about computer programming, using terms like "tabular data stream" and "optimistic concurrency control mechanism", I found him to be one of the world's great paradoxes: The Super Sexy Nerd.

The Super Sexy Nerd was an up-and-coming niche of the dot-com populous. They grew in places like Seattle's Eastside and Silicon Valley, and started out as regular nerds but after becoming rich and cultured the lures of the modish and fashionable began to ensnare them. At the beginning of their twenties they worked 80-hour weeks for little pay in an anonymous, windowless office. But by the time they reached 30, or in Blaine's case 29, they were insanely rich, giving them the time and power to attend society fair. They used designer skincare products and exercised religiously, making them a gorgeous paradox within the tech industry.

As Loren and Blaine gossiped about the other members of the group, getting as much in as they could before their arrival, I found it alarming that Blaine kept insisting on my consideration and input. He was an absolute gentleman in trying to get the new guy involved in the vernacular.

"You ready to meet the most neurotic group of people in all of Seattle, Jimmy?" he asked, sipping a booze laced cappuccino.

"I don't suppose they can be any more neurotic than I am," I replied. He laughed briskly as Loren gave me one of *those* looks, this one meaning "I wish you weren't so goddamn witty."

"Oh Blainey!" Loren said, using the nickname she had coined for him. "I'm moving into my new place tomorrow. You have to come over and see it."

"What new place?" he asked, licking the luscious foam off his upper lip.

"My fabulous new loft at the top of the Smith Tower!" Loren screamed, her voice the loudest in the entire restaurant. "It's like a mansion on top of a skyscraper. You won't believe it when you see it."

"I don't believe it!" he scowled, "How in the hell did you get that loft? I've been trying to get the Smith for three years." Blaine then switched in to a sailor's accent to ask drunk and mockingly, "How'd ya snag it?"

"Baby you're a nobody in this town," she tried to rile him. "Or any town for that matter. I snagged it with money. They had the top of the tower split up into four rental units so I knew I'd never be able to buy each one and if I did it'd take years for each of the tenants to vacate. So, I did what any good real estate tycoon would do," she explained, causing Blaine to laugh.

"What'd you do?" I asked, not understanding the apparent joke.

"I bought the whole building. Probably paid way too much for it but who cares? It can only go up in value. It's real estate, right!" Loren declared as swanky Sonya Klein walked in and sat down at our table. For a very-late-twenty-something (according to her), Sonya wafted in with a stench of class. She wore a long flowing white dress, her elegant red hair was swept up in a bun and the jewels decorating her hands and neck had to have been worth a yacht. My first thought when I saw her was that Rita Hayworth had stopped by the Space Needle for a quick bite to eat.

"Sorry I'm late, looks like everyone else is running a little behind, too," she said eloquently and with such breathy politeness I wondered if she hadn't been imported from a vintage Hollywood romance. Sonya glanced at me and said, "You must be Jimmy, it's nice to meet you. Loren said you were adorable, but I was thinking boyish, but you... you're *positively* a grown man."

Sonya's flirting was more than welcome. I was dying for some attention and who better to give it to me? She was rich and as a senior fashion executive at Nordstrom, likely the most influential in the group. Her taste in clothes dictated the wardrobes of millions of women across the country. Forget Anna Wintour as the arbiter of taste. If Nordstrom didn't buy it, nobody did. Sonya Klein was front-and-center at every runway show she attended. In terms of dollars, nobody had the purse she did to buy both haute couture and ready-to-wear. I trembled just sitting next to her.

At about that time Chelsea Hudson arrived in a loud fervor. She was hurried, angry, and still taking a call on her cell phone (just as Loren predicted) when she sat down. The others didn't find it rude Chelsea carried on with her phone conversation in the restaurant. The other patrons were certainly aware of her lurid, high-volume dialogue about whether or not showing airborne semen in a cover photo was "too explicit for the public to digest" (her words exactly). Sonya was polite enough to introduce this crude creature. Apparently Chelsea was a sociopath who'd been given the nickname "The Dictator" at *The Sound*. She was also the town's most celebrated lesbian novelist who'd recently penned *The Pussy Who Flew Airplanes*, the fourth installment of a series of books that'd made her a millionaire. The ilk of her novels integrated graphic portrayals of women being raped by male brutes who vengefully slaughter their rapists and go on to become horny lesbians in Nazi-esque prisons (where lesbians apparently flourished).

As several conversations persisted around the table, petite and reticent Nina Kensington arrived with sly anonymity. She sat down unnoticed by anyone other than me. She nibbled on bread and sat silently flipping through the wine menu, continually unnoticed by everyone. It wasn't until Loren spilled sangria on Nina did anyone acknowledge her presence. As I continued to be primarily observant of the group I would notice the waiters never once conversed with my acquaintances, just me. Their drinks were refilled, appetizers replenished and upon the arrival of our first course it became evident these five people frequented the restaurant so much the staff knew their demands before they could demand them.

To my delight, Blaine raised a glass as well as his voice to announce my presence at the table. At this point Chelsea had ended her boisterous phone conversation/argument, and Sonya and Loren had finished their gossip-fest, so all eyes were on me.

"I hear he's a gorgeous photographer and an all around great guy. Here's to getting to know Jimmy," Blaine announced. He was so loud that nearby diners gave our entire group woeful glares and shook their heads in disdain.

The group continued about their mingling. I didn't get so much as a "what kind of a photographer are you" from anybody. I felt like the lonely and presumably outcast Nina sitting to my left. I finished somebody's glass of wine and decided to do something unusual: start a conversation with someone I didn't know!

"So Nina, how are things in the music biz?" I said as friendly as possible. I considered the reason she wasn't talking to anyone to be because she didn't like doing so.

"Fine, just fine I guess," she groaned with the most subtle British accent.

"Fine you guess… you're not sure?" I said, unintentionally bothersome.

"I don't know!" she blasted, surely frustrated that I didn't know at what.

I lowered my voice and politely asked, "Is it me or the group? It's as if they don't know you. They haven't said a word to you. I thought maybe you were seated at the wrong table."

"The music label is going under," Nina confessed. "And I have a lump. You'd think with tits as small as mine cancer would have a difficult time finding any tissue supple enough to live on. Regardless, I have a lump, can you fucking believe it? Where is that prick waiter, I need another drink!"

"Are you sure it's cancer?" I said, wanting to remain optimistic.

"Yes. I have breast cancer at 25, can you believe that... what was your name again?"

"Jimmy."

"Well Jimmy, can you believe it?"

I truly didn't know what to say. How often are you prepared to comfort a stranger who's admitted to you they have cancer? Lucky for me, a drunken Walter Dennison stumbled in and sat down to make an announcement.

"I'm going to fucking kill myself!" Walter barked.

The group gasped. A waiter spotted Walter's entrance and quickly jaunted to the bar to order him a double gin and tonic.

"Don't be absurd," Loren jeered, "your life isn't that wretched, Walty," she said while patting him on his slightly balding head.

"Yes it is. I'm pathetic," sneered Walter.

"Not really. Meet Jimmy. He's much more pathetic than you could ever be. He's not even a millionaire like the rest of us," Blaine announced with such blatant rudeness I felt both embarrassment and a rage so robust I knew not how to respond. All I could do is sit there and absorb the verbal affront.

"I'm not a millionaire," Nina chided.

"Blaine, Jimmy is not pathetic..." Loren defended, but elaborated in retraction. "Well he won't be in a couple weeks when I'm done with him."

Quickly the table's hostility made way for a very welcome eighth round of drinks. However, the drama would recommence around eight o'clock when an elderly group of delegates from the Japanese consulate were seated at a banquet table next to ours. They were talking quietly and gave several members of my group a dirty look whenever they raised their voice for dramatic purpose or even to laugh. By the time nine o'clock beckoned one of the women at the consulate's table summoned a waiter in order to complain of Loren's smoking inside the restaurant. The waiter came over to Loren and said "Miss, one of the other patrons has noted that you're smoking. I might remind you that it is illegal to smoke indoors." Loren and the waiter both giggled. She shot a disheartening glare over at the neighboring table and casually handed the waiter a handful of large bills. He proceeded to call several of the busing staff over to clear the consulate's table, whereupon the group was asked to leave. It was subtle, but the incident was probably the most spectacular social triumph I'd seen.

"Decadence truly is exquisite!" Loren cackled as she waved goodbye to the dignitaries who were carrying their coats out of the restaurant, each of their faces preserved in a hideous grimace.

The night proceeded as smoothly as riding a bronco through a carwash. I can remember discussing the pros and cons of being a slut, the pros and cons of being rich, and the pros and cons of being stalked, topics of which I had no experience in whatsoever.

The limousine ride home with Loren and Blaine was confusing. The entire journey I found myself confounded as to whether Blaine wanted to go home with me or Loren. Blaine put his arm around my shoulder like a football player might do to one of his teammates after a touchdown. It's also the kind of affection a guy might show his boyfriend. I was aroused and puzzled at the very same moment. What was more confusing was how Loren and Blaine acted around each other. She would set her folded hands on his lap, occasionally gripping his leg. When he had something to say he would whisper it in her ear. But then he'd scoot over and casually grip my shoulder gently and smile so warmly at me it was as if he wanted to kiss me.

"Where are we going?" Blaine asked Loren, surely recognizing we weren't stopping at Smith Tower.

"We have to stop at my old place," Loren barked. "I have to change. This dress is hell. You can hang out at Jimmy's while I change."

I celebrated the thought of Blaine in my apartment. Quickly I tried to recall if I'd left anything incriminating out in the open before I'd left for dinner. Underwear: neatly folded and placed in proper drawers. Porno: locked tightly in bedroom nightstand. Other unmentionable objects: nowhere in sight.

On the walk from Loren's limousine to the lobby I was riveted to find touchy Blaine had clung on to me as we both observed Loren digging through her purse for her phone. As we walked he whispered cute, drunken questions in my ear the same way he did at the restaurant with Loren. "What do you want to be when you grow up?" and, "When was the first time you had sex," were among his questions. I hesitated to answer having blushed at each one. Finally he asked, "Do you like girls or boys?"

I blushed once again, this time an intense, scorching fuchsia, the result of my pulse racing further in to excitement. Why did he want to know?

"What do you think?" I replied with a sweet murmur in his ear, delivered so close I could have licked his lobe if I extended my tongue.

He speculated a moment and came up with a conclusion, "Well you're definitely bi, if not gay. I can tell by the way you look at me. The way you acknowledge me touching you. A straight guy would be uncomfortable."

"Maybe you're right," I said.

"Are you hard?" he asked, sliding one of his hands across the top of my leg on to my crotch. "You are!"

"Blainey, I can't find my phone!" Loren screeched and whimpered.

My memory of what happened once we got to my apartment is distorted. I can remember eating pizza in the kitchen, serving Blaine and Loren gewürztraminer in martini glasses and laughing at everything they said. However, what they said is muted in my memory and the reason Loren left after finally finding her telephone is also unknown. A vivid recollection of events isn't clear to me until the next morning when I woke sleeping on the floor next to my bed face down on the hardwood with my arms tucked underneath my chest. To my relief I had all my clothes on, even my brilliant Dior oxfords. In fact I was even wearing a John Deere farm equipment hat that wasn't mine. This would be the first time I'd hit the town, got smashed, and woke up with *more* clothes on than fewer.

My phone was ringing madly, as if it were trying to warn me of a fire. The only fire I could locate was the one in my stomach. Inside me was a concoction of expensive liquor that wrestled with a hot molten beast of masticated cuisine. I answered the phone only to be subjected to one of Loren's grand statements in defense of her ever wavering morality: "Haven't you ever just wanted to get fucked? It didn't matter who it was, it was just a fuck. This whole week has been so frustrating." She was trying to make herself feel better by pleading to me how animal, carnal and passionate unplanned sex with a stranger could be. It was really a needless effort. I'd longed for sex with anybody, so be it a random stranger.

"What happened to Blaine?" I asked, having no recollection of how the evening ended.

"I don't know. I forgot to get him before I went to my new place."

"Hold on," I said, standing up to examine my apartment. I found Blaine watching Saturday morning cartoons in my living room as he smoked a cigarette and ate Trix cereal. He smiled at me, his teeth cluttered with a rainbow of fruity flavored cereal. I returned an ironic grin and went back in to my bedroom.

"Shit," I said, not knowing what had happened.

"What?" Loren begged.

"He's still here," I said. "Why is he still here?"

"You tell me!" Loren railed. "If you turned Blaine gay I'll kill you."

I stepped back in the living room to ask, "Blaine, why are you here?"

"You told me to stay the night because you said I was too drunk to make it home by myself. So I slept on the couch. You passed out in your room and I thought if I left and you woke up and I was gone you would have flipped out."

"Oh yes, that's right," I said as if I remembered any of it.

"Meet me for brunch," Loren insisted, "and bring Blaine."

We met Loren at a tiny vegetarian bakery named Garden tucked inside an alleyway in the charming Pioneer Square district. Loren told us of how one of her moving men had been just what she was looking for: a slightly older and obscenely muscular "dirty fucker" who she knew wouldn't call her even if she'd given him her number. I envied Loren and her lack of inhibition. Listening to her recount the sultry details of her evening only made me feel lonesome. I looked over at the delicious looking Blaine as he ate his scone, wondering if I would have been successful in seducing him had I not fallen asleep on my floor. No matter how hard I tried I could not evoke the memory of telling him to stay the night at my apartment. I began to wonder if he made up the story and had lingered at my place in the hopes that some sort of sexual encounter would transpire. Regardless of whatever happened, sex wasn't part of it and I decided the previous evening was just another one of my many lost opportunities at romance or intimacy.

Loren must have been thinking along the same vein as she prodded, "Blaine, you didn't take advantage of Jimmy last night did you?"

"No!" he said, shaking his head, just as every straight guy is required to do when asked such a gruesome question.

"Jimmy, you didn't rape Blaine last night, did you?"

"No comment."

. . .

Rich people really do have the best of everything; the best cars, the finest homes, and certainly the most brilliant physicians and therapists. I had been complaining to Loren that I felt depressed even though I should be happy. She told me to go to her psychiatrist and get a diagnosis, so I did. Five minutes into my first and last consultation I was given a bag load of different samples, one of which was called Cynexia, a lovely little pill that came in seven different colors, one for each day of the week. Cynexia was a drug unavailable to the general public because it has not been approved by the FDA. Only people like Loren Anders who owned their own pharmaceutical corporation had access to these types of experimental and sometimes "custom-fit" drugs like Cynexia. I was a bit apprehensive about taking the anti-depressant because I had to sign a 16-page waiver stating I wouldn't sue the company if the drug killed me or made me want to kill myself. I felt I had nothing to lose and signed the waiver, and I'm glad I did. I fell in love with Cynexia right away. She was simple and divine, and the little maroon pill I took on Sundays reminded me of the worm medicine I gave to Harriet, the English Sheppard I had as a kid.

Everything was better with Cynexia. Suddenly I loved my life. I didn't consider Cynexia to cause artificial joy, rather it just let me forget about the bad things in life, similar to liquor but without the hangover and it could be consumed first thing in the morning. And even though I wasn't legally permitted to operate machinery or tattoo needles while on Cynexia, I think I was sane. I knew there were side-effects because one night while on the dope I passed out while masturbating. When I woke up I didn't know where or who I was. It was so confusing waking up on the floor with my dick hanging out of my pants. I thought I'd just gotten laid, but no, it was only Cynexia. But as great as the drug was in boosting my mood, it did little to squelch my anxiety when it came to socializing.

Alone at home on a Saturday night, I was quite aware of how pitiable I was. But for someone to call and remind me was downright humiliating. The phone rang around ten and of course it was Loren (who else would it be, my mother?). She asked if I wanted to get fucked up, and me, being bored out of my mind said, "Yes, when and where?"

Miss Loren explained she was over on gritty but edgy Capitol Hill at a club called Blow, a place she described as the "only dance club worth going to in the whole city."

Despite the blatant stereotype, not all gay guys like dance music. In fact I preferred to stay as far away from the disco-throbbing joints as possible. But with a newfound optimism courtesy of Cynexia, I eagerly met my new friend at Blow, ready to get down to whatever the DJ was spinning.

Ever since Loren and I began a friendship she'd become very protective of me. In what I estimated as a maternal instinct, Loren purposefully ensured I was always in a good mood. She would always go out of her way to make sure I was having a nice day, no matter how bad hers may have been, and she'd buy me gifts because they reminded her of me. She was the most generous person I'd ever come to know. The only other person I knew to be so giving was my mother. But Loren provided for me in a different way. She saw to it that I wasn't lazy and I was also striving to do something with my life, even if my actions were in the hypothetical or remained in the planning stages. Loren would constantly remind me that a job in accounting didn't seem to be fulfilling me professionally, and that I should pursue a career that did. Loren would also chronically reassure me I was talented. She always liked to use the word "talent" but I'm not sure why. It's not like I could sing or play the cello. I'm not sure how she came up with the idea that I was blessed with any sort of genius or skill. Maybe she saw something I didn't.

Blow turned out to be unexpectedly mellow. The disco queens were confined to the basement trance level while the main level swung to upbeat West Coast jazz. Loren met me in a room titled The SmoothBar where the young-and-beautiful lounged, drank and discussed current events and politics. The hot topic that evening was: Where would Dior be without John Galliano?

At a table for two Loren told me she had serious news. In the few short weeks I'd known Loren "serious" meant she had either lost her appointment with her dermatologist or she was considering the purchase of a new credenza. However, this time "serious" meant she wanted me to photograph her.

"Just a couple shots, nothing big, just to see if something happens!" Loren begged. Unsure of my remaining ability behind the camera, I reacted to her gesture without enthusiasm, saying that I'd consider it. But she persisted. "I'll give you money for time and expense. I just need somebody I can trust and you're such a good photographer. It's not as if you're so busy you can't do it."

I paused before giving her an answer. I truthfully never considered myself to be a photographer before, just someone who enjoyed taking pictures and happened to be good at it. In that moment I was unsure I could come up with a concept that could be worth shooting, let alone so good that it would be worth adding to her portfolio. This was a woman who'd been shot by the greatest visionaries of the day, not to mention the wolf packs of paparazzi that often hunted her in public. She didn't need me to add any content to her portfolio. She already had one of the most impressive in the industry. What she wanted was to motivate me, and having realized this halfway in to the conversation, I couldn't help but feel grateful for her attempt.

Before I could tell her that I would photograph her, she said, "I'll give you a hundred dollars a picture!"

"Done!" We toasted and our work began. I didn't anticipate that she wanted me to get to work that night on the photos.

At three o'clock in the morning in the desolate Financial District of Seattle, Loren and I set out to capture her in the gloomy urban jungle. We were calling it 'Beauty and the Bleak'. Prior to that night I'd never seen this part of the city so empty. Electricity conservation made streets that in the day were crowded with thousands of pedestrians a stark opposite of black emptiness. The air was cold and dewy. Homeless men rested peacefully in the doorways of banks and luxury boutiques. Despite the fearsome atmosphere we were determined to create something as memorable as the fear we felt. The creepy ambiance was a mesmerizing theme, we only had to capture it.

Thanks to my pre-planning we quickly found a sculpture garden for Loren to pose in. Loren's inventive thinking provided her a duffle bag of hair and makeup options. As for fashion, everything from Alberta Ferreti to Yves Saint Laurent had been packed inside a rolling Louis Vuitton armoire. The camera's bulb shot blinding blasts of light across Loren, standing at perfect akimbo in front of the monolithic skyscrapers of downtown that sparkled in the headlights of occasionally passing automobiles. She was a small angelic figure trapped between giant beasts of cold architecture, a gorgeous juxtaposition of warm fragility and steely strength. In several shots I would even capture the looming AndersCenter towers in the background, something she had told me to avoid but I couldn't help snap.

As we moved around the city we began to cause a stir amongst the abundant homeless population. At one point I captured a shot of a transient woman asking Loren for a dollar. In one of the photographs Loren is seen handing the woman a dollar and some change from a Fendi bag that retailed for $3,900.

Once the shoot was complete we found ourselves over by the Pike Place Market, just a few blocks from my apartment building. There we examined our creation to find before us a series of provocative photos. Loren had never looked more glamorous and I'd somehow become a professional photographer. To both our surprise the shoot ended up having a theme I had not predicted: capitalism. Loren and the skyscrapers represented power and money; the black night and maligned homeless symbolized depravity. These photos perfectly captured the hedonistic and anxious era in which we frolicked.

"I can't wait to show these to my agent, he'll love them!" Loren gleamed as we reexamined each photo. I had a very different reaction than her, one I can only surmise as being in love. It was not love for the photos or for feeling redeemed through creating something viable, but love for Loren. She was a strong, compassionate young woman who, for some unknown reason, had flown down from her perch, swooped me up, and made me realize I was worth something. In the early morning when any other heiress would have been asleep in her royal suite, there she was, convincing me I had a talent.

That moment Loren Anders would destroy some of the theories I'd let fester in my mind about the independent life. For so long I'd romanced the idea of being a person on my own in need of no one else to make me happy. But there with her looking at our handiwork, I conjured not needing anyone as a type of immense handicap. I needed her more than anything. As she savored each photograph on the computer's screen, I began to consider that she might need me too.

APRIL

When I woke up at 6:09 am on April 1ˢᵗ I was overwhelmingly delighted and proud to say: "This is the month I go to New York City!"

With my now over-booked society calendar I'd somewhat forgotten about my impulsive purchase of non-refundable airline tickets and hotel fare in The Big Apple. I kept telling myself "it's still months away" and then suddenly it wasn't. The trip was now only three weeks off and a dizzying bout of anticipation fused with fear began to mount.

Just as my horoscope would preface good fortune, my nasty boss at OmniCare, Guinevere, had been replaced in recent weeks by a flaming queen who went by the name Stefan (his real and legal name was Steve). Stefan was charmed when I told him I'd frivolously purchased a trip to Manhattan prior to having the time off from work formally approved. He described my blithe ambition with the phrase "you're only young once!" and would later describe his first time in New York, circa 1982, including the time he tried to buy marijuana in Washington Square Park from a break dancer and got arrested. "Mom and dad were so ashamed!" he wailed, recalling the arrest.

The tired wardrobe I once loathed had been replaced by a chic array of this-season designer pieces I gleamed at every time I saw them. I couldn't wait to pack it all up and strut them around the island of Manhattan. The indulgent shopping spree Loren treated me to had been further expanded after she paid me $11,700 for our late night photo shoot, a fee I spent on a new computer and Prada sneakers. The rest was put in savings. The best part of spending the earnings came when one of the sales clerks at Nordstrom referred to me by first name. I'd become one of their most frequent customers.

It seemed life couldn't get any more frivolous. I was attending the Opera in designer suits and taking cabs to work. Forget that sultry bus. Not until something so extraordinarily gruesome happened was I reminded that it all was not to be had without a sense of other people's peril or mortality. Loren and I were strolling down First Avenue on a busy weekday afternoon. Rush hour was in full effect and we were minding our business, talking about things I don't recall. One of those California girls imported to Seattle was talking on her cell phone and drinking an espresso while smoking a cigarette. I had noticed her because I had wondered how she kept the ashes from falling in her coffee. She was one of those types that wore tight spaghetti-strap T-shirts all year-round and who would broadcast their cell phone conversations to everyone within a five mile radius. Her type really annoyed me, mostly because they seemed to have everything they wanted and didn't have to do anything to earn it, yet were the most miserable beings you could ever encounters. These girls had beautiful, muscled boyfriends, drove expensive cars, and lived in tremendous condos overlooking the bay. They had everything they wanted and seemed to hate it.

"Look at her," I murmured to Loren. "She's MTV on two legs." We both laughed mutedly.

"Pants are supposed to cover your ass, not be lodged in it," Loren noted quietly. The girl's jeans just barely crested her ass crack, the tops of her lacey panties exposed intentionally. A moment would pass as Loren and I continued to gawk at the absurd creature of modern day – her slutty heels, cheap knock-off handbag, and other counterfeit wares all came under fire from the two of us.

Loren and I got a real close-up view of the girl as she waited for the crosswalk light to change. For some unknown reason this girl who blatantly flaunted everything wrong with the generation, decided she was too good to wait for the 'WALK' signal and just headed right into traffic. I don't think she even looked both ways before she crossed. I'd seen lots of people do this and usually the cars, buses, trucks, and other vehicles careening down the street would stop, or at least slow down. *Usually.*

I heard a giant gasp from Loren and then a giant boom, the screeching of tires and the sound of broken glass hitting the sidewalk. I looked around to see what had happened. A metro bus had hit this girl at around forty miles-per-hour and she was gone. There were bloody bits of her all over the road, the bus, and other cars, as if she'd just combusted. It was a ghastly, bloody mess like nothing I'd ever seen. The thick crowd of tourists we were in immediately began screaming and weeping.

"That was dumb," is all I could say. I knew the comment to be insensitive but it's just what came out of my mouth, I couldn't stop it.

"I can't believe it," Loren said, her voice weak and trembling. I sensed she was about to cry. All the people around us had the same reaction. Immediately we walked away from the gory scene and headed toward the Harbor Steps where we both sat, shaking our heads in disbelief. As I sat there I'd discover my legs were trembling. I looked at my hands to see they were blue and shivering like it was a winter day.

"I've never seen anything like that," Loren said in a daze.

"Neither have I," I replied. Both of us just stared at the ground, unsure of what to say and both of us feeling guilty for having teased the dead girl. We just sat there, not knowing what to do or how to do it. As the sirens came, Loren angrily said, "Why didn't that bitch watch what she was doing?"

"I don't know," I mumbled.

"She was so fucking caught up in herself. What a dumb ass." Loren's words were shocking. She was calling a woman who'd just been killed a bitch and an ass. Some people deal with tragedy strangely.

"I guess it's just survival of the fittest," I said. "The city is a predator." Loren shook her head, brushing off my comment. At the same time she wiped a rogue tear from her cheek.

We waited and waited, sitting on the Harbor Steps, listening to the ambulance and police arrive – not to rescue or revive but to clean up the horrific mess. We sat there for I don't know how long, talking about things that didn't matter, maybe to comfort each other in our shock, or maybe just because we could, celebrating the luxury and burden of still being alive.

That horrid day changed Loren Anders. As we walked down to Pioneer Square her cellular phone rang. Startled, she tore the phone out of her purse and threw it in a garbage can. Days later she would quit smoking and begin the pursuit of a deeper spirituality. The outlandish and frivolous Loren Anders I had come to know suddenly became a more thoughtful and appreciative incarnation, if only temporarily.

I can't say I wasn't changed by witnessing the accident. The optimism I once possessed had been replaced by inexorable frustration. I guess it was my sudden realization that no matter what you make of yourself, it can all be gone in the time it takes to cross the street. A speeding metro bus could just suddenly erase your existence, regardless of how fabulous your job, supple your bank account or glamorous your friends and acquaintances.

My new, reluctant and passive attitude toward everything became ever present. At the monthly social summit at the Space Needle the pressure to look good in exchange for acceptance was gone and I was free to just sit there and get drunk. During a group conversation on why tourists are were flocking to Seattle for romance and adventure (seemingly overnight the city had become known as "America's Paris"), Chelsea disclosed that *The Sound* was putting together a Seattle travel guide geared toward the trendy traveler. She asked us all what we thought should be included in the text.

"A shopping map," Sonya chimed first, an essential request.

"A guide to the best theaters," suggested Nina.

"I've got it," Blaine announced with fanfare. "How about in the section where it describes the neighborhoods outside the downtown core you could honestly and poignantly describe each neighborhood."

"Well of course," Chelsea persisted. She wouldn't have it any other way.

"I don't think you do." Blaine began his agenda, "Instead of saying these so-and-so streets are scattered with beautiful linden trees, it could give a cultural exploration into each neighborhood. A true look at the dynamic social conflicts within each neighborhood!"

"It is a tourism guide. We want the tourists to go home with a feeling they saw something they haven't ever seen before," Chelsea summarized, reciting the instructions she'd given to her staff verbatim.

"I know," I blared, "Just tell them how it is. The Seattle suburbs are filled with blue-collar hillbillies and food stamp whores. Most of which were drawn here because of an abundance of high-school education entry-level jobs at Boeing where they can work in departments like Nuts and Bolts with exciting job titles such as Blinking Light Technician and Assistant Screwdriver Supervisor. That's pretty fucking honest."

The group howled with laughter, except for Chelsea who felt we were only demeaning her call for help. She took a passive stance in every conversation throughout the night. It was not my intention to dissuade Chelsea with my comment, however true it was. Her silence yielded no apology from me and that was probably the last interaction I ever had with the beast.

My comfort level in the group had grown so nonchalant that I misplaced the number of drinks I'd consumed. After hearing of how Nina had met Woody Allen, her hero, by accident in Atlanta the previous weekend, I began telling the group of an embarrassing story of a girl who'd fallen madly in love with me on a plane ride to San Francisco. "On the flight she's telling me about how she wants to find a boyfriend who won't treat her like garbage and before I know it we've landed, she's taken me to her place, she's slurping on my half-hard dick and trying to tell me how it was fate that we met. And just then I got the balls, so to speak, to tell her I was gay and that I didn't want to sleep with her. Well she's nice enough to carefully zip me back up and asks if I want to go see the Woody Allen film playing at the theater down the block."

"So that's how you met Loren," Blaine joked. Everyone in the group, including the bitter Chelsea, roared with laughter. And even though she was the butt of the joke, I think Loren laughed the hardest.

"Great story," Sonya praised. She must've been as drunk as I was for she began telling of a similar tale: "On my way back from Milan a man who was sitting next to me asked if I wanted to join the mile high club. I told him I was already a member and he then asked if I would help him gain his membership." She paused to take a drink.

"Here we go," Chelsea pouted.

"We get into the bathroom and it's tight. We start kissing and he's groping my breasts and soon he's ripped my panties off and he's fingering me and all that. I really started getting hot and wanted it so I began unbuckling his belt and see he has a small gun strapped to his waist. So I start screaming."

"Because you're coming already?" I foolishly asked.

"No. Because of the gun. So I ask why he has a gun on an airplane." Just then her jaw opened and made a dangling motion for dramatic purposes. "Do you know what he says?"

"He's a Palestinian terrorist planning on hijacking the plane?" Blaine guessed.

"No! It turns out he's the sky marshal. Can you imagine terrorists taking over the plane and the sky marshal is in the bathroom fucking? It just goes to show you we need better security in the skies."

"Right on!" Loren applauded mockingly. Even through my veil of drunkenness I could see Loren was not happy. She was obviously annoyed by the group's sex banter. It was then I noticed she'd not had one cocktail the whole evening. Her lone sobriety made the rest of the group uncomfortable, not to mention curious.

After dinner when even more crude banter proliferated, Loren demanded we leave, and we did. After exiting the Space Needle we were escorted by her entourage to her limousine. I found the late winter breeze fairly unpleasant. The only thing more brisk than the air was Loren.

"Is something wrong?" I pried. "You seem very distracted."

"I understand you for being friendly and all," she began, her voice restraining anger. "But we're there for a reason. It's to enhance our careers, not talk about who we've fucked. And don't get too attached to Sonya, her days are numbered. I can tell you've taken a liking to that old hag."

Her comment stunk of jealousy.

"She's the only one who makes any sense," I replied. "Maybe it's because she's older but she isn't there to improve her career. She's there to have fun and have an excuse to get tipsy. Fuck Loren, I don't even have a career! What am I doing there with you?"

"I don't know," Loren agreed. "Unless you want to have a long and tumultuous career in the exciting realm of accounting then you'd better do something with your life."

The limousine ride home was silent until the car stopped at my building. Loren kissed me on each cheek and said she was only angry because she loved me, then sent me to my apartment.

In a cognizant drift I rode up the elevator, beginning to feel weary of what Loren's sudden irritation had been caused by. I feared she hated me for having no direction in life, for not having a future and becoming more accepted among her friends than she was. All those worries were joyfully erased as I hit the pillow that night, my merry slumber orchestrated by $200 worth of delicious alcohol.

• • •

I spent the rest of the weekend cleaning my neglected apartment and finalizing the clothes I planned to take to New York. Randomly I would have the impulse to call Loren to talk about stupid, petty things like always. Then I considered her frustration with me may have come from the fact I was around her too much.

On Monday I went to work in a daze. As I stepped out of the cab and tried to prepare my mind for the day's upcoming tasks by recalling what had been done the previous week, absolutely nothing came to mind. I trusted that checking my inbox would bring back a flood of memories. When I sat down at my desk and checked my voicemail I discovered a curious message from Tom Jennings in Human Resources.

"Hello James," the message started, strangely as everyone in the company including Tom usually called me Jimmy. "When you get in today could you please come over to H-R. We need to go over some things with you. Thanks, bye." The message was oddly stern, the tone so callous I felt as if I were being reprimanded. My pulse immediately quickened.

I wandered over to Human Resources and greeted the receptionist warmly with a smile. She did not return any sort of friendly gesture and told me to have a seat in the waiting area. Moments later Tom Jennings, who'd recently been promoted to H/R Associate, up from H/R Clerk (receptionist), called me into his window office. His manner was frank, the absolute opposite of the giddy young boy he previously typified.

"James, let me start by asking you how your health is," Tom began. The question was preposterous as I was a healthy young male in his prime.

"Great, why?"

"Since the beginning of the year you've called in sick seven times," Tom said as he set a calendar in front of me, seven days highlighted in bright yellow. It looked like a lot compacted in to just over two months.

"We're concerned you might not be well," he falsely stated. Omnicare didn't care about my health, only the cost of their group health insurance premium. It was H/R's responsibility to creatively terminate the career of anyone who might actually use the company's health insurance plan.

"It's cold season… isn't it?" I tried to cover, only making an ass of myself. I'd suddenly made the biggest mistake of my medical accounting career! *How could I be so stupid?* And how could this be true? Seven seemed like a lot and I questioned it initially. But quickly I realized the number was correct. I remembered the first time was because I had a cough, the second to see a movie. The third time was due to a sporadic helicopter ski trip to Whistler with Loren. The fourth was a hangover (I really was sick that time). The fifth was a Hugo Boss sale we had to fly to San Francisco for. The sixth time was the result of a sudden teeth-whitening session I had to attend at the dentist. And the seventh, occurring just the previous Friday, was the result of being too tired to go to work given the fact I had stayed up all Thursday night having assumed it was Friday.

"Unfortunately James, if you reference page eighty of your employee handbook you will see seven sick days within a ninety day period is a violation of the Employee Wellness Integrity agreement you signed when you were hired." What he said was absurd and yet he delivered the line flawlessly.

I had no words. What Tom was saying sounded very grave. But who was he to tell me about employee integrity? This was the same amateur musician I'd caught mass-producing promotional fliers in the copy room.

"We know you've been very productive here at the company," continued Tom, "But we must enforce policy. They're meant to protect all employees. In light of all your contribution to the company, we're offering you a two-week suspension as opposed to termination." This meant they wouldn't fire me because they didn't think they could find another fool to work as hard as I did (when I showed up) for what they paid me. I felt I had worked harder for OmniCare than anyone of my colleagues. But I was grateful for not being terminated, and simply stated, "That sounds reasonable."

Tom told me to go home immediately and return in two weeks for a post-suspension interview. The problem was in two weeks I was scheduled to be flying to New York City, not sitting in a cubicle writing up spreadsheets. Before the elevator could even get me to the lobby I began to believe my suspension from OmniCare to be the result of fate. I had two weeks to find a new job.

Once I left the OmniCare building I immediately called Loren on my cell phone. I didn't tell her the news right away. I feared she'd be mad at me. However, I did tell her I had important news, so she invited me over to her place.

Those familiar with the rapidly changing skyline of Seattle know it to be a mix of towering glass, suggestively pornographic high-rises, and a gleaming renaissance of historic brick and terra cotta. An iconic gem amongst the madness, the Smith Tower, was in 1914 a behemoth of what man could create. It is to Seattle what the Chrysler Building is to New York: a stunning marvel of art and architecture that remained spectacular despite being dwarfed by some nearby modern skyscrapers. And furthermore, like the Chrysler Building or Arc De Triomphe, it had to play the role of second-fiddle to some *other* landmark that floundered in fame and attention, all the while remaining regal, and in its own way, superior.

When I arrived at the Smith Tower I found that Loren's apartment had its own exclusive elevator, secretly tucked behind a statue of Chief Sealth in the ornate marble lobby. To call Loren's home an "apartment" would be inaccurate. It was a mansion perched on top of a skyscraper, similar to her office at the AndersCenter.

Once inside Loren's home I gasped, it was like nothing I'd ever seen. The foyer was a grand chamber of contemporary metalwork and Chihuly glass, flanked with a massive Art Deco double-door that brought to mind the entrance to a Royal's throne room or maybe the diamond vault at Tiffany's. Like a medieval castle, the entrance was guarded by a uniformed officer. He smiled and nodded at me. I recognized him as one of Loren's closest bodyguards.

The giant metal doors swung open with the help of a whirring motor, revealing a giant circular staircase that ascended over fifty feet, each of the four levels above the entrance accessing the stairs via several elaborate arched bridges.

I found Loren in what she called the Harbor Room, a giant den overlooking Elliott bay. She had taken the day off and was watching *How To Marry A Millionaire* with Sarah Madison, her personal assistant.

"Hi honey!" Loren greeted me with a giant smile. I was relieved our verbal scuffle of several evenings past had been forgotten. "This is Sarah, my assistant. Have you two met?"

"No," I said smiling at Sarah. We briefly shook hands. I noticed Sarah was obese and not very pretty. Her hands were cushioned with fat and I wondered how she'd made it into Loren's ideal world filled only with the most beautiful of objects.

"Nice to meet you Jimmy," Sarah asserted.

"What's your big news?" Loren asked.

"I got suspended from my job," I said, hoping her reaction would be sedate.

"Why?" she asked without emotion or surprise.

"Calling in sick too much."

"It was only a matter of time. I told you," Loren gloated, "if you were one of my employees I would have *fired* you." She was only being dramatic when she said this.

"No you wouldn't," I replied, "you're in love with me."

Loren sent Sarah home not long after my arrival. I assumed she preferred my company to hers. We discussed how bored we both were with life, how unfulfilling and tedious everything seemed. Then I began demanding Loren entertain me while I was out of work.

"This whole week is a mess Jimmy," Loren flustered. "We're in the middle of acquiring a giant soft-drink conglomerate in Japan and I'm beyond stressed. I took today off to prepare myself for the rest of the week."

I found a bit of tragedy in knowing that I wanted so desperately to spend every moment with Loren. And now that I could, having been suspended from work, it angered me that she didn't seem to want to be around me anymore. The next two weeks began to look like an expanse of unwanted solitude that I'd have to spend sifting through the job listings. While Loren strategized and implemented a global corporate warfare campaign, I'd be scouring the Internet for a new entry-level job.

The next morning Loren unexpectedly arrived with breakfast. Her chef sent over crepes with five different berry sauces. Together we dined al fresco on my balcony, watching and listening to the morning chaos of downtown. It was glorious to recline and eat as we witnessed the madness of people, buses, cars and cabs flooding the once desolate concrete landscape. As we ate Loren became curious as to what I'd do with myself while suspended from work.

"I know for sure I'm going to the art museum," I rambled. "They're having a Lichtenstein exhibit. Maybe I'll see a movie... oh, I keep hearing great things about Tacoma. I might take a day trip there to witness the renaissance."

"I think I want to leave town," Loren said, "I'm sick of it."

"What, like move?" I asked. I would have gone in to cardiac arrest if she told me she was leaving Seattle.

"No. Just for the week." Relief hit my face like a splash of cold water.

"You can't leave town in the middle of an acquisition,"

"There is no fucking acquisition," Loren rebuffed. "AndersGroup can't acquire Japan's largest soft-drink company because we already own their fourth largest soft-drink company. The government said it has something to do with an anti-trust agreement or anti-monopolistic principles, I don't remember which, probably both."

"I'm sorry," is all I could say. I hadn't been prepared to console someone for losing out on a corporate takeover.

"Let's get a car and drive up to the islands," she suddenly vented. The idea sounded superb. Then I recalled Loren owned a helicopter and was about to suggest we take it up to the islands. But something stopped me. I didn't want to be perceived as one of *those* friends who relish in another friend's riches.

"Sounds terrific!" I cheered.

"I know this great little spa up there on this tiny secluded island," Loren beamed. "I think you'll really enjoy it. " Then she stuffed an entire crepe into her mouth. How she maintained her slim physique was a mystery that only her personal chemist was privy to.

Loren's description of the accommodations disappointed me at first. I had heard rumors that her family owned a vast estate on a private island somewhere in the San Juan Islands. At the time I knew very little of Loren's widespread wealth. Unlike other billionaires, Loren's riches were well obscured. All the family assets had been hidden using front companies, not for the purpose of evading taxes, but maintaining privacy. In their very public Queen Anne Hill villa, her parents had been constantly dogged by media like it were 10 Downing Street or something. That home's vulnerability to the media explained why she preferred living at the top of a skyscraper. Any other home she owned was absolutely private, separated by the outside world by gates, acreage, and lethal security. I would only get to see what she wanted me to see, and nothing more. Her family was known for discretion and had raised her never to flaunt what she had been given. Even as the world's richest woman she was very reserved and never boasted about her massive assets. Sometimes I considered she was embarrassed by the whole inheritance thing. Loren had a very strong work ethic and to have been given one of the largest inheritances in the history of inheritances was defeating. She wanted to work for what she had, which explained why she was at AndersGroup every day. She could have sat on her billion-dollar ass, but didn't. Every day she woke up with the intent of earning what she been given, as if it were a loan she had to repay.

The Anders Family riches would naturally lead to a sheltered upbringing for Loren. But I, a representative of the working class, was happy to enlighten her on all her inaccurate assumptions she had mistakenly made about middle-class culture. Loren had assumed Kool-Aid was something you might apply to a burn and The Dollar Store was a place that sold rare and exotic coins. Even her knowledge of slang was limited and uninformed, so much so she believed that a pimp was the same thing as a gigolo and tits were small versions of boobs. If it weren't for me she'd have been lost trying to navigate the confounding avenues of the hoi polloi.

Shaw Island was a rolling forested mound in the complex chain of rocky bluffs that make up Washington's beautiful San Juan Islands. What was so great about the island was there were only two things on it: a tiny spa appropriately named Shaw Spa, and a giant convent of Catholic nuns who controlled the tiny local government and all commerce on the island. There was a nun mayor, nun police officer and even a nun pilot who flies tourists back and forth from the island to Seattle and Victoria.

Loren's idea to go out to the island was not purely for pleasure. I could tell she was aggravated by her work and needed some sort of release the city could not provide. Her vow to stop smoking had been thwarted by events at AndersGroup. Not only was she smoking again, her trademark extra-long Italian Firenze cigarettes, but now every three minutes she seemed to light up a new one. And our weekend ritual known as "happy hours and hours" (the consumption of unlimited cocktails and champagne) was being celebrated daily, sometimes prior to noon.

Loren would have me believe that it was the botched soft-drink acquisition that provided her so much stress, but I detected it was something else. All the big fashion houses in New York, London, Paris, and Milan were all preparing their fall and winter ad campaigns and Loren didn't have a single photo shoot booked. Loren's modeling agent Ghiann (pronounced "John") hadn't called her in weeks. This had to have been the true source of her anxiety, and if it wasn't, there was a realm to Loren I never had access to.

On the day of our trip I met Loren at her place for a quick breakfast before heading out. While I feasted on raspberry tarts she had three Benadryl tablets and a glass of champagne. It was a recipe for a coma.

"I have a surprise for you," Loren squeaked as I laced up my new Salvatore Ferragamo mountain boots, courtesy of her.

"What? You bought me the Burberry computer case?" I asked, hinting at the next present I wanted her to furnish me with.

"No, I didn't buy you that bag," she said, "I'm going to let you drive my car!"

"Shut the fuck up," I said, not wanting to be riled or teased with such an absurd treat. Loren's infamous car, a modernized 1939 Jaguar SS-100, was tagged "the Batmobile" in the local media. It was only seen on very special occasions, such as when Loren attended the ballet or was romancing a celebrity boyfriend.

"No, you shut the fuck up," she snapped with a smile, holding up a set of keys. The platinum key chain, a relic from the 1930s, had the phrase "Jag Hag" inscribed on its back. She added, "Normally I'd prefer to drive one of the Duesenbergs but they're all on loan to MOMA."

"What's a Duesenberg?" I daftly asked.

Loren gave a cackling laugh to my questioned and said, "You really are middle-class." She had such a warm smile on her face that I failed to take offense to the comment.

The elevator seemed to take years to descend those 40 floors down to the street. During the descent Loren quickly explained how I was not to tip off the "Gestapo," her nickname for the posse of bodyguards hired to protect her from the bane that massive wealth brings (stalkers, paparazzi, lawyers, commoners, terrorists, distant relatives). But as the doors finally swung open and we exited to the street I saw before me Loren's automobile steward standing guard over her silvery Jaguar. Smaller than I expected, the car radiated in the faint sun lit. The inside had been completely restored and modernized. It was both deco and delicious, and so British it made my mind spin with how chic I would look behind the wheel. The car was a vintage dream to get inside, every handle and button a work of craftsmanship. As I got situated behind the wheel Loren explained there was a brand new BMW engine under the hood so we wouldn't have to worry about breaking down or being passed on the freeway. Then in horror I peered down and beside my leg found the most revolting sight: a manual shift!

"It's a stick!" I declared.

"It makes it more sporty, don't you think?" Loren heralded. "So damn European, like we're going to speed through the Alps!"

"I can't drive a manual," I said with a synchronized huff and pout.

"Then you better let me drive," she giggled, almost as if it were her original plot to dangle something so beautiful and well-crafted before me and then snatch it away just before I took complete control.

Loren was all smiles, snickers, quips, and puns as she started the engine. She was the happiest I'd ever seen her. If driving was able to do that to a person I figured I should save up and buy a car. It's funny how those who have everything they could possibly want can still get satisfaction from having even more. Loren proved the old catechism that the rich eventually became bored to be utterly, and profoundly wrong.

It didn't matter how many roads they built in Seattle, as there could never have be enough to accommodate the kind of traffic that clogged the thoroughfares and freeways. Just getting to the freeway onramp a few block from Smith Tower was a nightmare with construction closing off roads and the overflow from that jamming up every detour. But Loren handled it well and within an hour we were far outside the city. Bored from scrutinizing my fresh issue of *L'uomo Vogue,* I decided to start a meaningful conversation devoid of hollow topics like fashion, celebrity or politics.

"Does my hair look thinner in the front?" I asked. Riding in a convertible made my scalp look more prominent than it had before. I began to worry I was losing my hair.

"No. It's because you got those highlights," Loren soothed. "You have nice thick hair. I don't think you'll ever go bald. Are either of your grandfathers bald?" she implored. She even put her hand in my wind-swept mane and tugged on it just to show how right she was.

"They're both bald. But that's because they're dead. I don't have to worry about male pattern baldness, just early termination."

"How'd they die?"

"Heart attacks. One was sixty, the other was sixty-seven."

I noticed Loren's little Christian Dior satchel was tossed on the floor, so I decided to go on a treasure hunt. With one eye on the road and another on me, Loren watched as I exhumed the contents of her handbag. Inside I found lip balm and lip stick, a bottle of perfume, a few condoms, a bottle of Cynexia, a pack of Firenze herbal cigarettes, and a Zippo lighter with an American flag on it. The flag's stars were made of 50 actual diamonds.

"I thought you said you quit smoking," I said holding up the pack of cigarettes. I received an icy glare from Loren that quickly thawed in to a reluctant, humbled grin. Even she was subject to something as human as addiction.

An hour in to our journey Loren gave me an impromptu course on driving a manual transmission. It was easier than I'd imagined and there wasn't a lot of shifting to do on the freeway. The car had been modified so much that that all the controls were electronic; there wasn't even a clutch to push in to shift.

So while Loren thought she knew how to drive a manual shift, the truth was that the car was an automatic that had been made to act and feel like a manual roadster. When we sped out back on to the freeway from our pit stop it felt so thrilling behind that wheel of solid polished oak. I put on a pair of driving gloves and sunglasses, relishing in the attention the classic beauty got us. Men stared at us from their minivans and economy sedans, their faces drooping with lust and envy, either for the car or for the model in the passenger seat. I couldn't have ever anticipated the kind of attention such a piece of art and engineering would garner. There wasn't a moment on the freeway that someone wasn't busting their neck trying to get a better look at us.

On the stereo Loren queued up the gentle crooning of Russ Colombo, a singer from the 1930s Jazz era. As his classic, weepy tunes roared, and we giggled like teenagers who'd just skipped out on sixth period, I couldn't help but feel as if we'd driven in to another, more graceful time.

We were far outside the city and alone on the highway when we came to a very special place. It was the Skagit Valley, a lush green refuge of burgeoning farms, fluttering hills, and shimmering rivers that wound through lush forests, and wildlife not yet encroached upon by swelling Seattle subdivisions. The sun was beaming over the sea to the west, proving to me I'd forgotten just how vivid the colors of the valley could be. It was refreshing to have the monochromatic hues of the city replaced by this sudden burst of light and color. So enticing was this landscape that I couldn't help but struggle to remember why I'd left it for the city.

Loren was still asleep as I pensively drove the car along the back roads of a farm. The fields appeared empty, only the long dark grooves of rich brown soil visible. Beneath those miles of dirt rows rested thousands of tulip bulbs whose grassy tendrils would begin to rise out from the earth any day now and create an ocean of various colors. At the driveway of a quaint farmhouse I parked the car and waited. I did not get out of the car as I did not want to wake Loren. I sat there and stared at the home, wondering what its inhabitants must be doing. Were they eating dinner? I knew they always ate dinner early in the evening. Everything they did was early because they got up before the sunrise. Their patterns were formed by the earth. Meals, work, sleep - all of it determined by what went on in the sky above them. They weren't slaves to a clock or fueled by caffeine like us city people. It had to have been nice to be so in tune with nature. It seemed the further humans strayed from the cycle of the earth the less human they became. I wanted in that moment to return to something that more closely resembled the harmony that nature provided.

As I examined the house I saw a tired black lab resting near a birdbath at the side of the home. I knew she must have been exhausted having risen with her owners early that morning. She would in her typical fashion follow them around all day, only to be the first one in bed right after dinner. She had earned the name Shadow for her ability to silently stalk her owners. I figured with a whistle or a clap I could wake her from her afternoon nap, but she looked so happy and serene in that yard, her black coat just a still lump in the acre of vivid green lawn.

As I started the car again I noticed Loren had woken up. She'd watched me examine this strange and anonymous house. As we drove away she recognized in me that the house must have meant something. She must have known it was the house I was raised in. It embarrassed me at first for Loren to see my parent's ordinary farmhouse. How rundown it must have looked to her. Since I was a kid I can remember wanting people to believe I had somehow come from premium stock, the descendent of noble gentry or something. I suppose everyone wants to believe their family is something special. As much as I wanted to be ashamed of my background, I couldn't be. Loren hadn't become friends with me because she thought I was like her. She liked me because I had a completely different adolescence and had a perspective on life that complimented hers, even though all my experiences were had in another sphere. And it was only fair for Loren to see where I had come from. Every business and finance publication known to man had documented her family and her childhood. She was famous the day she was born. Everybody knew about her and nobody knew about me. We were opposites in so many ways, and because of this, the perfect pair. Our common interest was good, stylish living. It was the only thing we needed to cement our friendship. How we were raised was perfectly irrelevant to our adult lives.

After a slow drift about a rusted ferry from the port of Anacortes to the dock of Shaw Island, Loren and I finally arrived at adorable Shaw Village. The town was a cluster of European looking stone buildings huddled on the steep shore of the rocky island, where the orange wood and green leaves of madrona trees slinked up from the stony banks. The moment we parked at the gates of the spa a throng of tiny nuns gathered around Loren as if she were the Pope or Julia Roberts. They took her coat, offered her some local nun wine and showed her right to the spa. I got our bags out of the back of the car and stacked them near the entrance to the nunnery, hoping someone would come around to fetch the bags and show me to our suite. I waited a good five minutes without anyone coming out to help me. It was apparent all staff were dedicating their time to Loren. I followed the stone path they had led her down to find the spa, a collection of wooden huts with steam pouring out the tiny windows.

"When does my treatment begin?" I asked one of the nuns who poured Loren a tiny little glass of icy Riesling. "Is there a separate section for the men?" Sister Mary Roberta instructed me to go to cabin #11 and wait for someone to meet me.

The Shaw Spa bellboy and masseur, Derek, a fit young man no older than 25, eventually arrived to take our bags and to show me to cabin #11. The cabin was a shingle style house attached to the side of a cliff several hundred feet above a sandy beach. Derek told me to disrobe and lie on the massage table assembled in the living room. I did just as he said while he lit some candles, sorted his massage creams and put on some relaxing chant music. He slathered my legs, back, shoulders, chest and stomach in fruity oil, massaging *almost* every muscle in a long, slow manner more arousing than I could have expected. An hour after the massage Derek drew me a bubble bath sprinkled with tulip petals and enhanced with several aroma therapy oils. I would soak in the giant bath tub for what seemed like a well needed year, savoring every bit of serenity and calm. I couldn't think of any better way to spend my time while being suspended from work.

Inside the cabin I speculated if the sisters had hired a Parisian interior designer to furnish the suites. The floors were glossy black hardwood planks soaked in lacquer that had been worn over time, making the place feel aged and timeless. The various drapes were a scheme of grey and black stripes, a fairly masculine color scheme for a resort run by women. It was the perfect backdrop for a photo shoot featuring Loren I called "Monochrome Dreams." Loren had the perfect blood-red Valentino ball gown to contrast the room. With just a dash of crimson on her lips and quick flattening of her luscious hair, she came off looking like a Hollywood screen siren.

After our shoot Loren and I took a dip in our private cliff-side hot tub that overlooked the water and other islands. The comfort provided by the warm bubbling water became the perfect scenario to discuss with Loren something I'd been tormented by: the future.

"What am I going to do with my life?" I questioned aloud.

"Whatever makes you happy," she vaguely suggested. "You can't work in an office for the rest of your life. It makes you miserable. Can you imagine if you didn't have me? You would have jumped off the Ship Canal Bridge by now."

Loren put an arm around me and molded my soggy head of hair in to a set of punk spikes. She laughed and giggled at her attempt to form me into the image of a Sex Pistol. But as she displayed so much enjoyment in altering my image and I became aware her molding of me was more than just metaphysical. The designer couture and her frequent suggestions about always changing appearances made it seem as if I were Loren's human clay.

"How come you're always buying me things?" I asked.

"We're friends," she replied plainly.

"No. I mean clothes, spa treatments, male beauty regimens," I began to inventory. "You're spoiling me!"

"Listen, this is America," Loren preached. "Friends represent compassion for each other by giving gifts. And I really like you. You're the sweetest boy."

"You don't have to buy me things," I leveled, "I know you like me."

"I know," she doled. Her reluctant response made me wonder if I'd found a crux within Loren. It was the first time I ever considered she might deplore being rich. It was possible she couldn't understand why she was born into so much gluttony and advantage. There had to be such a thing as being exhausted by luxury.

"What?" I asked gently as she hung her head in contemplation.

"It's j-just," she uncomfortably stuttered, "I know *you* know I like you."

"Oh, I get it!" I smiled, identifying her agony. "You're worried I don't like you because I haven't bought you anything."

"No," she denied.

"Loren, I like you so much you don't even know," I began. "You're the strongest, most influential woman I have ever met. Before we knew each other I was depressed beyond belief. Unlike all the other people back in Seattle, you decided to accept me for what I am. You didn't want anything from me other than companionship and I want to thank you for that. Sometimes I think you saved my life." Our friendship was still young and fragile, so I hesitated to confess to her just how devastated I would be if ever she left my life.

"Jimmy, I think you just said to me what I've been trying to tell you for the last month." Loren turned and stared at me, "Until you, I had nothing." It may have been the hot tub's chlorine vapors, but at that moment my eyes began to moisten. Not wanting her to see how she affected me, I dunked my head under the water and came up to shake the spikes out of my hair.

The island air was unexplainably warm for mid-April. In celebration of the warmth and out of daring, Loren and I took several blankets down to a small patch of sandy beach in front of our cabin. At dusk we roasted veggie wieners and toasted marshmallows and laughed relentlessly at stupid jokes told while sharing a bottle of nun wine. The wine was so intoxicating I wondered if we hadn't accidentally been given one of their secret bottles of purple moonshine.

"This is the closest I've ever come to camping," Loren relinquished. "I feel so woodsy!"

"Come to think of it," I said, "it's the closest I've come to camping too." We both chuckled at how a farm boy like me had never been camping.

After nightfall, and for reasons I can't exactly explain, we both took off nearly all our clothes and ran into the water. The ocean water was brutally cold but we both got a kick out of the extreme sensation of chill and nakedness. After our swim we huddled together on the beach under a much too thin blanket. Shivering, we warmed each other with our hands, giggling under the blanket in amusement of our drunken antics.

We had become physical for the first time. It certainly wasn't sexual, but that night on the beach was a turning point for me and Loren. Those moments of laughter and closeness perfectly symbolized what our relationship was: two unabashed friends who undoubtedly needed one another and had nothing to hide. There on a brisk spring night on a pebbly beach we lay nearly naked together, she wrapped in my arms huddled on top of my chest.

"What are we doing?" Loren cackled, the both of us shivering.

"I don't know. We're the craziest people I know of."

"You're a lot warmer than I am," she screeched, "it's not fair."

I held her closely in my arms, the tighter I squeezed her the more appreciative she became. As I held her I became aware of her frailty. She was so thin I feared holding her too tight could break her.

"Jimmy I love you," she said, "like nobody I know."

"You *love* me, like how?" I asked, weary this might be going someplace I wasn't sure Loren wanted to go with me.

"Like a brother," she clarified, "if I had a brother." Prior to her comment I'd never realized we were both from single-child households. Together we formed a sort of urban siblinghood.

"Loren, I think I love you like a sister," I said, then kissed her on her cheek. "Like a perverted sister who gets naked with her brother on a beach blanket."

"I want to ask you something," she said, pulling her head up to look me in the eyes.

"No, I won't marry you," I joked.

"Not that." Then there was silence from her and I became a bit apprehensive. "I want you to work for me."

"What do you mean?" I asked. Delight enveloped me as I imagined how glorious it'd be tell the bastards at OmniCare that I was going to work for a *real* company like AndersGroup.

"Be my personal assistant," Loren insisted.

"What about what's-her-face, Sarah?" I asked. "Did she quit?"

"I'm firing her," Loren exclaimed bitterly. "She's not very nice. She's rude to my other employees and I think she took money from a tabloid for a story that was printed about me." Loren became sour, "And she's a fat ass. I can't have a fat assistant. She just can't keep up with me, and I have an image to uphold."

"Are you joking Loren?" I had to ask. I couldn't let myself think she was serious. A job offer from her just seemed too good.

"Yes!" she yowled, as if what I was asking was offensive. "Who better to be my personal assistant? You already know everything about me."

Without further hesitance I said, "Yes, of course I'll be your assistant!" As I said these words she smirked and stared at me, as if she were studying my thoughts.

For hours the two us would lay there swigging wine on the silent beach. We stared at the black sky freckled by stars that became more blurred as drank. It was then I thought of the trust Loren must have had in me. During the day, back in the city, this woman was always surrounded by security. But now it was just her and I, alone and together. She'd fled the constraints of modern aristocracy and pulled me out of my own dejection and isolation. For her to be offering me even more was surreal.

Six misplaced hours later I woke up wearing sumptuous silk pajamas, sprawled about in a bedroom aboard the Cathryn Anders,

Loren's Pacific yacht (her Atlantic yacht was fittingly known as the William Anders). At the end of the bed Loren sat, draped in an elegant robe reading the *The Economist*. She did not notice me wake up and I preferred it stay that way. I needed time to reassemble my memory.

"Good morning sweetie," she murmured, spotting my open eyes in the mirror that flanked the nearby armoire.

"What are we doing?" I moaned, my voice echoing around the aching chambers of my brain.

"Don't you remember?" Loren asked as she slid open the drapes to the giant bedroom. As the early morning light filled the room I could see on the sea's horizon the razorback towers of downtown Seattle not more than three miles away.

"Not a clue," I said, sitting up to survey my surroundings. Nothing about the room brought any recollection of how I'd arrived on board.

"Our luxury excursion has been unfortunately cut short," Loren explained. "Ghian booked me a photo shoot at Chanel in Paris on Monday and some other shoot in Madrid on Tuesday. Or was it Milan? I always get those two cities mixed up."

"No way!" I blared in excitement. For Loren to book a modeling job with Chanel symbolized a great boost to her fledgling career.

"You fell asleep on the beach and I was reading a book when one of the nuns came down and said I had a call. It was Ghian!"

"How'd I get on the boat?"

"Some of the yacht boys dragged you aboard," she said. "I think you may have been drugged because you were out like a corpse. I had my doctor check your vitals just to make sure you were still with us."

A doctor travelled with Loren at all times. So did her security personal. Even though we'd escaped town we hadn't evaded her 24-hour staff of caretakers. They were no further than a five cars back when we'd driven up to the San Juan Islands.

"Was I wearing anything?" I asked, suddenly embarrassed that we'd been nearly nude on the chilly beach.

"You were wearing a smile," she cajoled.

"How'd you get a shoot at Chanel?" I asked.

Loren set a fresh copy of *Women's Wear Daily* on my lap. On the cover roared the headline STARK REALITY. Beneath it was one of the photos I'd taken of Loren in front of her silvery AndersCenter. She donned a platinum blonde bob wig and wore a Mod-revival Gucci dress that rung out in vivid rainbow color. Loren explained her agent loved the photos we'd taken and got the series in *WWD* with nothing more than a few strings being pulled.

As I dressed, the yacht docked at Pier 66 downtown, right next to all the other enormous billionaire's yachts. Loren's limousine and entourage sat parked on Alaskan Way. I felt rushed seeing that the entire road had been blocked off by police as they waited for us to get in the limousine. The security was like nothing I'd ever seen before. Usually Loren travelled with only two or three bodyguards. But as we strolled down the pier, escorted by Seattle's finest and some agents from the Department of Homeland Security, I began to consider something had happened. Our sudden desertion of Shaw Island felt so abrupt I couldn't help but feel we were evading something.

Loren unleashed a shock in the limousine on the way to Smith Tower: "I'm moving to Manhattan."

"WHAT!" I shrieked, the confession coming much too early in the day.

"I've been thinking about it," Loren confessed, "and my agent agrees, that if I'm serious about modeling I have to live in New York. Seattle is just too far away from the fashion industry. To fly to New York every time I have a modeling job is just too much work. I need to live in New York to be taken seriously. It's what the designers want."

"But what about…" I almost said 'us' but didn't want her to think I'd be devastated by her leaving me. "What about AndersGroup? You're the President! You can't just leave!"

"It really won't be an issue. You've seen what I do… sitting in my office all day reading fashion magazines. I can do that from our New York office. And maybe instead of reading magazines I'll be in them!"

"I don't know what to say," is all I could utter.

"You don't have to say anything. You should just be happy. You had that vacation to New York planned, so cancel it. Why *visit* New York when you can *live* in New York?"

Live in New York? Did she just say I was moving to New York with her? She did. How can this be?

"Loren, this is too much to handle. I can't just move like this. I have a job, a life," I panicked. She laughed at me and my trivial little worries.

"Jimmy, you don't have a life. And you're right, you may have a job but you don't have a career. I want to make you happy. I see how miserable you are. Why not leave it all behind? Take a break. Go with me on this adventure." She finally gave up trying to sway me and just affirmed, "You're going to Manhattan!"

As we rode to the penthouse I felt the universe tilt a bit. The dismal world I once inhabited was gone and a new, more fabulous and idealistic one enshrouded me. Every worry I possessed about a job, money or subsistence was released. A pressure lifted and I was free from the force that seemed to always follow me.

· · ·

PacificAnders Properties, the real estate subsidiary which owned my apartment building, voided my lease upon the orders of Loren Anders. I didn't even have to movie my belongings out. They let me keep everything as it was. My tine apartment was now just a storage unit, which it had always resembled in size. To be closer to my new job, I took up temporary residence in a bedroom at the Smith Tower penthouse. There I would begin my first task as her personal assistant: coordinate Loren's massive move to Manhattan, tagging all sentimental items she wanted to take with her, not that she was vacating the place at Smith Tower. It would remain her Seattle residence. Not even a month after it had been completed she was already moving on. Her extravagance was wasteful and divine.

On an unusually hot early spring afternoon I found myself bored and alone. With the Lady of the home away, the staff was nearly completely absent. Loren had jetted off to her shoot in Paris, and being that she was my only friend, I became lonely in her giant penthouse. I turned on the television to find one of those do-it-yourself home improvement shows. Unexpectedly I was drawn to the sexy, rugged carpenters scaling the grout of a bathtub. Everything about them screamed sex; their worn jeans, inexplicable bulging crotches and tight T-shirts with thick hairy arms all drove me crazy with lust. It didn't take me long to realize I was horny. With my stash of porno back at my old apartment, I decided to treat myself to a brand new XXX video. I walked down to the seedy Showgirls Boutique a stone's throw from touristy Pike Place Market. It was a store I'd never been in but from their giant ad in *The Sound* knew they sold all sorts of videos, including the kind that didn't feature any women. After browsing the entire store pretending I was interested in everything, including the sections labeled Black Soul, Asian Delights, Lezbos, Anal Action, and my personal favorite, Any Which Way But Straight, I finally picked a queer British title named *The House of Girth*. Unable to bring myself to take the video to the cashier, I began to browse the store some more, looking over their fine selection of butt plugs, dildos, lubes, and other synthetic genitalia. I was in awe of how lifelike some of the items appeared, yet was baffled by how unrealistic some of their dimensions were. Any woman or man who could fit a two-foot long rod of vibrating plastic in one of their orifices and become aroused by it was surely a pervert.

Wanting so bad to run back the penthouse and watch the video, I finally got the nerve to go to the counter and purchase the damn thing. With my head lowered I schlepped up to the counter and placed the video in front of the clerk along with a handful of cash. I was such a coward that my outstretched hand vibrated with nervousness. Just as she began to ring me up the girl behind the counter shouted in delight, "Jimmy Minor, is that you?"

I looked up to see Stacy, my high school pseudo-sweetheart. With bright pink hair and a few dozen extra pounds than I recalled, she smiled at me like she'd just won the lottery. I was too embarrassed to react calmly. A bundle of nerves inside me seemed to all explode at once and I could feel sweat beads bunching up on my neck and forehead. How perfect that the girl I'd let believe that I liked her witness first-hand as I attempted to purchase a gay porno video.

"Yes?" I said with just enough befuddlement to make it seem as if I didn't recognize her.

"It's me, Stacy Rosen, from high school. Remember?" She replied with such passion it was if I'd break her heart all over again by not admitting that I knew her.

"Stacy!" I roared, acting as if her transformation into a pudgy punk had fooled me into recognizing her true identity. "How've you been?" She was so pleased that I remembered her that she reached across the glass cabinet they kept the premium videos in to hug me.

"Good. It's been so long."

"Yes, it has." The awkwardness of meeting one another in such a place quickly overtook us.

She examined the video I was buying and began to laugh nervously with compulsion. "Now I see why you didn't want to go to the prom with me." I turned bright red as she slipped the video in a brown paper bag. I could feel the other half dozen store patrons staring at us.

"Do you live in Seattle?" I asked, trying desperately to derail the direction the conversation was barreling.

"Yes, I live in Fremont," she said. "Do you live here, or you just visiting?"

"No, I'm just visiting some friends," I lied emphatically.

"You still live in La Conner?" she assumed with a giggle that felt like some sort of judgment or derision.

"No," I shrugged. "I live in New York City." How glorious it felt to say that.

She gasped, "Wow, New York!" My response had dazzled her. "Listen, if I gave you my phone number, would you call me?" She said this in an almost flirty way. It was bizarre. This girl who had a raging crush on me in high school, and had just witnessed me purchase a video proclaiming itself to contain '5 HOURS OF HOT MAN-ON-MAN ACTION,' continued to pursue me. She was clinging to the idea I might still like her after all those years.

Discovering Stacy Rosen as a tired-looking porn shop clerk made me feel morbidly good about myself. Seeing her made me recall how inadequate I'd felt throughout high school, having been a skinny geek with a droll sense of humor. I felt myself to be in the midst of a cathartic climax when I left the store. For so many years I had feared what classmates in high school had thought of me. But as I embarked on a journey larger than any of them would ever know, I no longer cared what any of them thought of me. They were the farthest thing from my mind. The chapter in my life called adolescence had closed and the realm of adulthood was finally beginning. Funny that it took place in an actual store labeled "adult."

On my walk back to Smith Tower I played with the idea of what all the people I'd went to high school were like. They'd all probably just let themselves go, had become fat, some of them surely got married, others had kids and worked at the same grocery store or gas station they did when I graduated high school. Some of them probably moved to the city like I had and were looking for a nice suburb to settle down in. I've always hated the term "settling down." It just meant to give up, to stop trying. To say someone is settling down is to say that ambition has escaped them and that they've began a transition in to mediocrity, security, and stability. I was filled with pride knowing I was far from settling down and that so many opportunities and experiences still lay out there for me.

As I prepared for my latest and by far greatest move, I traced back in my mind all the strange and interesting places I'd found shelter. As if it were a billion years ago I laughed thinking out my first home, my freshmen college dorm in the U-District and the nasty apartment I shared with some college friends in Ballard. After only six months in the apartment I found a new place in a cheap and not so hip SoDo warehouse. After the warehouse burnt down I had to move back home. I was ashamed of the fact I had to move back in with my folks. Thank god it was only for two weeks.

My parents were two perplexing and wonderful creatures. A tulip farmer and a medical assistant at a hospital, I always thought of my father and mother as just a pair of backwater know-nothings. But my experience in the city, a place they didn't care for and avoided fervently, taught me just how wonderful they were. Mom and dad were hard working people who only asked that others work as hard as they did. From their vantage they only saw the poor who were fed and the rich who seemed to steal their wealth. Their world view was warped by assumptions and ignorance, something I learned early on to avoid. Had it not been for what seemed like narrow-mindedness on their part, I'm not sure I would have been so motivated to seek out the city. Unlike the modern American parent, my mother and father didn't attempt to be my best friends. They were mentors and resources to me. Sometimes they would let me fail, and watch me fall flat on my face. They taught me that this was a part of the human experience. Neither of them would fuss, they would just instruct me to get up and attempt what I was doing again. It was a masculine kind of upbringing. There were some tears, but just as many hugs.

After moving out of my parent's house for the second time, I landed in Seattle's Belltown, the sub-cultural incubator and incinerator of the grunge music and fashion movement. Here I lived with a lesbian couple, Dawn and Jo, who'd placed an ad in *The Sound* for someone to rent their extra bedroom. The living arrangements were plush with two women in their early thirties taking care of me and assuming the role of my parents. Dawn was a lipstick-lesbian who was there for emotional counseling and encouraged me to express what I was feeling. She also encouraged me to explore my artistic psyche. Jo was a butch-dyke who changed the oil in my car and liked to go to Volunteer Park to play baseball.

Eventually I was forced to move out of Jo and Dawn's place because Dawn got pregnant via anonymous frozen sperm donor. They would need the room I was renting for a nursery. Moving out of Jo and Dawn's home was more emotional than moving out of my parent's as it was not my choice. Jo and Dawn were the first friends I'd made in the city. They were also the only ones I felt comfortable enough with to tell I was gay.

I ended up moving downtown to Seattle's Pike Street corridor. Once a resting hole for transients, prostitutes, and drug dealers, the touristy neighborhood between the Pike Place Market and retail core had in recent years pulled off a gentrification ala Times Square. I was lucky enough to snag an apartment who's landlord, a monstrous global corporation owned by AndersGroup Inc., was unaware the area had rebounded and was foolishly charging ghetto rent for spacious lofts, some with views of the bay.

Suddenly I found myself living in Seattle's trendiest urban locale where I would meet Loren Anders and her enigmatic circle of successful friends. And as I prepared for yet another move I realized I had been lugging around a set of small boxes with me over the years. I'd packed these boxes the first time I moved out of my parent's house and along they went with me from home to home. I'd become so used to ignoring them that I forgot what was inside. Opening each box was like opening a time capsule. Inside were newspaper clippings of photographs I'd taken for my high school newspaper. I recalled thinking of how great I thought they were. In my state of naivety and youth, the pictures seemed brilliant. Now they just appeared unexceptional and disposable. It's funny how an artist's perception of his work can change with time.

The next box I opened was one sealed just after dropping out of college. This box's contents were more frightening than the first. Inside were rejection letters from magazines and newspapers who were uninterested in the photographs I'd taken and sent to them. Overwhelmed by the heap of negativity and rejection I received, I thought of burning the box in a dumpster behind Smith Tower. But I dismissed the idea and instead placed it in the box with the copy of *Women's Wear Daily* that had my photo of Loren on the cover. I decided to keep the box because one of the most important things an artist can have is rejection. Without it, there is no true analysis of one's work. Without rejection there is nothing to strive for, nothing to overcome, and nothing to work against. Artists devoid of humility often resembled tyrants. If it weren't for rejection, and the anguish it can cause, many artists wouldn't find the motivation to work.

Mixed in with the rejection letters was one of my journals I'd kept in college. Inside was a collection of lewd illustrations detailing my aggravations drawn while sitting in class listening to my professor's candid criticisms. Comments like 'FUCK COLLEGE, JOIN THE NAVY' were drawn over a picture of two muscular sailors holding hands on the deck of an aircraft carrier.

• • •

In preparing for Loren's complex move to Manhattan, I'd forgotten I would be leaving a city I both loathed and loved. Seattle was a mystifying city in an age of rapid change. I always anticipated moving on to another city, one more foreign and historic, such as Paris. So saying goodbye to Seattle was something I'd thought about but in actual reality made the hasty move all the more distressing. I decided I would have to find some proper way of saying goodbye to the place that had brought me in to adulthood.

As Loren's personal assistant, I'd been furnished with my own chauffeured sedan whenever I needed one. On my last day in town I decided I would go to the neighborhood of Capitol Hill and visit Volunteer Park, a site I'd imagined to be a miniature Central Park as it too had a conservatory, museum, reservoir and band shell. The ride from downtown to the park seemed to take forever. Each street we traveled had some sort of special meaning to it. Every café we passed seemed to contain a special memory spent reading the Sunday morning paper or listening to people discuss the banalities of their lives. Having developed a life in Seattle, a city I was still discovering, I wondered what it would be like living in a city so fresh and new like New York.

At the park I would stroll aimlessly past the conservatory towards the reservoir where I found a seat and attempted to extol my fear, anticipation and other thoughts on my new notebook computer. I realized Seattle was not the ugly, lonely place I often thought it to be; it was just a city. And much like life, a city is what you make of it. Now I had to prepare myself for the unknown, the result of accepting offers that required me to leave my noble city to discern a new one touted as being superior. The panic of uncertainty began to escalate as I noticed my driver looking at his watch. I had but only a few hours left in the city and wasn't certain I was ready to leave.

Both Seattle and I would live on, apart, but in fair regard of the other. Upon a whim I had my driver take me out to West Seattle where from Alki I would exit the car and stare across Elliott Bay at the Seattle skyline. Behind me the sun would begin to set and the reflection on the various towers made the city look as if it was on fire. The massive AndersTower stood the tallest but was neatly and symmetrically surrounded by the other hordes of glistening skyscrapers, most of which had been built within my lifetime. I would soon trade it for a city that had been a behemoth for over a hundred years.

Back at Loren's penthouse I made sure everything was in order and took in one last sweeping view of the city from the observation deck. We were ready to part.

At around nine o'clock in the evening a piloted corporate jet from the AndersGroup fleet met me at Boeing Field. A group of uniformed staff loaded all my belongings into the jet. The plane had a seating capacity of 25 but I was the only passenger onboard. It was lonely. I wished Loren was with me. We hadn't talked in over a week. She was somewhere in Europe jetting from one fashion shoot to the next, networking with designers and eagerly awaiting bookings for fashion week in September. I would have thought she'd forgotten about me if it weren't for the emails she kept sending me. They weren't really even correspondence, more like instructions I were to follow when I got to New York. Those emails were the first indication that being Loren's assistant could supersede my capacity to be her friend.

The jet took off minutes after I got on board. We flew north a bit and as the jet rolled gently to head east I could see downtown Seattle twinkling, the streaming freeways bustling with sparkling activity. The Space Needle was ablaze in white lights that shot for miles into the sky. Equally illuminated was the giant AndersTower, so mountainous I wasn't sure we were flying above it so much as in equal altitude to its pinnacle.

The most ridiculous aspect of the flight was the flight attendant, Helen. She was the loveliest older lady you could meet. But her presence unnerved me as I already had a driver, a pilot and now my own stewardess. She must have certainly been confused having been booked to serve a cabin of 25 spoiled executives and then arrived to discover she was there to serve the needs of just one thoroughly content individual, myself, who'd never flown in such a luxurious manner. She sat near the front of the jet the whole time and would cook my dinner and serve me cocktails.

"Wanna play cards?" I asked Helen who sat calmly staring out the window.

"Sir, I don't think I'm allowed." Her response was hushed, like there was a rule against her speaking to the passengers.

"Says who?" I goaded.

"The company. My job is to serve dinner."

"Well I demand that you play cards with me," I said with sudden gusto. "I'll fire anyone who questions you do such a thing." Helen must have thought I was Loren's brother or husband or something as she immediately got up, sat across from me, and began dealing. She played cards with me for almost two hours until we both got restless. I watched television for a while and turned it off, unable to find anything on so late at night.

I don't remember much of the flight thereafter. Idaho, Montana, the Dakotas and whatever else we flew over was dark. I thought we might have accidentally flown out over the ocean it was so void of civilization. Perhaps clouds had sheathed the twinkling landscape. I was asleep before we soared over the Midwest and woke up when the first traces of the sunrise could be seen. I asked the pilot where we were and he said Western Pennsylvania. I was so excited, realizing I'd be in New York within the hour. But I remembered then I was supposed to call Loren in London when I reached Illinois. Flustered, I was suddenly convinced she was probably already plotting to fire me. This kind of irrational paranoia would become common while working for Loren Anders.

I dialed her and she answered right away.

"Sorry, I fell asleep," I announced.

"Honey, where are you?" she asked. I could hear girlish giggling in the background. It sounded like some of the other models were having a really good time.

"Somewhere over Pittsburgh. I can't wait to land! What are you doing?" I could hear a French man cursing at someone in the background.

"I'm in Paris. Me and some of the other girls are having fittings at Dior."

"Are you having fun?"

"It's a sheer delight. My dream job," her tone giddy. The French man was now screaming for someone to find his hot glue gun.

"I was about to say the same thing."

"*Really?*" She was doubtful of my sincerity.

"Yes!" I replied, "I've never felt so free."

I told Loren the truth, just not the entire truth. After I hung up and we landed in New York I found myself to be more frightened than I'd ever been. My life had changed so drastically in just three short days. I genuinely didn't know what was happening, or how big this sudden move to New York City would affect the rest of my life. It was all just instinct that made me function, my body running on standby as I frolicked around in this outlandish new world of supreme excess.

As my luggage was unloaded into my waiting sedan, I noticed I kept looking at my watch. Every minute or so I had to know what time it was. The anxiousness didn't cease when I got in the car. In the back seat I unloaded my briefcase and I went over the checklist Loren had emailed me. None of the tasks were due to be completed that day but I was still worried. I had become frantic thinking I'd inadvertently fuck up my new career as personal assistant and the glorious world in which I had been admitted to would once again become a realm I was no longer welcome.

I swallowed an extra Cynexia tablet to calm myself down. I stared out the window as we drove through Queens toward Manhattan. Along the road were the biggest ghettos I'd ever seen. They were whole cities without life, streets with no people, just transients looking for some breakfast, a morning fix, companionship, and a decent life they were sure to never find. *This couldn't be New York!* This infinite wasteland of dilapidated brick towers made for public housing couldn't be the city I wanted so much to adore. Disappointed at the despair I was witnessing, I became flustered in the car trying to organize myself. Despite not having to complete any of the tasks on my list of duties, I still had a busy day ahead of me. I would now have to situate myself in an unfamiliar city. In my stupor to make several phone calls as the car scaled the length of the Queensboro Bridge, I peered down the East River to the long strip of land before me. Suddenly there were skyscrapers as far as I could see lining the banks of the river. The realization I was in New York City hit me violently. I'd become so paranoiac organizing the move I'd forgotten these first couple of days were supposed to be a vacation, not a job. As the cab sped further towards Manhattan and the skyline drew closer I looked down river and saw the illustrious Empire State Building. A feeling of arrival overcame me and as I stared at that tower, so stately and strong looking, I said to myself, "There Jimmy is the Center of the Universe." And I really believed it. The overwhelming rush of excitement an urbanite experiences the first time he arrives in Manhattan is unforgettable.

The cab entered the enormous man made mountain of steel and concrete and at once I was perplexed by the vastness of it all. It wasn't the height of all the structures that stunned me, it was the overwhelming amount of them. Every building was massive, but here in such a densely populated forest of skyscrapers it was hard to even appreciate each building's architectural beauty as every one of them seemed obscured by another. As the car sped along the bridge above First and Second Avenues I peered down massive canyons the streets of Manhattan formed. It was unreal. I wondered how a city could be so large. These grand avenues, lined on each side by skyscrapers, stretched so far they crested the horizon. Movies and television hadn't done New York justice. She was the biggest, most intimidating thing I'd ever seen.

Adding to my sudden bafflement, the car exited on to a busy thoroughfare. As I tried to take in the stimulation of finally being in the metropolis, the car made so many quick, tight turns I lost all sense of direction. It wasn't until the car stropped and my driver announced "We're here sir," I celebrated, knowing the confusing car ride was over. I would finally be able to explore the city on foot at a pace I determined.

My door was opened by the concierge. I got out and found a team of bellmen loading my luggage on to a trolley.

"Welcome to the Waldorf=Astoria sir," the concierge greeted. I smiled at him and he returned the warmest grin I'd ever seen from a hotel employee. I instructed my driver to take the rest of the day off and to meet me the next day at eight AM in the very same spot.

Before I entered the hotel I just had to have a quick look at my surroundings. There I was, standing on Park Avenue with a team of people managing my luggage and waiting for my next command. I glanced down the great thoroughfare to witness the northern entrance to the Grand Central Terminal. A river of impatient pedestrians flowed around me as I looked all around, savoring the view of finally being in blessed Manhattan.

Inside the hotel the majestic entrance to the Waldorf=Astoria reminded me of a fourth grade field trip to the state capitol in Olympia.

Every surface of the hotel's interior was either marble or polished metal. The grand dame of hotels had created drama through décor. A myriad of floral arrangements punctuated each table in the entryway that led to the Park Avenue Lobby. There are few lobbies like the one at the Waldorf. Similar in size to a great railroad depot or airport terminal, the lush and vibrant space percolated with activity. Business professionals in suits chattered as old women gossiped on a sofa. It was the kind of thing only seen in a movie. But there it was in front of me, real and alive.

Some arrangements had been made so I was already checked-in. No need to actually go to the lobby. The bellmen led me to an elevator and I soon found myself in my suite overlooking Park Avenue. I'd never been in such a magnificent hotel before. My suite, larger than any apartment I'd ever occupied, was festooned with antiques and other furnishings that just seemed so Art Deco, and so New York. I had a real, working fireplace, a full bar and a bed about an acre in size. The bathroom had so many knobs, switches, and other features I didn't know what function half of them performed.

My team of three skilled bellmen unpacked my luggage, hung up all my shirts, refolded my pants and put them in my armoire, organized my shoes by color and occasion and quietly left me alone after I tipped them. They were so skilled that in just those few short moments they were able to perform an hour's worth of unpacking and organization. I couldn't have felt more welcome at the hotel.

Exhausted from the overnight trip, I sat on my bed and slipped off my shoes. I hadn't been to sleep in over twenty hours and was feeling it throughout my body. But more powerful than the jolt of a thousand cups of espresso, the thought of "I'm in New York City!" awoke me to full alertness. I washed my face and took a piss and then set out to discover The Big Apple, the city I considered to be the epitome of urban sophistication. I would now have to go confirm my assumption.

That first day in Manhattan I walked everywhere. Perhaps I was too afraid to ride the subway or uncertain of how to hail a taxi cab. But it was fine taking the island on foot. I never walked so much in my life, or even wanted to. New York was so easy to walk around because something interesting or beautiful or humongous always seemed just a few blocks away. I must have strolled 20 miles that day, dazzled by the history and size of the city, made all the more massive by the crowds of people flowing through it. Not one square inch of the place was dull.

Starting my journey at the hotel in East Midtown, the first thing I wanted to see was Times Square, the heart of The Center of The Word. I walked west for what seemed like miles, discovering the blocks in New York weren't like regular city blocks, rather they were long rectangles, some a sixth of a mile in distance. On my way to Times Square I passed by the gorgeous Rockefeller Center, the size of a city itself. Seeing it firsthand made me recognize the inspiration this collection of structures had on Loren's AndersCenter back in Seattle.

When I arrived in Times Square I was astounded by its size. The place was a massive valley of lights and video billboards. Just like stepping into another world, a vision of a radical future that had never been captured fully on film. I had assumed that Times Square was just an intersection of streets that had been decorated with its trademark advertisements. What it turned out to be was a massive district of many streets and intersections flowing from one avenue to the next, forming all sorts of squares and plazas. Every one of the giant advertisements were cutting edge with video screens and other special effects, like smoke or strobe lights. Being that there were so many of them, I wasn't sure how effective the individual ads were. I don't think that was necessarily the point. Time Square was more like a giant workshop for the nation's advertising industry over on Madison Avenue — a kind of testing ground for other billboards and visual displays. Collectively it created a vast temple to consumerism and free enterprise.

After about an hour exploring Times Square, I walked up Eighth Avenue to Columbus Circle where I'd encounter the magnificent Central Park. I was overcome with glee witnessing the entrance to the park, it's giant statues welcoming me. To observe the chaos of cars right next to the park, while it remained a green oasis of serenity, only heightened the sense of nature and calm it provided the city. I would literally run across the street and into its hospitable flora and wildlife, celebrating its beauty. There I'd spend hours roaming the regions of the park, all the while impressed how this giant tribute to the natural world was all manmade. Standing at the Bethesda Terrace in Central Park made me drunk with optimism, knowing that in some way the decisions I'd made in life had got me to where I was. It wasn't just Loren who'd brought me here. I had a role in all of this.

Eventually I became overwhelmed with Central Park and decided I would need another day, and maybe a bicycle, to fully explore it. I cut across the Great Lawn to Fifth Avenue and then to Madison Avenue. I would head south towards where I believed the Waldorf to be, passing boutiques with names so famous and familiar (thanks to the pages of *Vogue*) I found myself popping in each one just for a glance. The film *Pretty Woman* had taught me that the people who worked in these stores were elitist snobs, however that was not the case. Every store welcomed me with a smile and a helpful insistence that I try something on. Sales people had evolved fathoms since the days of Julia Roberts on Rodeo Drive.

I walked back over to Fifth Avenue near Grand Army Plaza and discovered the exceedingly chic department stores of Bergdorf Goodman and Saks Fifth Avenue, the stores I read about and dreamed of patronizing. Smartly, I'd planned for such an occurrence and had some cash on hand to spend, picking up a new pair of shoes and a light jacket. After my dalliance at shopping I returned to the hotel around sunset where I ordered room service for dinner. I ate, off course, a Waldorf salad.

The City of New York was now mine to discover and I would spend the next several days surveying her landscape. I'd quickly lose my fear of riding the subway and found it was the fastest way to travel from one end of the island to the other. And it was cheap too, not that I cared. I still used my driver whenever I went shopping but would take the subway any time I just wanted to feel free and run around from neighborhood to neighborhood. I was like a little kid capturing a playground fortress, except now my playground was the greatest city man had yet to build.

MAY

After numerous days of indulgent hedonism, I took strife in reminding myself I was no longer in New York on leisure, but business. As Loren Anders's new personal assistant I was now her highest ranking domestic servant, in charge of supervising her yet-to-be-hired maids, butlers and chefs, and responsible for providing a buffer between her and the omnipresent entourage of invisible security. I was the thin veneer of artifice between her fantasy world of constant indulgence and the hastened team of laborers making everything in her life fabulous. As Loren galloped the globe posing for every designer's fall and winter ad campaigns, I'd arranged to meet with her Manhattan realtor, Andrea Haas, the queen of East Coast real estate.

In New York City the neighborhood you live in says as much about you as your hairstyle. If you live in Chelsea you're gay. If you live in SoHo you're too trendy for your own good. Knowing Loren, I knew she would spend hours and hours contemplating what address she would call home. She'd been known to spend 90 minutes choosing a hue of fabric for a pillow. However, she was in Europe somewhere being fitted in couture while being paid top dollar for doing so. Simply, she didn't have time to go house hunting. She was a very busy girl with two careers. That's where I came in.

The instructions I received from Loren were simple: "Trendy, but not *too* trendy. Old New York but not old news." I gave these directives to Andrea Haas who assembled a supple list of residences for me to tour. Immediately I ruled out all co-ops, as their boards were notorious for refusing sale to anyone with even the most minor of celebrity statuses. A week didn't pass that the *New York Post* didn't tell the tale of a co-op taking pride in declining the tenancy applications of movie stars and musicians. I didn't want the first item in the New York press about Loren's move to Manhattan to be about how she was refused residency at a Park Avenue high-rise.

All condominiums, no matter how swanky, were eliminated from consideration. Condos were a fairly new type of housing in Manhattan, and for all their sleek beauty and style, I wanted Loren to have a home that recollected the feel of an embassy, not an office tower. Loren needed a home that would put Gracie Mansion to shame. It was just our luck that the former French Embassy located a few blocks from the

Guggenheim on Fifth Avenue had come on to the market. Andrea Haas described it as, "the New York mansion to end all mansions," and I certainly agreed. The 1895 mansion was enormous, with over 30,000 square feet of living space. It featured an underground parking garage and rooftop swimming pool. It was exactly the gaudy, super-extravagant home I knew Loren would love to start her new New York life in.

While the mansion was regal and historic, it was far from chic. The faucets were rusty, the lighting dim and dated, the hardwood and tile floors cracked and worn. Ceiling moldings had been ill-preserved and the climate system fairly medieval. The price tag of $43-million was steep, even for the size and location. Andrea Haas showed me other properties, but none of them came close to the embassy. There was so much potential in the property I couldn't help but keep it in mind. And while the price was at the very top of Manhattan real estate, it wasn't considered all that substantial of a purchase to Loren. She had a collection of yachts and jets worth much more, but I would still need her permission before closing on the property.

Loren was in London for several days shooting a Bombay Sapphire campaign, complete with print, TV, and Internet ads – in terms of dollars it was the largest campaign she had been involved with, having been described by executives from Bacardi as a "brand re-launch." After her stay in England she'd be jetted off to Italy as she was the face of Armani's newest women's fragrance. After that she would return to New York where she expected me to have found a new home for her. I'd have just two weeks to prepare Loren's new place with décor and all the other luxuries she expected. After a three minute pitch to her about the property, Loren and her accountants gave me the go-ahead and I had Andrea secure the embassy. The Anders Family Trust purchased the house with cash upon my request and the mansion was now mine, figuratively.

My suite at The Waldorf=Astoria became ground zero for the restoration. I hired contractors to work round-the-clock preparing the new estate which we formally re-named AndersPlace. I had, thankfully, remembered Loren's requisite of not wanting to live in a place that had not been freshly renovated. The floors, ceilings, windows and plumbing would all be completely overhauled. Only period details were spared, mostly for charm. We even hired a historian from the AIA's Center for Architecture to make the homes restoration was a celebration of its legacy and not a debasement or mockery of it. Elegant perimeter fencing and a new security detail certainly caught the attention of neighbors. As bulletproof windows were being installed a passerby asked me "What's going on in there?" I said: "We're just getting the place fit for a queen!" The comment made rumors swirl, and the *New York Daily News* printed in their *Overheard* gossip column that the Queen of Jordan had acquired the property and was to make it her official American vacation house. They had no idea someone far richer and far more beautiful was to take up residence.

The most enjoyable part of being Loren's assistant was spending her money. I hired one of Manhattan's most glamorous and flamboyant (whilst still talented) interior designers to make the drab place the most spectacular of all the mansions on Fifth Avenue. Franc (pronounced "fronk") of Franc Carlton Designs & Associates was eager to turn the mansion into something worthy of an *Architectural Digest* spread. In fact, photographers from the magazine shot the place before, during and after for their annual issue on renovations. Franc's handy work for the mansion would also be the scenario in the pilot of his new TV show *Franc Living*, a show that would later be picked up by many major network television affiliates around the country. Given the television exposure, Loren's New York residence would become just as famous as she was.

Once all the major renovations were complete and the paint done drying, Franc set out on several breakneck days of careful redecoration, turning the former embassy in to Fifth Avenue's finest modern masterpiece. The place radiated sophistication while maintaining a modern fusion of classic designs and cutting edge art pieces. I anticipated Loren would find the place more than suitable, and remain unaware of the turmoil and strife we'd endured to make it so.

On the afternoon prior to Loren's return from Europe, and just a day after Franc Carlton and his team finished their work, I found myself alone in Loren's new manor. It's size felt more like an emptied hotel than a single 22-year-old woman's pied-a-terre. I strolled lackadaisically throughout the place, burning countless calories ascending and descending the giant marble staircases. Appropriately, it was in the Receiving Room off the Grand Foyer where I would receive a call on my cellular phone.

"Hello," I greeted, assuming it was Loren.

"Hi, is this James Minor?" A queer yet familiar voice asked.

"It is. Who's this?"

"Hi, this is Thomas Jennings from OmniCare. How are you?"

"*Fine*," I said, baffled as to why this fool would be calling me.

"James, I'm calling because you didn't return to work today."

"Oh yes, that," I said, trying to find the most eloquent words to describe what had happened. I then realized there was no consequence to be being honest. "I quit. You're an idiot and your rock band sucks ass."

"That's unfortunate to hear," he replied, his voice pinched. "Where do you want us to send your final paycheck? Will it be to..." he began to rattle off my former address in Seattle, at which point I interrupted him.

"No. Please send it to The Waldorf=Astoria, attention James Minor. That's 301 Park Avenue, suite 4202. New York, New York." After I confirmed he'd written the address correctly I hung up. It felt so good to tell him I'd relocated to Manhattan. For a moment when I hung up the phone I imagined him sitting at his little desk in that horrible office envying me for escaping it all.

*　*　*

My excitement to have Loren return to New York and behold the work of art I'd created for her became burdensome. I began to fear that she would not like the home. In just two short weeks we'd spent nearly $11-million dollars on renovations, a number I had a difficult time comprehending. I imagined if Loren were to abhor the project and demand I pay her back in labor, at my $3,000 a week salary it would take over 70 years to repay her. In order to distract her from the house, I decided I would throw her a house warming party. After all, what good is a ballroom if you're not going to throw a party every now and then?

I contacted Loren's publicist to organize the event, her modeling agent to secretly invite all her industry friends, and hired Loren's favorite vegetarian chef from Nepal to cater the event. I even sent invitations to the CEO of AndersGroup and all the executives of the company in Seattle, New York and London. Not long into planning the event I had a list of 500 of Loren's closest friends and associates confirmed to attend. It would be the largest event of its kind that month and give Loren a footing in the precarious New York society scene. And it was more than just an ordinary house warming.

The opening of AndersPlace symbolized both Loren's arrival on the eastern seaboard and the presence of AndersGroup in New York City.

On the night of the event a host of black limousines clogged Fifth Avenue in front of the mansion. Paparazzi, tipped off by our publicist, gathered in front of the mysterious new residence. I even spotted several tourists congregating outside, having confused the party for a movie premiere. I'd overlooked no detail in making sure Loren's party was as glamorous as could be. A long red carpet draped the front steps and a giant ribbon hung across the front door awaiting Loren to cut it.

In the biggest show of her entourage I'd yet to see, Loren Anders's armored limousine, built by the same agency responsible for furnishing the President with his, arrived in style, flanked by a dozen NYPD patrol cars. Dressed in a tuxedo and smiling widely, I stood at the top of the stairs to the entrance of AndersPlace. I would watch Loren emerge from her limousine, the camera bulbs flickering madly as she made her way up the stairs. I could immediately see Loren was dazzled at my creative way of welcoming her home. I handed her a bottle of champagne which she broke over the front door, christening AndersPlace as her official residence. She would proceed to cut the ribbon and enter the Grand Foyer, empty as I had specifically requested all partygoers move to the Grand Ballroom.

As we entered the foyer hand-in-hand, Loren became breathless and teary-eyed.

"Jimmy, this place is unreal!" she crooned with excitement, her head arched back as she examined the giant chandelier hanging from the top of the ornate domed ceiling. It was a tremendous relief to see her embracing the home. Loren could be the most opinionated person, with an eye for craftsmanship and taste I'd never known before. To watch her become enrapt by the décor and ambiance was to have the weight of $11-million dollars lifted off my collapsed chest.

"You don't hate it?" I made sure.

"No," she cooed. She took her eyes off the house and put them on me. "I couldn't love it any more than I do."

"Wait until you see the rest," I baited.

I took Loren into the ballroom where her 500 guests waited. She was stunned to see the scale of the party. Its size was like that of a wedding or bar mitzvah. Her model friends, all singularly named (Bali, Jasmine, Sky, Persimmon), would flock to her in a cloud of cackles and girlish screams, one of them foolishly decreeing, "I knew you were rich, but not *this* rich!" Loren introduced me to her troupe of new friends, all of them tall, giddy, drunk and dazzled. I was heartened to find that some of them already knew who I was.

Loren would not leave my side the entire evening. She clung to me like a small child who'd just been picked up by their mom or dad at day care. I'd feared being separated from her for nearly a month would create a rift in our somewhat infantile friendship. However, the time apart made her even fonder of me. I didn't understand why, but I went with it.

The liveliest man I would meet at the party was the CEO of AndersGroup, Hubert Redding. Loren would explain to me that Hubert was the head of Deutsche-France Holdings when AndersGroup procured the company in the late 1990s. She helped form the coalition that appointed Hubert the CEO of the company when her father died. Hubert was a good looking man, even at 61 years-of-age. His face remained youthful, his manner of dress as contemporary as they came. Meeting him made me dream of how handsome he must have been in his twenties or thirties. His wife, Margo, reminded me of the First Lady with her extravagant black ball gown furnished by Balenciaga. I became bashful upon meeting the prestigious couple.

"This is Jimmy," she introduced. No last name, nothing, as if I was famous or something.

"Jimmy!" Margo chanted, "It's very nice to meet you. Loren is just smitten with you."

"Uh-ho," I said, weary.

"Quite the influential fellow you are," Hubert lectured jokingly. "Convincing her to leave Seattle for the foolishness of New York."

"I did no such a thing," I squealed, mistaking his humor for a true accusation. Loren shot me the kind of look that was an appeal for silence.

"She also says you renovated this place," Margo delighted, "and threw this party. If I could find a personal assistant with your taste and creativity I'd hire him."

"I'm always entertaining offers," I said. All three of them laughed hysterically.

"I remember meeting the President of France here back when this was the old French consulate. You've done a lot with it," Hubert feted.

The Reddings were charming people, like grandparents to Loren. There was something calming about being around older people with similar financial circumstance. They weren't shocked by anything and had seen everything in their day. I would hover around them the rest of the party, not knowing anyone else in the sea of black and white. Margo would tell me stories of what Loren's parents were like and how they struggled to bring her up with a level head. We would watch her greet and mingle with everyone in the crowd. She was a public relations veteran and I envied her ability to walk up to anyone and be able to charm them.

Near dawn the party finally ended and I had time to ask Loren why she told the Reddings I'd convinced her to leave Seattle.

"They think the modeling thing is a waste of time," Loren scoffed. "If it were up to them I'd have a much greater role at AndersGroup. I couldn't tell them the real reason I moved here."

"I was your scapegoat?" I prodded.

"Yes," she confidently admitted. "I used you as an excuse to rebel. I hope you don't mind."

"You gave that man his job. What is there to rebel against?"

"Everything."

The next day, Loren, her giant circle of beautiful friends, the entire Board of Directors of AndersGroup, and some of the perennial New York socialites who'd attended our event, saturated the pages of every society newspaper in Manhattan. Never had the town seen such a sudden confluence of unknown wealth and glamour in one unforgettable night. The aristocracy of Manhattan gentry had been given a new shining star that night, and I had helped place her in the galaxy.

* * *

Being a personal assistant was a lot harder than one might expect. My daily tasks and responsibilities had become vast and sometimes all consuming. If Loren hadn't paid me loads of cash and kept my closet brimming with the latest menswear I probably would have quit the job not long after she hired me. The most surprising aspect of being Loren's personal assistant was finding out just how good at it I was. I'd always had a keen eye for minding the details, but never had a job where such a trait was merited.

My most important duty was to take care of Loren's two children, the recently adopted Kitty Cartier and Puppy Pucci. These two brats were a nightmare to potty train but eventually showed great skill in paying their master some affection. They quickly became a welcome addition at AnderPlace, given that the faces of the staff changed so often but theirs remanded smiling and content. They rarely quarreled, having been adopted so young they had no clue dogs and cats weren't supposed to get along. As far as they knew, Cartier and Pucci were brother and sister, happy as could be in their mansion in the city. Having the pets around made AndersPlace feel even more like home and there would be many nights where I wouldn't return to my suite at the Waldorf because I so preferred their company.

Besides cleaning up after her two pets and helping decorate her abode, I was also in charge of managing her closet. At nearly 3,500 square feet, it was like another residence within the mansion. The size of the closet was rather embarrassing, as it wasn't like Loren purchased all that much apparel and accessories. The stuff just seemed to accumulate. Designers would send her things faster than she could wear them. Once I playfully suggested to her I could make a fortune selling all the goods she couldn't find time to wear. The idea spawned a website where we auctioned over her castoffs to raise money for various charities. In our first month we raised nearly $37,000 for breast cancer research.

The countless hours spent alone supervising her cleaning staff, organizing belongings and managing general household functions were not in the least boring. It reminded me of the summer break when I was in elementary school and my parents would make me clean their house. The time alone allowed me to think about where I was headed in life and why I was without a companion, a line of thought which always haunted me. Everyone around me seemed to so effortlessly find a partner in life. So far I hadn't even come close to tasting romance or companionship. It was something I wanted to work on, but given my new, all-consuming job, was one I was afraid would have to wait until retirement.

As creative and empowered as being Loren's personal assistant made me feel, the responsibilities of the job never ended. It wasn't like I just clocked out at the end of the day and headed home. Just the other night while eating dinner in my room at The Waldorf and talking to Shaneela, a customer service representative for the Pottery Barn catalog, Loren called on the other line to inform me she was having a culinary emergency. According to Loren, her chef Helska was nowhere to be found and she was "mother-fucking starving." I had to hang up on Shaneela in order to dial Helska. When I asked her why she wasn't at AndersPlace making Loren dinner, she said, "if she is so hungry she can eat me!" I switched over to Loren and asked her why Helska would say such a thing. Loren had a bad reputation among the cooking elite. Her finicky eating habits drove many to quit, one French chef would threaten a lawsuits because of "creative infringement," claiming their cooking was art and not something a prissy vegan snob could customize. Considering how much we paid the chefs, I always came to Loren's defense, telling one of the sushi chefs, "If Loren orders a hamburger then make her a hamburger."

"I requested Helga put ketchup on my perogy, is that so much to ask?"

"First of all," I scowled, "her name is Hel*ska*, not Hel*ga*. And I've told you not to add anything to what they make you. They get very offended."

"I pay those mother fuckers ten-thousand dollars a month for mashed potato turds and I can't even add ketchup without offending them? This is horseshit Jimmy!" She must have been starving because she only cussed like that on an empty stomach.

"I know darling," I tried to mend, "but you insist on getting these very famous chefs and you know they come with very famous egos."

"I know," she relented, "Just get me someone who cooks good food."

Within a week I would hire the loveliest Louisianan chef. Her name was Georgina Chase. She owned a trio of fine restaurants in New Orleans and was being featured on a morning television program in New York. She created the most radiant looking meals, nothing regional or strictly southern. Georgina's dishes were worldly and completely original but done in a manner that made the most exotic of feasts feel like comfort food. When I told her Loren was a vegetarian she didn't respond with an annoyed sigh like some of the other chefs I'd hired. Instead, she proclaimed "I love a good challenge."

Loren fell in love Georgina Chase, confiding she savored the chef's food, her warm personality and indelible southern charm. I too would fall in love with Georgina as she was always sent dinner to my hotel room knowing I'd tried everything on the Waldorf's room service menu a hundred times.

Living at the Waldorf=Astoria became more and more impractical every day. It was further than walking distance to AndersPlace and no matter how homey it felt in my suite, walking outside and going down to the lobby was like attending a black tie wedding. When I wanted to throw on a pair of jeans and a T-shirt to go fetch some groceries, I felt pressured to put on slacks and a coat as to not appear like a transient wandering through the posh lobby. I soon decided I would need to rent a place of my own near AndersPlace. In Manhattan's Yorkville, a quaint starter neighborhood on the Upper East Side, I found myself the ideal flat. For just over half of my monthly wage, this top floor apartment had beautiful refinished hardwood floors, an eat-in kitchen and a bathroom with both a shower and bathtub. All the rooms overlooked a quiet, wooded side street and the entire building was air conditioned. I felt fortunate to find a classic New York walk-up. Its location of just eight blocks from AndersPlace made it all the more wonderful of a find.

After a week of negotiating the lease with the feisty Russian landlady who was unhappy with me because I was an out-of-towner, she made me pay four months rent in advance. The real estate climate in New York made me miss Seattle. It was shocking to see housing so overpriced. Standard amenities like a dishwasher and washing machine were luxuries in New York. I would have to pay extra to have these installed in my apartment. I didn't understand why people would pay so much for so little, but neither did I care. On many occasions I had AndersPlace all to myself. As far as I was concerned there was no more luxurious of a place to stay.

Upon finishing the triumphant task of supervising the decoration of AndersPlace, I could hardly wait to furnish my own. I consulted with interior designer Franc Carlton, now a close acquaintance, on what I should do with a small yet fabulous pad. Franc suggested for a bachelor such as myself, a scheme of gray hues accented by bright floral colors. I agreed, painting the walls a shade called "gun metal." In SoHo and Midtown I'd go bonkers buying furniture and other decor, spending much of my savings on a couch. Once everything was delivered, in place and meticulously rearranged, I at last had the perfect Manhattan starter apartment I'd been dreaming of. The decorating spat may have put me a further ten grand in debt but I didn't care. I was making lots of money, had very few bills and figured my career as a personal assistant could only further thrive.

My neighborhood, Yorkville, was the new Greenwich Village, according to *Rag* magazine, the premier pop-meets-subterranean culture magazine every hip Manhattanite seemed to be lugging around. Because the rents were a huge value in a city where even the slums are pricey, the starving artists had flocked to Yorkville. The walk to Lexington to get to the subway could be arduous but the neighborhood had great restaurants, tree lined streets, and was very close to all the Midtown jobs. An added benefit of living in Yorkville was that you could truthfully tell people that you lived on the Upper East Side. Then again, all of El Barrio could say the same.

Moving into a place of my own made me feel like a real New Yorker, upon which I discovered the everyday hassles that every New Yorker must face. My biggest peeve being grocery shopping. They cost me a fortune and they didn't have real super-markets in Manhattan, just little markets that specialized in certain types of food, like Kosher or organic. To buy ingredients for a single meal could mean stopping off at two or three different markets. The grocery problem would cause me to eat delivery almost every night that I didn't eat at AndersPlace, which was becoming all the more regular.

∙ ∙ ∙

In a city as crass and intense as New York, I found it was easy to overlook her shining triumphs. For instance, the wonder of New York's subway system doesn't simply lie in the fact it moves millions of people thousands of miles every day. Something I discovered early in my initial Manhattan daze was that passengers aboard the subway can touch and be touched, even suggestively, right out there in public with no apologies or permissions issued or granted.

It was a sweltering Monday afternoon and I had gotten lost while shopping in unpredictably pleasant Lower Manhattan. This was truly *Old New York*. Walking down winding William Street made me feel as if I'd travelled back in time and was navigating New Amsterdam. After becoming frustrated with my disorientation I found the closest subway station and decided to board the green line in order to head uptown to Carnegie Hill. I was suddenly horrified to see the platform crowded beyond belief with a teeming sea of well-dressed bodies. After what seemed like an hour, the already crammed train arrived and the sea of bodies pushed itself onto the train like a crowd pushes itself against a stage at a rock concert. There didn't appear to be room on the train but somehow the crowd already inside contracted to let all of us in. As I moved I could feel hands and hips and thighs and purses brushing up against me. Inside the train I was wedged up against one of the cutest Wall Street types I'd seen all day. Having been pressed against such a cute young man made me nervous at first. I worried if the train swayed and I brushed my hand against his crotch (accidentally of course) he might accost me. However, when it was his hand brushing across my ass the nervousness I felt turned immediately in to excitement. I assumed his motions were from him trying to retrieve his wallet so he could put away his metro card. When his hands just kept molesting me I started to question whether or not this was his way of flirting. When the train hit another bump I leaned into him pretending to lose my balance, but the hand didn't back away. It remained there, cupping my buttock like a cup of coffee. When we reached the next station and the doors opened I turned to see if he'd make eye contact with me. I turned to find an elderly Asian woman's loaf of naughty French bread sticking out of her grocery bag.

This flirtatious subway train cramming concept didn't end with one disappointment. I took it up as a new way to pass the time. Every couple of afternoons I'd take the green line down to the Financial District around four, wait for the market to close and watch as the trains filled up with cute Wall Street types. I now know for a fact I'm not the only one taking advantage of the close quarters. During several adventures in which I was poised to touch some hunk I would end up at the receiving end of a public groping. But every time I would turn to look at my assailant, even the cute male ones, they would say "sorry." Maybe I looked too straight or intimidating. I blamed my new military inspired haircut, the one I'd gotten after seeing some attractive American soldiers on television who were blowing Baghdad to shit.

Instead of just giving up on my new method of meeting hot professionals, I was determined to make these subterranean happenings lead to at least one date. I did have qualms as to the dangers of my practice. I feared one of these men might take my flirting as an invitation for a hot bathroom jerk off session, something I would never consider doing. It seemed so foolish to jerk it in a dirty, poorly lit, cramped bathroom when I paid very good money for a dirty, poorly lit, cramped apartment.

My adventures on the subway turned into a fascination. I would find myself utilizing the crowded downtown lines in the morning, lunch and afternoon, looking for a car crammed full of cute young executives. I was beginning to think my follies on the subway had turned into a long term hobby until I was the victim of an unwelcome subway grope. It was morning around nine o'clock and the markets were about to open. All the trains headed downtown were packed and I was on one of them. I was standing by the door because it was the farthest I could make it into the train. Unfortunately for me, a decrepit old man crammed his way in behind me. I could see the man's reflection in the glass behind me. He looked harmless, possibly homeless. Just as the train left Fulton Street I felt the seedy homeless man place one of his greasy hands on my ass. Initially I hoped he was pick-pocketing me. I attempted to turn around and to look at him but the train was so crowded I couldn't. Moments passed and he didn't take his hand away, he just left it on me. It was like the incident with the French bread all over again. I strained my neck to glare at him and he actually smiled at me. I didn't smile back and turned away. He then put his hand down. But suddenly he touched the front of my leg and it was suddenly blazing a trail towards my naughty zone. I didn't know what to do. As a goodwill gesture I briefly considered letting the man have a feel. After all, everyone deserved to get their kicks. And wasn't I being discriminatory by only letting handsome and wealthy men touch me? Maybe I'd feel him back and discover he had a huge homeless cock. As I reexamined his reflection in the window I found he wasn't *that* revolting. He had a nice chin and beyond his bushy eyebrows were a set of charming, if not beady, sky blue eyes. Before I had a chance to turn and take a grope, an undercover NYPD officer pulled the man aside after the train stopped and arrested him. Another officer took me aside for questioning, asking if it was the first time such an event had happened to me. I told the officer it was and that I didn't react because I was too afraid do anything. I pouted and claimed that I was worried the man might have a knife or a gun. I'm not sure the officer believed me because when I left the subway station he said, "I don't want to catch you getting groped by anymore dirty old men on the subway again, okay?"

◦ ◦ ◦

Near the end of May it was announced that Loren Anders was to become the new face of Coca-Cola. The envisioned campaign was one similar to what Bacardi had done with Bombay Sapphire, just on a greater scale. Loren would be used to redefine the global brand and move the soda makers image up market. Coca-Cola was going to put her on everyone one of its billboards in every single country it did business, which was pretty much every country in the world. Loren's fame would begin to rise to a greater level than either of us could have predicted. When the campaign was announced I discovered her dancing alone in her ballroom. She was the happiest I'd ever seen her.

"Jimmy, this is big," Loren gasped.

"Why? It's just Coke," I shrugged passively to tease her. She slapped me on the shoulder and made me dance with her to celebrate the campaign.

Loren's unbridled excitement was even more animated as she declared with giddy revelry that her newest real estate project, AndersPlaza, a skyscraper under-construction on East 35th street, was ready for its first viewing. When we arrived at the site I expected to see a towering mass of concrete and steel but found only an immense hole in the ground. The hole was so deep I couldn't see the bottom until I stood near the edge of the vast worksite. With the two us wearing bright blue hardhats stamped 'AndersGroup' on the sides, Loren and I were lead down into the damp smelling hole by a well-dressed group of engineers, architects, and contractors.

Although I was disappointed at first by the site, the engineers gave the two of us a fascinating tour of the project and would explain the complexity of the building. The soon-to-be tower's foundation rested 135 feet below the surface of the East River. Crews had spent over a year constructing the equivalent of a dam around the hole to ensure the site did not become deluged with river water. A collapse would have meant disaster as several buildings bordering the site would have surely been affected. Another unique aspect of the project was that a third of the building would be constructed above the Eastside Drive highway. Had anything gone wrong during construction, both a major highway and neighborhood could've been compromised. After being told of the unthinkable amount of work that had gone into the design of the building, I gained a sudden respect for the brave construction workers who slaved away daily erecting yet another monument to AndersGroup Incorporated.

Standing in the base of the hole was unnerving. The warm atmosphere of the springtime air had been replaced by a cool, dewy haze, chilled by the East River flowing past us just yards away. I couldn't help but wonder what would have happened to the site if there'd been an earthquake. Foolishly, I asked one of the foremen, "How strong of an earthquake can this wall withstand?" His face went from hospitable to hostile.

"Puhleez!" The man cried, "this is New York. We don't have earthquakes."

"Isn't it amazing," Loren dazzled, spinning around looking at each massive wall of concrete surrounding us on all four sides. "It's going to be breathtaking."

"How tall is going to be?" I asked.

"A thousand feet exactly. They wouldn't let me build any higher, not this close to the river and all. The project is complex enough."

"Close? We're practically in the river," I said.

"I showed you the drawing didn't I?" Loren asked. "The east side of the building will actually slope down to the shore and appear to be in the water. It's going to be breathtaking, like the building is a floating skyscraper parked here in East Midtown. From across the river in Queens you'll be able to look over the river and its reflection in the water will make it appear twice as tall."

"It wouldn't be an Anders building without a little controversy," I plainly stated.

"What do you mean by that?" she asked, glaring at me.

"It's as if you seek out the most avant-garde of projects," I replied. It was a fact that all her monstrosities, be it her AndersCenter, AndersTower, and AndersHall of Seattle, the AndersPacific building in Los Angeles, the Deustche-Anders complex in Frankfurt, or the AndersNippon National Tower in Tokyo, were all architectural bastards, created to offend the locals with radical shapes and unconventional flair. New York's AndersPlaza was no different in its design, consisting of a double-domed lobby adjoined by a 90-story tower topped by another dome. New York newspapers were calling it the largest phallus ever conceived. After mindful consideration of what the towers resembled, Loren would have her architects turn the domes into pyramidal shapes, only after the project had been dismissed as obscene by nearly every architecture critic in the city.

The construction of the AndersPlaza was possibly the most controversial new building in New York's recent history. As Loren and I were escorted out of the site toward her limousine I noticed a line of several dozen protesters holding signs and marching behind police barricades. The NYPD was doing a marvelous job in holding back this flash mob that had formed within just hours of it being made known that Loren would be visiting the site that day. They roared with anger and held giant signs of protest that shocked me: "Environmental Time Bomb," "WTC2," "Daddy Can't Buy New York," and "Capitalist Bitch Go Back To Seattle." This group – a radical coalition of socialists, environmentalists, libertarians, and anti-intelligentsia – were a staple to any public event Loren attended. Having recently passed on Bill Gates as a target for anti-capitalist demonstrations, Loren had become their new icon of revolt. She was their new cover girl for conspiracy theories on alleged plutocracy, as evidenced by the multitude of websites that popped up claiming she was a freemason and demonized her for being a Unitarian Universalist.

As we sat in the armored limousine and we drove via police escort back to AndersPlace, I would confide in Loren by telling her I felt like crying when I saw the protestors. Several raw eggs would burst on the window of the limousine, the sound of their impact as startling as gun shots.

"What a shame?" Loren sighed looking out at the crowd that denounced her.

"What do you mean," I asked.

"I don't know." Loren would offer, "I mean, why not protest something really horrible like deforestation or cruelty towards animals. Or the rising cost of prescription medicine. That's a real tragedy. Every day thousands of Americans go without much needed medical care because we've failed to pass healthcare reform in this country. And yet despite that, these fools have it in them to stage a rally against something as innocuous as me."

"That's a really good point," I said.

"Those protestors out there, Jimmy, are the same people who think we should do away with the capitalist system and barter for things. Countless societies have tried that with no success. To be without a currency is to have vast inefficiencies in trade. These same people believe that a mother should go to jail for spanking her kid, or that burning logs in a fireplace is an environmental sin," Loren laughed, "they don't live in the same world as you and me."

"What world is that?"

"A world where one is expected to shower daily and hold down a job. Like it or not, but a job is not just something you do to make money, it's a contribution to the larger society. Our world is one of choices and consequences, where a person is expected to contribute. Every economic system has its faults, but what they promote has been proven to fail time and again."

When we returned to Loren's house she explained in great detail over lunch how she dealt with the constraints of extreme wealth. "I look at it this way: Money can only buy so much. I still only get one vote. I have to stand in line at Starbucks along with everyone else. Money only buys material things. For instance... I still, for some god forsaken reason, cannot hold down a boyfriend."

"Maybe you should buy one," I proposed.

"I probably could," she laughed. "But these men I'm attracted to, they're all scared of me. Every single one of them. They think that if I have everything money can buy then they can't provide for me."

"It's as if your wealth affects them more than it does you."

"I know! As if money could make a man obsolete! What a sad idea."

The next day Loren would jet off to Atlanta to meet with the executives of Coca-Cola. There she would witness the creation of the campaign they'd envisioned she be a central part of. I would spend the rest of the week leisurely entertaining myself, continually discovering my new city and taking up a cavalier interest in what the anti-capitalism movement was about. Their website proclaimed Loren Anders to be everything that was wrong with America. As valid as their concerns were about the disparity between the rich and poor, they deflated every argument they had by pointing to Loren. There was no way that one person, no matter how rich, young or beautiful, could become the catalyst for America's downfall. Or so I hoped.

Undoubtedly, Loren had her faults. Everyone does. Loren Anders liked to appear as if she were a typical girl, living fast, partying, and enjoying the company of her many friends. The truth was much more tiresome. Loren may not have been in absolute executive control of AndersGroup, she didn't want to be, but her lifestyle of indulgence and metro-hopping always played a secondary role in her relentless supervision of all of AndersGroup's operations. On many occasions she'd tell her friends, "I'm too hung over to go out tonight," when in fact she would stay home to make conference calls with business associates. Her lifestyle, however heralded as outlandish in the press was all just a show. It was Loren saying to the world, "I am America's Princess, I know how to have a good time and I don't care what you think of me." Meanwhile she knew exactly what put food on her table, couture on her back and diamonds on every one of her limbs. Her reckless image was a ploy for publicity as the world was constantly fascinated by unstable celebrities. It was America's favorite storyline: the girl who has it all and can't cope with the pressure of publicity. She recognized this and made it appear as if the pedestal which she stood atop was about to fall over, when really it couldn't have been more sturdy.

Loren Anders would always blame her exorbitant excess of wealth for the reason she seemed unable to fall in love with a man. I observed the truth as her clockwork tiring of men. Every time she ever met someone she though she liked she would attempt a relationship with them. But after a couple days of romance she would sicken of it and wish for nothing more than to be single again. I'm not sure she's ever been in love with a man, although I am undoubtedly positive many men have been in love with her.

JUNE

Through the personal assistant grapevine I heard many PA's, like those hired to mind after celebrities, often had to perform strenuous labor, like washing cars and vacuuming. Fortunately, I never had to do any of that. As Loren's top ranking PA I simply supervised, making sure that the maids were cleaning everything they should've, the chefs were preparing exactly what Loren desired, and everything else that went into making the Anders home perfect was being done to *my* exact specifications. If my attention to detail was not met I didn't mess around. In our first month at AnderPlace I had to let three housekeepers go because of their inability to mind certain details.

Much of my supervising was done covertly, as you never know if a maid might take her frustrations out on her boss by inserting her employer's toothbrush in an orifice. It's often during these times of clandestine supervision I learn if a housekeeper is really loyal or just fearful, astute or dreadfully two-faced. Gossip was never tolerated on my watch and it broke my heart to find that even the best housekeepers loved to shoot the shit with each other all day. Eavesdropping on these poor souls often involved hearing them talk of me. One day I overheard Loren's Lead Housekeeper and First Assistant Chef discussing how I was a "tag along" and a "mooch." I would have fired them if what they said had been untruthful. I felt like both those things. What I didn't like was that it had been so obvious to the staff.

As Loren's modeling career continued its ascent, my assistant tasks for her did as well. Because I spent many long nights at AndersPlace, I even had my own bedroom there, complete with several days worth of clothes and a few personal items. In a strange facet of human nature, when Loren was home we'd tend to hang out together all day in my tiny room, like it was my apartment back in Seattle. How absurd it was for us to have that giant palace to ourselves and only use but a few rooms of it.

Given that my job as personal assistant really entailed anything that was assigned to me, there were certain tasks that seemed a bit too absurd to be real. There was one mission so covert I felt it necessary to consult with several lawyers before writing about it: I was to destroy the career of a model who was encroaching on Loren's trademark look. Her name was Lark, singularly named like all great supermodels and the young girls who emulated them. She was Loren Anders's arch-nemesis and cat-walking doppelganger. A complete mess who couldn't walk a runway without a nose full of cocaine, she was a notorious gold-digging slut who'd go down on any man worth more than $50-million dollars. Beside her trajectory toward the tragic, it was made clear to me that I was to infiltrate her circle of friends, charm her, and do what was necessary to end her career. Of course I wasn't instructed to kill her. Rather, I was to find out what it was that could end her career as a model.

Lark had been seen at the same variety of pro-education, pro-vegetarian, pro-African debt relief fundraisers held throughout Manhattan that Loren was known to attend. It was no surprise that Page Six of the *New York Post* would carry a half page feature on the two who looked strikingly similar to one another: both tall blonde stick figures with large eyes and a wide pouty mouths. The article in the *Post* hinted that designers who wanted Loren but wouldn't pay her $20,000-an-hour fee would often seek Lark, Loren's composite, for a mere $5,000-per-hour, a bargain if you considered that most people viewing a Lark ad campaigned assumed it was Loren in the photos.

Lark was very much the Pepsi to Loren's Coca-Cola. In Loren's own words, "All great products have their imposters." But what drove Loren over the edge was the charlatan's recent announcement that she was soon to be a published writer, penning the said-to-be fashion epic, *A Model's Story: The Secret To My Success*. It was a move that infuriated Loren as she too was working on her own modeling exposé, tentatively titled *Model of Success: My Secret Story*. Loren was being copied faster than she could even produce her work. Loren called me from Miami one afternoon having just heard of Lark's book. She was calling to seek my advice on some way to sabotage Lark. I suggested a two-part poison that would make an autopsy inconclusive as to what killed her. It was a method of homicide I'd learned about from a *Columbo* episode when I was a kid. Loren had other ideas.

"We can't kill her," Loren moralized.

"She's a model. No one will object," I cited. "They'll just understand that it was her time. Live fast, be beautiful, die young. How old is she?"

"That's a carefully guarded secret. But backstage at the Donna Karan show I got a look at her ass. A little wrinkly if you ask me. She might be 25."

"25!" I gasped. Any model over 23 was insanity. This was an age where models retired at 17. For he to be strutting the runways at 25 was actually remarkable.

"How dare she title her book *The Secret of My Success*!" Loren fumed. "Her success is a direct result of *my* success. If it weren't for me she'd be back in Phoenix or Houston or whatever sweltering shit-crevasse she emerged from."

"What possibly could be the secret of her success anyway?" I invited ridicule.

"A push-up bra and transparent panties," Loren offered.

"Or the absence of a gag reflex?"

"The tragic result of binge and purge!" Loren announced, not catching my insinuation.

"No. She's a whore."

"Let's not go there."

"Well fuck you, I'm trying to demonize her," I scowled.

"That wrinkly bitch is history!" Loren shrieked, thus putting the hit on Lark.

* * *

"I'm James Minor, here to see Ms. Ritzburg," I told one of the receptionist clones in the lobby of Chic Models Limited. She was just one in a series of eight answering telephones at the front desk. By their appearance - youthful, pure, and hollow-minded – I assumed they'd all submitted their portfolios to the agency for modeling gigs but were deemed only pretty enough to answer the phone.

"One moment," the girl replied as she examined a list of scheduled visitors on her computer. For a moment I feared my undercover mission had already been foiled for it was taking a long time for her to find me on the computer. The delay was probably due to her inability to remember the alphabet.

My press credentials were attained using Loren's miniscule fractional ownership of the *New York Times*. I was sent to the modeling agency as a fact gatherer for a story that was to coincide with a larger fashion feature. Because of the newspaper's clout, the agency felt I should speak with Barbara Ritzburg, founder, president and chairwoman.

"Oh, here you are," the receptionist said. "Ms. Ritzburg is on her way back from lunch. I'll let you know when she's arrived."

I took a seat in the lobby that looked like a space age set from a 1970's James Bond film. The floor, walls, and furniture were all bright white, lacquered and shiny – a virtual tribute to Pierre Cardin. In this waiting area the agency did not have plain old magazines on display but what are called Look Books, each page that featured a Chic model having been flagged. These are limited edition photo magazines of fashion collections. These books were coveted in the industry because of their restricted distribution, reserved for celebrities and buyers at department stores. So when I got the chance to finger through one of these nifty compendiums I told my moral conscious to hit the road and swiftly stashed the Dior menswear book in my briefcase.

Moments later I was in Barbara Ritzburg's office. She was a frail, elderly woman. By counting the wrinkles on her face I assumed the Chanel suit she wore had been a gift from Coco herself.

"So you want the dirt, don't you!" Barbara insisted as she mixed herself a cocktail. She had enough liquor next to her desk to open a bar. As she swilled her drink I identified Barbara as one of those rare women whose directness and curtness got her to the top of her field. I began to like her.

"By dirt you mean?" I yearned. Playing coy had always been a natural inclination.

"You want to know the foul secrets, right?" She rattled on, "Like what we do to the poor girls, what they have to go through to get this far. Who they have to... *entertain* to get to this agency?" It became apparent I was not the first writer to try and uncover the furtive dealings within the more prestigious modeling agencies.

"Although that sounds interesting," I said, beginning a spiel I hoped would justify my genuine interest in the industry, "I'm here to expose what an up-and-coming young girl or guy might want to know if they were interested in modeling." My delivery was excellent. "It's more of a how-to piece, not a gossip and hearsay story. After all, I'm from the *New York Times*. Gossip and hearsay are for other publications."

"I see," she replied with a flinch in her chin. "You're the first journalist from any paper who didn't want me to start with the filth. Are you sure there's no backstage squabbling you want me to make public? What about the rumors of drugs and alcohol abuse?"

"Mrs. Ritzburg, I'm sure those are interesting tales. As a casual reader of the *New York Post* I know many of those stories have already been written. The last thing I need or want to write about is a scandal article. Fashion is art. Your agency helps artists realize their vision. I am here to pay respect to modeling, not deride it."

She was satisfied with my answer but not the way I addressed her.

"It's not *Misses*, it's *Ms.* and as a reader of the *Post* I'm sure you're aware of my very public divorce."

"Yes, but as a member of the press I'm also very careful not to believe everything I read," I said. She cackled loosely and the ice that had been present in the room the momentarily thawed.

"Well then," she said, standing up from her desk to pace about the room. "Seeing that you're doing an honest piece on the modeling industry and not the pesky fictional stereotypes of it, I feel it is my duty to give you an accurate picture of our world."

"Thank you. I must admit," I began to lie, "I have tremendous respect for models. They're no different than say an actor, or a dancer. They tells us stories with poses and expressions. What's more beautiful than that?"

"Exactly!" Barbara proclaimed as she lit a giant cigarette and paraded me out into the office where the failed models furiously answered phones. "You seem like a nice boy, I hope you have enough time to do extensive research on your topic."

"Why yes, I do!" I chirped. "When I'm writing a story I dedicate my life to it. Nothing but the story exists. I go all in."

"Great. Let's go to Paris!"

* * *

In the month of June, the City of Light hosts its haute couture shows. These are not just regular showcases of priceless wares, but the elite-of-the-elite. And Barbara Ritzburg's models at Chic had a stranglehold on these runways.

"Never been to Paris!" Barbara blasted in disbelief as we entered her waiting sedan on Seventh Avenue. "You haven't been anywhere until you've been to Paris!" That sort of statement suddenly seemed so cliché, so applicable. *You haven't been anywhere until you've been to Omaha!*

"Fuck the French!" Barbara blasted as she recalled the nostalgic days of traveling on the Concorde. "And the British too. Do you know how long it takes to get to Paris now?"

"No." I really had no clue.

"Forever!" she growled.

I almost mentioned that my good friend Loren Anders owned one of the Concordes that Air France had sold when they liquidated their fleet. Such a confession would have completely blown my cover and I scrambled for something else to say.

"Beats the boat," I joked, hoping to receive at least a small chuckle. Then I winced when I considered Barbara's age. She probably had taken a steam ship to France in her younger years.

"Thank God they still have first-class," Barbara said, shuttering as she imagined riding alongside the middle-class.

"Oh yes… thank God!" I groused. I'd never traveled first-class on a commercial flight.

"Sweetie," Barbara addressed me, "you're coming to Paris with me for a couple days. I want you to see it all. I'm going to throw you right into a model's environment. You'll be shocked… appalled… and maybe a little enlightened."

"That's great!" I truly did want to go to France and was thankful that I had gotten a passport earlier in the year for a ski trip to Whistler, BC with Loren. As big as an industry as fashion was in New York, fashion as an art form seemed to be in its prime in Europe.

Barbara was chauffeured off to her Gramercy Park penthouse to fetch some items for the trip and kiss her cats goodbye. I was taken to my place where I collected a bag of only the essentials. Going undercover meant compromise, so only the core of my skin care regimen was able to make the trip. The two of us rejoined at the airport where we boarded our flight.

Inside the first-class cab of a jumbo jet headed for Europe, I found myself in the company of approximately thirty male fashion models Barbara had rounded up for a photo shoot at Versailles. These gorgeous, sculpted men, some of them wearing no shirts, would gorge on champagne and lobster for hours. They made raucous noise, laughing, joking and fighting with one another. Nowhere did I see a flight attendant raise an eyebrow. In Europe these guys were the equivalent of NBA all-stars. They did as they pleased, no matter how crude or vulgar. It was glorious!

"So Jimmy," Barbara moaned, "which of these boys should make the cut and which should be cut from the show?" I had no idea why she was asking me. They were all beyond perfect, their beauty fragile while their bodies chiseled and strong.

"I don't know," I said. "Why are you asking me?"

"Brutality is fashion. Fashion is aesthetic. We survive by manufacturing beauty. Decisions must be made that realize our goal of producing fashion. I want your story to depict this. I think readers will be fascinated to know the challenges we face in this industry."

"I've never heard that before Barbara. I will definitely consider incorporating it in the story."

"Now go on," she snarled, "tell me which one should lose his modeling contract." The boys were all game for this little modeling competition and lined up the aisle striking poses and sulking.

"I don't know," I shrugged, "they're all wearing so much clothing." Immediately the boys began removing the scraps of clothing they had on. Before me was a line of thirty flawless boys wearing nothing but their man panties.

"They're all kind of nice," I said indecisively.

"Be honest. Who's the ugliest?" she growled crudely. Picking an ugly one would've been impossible. I'd never seen such a large collection of good looking men. I decided to be playful and pick the cutest one I could find.

"Him!" I pointed. "He's hideous." All the boys laughed for we all knew just how stunning the boy I picked was. These men all knew they were beautiful. If they were less than stunning there was no way they'd be on a jet with Barbara Ritzburg on their way to Paris.

After my eighth glass of champagne I fell asleep and when I woke up we were beginning to land. With glee I'd find the very same model who I called hideous had fallen asleep with his head on my shoulder. When I stood up to use the bathroom he grabbed my hand and said, "Jimmy, don't leave. I'm sorry."

"It's fine. I just have to use the bathroom."

"Can I go with you?" he sniveled.

"No." Fear prompted this response.

As I made my way to the restroom I found all the models had fallen asleep, some of them on the floor. When I returned to my seat I found the model who'd fallen asleep on my shoulder packing up his belongings in preparation for the landing.

"I've never been to Paris before," I said to him.

"You'll love it… or you'll hate it. One of the two," he replied, his English affected. I suspected he was French or Austrian.

"My name is Jimmy," I said, giving him a hand to shake.

"I'm Jules." When he said his name his lips puckered like he was blowing a kiss. I began to wonder if he had filler put in his lips. They looked swollen, as if he'd been stung by a bee. Either that or he'd sucked someone off while I was in the bathroom.

Before long we landed to meet a fleet of limousines that would take us into Paris city proper. I would shadow Barbara, asking her the types of questions I thought a reporter might, like how many times a year she made it to Paris and if the boys and girls who worked for her agency always had people watching after them. As the male models were herded off to be primped for a magazine shoot, Barbara and I were taken to her office on the Champs-Elyées. The entire time I talked to Barbara I was in disbelief that I was actually in Paris. I tried to take in the view out the window but she kept talking, babbling on about the myths of "modeldom." I found it necessary to write down much of what she said, even if the notes were destined for the recycling bin. Babs told me she was going to show me how rank the Parisian girls were and how her agency revolutionized modeling in Europe. Just as she was telling me, "These Parisian bitches never even waxed their bushes before we hit town," unexpected news broke over the radio, announcing the tragic passing of a fashion designer while he was vacationing in Mallorca. Barbie was aghast and broke down in to what I believe were tears (her face didn't actually move, she just patted her eyes with a tissue). She insisted the driver take her immediately to her house on the Left Bank. In a fit of shock and sadness she apologized for ending our interview. I was dropped off at the Chic modeling office a few yards from the Arc de Triomphe and told they'd arrange accommodations for me there.

My arrival at the studio must have been preceded with some sort of announcement because everyone knew my name and the newspaper from which I supposedly hailed. A frail waif known as Lark introduced herself to me a team of experts tried to squeeze her into a pair of skyscraper size white go-go boots. It wasn't a conventional fashion shoot, rather a set of photos that would be used to promote the agency.

"Where's Ms. Ritzburg?" Lark asked me, her voice docile. Most models I'd met were brash paladins. Lark was so unassumingly feeble.

This is who I've been sent to destroy?

"She was taken to her home," I said. "She's mourning the loss."

"What loss?" Lark snorted, "The guy was a fiend. I'll tell you right now it was his dope dealer who shot him!"

"What's your name?" I faked naivety.

"Lark," she said, breathy and rehearsed, like she'd practiced saying her own name.

"I'm Jimmy Minor." We shook hands. Her hand was no larger than a mouse's with claws just as sharp.

"What kind of a piece are you doing?" she asked passively. "Something on how glorious the fashion industry is…because if you'd like some breaking news, it's not."

"It's basically a puff piece," I said with a slight giggle. "My editors want something romantic, a tribute to the great designers. The kind of article lanky girls and prissy boys all across the American heartland can read just before going to bed and dreaming of what it must be like to be you."

"Really?" Lark questioned cautiously, the concept of a newspaper article honoring fashion seemed foreign to her. "I'd say it's long overdue your paper realized the importance of fashion in today's culture. It's a goddamn art and they treat it very acrimoniously, like it's a circus or something."

"Well it's not just about fashion," I countered. "It's about the entire culture. People like you, the models, the designers, everybody." I elaborated, "fashion really has little to do with clothing. It's both an industry and an art. A discipline and an addiction."

"Absolutely" she howled. She and I were reading each other quite well, so much so that we went out for coffee after the shoot. After that we walked over to her apartment just off the Rue de Rivoli overlooking the Jardin des Tuileries. If I were at all interested in women I would have been in paradise. Not that Lark was superior to my closest confident Loren, but she did have a refinement to her that Loren lacked. Where as Loren was a crass wild flower, Lark was a quivering and delicate blossom crafted by nature and polished with education. Lark possessed a demeanor of someone who'd been beaten all her life, someone who's been deprived of notice and someone you feel compelled to give adoration to, not out of obligation but because she seemed to enliven with it.

"You know I'm so sick of people shitting on fashion," Lark professed, pouring us both a glass of Chateau Margaux. We sat on her terrace and drank. The Eiffel Tower gleamed a fiery yellow no more than ten blocks away. I so wanted to snap a photo of myself on the terrace but didn't want to give myself away as a Paris virgin.

"Fashion is the least harmful thing in the world," Lark went on, "and yet half the globe seems to be protesting against it."

"Isn't fur harmful?" I asked. "To kill an animal only for its pelt is something that really turns people off."

"Fur *is* disgusting. I told Lagerfeld if he tried to put a hide on me I'd quit the show. And has he? No way!" Lark sounded just as strong willed as Loren when it came to animal rights.

"How did you get into modeling?" I asked, prompting her to swig her wine.

"My mother. My stupid mother," Lark replied and stopped hastily as if wanting to change the subject. Of course this drew me to persist.

"She pressured you into it?"

"Oh god yes. It was horrible," Lark lamented, her chin in her palm, her eyes wide and misty. "She made me into one of those toddler beauty queens, like that Colorado girl that got killed."

"What is your relationship with her like now?" I asked delicately.

"You're a journalist so I have to be careful what I tell you," she keenly prefaced, "so I'll just say, my mother and I talk on the phone about once a week. She was my manager for a while when I began getting the big jobs, like Avon and JC Penney. She became an alcoholic about two years ago. I made her enter treatment soon after that and she's been in and out of rehab since. Our relationship, if you can call it that, works great for the both of us. We respected each other's boundaries."

I was stunned. Loren's so-called biggest threat, Lark, a supposed diva-super-bitch was shockingly human and had a family not unlike most people's. Just like Loren, Lark's relationship with her parents was fractured. They both knew tremendous pain, but in that moment with Lark, I felt she had a better, more managed grasp on her grief.

For dinner, Lark took me to Pongal, the spiciest Thai vegan cuisine I'd ever tasted, but also the best. Over dinner she explained her hectic schedule that week. Every morning she was to fly to a new city somewhere in Europe and each night return to Paris. She begged me to go with her to Rome the next day where she was being shot for a new Versace campaign. She said it would be perfect for the piece I was writing, and I agreed.

"You know what they say," I alluded.

"What?"

"You haven't been anywhere until you've been to Rome," I replied. Her eyes squinted in response.

"I thought they said that about Hollywood."

After Lark went off to meet some model friends who she described as the "dumbest women east of Orange County," I headed back over to the Chic modeling agency. The glamour of Paris never ended so the agency was open twenty-four-seven. There I found one of the almost-gorgeous receptionists had a message for me. It read: "Jimmy, Jardin du Luxembourg ASAP." Unaware of what it meant, the receptionist told me to take a cab over to the Palais du Luxembourg where the house of Dior was showing its menswear line in what was described in the message as a "very classy nighttime setting."

"Sweety," Ms. Ritzburg hummed as I entered the production tent of the gardens. "I want to take you to see my good friend Sebastian, he does everyone's hair. He's got a great perspective on the goings on backstage."

"Great, I can't wait." I began to wonder if he was going to do my hair, not that it needed any coiffing.

I pictured Sebastian to be a skinny little priss wielding a brush and blow-dryer, wearing all black with some sort of hair barrette or rainbow colored earrings. Barbara introduced me to a three-hundred pound gorilla with shoulder-length blond hair and a very tight "I ♥ NY" T-shirt. Despite the low maintenance look, he was just as feminine as any other hairdresser.

"Darling, this is my friend Jimmy," Barbara explained to Sebastian as he molested the hair of a tiny French model that looked hungry and frightened.

"Oh, doll, this is the journalist?" Sebastian quizzed glancing at me while blindly ironing the long black hair of the model. "Delicious, I'll be done in three snaps." Steam shot out from the iron, the models head being tossed around like it weren't attached to anything.

"Fantastic," Barbara said. She turned to me to say, "I'll see you later. I have a room for you at the Hotel Bristol. You're staying under the name Jim Stark. Call you later!"

Barbara left with a tiny little boy model whose only job was to carry her enormous black and white Chanel purse.

"Okay, what do you want to know?" Sebastian asked as he sorted through a giant pile of the left over hair extensions.

"Nothing in particular," I replied. "I'm writing a story on what a girl has to go through to become a model."

"Oh," he sounded stunned, "most writers want to know who hates who, who's fucked who, and who hates who after they've fucked their boyfriend." He chuckled loudly and disproportionately. He was one of those people who thought he was funnier than he actually was. He walked me out of the tent and over to the Rue Guynemer where he lit a cigarette. I got out my pen and notepad and began the interview.

"From your experience, are you able to tell right from the beginning if a girl has what it takes to make it?"

"Definitely. The girls who last one season, they'll do anything and wear anything just to be on the runway. Designers hate that, they want attitude. I once saw a girl spit in a designer's face because he'd paired these hideous boots with a ski parka. She's been on that runway every year for last eight years. The girls have to bring themselves to the show. The only thing that should be molded is the exterior."

"Which young model do you think is going to be around for the next five years?"

"Five years. That's a long time in modeling," he said, pausing to reflect. He rattled off a bunch of names I didn't recognize, then came to the one I was fishing for. "I think Lark will be around for a while. At least in the industry, if not a model then a designer."

Hold on. Lark designed clothes too? No wonder Loren was so afraid of her.

Sebastian said he had nothing to do for the rest of the night so I proposed I interview him at a café. He said he knew a great place just down the block. I was expecting an eclectic smoke filled bistro, something very Parisian. I became dismayed when the two of us were seated in a Starbucks inside a Barnes and Noble. Not exactly what I dreamed of when I thought of Paris, coffee, and French literature.

"How does a girl go from shit to chic?" I asked. Sebastian chuckled, sipping his Americano, flipping through the day's *New York Post*, a copy which he said he snagged from Natalie Portman. According to Sebastian she'd given it to him "just moments ago at the show. Me and Nat go way back. I did her hair in *The Clone Wars*."

I tried to take our conversation back to fashion by asking: "In so many words, what does the average model's career look like?"

"To become a model a girl has to sleep with the right casting agent, be it male or female," he propagandized. "Take up smoking and bulimia, find a rich Hollywood actor boyfriend to subsidize her heroin and cocaine addictions, and finally after retiring at age nineteen-and-a-half, write a tell-all book on her experiences. HarperCollins loves that shit." I could see that Sebastian was just as big a cynic towards modeling as I was. "Seriously, I don't know how the girls get from Missouri to Milan, but they do. I just do their hair!"

"I'm not going to find the secret with you, am I?"

"Afraid not," Sebastian admitted. "But if you ever write an article on ringlets give me a call."

We chatted for a while over the gossip page in the *Post*. I knew we were going to part ways the moment we finished our drinks but I didn't want to leave without getting his take on Paris. All around people were speaking French and I didn't know a scrap of the language. I wasn't ready to set out in the city in search of a hotel called Bristol without at least a little guidance from a fellow American.

"Would you happen to know Paris very well?" I asked. "I've never been here before."

"Sure!" He rang, "I know Paris, like I know men… up-and-down and side-to-side!"

I spent the rest of the evening with Sebastian. He was kind enough to show me the sites, especially the ones involving seedy nightlife and where American celebrities hung out whenever they were in town. I'd also see the touristy places like the haunting Notre Dame and Hotel de Ville, Paris' city hall. I recall it wasn't the landmarks that intrigued me most about Paris, it was the city itself. It was just so ornamental. Every stone and surface was crafted and worn, every building emblazed with decoration. Not a single thing was dull, not even in the dead of night.

At around two AM I wound up at the Hotel Bristol, not far from the Chic agency. The hotel wasn't the biggest or the most expensive I'd seen (compared to the behemoths of Manhattan) but it was certainly the most charming. It was the ideal Parisian inn, with staff dressed in clean, tailored uniforms, and handsome bellman that could have doubled for models. The rooms were so cozy and thoughtfully decorated I dreaded ever having to leave. My first night in Paris I ordered room service, wildly picking things I'd never heard of. I would end up with, of course, an array of grotesque looking meats which I forced myself to eat out of principal, considering the animal was already dead. As gruesome as the meat seemed for this vegetarian, I found all the dishes were rather delicious and painstakingly prepared, like only the French can do. A meal I knew I'd have to eat again was called Coquilles Saint-Jacques, a dish of oblong shaped mashed potatoes housing a center of scallops and sliced mushrooms. I laughed when I first saw the meal and thought it too handsome to destroy. But my stomach and taste buds celebrated as I devoured it and the rest of my distinctly French feast.

By the next morning I hadn't received any calls or messages from Barbara or Lark, so I decided to spend the morning exploring Paris. Seeing that I didn't speak a word of French, and was fearful I'd get myself in to a situation what it was required, I headed some place safe and touristy: the Louvre. When I got there and saw a map of all the exhibits I decided it was too big to even preview. Instead I kicked around Paris for a couple of hours by myself, marveling the architecture and layout of the immensely ornate city. At a hip café near the Place de la Concorde I took a break from walking and asked for a bottle of Evian, thinking it was a national standard at restaurants. The waiter replied with "vhut?" to which I said "you know, water!" and he gave me a bottle of Crystal Geyser, imported all the way from California.

Just as I was starting to tire from all the walking and exploring, I got a call from Lark on Sunday night telling me to meet her down on the street.

"We're picking you up, we're flying out tonight," Lark said hurriedly. She had just learned the Rome photo shoot had been rescheduled.

A fashion shoot is an event in Italy. Just like a major motion picture shoot in America, streets are closed, traffic redirected, and security heightened. For a Versace shoot in Rome, the design house pulled out all the stops. The shoot was to take place in the middle of a street in front of the Trevi Fountain, a major tourist enclave. And just like a film shoot, the models had their own trailers, and Lark's was the biggest. As her new best friend I was in charge of watching the trailer, making sure no paparazzi snuck in or any crazed men claiming to be her ex-husband came in and raped her. In Europe, a place devoid of global movie stars, those associated with the fashion industry (supermodels, designers, editors, photographers) were some of the highest ranking celebrities, just behind soccer players.

The theme of the fashion shoot was Hollywood Vs. Europe. Lark was to portray a spoiled Beverly Hills actress who was struggling to find her character on the set of a film about the dark and seedy Roman street culture. The scene was to depict a rich woman walking down the middle of a street as a few dozen men held handbags out for her to choose from. A very attractive young man was to pose as her American boyfriend who's pleading with her to return to Los Angeles. The concept of the shoot was brilliant. The creative force behind it, Cecilia Graham, was a Brooklyn photographer I had coincidentally met while on a photo shoot with Loren. Cecilia even recognized me and gave me a European double kiss on each cheek. I felt so elite but worried she'd ask me about Loren. She didn't, assuming I'd simply made more friends in the fashion industry.

Barbara Ritzburg arrived a short time into the shoot with her entourage of boyfriends and bodyguards. She brought with her a pair of twin terriers who'd just gotten back from holiday in Capri with Barbara's ex-husband. Even Sebastian, the stylist who'd been my guide around Paris, was there. I felt so comfortable and glamorous. I was amongst people who I liked and who seemed to like me. The situation would have been perfect bliss if I hadn't been there to destroy someone's career.

The young male model hired to play Lark's boyfriend sat between me and Barbara as she yelled at her "dipshit slut" personal assistant, a term I felt was harshly used, even in Italy. The model, another of Barbara's latest finds whom she stole from another agency, was laughing at her telephone antics when he tapped me on the shoulder and asked, "Are you in the shoot?"

Laughingly I shook my head, then I examined the model more closely to find it was Jacques, the same model I'd met on the jet ride to Paris.

"Me, a model?" I snickered, "you must be kidding."

"You could be a model," he defended his statement. It was an obvious attempt at flirtation. "You look just like one of the guys in the new Yves Saint Laurent campaign."

"I'm too old to be a model," I bashfully replied.

"What are you, 22?" he guessed.

"Yes."

Jacques and I talked for hours in between the lengthy setups. For just a few photos the crew worked for eight hours. It was really incredible how much labor went in to the effort. This crew was relentless in getting every shot. What made the process take so long was that every garment from the designer's collection had to fit in somewhere. Each setup became a dynamic puzzle of clothes and accessories where the inclusion of one could result in the elimination of others. It was a complex spectacle to watch. As we chatted Jacques found everything I said funny. I figured he was drunk, nervous, or absolutely smitten with me because what I was saying wasn't all that funny. After the shoot wrapped everyone from Chic, including me, hopped on a flight over to London. Barbara had chartered a jet to take all the models to England for a photo shoot the following day. It was on that flight Jacques and I would cozy up in a pair of seats near the rear of the jet. As we gabbed in to the night I fell madly in lust with him. The jet was far from full and we found we had just enough privacy for a few gentle kisses here and there.

When the jet landed at Heathrow and taxied in next to the other private jets I glanced out the window just briefly enough to see the shiny black fuselage of Loren's Concorde parked next to us. I began to wonder if a face-to-face confrontation with Lark and Loren was in the works.

From the men's bathroom in the airport I called Loren immediately, thinking how surprised she would be to find I'd just landed in London. As I was dialing a torrent of disbelief swept through me, realizing within one whole day I'd been in Paris, Rome, and London.

"Hello," Loren answered with in anticipation.

"It's me, where are you?" I chirped.

"Home." Loren said, the answer ridiculously vague as she had dozens of them spread across the globe.

"In Mayfair?"

"Yes, why?" Loren asked, annoyed. I was being a bit too forceful.

"We just landed at Heathrow. Barbara, myself, and Lark."

"Why, what are you doing?"

"I'm staying at the Ritz in room 907. Come meet me in one hour."

Barabara Ritzburg put me and my new guy-pal Jacques up at the Ritz like the doll she is, warning us not to get into too much trouble as pretty little Jacqy had a dozen shoots lined up in the next couple of days and didn't have time to have some jet-setting journalist break his heart. Some very important designers were sure to be upset if he was to look even a tad less gorgeous than he naturally was.

After Jacques and I unpacked our few things, I told him I had to meet a friend in the lobby. He offered to accompany me and I figured his presence would be welcome. I would have been a fool not to show off my new boy toy.

"Honey!" Loren bellowed across the hotel lobby, her arms spread, hair waving in the wind as she ran toward me and Jacques. As she approached I saw that her gleaming wide-eyes were not fixed on me, but Jacques.

"Jimmy, you met Jacques?!" she said, hugging and pecking me on the lips. I just shook my head and looked at Jacques who appeared sullen and frightened.

"How'd you meet?" Loren asked.

"Versace," Jules disclosed simply. Anymore would have exposed his indiscretion.

Loren was selectively oblivious to Jacques' gayness. As one of the few people who didn't allow anything to get by her, I wasn't about to play along with it. I was the only person in the entire world Loren trusted and it was my duty to tell her what I knew of little Jacques. I pulled her aside and politely whispered, "He's a gold-digger honey. We made out the whole way from Rome."

"Shut up I'm totally in love with him," Loren said and pretended to pout. I saw the devil in her eyes. She was fully aware of Jacques' true motives and had to dangle her riches in front of him so she could use it to get what she wanted from him: sex.

"No you're not," I replied.

"I know," she grinned and nodded, "I'm just fooling around. I'm a whore. A big whore who uses her money to romance bisexual male models." It was the greatest line of truth I'd ever heard Loren say.

That night at a private dinner between the two of them, Loren broke it off with Jacques, citing her "reckless endangerment" of his emotions. He would openly cry over his dinner and angrily beg for her to continue to see him. She wouldn't have it and left before her water glass could even be refilled.

Despite having a fantastic suite at the London Ritz facing Green Park, courtesy of my new elderly best friend Barbara Ritzburg, I couldn't resist taking a gander at Loren's English manor. Walking to the townhouse would give me a chance to stroll through London's fabled Mayfair district. I wasn't particularly certain if this was an important quarter of the city as the sidewalks were very narrow and the streets clogged with cars failing to travel anywhere, their patient drivers acting as if they had all day to get to their destination.

Like all of Loren's commissions, the Anders's London home was an architectural standout for such a historic neighborhood. Unlike the many 18th century homes lining the block, Loren's place was a five story glass and steel abode adjacent to Grosvenor Square. I assumed the shape of the house was likely inspired by that of a rare crustacean living at the bottom of the ocean. Its shape was both organic and mechanical, like a giant glass scorpion that was resting in the heart of London. It was refreshing to see something modern in traditional old London.

Inside I found Loren with some models and her stylist, Ralfeo, who was talking on his cell phone to a photographer and serving glasses of champagne to everyone.

"Darling!" Loren celebrated as I entered. She would introduce me to all her industry friends. They all gossiped about celebrities and designers while drinking champagne and listening to French techno music. All was swell and fabulous until I got a call on my cell phone from Lark. I exited to the foyer to take the call.

"This is Jimmy."

"Darling?" Lark moaned as I answered. Never in my life had I felt so adored.

"Larky, what's up?" I asked, creating a nickname for her on a whim.

"What's up is I'm freaking out!" she cried.

"Why," I pacified, "What could possibly be wrong? Life is fabulous!"

"My idiot agent booked me a photo shoot with Estee Lauder in New York tomorrow, I have to fly back tonight!"

"What's wrong with that?" I asked. Estee Lauder was one of the biggest cosmetics accounts a girl could land.

"I'm filming a pantyhose advertisement here in London tomorrow. If I cancel I'll have a horrible reputation."

"I'm sorry baby," I said trying to figure out a resolution. "Why not cancel the Estee Launder thing? It doesn't make since to fly to New York if you have bookings here all next week."

"I'm under contract," she huffed, likely on the edge of tears. "If I ditch the shoot they can sue me for breach of contract."

I didn't know what to tell her. She sounded like a helpless, whiny little girl having been dealt a crisis she was ill prepared to handle alone.

"Where are you staying?" I asked, thinking that a face to face counseling session would be much more effective.

"The Ritz. Where are you?" she asked. I couldn't possibly tell her the truth.

"Harrods." It was the only London locale I knew of off-hand.

"I'll pick you up," she said and hung up the phone. I freaked out and went back out to tell the crew what had happened.

"Does anyone know where Harrods is at?" I shouted over the hubbub, hoping it was not too far away.

"My driver can take you honey, why?" Loren inquired.

"I'm meeting Lark. The sabotage is still in progress."

Loren's driver dropped me off in front of the giant department store just as Lark, riding in a long limousine, pulled up.

Lark's hotel suite, approximately seven times larger than my own, was strewn with clothing. A solid heap of apparel and accessories lined each hallway and room. Judging by the number of empty champagne and wine bottles, I guessed she had been staying at the hotel for weeks and only went to Paris when she had a job there.

"Oh my god," I gasped, looking around the room.

"I've gone psycho!" Lark admitted.

"That's obvious."

"I ordered room service," Lark said, pointing to three rolling carts piled with silver serving dishes. "I'm starving. Today was horrible. Help yourself."

I piled a plate with fruit, a couple of sandwiches, and poured a cup of proper English tea, which was fresh and piping hot. As I nibbled and sipped I listened to Lark bemoan the horrors of modeling.

"It all seems so worthless, strutting down the runway in rags. Who the cares?" Lark would vent. "There are people in this world who can't afford to feed themselves or their families, and I work to promote companies that charge thousands of dollars for a scarf. How did we come to this?"

"Are you sure you want to be a model?" I asked candidly. It was a question I considered she hadn't yet asked herself. She didn't answer me but just lay across two of the dining chairs next to the table. All I could hear was a childish groan come from her face, which she had covered with her hair.

"Why aren't you answering me?" I asked.

"No."

"Why won't you answer me?"

"I just did." Lark sat up to explain. "*No*, I don't want to be a model. I was forced into it. My stupid mother made me a model. And now, here I am!" She was in a state of absolute exhaustion. Under her eyes were dark bags and the little makeup she did have on was smeared and flaking, far from the epitome of glamour she embodied while on the set.

"If you don't want to be a model, what is it you want to be?" I asked. Lark put her head back down on the chair.

"That's the worst part," she said, tears beginning to pour from her face. I gave her a moment to elaborate. "My life has been one big fucking hurry. Always going here or there, always racing to the next shoot or audition, or whatever. I never had time to stop and think what I wanted."

Just then Lark's tiny cell phone rang. She wiped the tears from her cheeks and answered the phone, her voice wrangled by emotion. Her conversation was at first subdued and boring, then ended suddenly with "fuck you bitch, if you had any respect for me this wouldn't have happened!" Lark had become volatile and irate. Her lewdness continued: "...you're the bitch, you never listen to me... that was two years ago!... I never said that, she starts rumors all the time... no, you're not coming down here... because I'll lock the fucking door!"

Lark threw the phone across the room and the tears began again. I hadn't a clue what to do or say so I just continued to eat until I was drawn into the conflict.

"Can you believe her, she's such a fake piece of trash!" Lark said, staring at me as I gorged myself. Traipsing around London had instilled an appetite in me I was almost embarrassed by.

"I don't know," I offered, my cheeks filled with rigatoni. "I've never met your mother. But from what you've told me of her she doesn't sound very nice."

Just then there was a fervent knock on the door. Lark stomped her feet angrily and commanded me to quickly lock it. Being the polite lad I am I rushed to the door and turned the deadbolt. Curious, I looked through the peep hole to find Barbara Ritzburg.

"It's okay," I cheered, "it's just Barbara." I unlocked the door and opened it, greeting Ms. Ritzburg with my prettiest smile. However, Barbara did not return any display of politeness.

"Where is that little hemorrhoid!?!" Barbara hissed. I was beyond confused.

"Jimmy, I told you to lock it!" Lark screamed in betrayal.

Again, I tried to plead my case, saying it was just Barbara, not her mother. Then I realized Lark was the spawn of the prehistoric Barbara Ritzburg. With this, Lark's career now seemed all so plausible. Her sudden, calculated campaign of fashion spreads and runway engagements, a spectacular rise from catalog model to the brink of supermodel status could only have been planned by an insider. It had all been orchestrated by a modeling industry tycoon, her mother, Barbara Ritzburg.

If I had been from a gossip rag or even a legitimate newspaper like Barbara and Lark thought I was, this dish would have been scandalous. As far as I knew, it wasn't public knowledge that Lark was a Ritzburg. But as I watched Lark and Barbara scream at one another, like only a mother and daughter could do, they both eventually began to cry and would end their dispute with a long hug and a friendly peck on each cheek. It was a gruesome scene of co-dependence that no matter how perverse or interesting belonged solely in the privacy of their hotel suite. Seeing the two of them together was like a scene of *Grey Gardens*, only with nicer clothing and fewer cats.

Barbara left less than 20 minutes after the brawl erupted, presumably to go tear another model to shreds. Lark apologized to me for having to witness such "tyranny" and suggested we watch a movie to ease the uncomfortable mood. She played the fight off like it was nothing, trying to smile and laugh, but it was all so forced I could tell that on the inside she was still embroiled in anger. It was apparent she held a deep resentment for her mother. Just as we began to see what movies were on the television, Lark erupted in tears she didn't see coming. She clutched her face like she was about to sneeze and shook her head as if to downplay or shake off the mood.

"Are you okay?" I asked.

"You know," she began, her chin wobbling, "I never even graduated high school."

Her statement was both absurd and typical of the industry in which she worked. Models her age were not unlike professional athletes who shined so bright in high school they'd skip college to pursue multi-million dollar sports contracts. Models were every bit the same, except it wasn't their skill that was so sought after, but their very youth which was the commodity. Some would return to school after retirement, but most would live a life devoid of a quality education.

"Who needs a diploma when you have millions of dollars?" I asked. My statement seemed to cheer her up, or at least she pretended as if it did. Lark stopped crying and we watched *All About Eve* in her bedroom. As we watched the epic I put my arm around her. I could see that her eyes were on the screen but her mind somewhere else, likely contemplating her entire life. Certainly she had to realize she was an invention of her mother Barbara. I hoped that she would consider the relationship with her mother and family, her career, and what she was going to do tomorrow when she woke up. She was such a determined girl that I couldn't imagine her doing nothing in finding a more balanced life. These thoughts must have exhausted her as she fell asleep next to me.

To be fair I'll admit Lark was a fantastic model. She symbolized naïve beauty, young elegance and a new generation of rebellion. As a novice photographer I would have loved capturing a few of her witty, flagrant poses. Witnessing her in front of the Trevi Fountain in Rome was like witnessing Picasso paint or Michelangelo sculpt. She made modeling an art. It's arguable that Lark's physical resemblance to Loren Anders was the worst thing that could have happened to her career. As hard working and talented as Lark was, she would never be considered anything more than a substitute for "the real thing." Not even industry magnate Barbara Ritzburg could have seen that coming. They were probably both furious watching a billionaire heiress from Seattle who decided to try her hand at modeling sweep the entire industry. Loren didn't have to work like other models did. She exerted her power and influence to land modeling jobs. Famously, Loren purchased one of the top Parisian couture houses just so she would be featured in its 16-page Spring ad spread in *Vogue*. That was something no other model could do. In contrast, Lark had her model agent mother, who no matter how powerful she thought she was, always had to bow down to what designers thought. It was only Loren Anders who could tell the designers who to hire.

As I lay next to Lark I questioned if encouraging her to flee the modeling world would be ethical. I knew I wouldn't have been able to live with myself if I was to purposefully attempt to ruin her career. But what about her life? As talented as she was at modeling, I knew there had to be a better world for her to inhabit. This was a girl who was falling apart. She didn't have the thick skin the other girls in the industry did. She was fragile and could only act tough, not be tough. I had been sent to ruin her career, or at least attempt to. If I succeeded it would be the best thing for Lark.

I suppose I'm used to cleaning up after models as I would straighten up Lark's room by placing all the room service trays outside the door and rearranging the pillows that'd been tossed about in the living room. I would leave a note which read "See you in New York" and left, walking back to Loren's house over at Grosvenor Square.

* * *

Walking in London was a joy, even at night. The confusing, meandering streets, an absurd concept to all right-angle loving Americans, weren't too perplexing, as I was able to cautiously find my way back to Loren's place without a map. On the way I would peak in to all the shops and flats that lined the streets. There was such a distinctly different style of street life in London. Compared to New York, London was like a charming village. Streets were quieter, flowers grew out of baskets and beds lining every curb, and the number of cars was far fewer than in Manhattan. Passing a home with an open window meant hearing children laughing and old folks gossiping. It was a city built for humans, not automobiles, and I liked that. As congested as the main roadways were, it seemed like I was never more than few steps away from a quiet enclave, be it a private garden or narrow pathway of hidden homes and shops.

When I returned to Loren's house I was prepared to find a crowd of drunken models, groupies and fashion industry people strewn seedily about. What I found was Loren on a conference call with some of her AndersGroup executives in Japan, her best live-in girlfriend and model Gigi cramming for the Massachusetts bar exam upstairs in her bedroom, and Loren's stylist Ralfeo glazing a terra cotta vase in the basement. All of it much more sedate than the debauchery I expected. The modeling world was beginning to reveal itself as one of vast make believe and illusion, where reality was more human and imperfect than it would ever dare to admit. When the makeup and couture came off the fantasy was gone. The concept of fashion was abstract, always changing, and never fully realized. Glamour was equally unattainable, as it was an idea, one of continuous pursuit which could only be attempted but never kept or preserved.

Once Loren finished her call I began explaining to her my quandary with Lark.

"Here's the thing," I began, "Lark is not strong like you are. She is at a breaking point. She doesn't want to be a model any more than you want her to be. But if I push her too hard it's going to be obvious."

"What do you mean she's at a breaking point?" Loren asked. Illustrating Lark's frailties enlightened her understanding of her perceived rival.

"Her mother is Barbara Ritzburg," I said.

"What!" Loren was flabbergasted.

"Yes. Her mother is the queen of the modeling agencies. Barbara never asked Lark if she wanted to be a model, she just crafted her into one."

"That's bizarre," Loren said, confounded.

"I know. You'd think it'd be in the magazines."

"Maybe they don't know."

"Maybe they're not supposed to," I proposed. Conspiracy was one of Loren's favorite ideas. Her eyes squinted and smoldered as she contemplated the details.

Loren Anders would become sympathetic to Lark's troubles as I professed their strange and wonderful similarities. I'd offer an apology to Loren, admitting that I wanted to be friends with Lark, if only on a temporary basis "for her own safety… she's not at all that stable right now." Loren would allow it, suddenly feeling guilty she'd put the career hit on such a frail, corruptible girl. If Loren hadn't come to this conclusion I was going to ask her to pick on somebody her own size. Lark was small potatoes in fashion, regardless of her connection to Barbara. For Loren to single her out was much more of a display of insecurity than anything else.

. . .

Loren would stay in London for two more days, not for modeling but on AndersGroup business, familiarizing herself with the European leadership of the company. The group was undergoing a restructuring of its European operations that included moving several of its divisions from Frankfurt to London. The project wasn't going very well because they'd lost nearly 10% of their executive staff who were unwilling to relocate to the other side of the English Channel. She lent me her unmarked Concorde jet to take me back to New York City, a trip that was remarkably short compared to the flight over. Initially I was reluctant to deprive her of the stallion in her air fleet.

"I can't take it!" I refused, "what if something happens and you have to get back to the America?"

"It's okay baby!" she fluttered, "I've got the *other* jet." She referred to her Gulfstream, which by most people's standards would have been the pinnacle of air travel. "I can live without the Conc for an afternoon."

"Just be careful. Last year Henri," that was her pilot, "…and I got an $800,000 dollar fine for flying supersonic over Newfoundland. As sophisticated as Canadians are, I can't believe they'd fine a person for such a thing!"

It felt premature to leave London already. The glimpse of it I had was satiating. Ancient looking dwellings were juxtaposed to gleaming new office towers. Construction and renovation crowded almost every block. London was undergoing a major post-millennial reinvention. Not only that, every person I came in contact with seemed downright delightful. I don't know why. The overcast weather was grotesque and oppressive, but despite that, everyone was cheerful and resilient. I suppose that's what made them so British.

The heartache I felt in suddenly leaving Europe was completely obliterated when I returned to Manhattan, realizing with sincere and overwhelming sentiment I was in love with both New York and America. Once again seeing the city's giant, wide avenues lined by soaring monuments to capitalism reminded me of New York's awesome stature amongst cities. I'd almost forget why I ever dreamt of roving the crooked streets of London, strolling the gorgeous gardens of Paris, or exploring in the many art museums of Italy. It wasn't often that people could cherish both America and Europe, but I did. To compare them was silly, as their differences and cultures were too vast and developed to contrast. This was the modern Free World – I could have both the old and new and appreciate them simultaneously.

I was laying on the floor staring at the ceiling of my infrequently air conditioned apartment one scorching afternoon having finished unpacking all my clothes and new acquisitions. Luckily I had found a few pockets of time to do a little shopping. I was on the floor dreaming of being back in Paris when I got a call from Lark saying she'd just landed and wanted to meet me somewhere, possibly for dinner. Lark explained she was in town for two days shooting a Coach ad campaign. I had prior engagements to represent AndersGroup at a benefit dinner for Manhattan's homeless artists, but decided to call in sick. I couldn't think of anything more tedious than listening to starving artists weep and wale about of how brilliant they were.

"It's so good to be back in New York!" Lark cheered as she sat down across from me. We met in the Crystal Room at Tavern On The Green, a very touristy New York restaurant on Central Park West. The restaurant was Lark's choice. I wouldn't have ever picked the place. I assumed she picked The Tavern because she was sure to be noticed in such a busy place. Until I entered the restaurant I'd never witnessed so many tourists packed into one restaurant before. If we hadn't managed a reservation we would have been put in the cattle queue along with the hordes.

"Enjoying it are you?" I asked, flipping through my menu. There were so many delicious sounding meat dishes I had to remind myself of the pact I'd made with Loren to remain a vegetarian until death.

"I forgot how fast everything is here," she replied, lighting a cigarette.

"Illegal!" I squeaked as I grabbed her cigarette and tossed it in a water glass.

"Oh. I forgot. Where the hell is the waiter? I'm starving!" As she spoke I noticed several pairs of people gazing at her as they walked by. They likely recognized her from the cover of *Elle* magazine.

"It was so nice of you to meet me here," Lark said. "I really feel like we're going to become the best of friends."

"Me too!" I said. "Let's celebrate. Champagne or gin and tonics?"

She looked down at the napkin on her lap. "I'm not drinking."

"You're not drinking, since when?" I quizzed. Just then the cheesecake trolley drove by.

"I can't drink." Lark said plainly. "And I probably shouldn't be smoking either."

"You're not becoming all healthy and shit are you?"

"No," she said in a whisper. I knew something was going on but at the moment wasn't really concentrating on the conversation. My stomach was roaring and as a woman across the room feasted on her roasted duck I contemplated for a moment ditching the whole vegetarian thing.

"I can't drink because… I'm…" she began to say, then waivered, "I just want to thank you first. For all the wonderful advice you've given me. I mean, I've been so surrounded by the glamour and excess that is f-f-fashion that I've completely l-l-lost touch with what's real and you've brought me back down."

Her stuttering got my attention. Lark was always so articulate, and not just for a model but for anyone. What she was about to say must have been difficult for her.

"I'm pregnant. I'm going to retire from modeling."

The restaurant went silent. Everyone had been listening to our conversation with at least one ear. A gossip reporter from the *New York Post* leaped for her cell phone and began dialing, surely to report the scoop.

"Are you joking?" I shouted by accident, maybe too dramatically. It seemed unlikely that a girl who'd been working so hard to get to the top of her field would retire after coming so far.

"No," she shook her head, "it's the right time to get out."

Our friendship was so new that I didn't even know who she was dating.

"Who's the father?" I asked without inhibition.

"He's a designer."

"A straight one?"

"Yes," she giggled and rolled her eyes.

Lark and I talked for another hour as we ate our meals. I don't remember what it was we talked about, I just remember telling her I thought her decision to be an intelligent one. She told me that the night in Paris when I'd seen Barbara and her fighting it was because Barbara was trying to convince her to have an abortion. A rift had opened between them that night that would never close.

Lunch was cut short when Lark told me she was meeting her boyfriend at his hotel and had to go. I didn't know it at the time, but that was the last I'd ever see of Lark. She went on to have her baby and marry her boyfriend. They would travel off in to the great black hole of anonymity known as the suburbs. Lark may have disappeared suddenly from the pages of *Vogue* and *Elle*, but it was not the last the world would see of the Ritzburgs. Lark was the oldest of seven children and Barbara remained adamant in turning one of them in to a superstar. Her siblings would all enter the fashion industry; her four sisters as models and her two brothers as a photographer and a set designer. None of them would ascend to the level that Lark did, but they all furthered the legacy their mother began.

As I walked down Central Park West I felt both victorious and cruel. I had deceived Lark, a truly wonderful person, because of Loren, her jealous rival. Lark possessed almost every attribute a legendary model was required to have: beauty, wit and style. But one element, and possibly the most important, longevity, she lacked. Lark was crushed in the glamour wheel, a ruthless churning of ego and prestige, where reality took a backseat to the imagined and desired.

The next morning in giant white-on-black type, the cover of one of New York's most laudable tabloids screamed FASHION LOSES ANOTHER TO PREGNANCY. Upon seeing the headline, Loren raised my salary to $5,000 a week.

JULY

As my life began to resemble that of a full-fledged cosmopolitan, attending book parties and art gallery openings, I would fitfully discover I was not the social butterfly I had intended to be. Being submerged in to a crowd of unfamiliar faces wasn't the delight I assumed it to be. Mingling was difficult, and boring, not to mention repetitive. At some point I stopped caring about meeting new people, finding I was more of a homebody than a wannabe somebody. For no apparent reason I'd offended several friends and acquaintances by turning down their invitations to various events. Even Loren was rebuffed when I ardently contested to be her date to The Billionaire's Ball. Loren, like all ordinarily neurotic Manhattanites, was experiencing her own romance problems and was attempting to substitute me for a boyfriend.

It was my belief that there was no reason to leave one's home if you had everything you wanted. At home I had great furniture, a blossoming music, video, and literature collection, and by way of Loren's chefs, had learned to cook excellent cuisine for myself. I was perfectly content being alone, actually preferring it over the company of others. I wasn't reclusive or anything. It wasn't like I was afraid to go outside. Most days I just cherished the little homestead I created for myself. And on some rare occasions I'd live it up and dine famously at New York's most elegant restaurants.

On a balmy summer Saturday night my wonderful friend Sonya Klein, the executive buyer for Nordstrom, flew in from Seattle to spend some quality time with Manhattan and myself. Sonya invited me to her hotel suite in Tribeca's newest five-star designer boutique hotel. It was the kind of night where I was hoping someone would ask me out, and when somebody did, I couldn't have been more enthused. When I got to Tribeca I found that Lower Manhattan's business core had gone to sleep. The only place that pulsated with any action was the hotel. Fortunately for us, it had a great restaurant just off the lobby, so we didn't even have to leave the building for a wild night out on the town. Sonya had stepped off the jet less than two hours before meeting me. I met her in her suite where we quickly slurped a pair of martinis and then set out for a wild night. She was in such a hurry to eat dinner she'd failed to use the toilet in her hotel room. As she tinkled in the ladies room I wandered around the restaurant lobby. Across the dining room I spotted a sexy young man in a tie seated at a large circular table by the window. At first I thought I recognized him from somewhere but couldn't place his name. I would've taken another glance at him but I didn't want to be caught staring by one of the half-dozen executives seated around him.

Sonya arrived and a moment later we were seated adjacent to the table of suits anchored by the cute young man whose name I couldn't place. As I began to reexamine him I became frustrated with my inability to figure out why he seemed so familiar to me. *Was he a celebrity? Was he a one night stand?* Suddenly someone at his table said something apparently funny, he laughed, and I as I heard his distinct, athletic chuckle I remembered who he was: Joey Hunter, my high school crush.

"Hello!" Sonya said, waving a hand in front of my face. I wasn't paying attention to her spiel on how the only items on the runways of Milan that season had been plaid or ruffles. "When you're done drooling can we have a conversation?" she hissed.

"Sorry," I said, "it's just that I know that hot guy over there. I think he was my high school crush."

She turned to glance at him. "Nice choice. What is he doing in New York? Aren't you from some farm town in Canada?"

"No. I'm not Canadian. I have no idea what he's doing. Stop talking about him. He'll hear us."

"Now, as I was saying, even Versace had bright floral plaid. It's like there's been this big shift in taste, like no taste is in right now, and … JIMMY!" She yelled again at me, this time some of the suits from Joey's table glanced over at the commotion. "You're completely obsessed. Why don't you just go over there and say hello," she yawned. Normally I would have found the notion absurd but the booze inside me agreed with Sonya.

Overwrought, I burst "I can't just walk over and interrupt his little meeting."

"Why not?" Sonya asked, "It's what people do."

There was nothing more frightening than running into someone I went to high school with. The probability of doing so was much lower in my case than most because I lived three thousand miles away from my hometown. I considered that an ordinary man would've stood up and went over and introduced himself to the person he'd dreamt about for so many nights. But another part of me wanted to avoid him. To see him stirred up memories of fear and guilt. He was the icon of my oppression. He was what I wanted but couldn't pursue because the danger to do so in a small town was too great.

With another glance over at his table I would catch an incidental moment of eye contact with Joey. Within that instant a torrent of memories were unleashed. I was taken back to high school, the days of my virtuousness, when I'd dreamt of only one man, him, and he was my motivation for everything. I recalled him as a standout soccer player and rebellious brat. His parents were both blue collar and I could often tell by his lackluster clothing he was lower-middle-class. From observing his competitive frustration in soccer, perpetuated by an intense desire to win, I suspected he had problems at home. Like me, he was trying to please a father he could never seem to satisfy. This gave Joey a reckless and uninhibited allure, a likeness that has only been documented in high-class porn films where the Hitchhiker Dude will do anything and anyone to get a ride out of Tulsa.

As I told Sonya of my situation and discomfort in introducing myself to him (I enhanced the drama of my story to her by telling her I once saw Joey brush up against another guy's penis in the locker room showers, a complete fabrication on my part), she came up with a possible way to determine his gender preference.

"I'll walk by the table," she plotted. "I'll drop my purse, bend over to pick it up, and accidentally one of my breasts will fall out of my dress. If he looks at it that means he's straight." Her plan was pure vulgarity. Her willingness to do anything for a friend was the reason I adored Sonya. The woman had exquisite taste in fashion but could be as crass and offensive as a homeless man.

"Sonya," I countered, "I'd look at your boobs if they fell out of your dress and I'm not straight."

"No, you're just perverted."

"Just never mind!" I protested, "This is stupid. This is just God showing me how pathetic I am. Confronting me with anything and everything I am insecure about."

My statement was pure blasphemy to Sonya. As a free spirit who did what she pleased when she pleased, she wasn't about to let me shrivel and hide in a corner. As clever as a frat boy, Sonya ordered a round of Bloody Mary's. They were so tangy we drank two more each. When our meals came I got even thirstier and began to just point at random items on the drink menu when the waiter came around. Before

I realized my judgment had deteriorated along with my verbal abilities I was caressing Joey Hunter's neck from behind with Sonya's cashmere scarf, saying nonsense such as "bitch, didn't I go to you high school with your hot ass," to which he was flattered. Despite the intoxication, I'd had the decency to wait until his business partners had left the restaurant to hail a cab.

"What the fuck," he said at first. He had no idea who I was, which I totally understood. In high school I was a baby-faced smudge with floppy hair. Since then I'd blossomed in to a polished, lean, elegant man with flair and style, or so I liked to think.

"Yo Joe, it's me, Jimmy Minor," I slurred.

"Who?" he asked.

"From La Conner high school," I said with a little extra inflection on 'high school.'.

"Oh my God," he said and blushed. It seemed the formerly bold and contemptuous Joey Hunter was suddenly shy? *Hmm*.

If I hadn't been so drunk I would have never said to him "You know Joe, I had the biggest damn crush on you back in the day."

"You're gay?" he made sure.

"Very," I said. I hadn't seen this man in five years yet somehow felt just like the scared boy back in La Conner peering up at him as he walked by my locker. The breathlessness, the anticipation, it had all returned with a simple glance. To stand before him was at once terrifying and exhilarating. I had no idea how our conversation would go but was thrilled simply by the fact of having initiated it.

"That's funny," he said in the way someone does when they identify irony.

"Why?" I asked, my intoxication making me both offended and intrigued.

"I kind of always thought you were…" he started, then hesitated.

"A dork?" I inserted.

"No," he said, "adorable." He laughed and revealed a delicate smile. His teeth were just as I remembered: movie star perfect.

My heart sank to the bottom of my stomach and I didn't know how to respond. I was so surprised by what he had said I got dizzy. The straight man I always dreamt about seducing had turned out to be gay. The dream of falling in love with him and him falling in love with me was now an astonishing possibility.

"It's bizarre how things turn out," I said in a murmur, my drunkenness overtaking me with sudden affliction. I began to stumble as I tried to stand still. He jumped and caught me before I fell over a chair. He guided me to the lobby with one of his arms around my back, his hand under my arm making sure I didn't collapse. I could see the elevator doors open. He guided me in and up we went to his room. Blackout.

* * *

I woke up with the echoing sound of my phone ringing through my aching head. I opened my eyes and saw Sonya's hotel room. Somehow I'd managed to make it safely to her room to sleep. I could hear the shower in the bathroom running and figured Sonya was getting ready for her first big shopping trip while in Manhattan.

"Hello," I answered the phone.

"Jimmy!" It was Loren, laden with worry.

"Hey babe."

"Where are you?" she asked, her voice quivering as though a ransom note had been left behind in my absence.

"I'm in Sonya's hotel room. I'm hung over, what time is it?"

"It's nine o'clock," Loren said. "If you're in Sonya's room why did she just call and ask if you'd made it home alright?"

As Loren said this I sat up in bed to examine the room. It was similar to Sonya's room, had many of the same décor pieces and the same sheets on the bed, but the view out the window was toward the river, not the street. I wasn't in Sonya's room.

"Loren, I don't know where I'm at," I pouted, then heard the shower in the bathroom shutoff.

"Sonya said you met a man. A very *attractive* man. He didn't rape you did he?" She said, suddenly playful.

"I hope so," I said mutedly. "I've got to go Loren. I'll meet you later and tell you all the immoral details just as soon as I find out what they are."

I hung up the phone and laid back down in the bed. I closed my eyes to pretend I was asleep. Just then Joey came out of the bathroom and I regretted closing my eyes. There was nothing more I wanted to do than open my eyes and see him dripping wet. I could hear him rustling through his suitcase and a moment later would hear the sound of him zipping up his pants.

In an attempt to appear sleepy and sexy, I made a big yawn and opened my eyes, stretching my arms while smiling at Joey, who smiled back at me in the mirror. I had no clue as to what we'd done the night before so I thought I'd let him answer all my questions.

"Wow, what a night!" I growled.

"You don't remember a moment of it, do you," Joey assumed.

"Nope," I admitted.

"*Nothing* happened," he said. "You tried." He laughed as he sorted some change on the desk. "But you Jimmy Minor, did not succeed."

"What do you mean I tried?" I had no idea to what he referred.

Joey explained how in my inebriated tantrum the previous evening I'd allegedly refused to leave his company. When he put me in a taxi I purportedly told the cabbie "I'm homeless, drop me off at Central Park West and 66th. I live in Madonna's bush!" Joey said he felt bad for me and let me sleep in his hotel room just so I wouldn't do anything extreme.

"So, you took pity on me?" I asked.

"Yes, this is New York City! A drunken young man can wind up in a lot of trouble on the street."

"I could have made it home," I said, defiant.

"Now do you remember where you live?" he asked as he adjusted his tie in the mirror.

"Yes!" I began to contemplate, "Yorkville... I think."

Joey began flipping through papers in his briefcase and getting ready for another day of meetings. He told me he had to fly to Chicago later that day but would give me his phone number, in case I was ever wanted to talk to somebody from "back home."

Joey Hunter was as heterosexual as they got. Before leaving he showed me, with great pride, his wallet packed with pictures of his wife and two young girls. Unlike the pompous homophobe I feared he'd be if I'd confessed to him my feelings, Joey was gracious claimed to be flattered by my interest in him. He assured me he was straight and was married to the most wonderful woman god had yet to create.

Not one to back down when first rejected, I asked, "are you sure you're not gay?"

"Yes," he said.

"How do you know?" I teased foolishly.

"Because… I just know."

"It's such a shame," I said, trying to make the saddest, most charming frown I could.

"Then again," he recanted, "being gay could be like Philadelphia."

"Philadelphia?" I slurred.

"Yes, Philadelphia." Joey explained, "nobody ever really thinks of going to Philadelphia, like on vacation or anything. But you might go there on business or on a road trip and you find, by accident, that Philadelphia is a very nice town."

"I see," I said, understanding his analogy to be flirtatious and suggestive.

Joey approached the bed and sat down next to me.

"Wanna go to Philadelphia?" I asked.

He shook his head. In a romantic movie we would have kissed just then but instead he just hugged me, very casually, almost like he would a colleague he's about to send on a very long business trip. Had we kissed I don't know if I would have been able to stop myself from doing all the things I fantasized doing to Joey in Spanish class six years prior. But then I thought of his family and how they were probably looking forward to him returning home in just a few days. He was so noble and kind. When he walked out of the room I had an even bigger crush on him than I did in high school. He was everything that I expected him to be and more, and his wife was the most fortunate woman in the world.

I slept for another hour. After waking and showering I took a cab home where I put on a fresh set of clothes. I took another cab back downtown to meet Sonya for brunch where she listened to me ramble on, romanticizing my night with Joey.

"It was so fantastic. So innocent and flirtatious, like the *Seven Year Itch*," I gleamed as I sliced my raspberry crepe into heart-shaped pieces. "It's like it's better off that he's not gay. He's still the perfect man, the same one I always dreamed of. I didn't get him but I'm happy he's happy. You know?"

"But you didn't sleep together?" Sonya pondered. How I could derive any pleasure from not having sex with someone was foreign to her.

"Nope. He let me have the bed and he slept on the couch. Such a gentleman!"

"So if he's straight, why did he let you stay the night?"

"I don't know. He said he was flattered. And I was trashed. What's he going to do, ditch me in an alley?"

"I don't know. He's the first straight guy I've heard of who lets a gay guy sleep in his bed."

"This is modern America. And *New York*. Joey is perfectly comfortable with gays."

"I'm just jealous. You were able to realize a fantasy."

"What fantasy?" I asked with a mouthful of breakfast.

"The fantasy of confronting your high school crush with the feelings you have for them," she said.

"Jealous?"

"Yes!" We both laughed. Sonya added, "my high school crush was Todd Matheson, a football player."

"What's he do now?"

"Rumor has it Todd is *assistant* manager of the tire department at Sears in Tacoma."

"What a dreamboat!" Her sentiment was a parody of 1950s teenage longing.

We finished our breakfasts and began chatting about frivolous crap.

"So how's the gang?" I asked, referring to the clan of elitists and social climbers Loren had introduced me to.

"What gang?" she replied, hinting of snide feelings.

"The Space Needle gang. The magnificent seven, or whatever the hell they were calling themselves when we left."

"Oh," she said, her face a dreary scowl. "I wouldn't know. After Loren left it all fell to pieces. Nobody wanted to go to dinner anymore."

"That's too bad," I responded. The dinners used to be so uproarious and vulgar. For a moment I felt nostalgic for the ritual. "What happened?"

"Eventually we sat there looking at each other asking ourselves 'What's the point?'"

"What do you mean 'What's the point?'" I asked, "It's dinner with friends!"

"Don't pretend. You're not any good at it," Sonya said. I detected a sudden change in her attitude. She was hinting at something that had been previously kept from me.

"Pretend what?" I demanded, her insinuations having baffled me.

"Pretend you weren't in it for the same reasons the five of us were," she tried to explain. I still didn't see the point she was making. She continued, "We all wanted something from Loren. We lassoed her into our little group, entertained her and when she wasn't looking jiggled the change out of her pockets. It was no secret the purpose of the group was to make connections. But the truth is once Loren left there was very little for anyone to possibly benefit from. I joined the group with the intent of getting her to appear in an ad campaign for Nordstrom. It never happened but it was worth a shot."

"But Loren said you've been a member of the group longer than anyone," I responded.

"No," she replied. "Loren started the group. Back before she was what she is now, she was just a rich little girl in the big city looking for friends. She started the group. I joined at her social secretary's request."

Once I understood the group's agenda I couldn't stop laughing. I was amused by their foolish judgment. How naïve they all were to think Loren hadn't seen right through them and how she'd kept a firm grip on her pocketbook the whole time.

"Appears as though you won," Sonya added. I was astonished and offended.

"Won what?" I replied defensively. It was clear she was implying I'd used Loren for personal gain.

"You got her," Sonya needlessly clarified. I already knew where she was going with the conversation so I looked at my watch.

"Sonya, let me explain something. Loren is my friend, that's it. I have never used my friendship with her in order to gain, either financially or socially. Anything she has given me has been from kindness. We became friends because she pursued me."

"I'm sorry Jimmy," Sonya replied. "But you have to understand that most people who come in contact with Loren are advantageous. She knows it. It's why she surrounds herself with people that can further her career. It's a two way street."

"But what about me," I asked. "I can't further her career."

"I haven't yet figured out what she sees in you," Sonya jested and we both laughed. The comment flouted the unease that had tainted the conversation.

Before Sonya jetted off back to Seattle we pillaged Madison and Fifth of everything and I'd end up alone in my apartment that night feeling imprudent. Ever since I'd finished furnishing my apartment I'd told myself not to buy another goddamn thing. But there I was again, staring at a great heap of clothing, none of it needed, much of it I didn't even like and would never wear. It was the *ability* to buy that made me purchase, not the actual desire to own the goods. Shopping had been turned in to a social sport and I consumed anything that the person who was with me shopping said I should buy.

When Loren hired me as her personal assistant and announced she'd pay me a whopping $3,000 a week, now raised to $5,000 a week, I was sure I'd be financially set for at least five years. I remember even balking at the notion of having to figure out what to do with so much money. But somehow, somewhere, I'd found things to buy. Stupid things, like the same pair of shoes twice. Buying things was like breathing and some days I purchased more items than I could inventory or process. Wares would remain in their bag for days, and if they weren't ever taken out and used, they would go in the closet where they remained unused and got buried under newer purchases. If consumerism was a disease I was a victim in its grips.

"Jimmy, you have a shopping problem," I told myself as I knelt over the new pile of goods. It felt good to confess it. I'd seen on TV that confession was the first part in overcoming an addiction.

I collapsed on the pile feeling as though I were about to cry and wipe snotty tears all over my DRY CLEAN ONLY fashions. I was an exhausted wreck.

Throughout my life I had always scoffed, maybe foolishly, at drug addicts, alcoholics, and smokers. Never having been addicted to anything myself, I'd considered addiction in any form a subtle sign of evolution doing what it did: eliminate the weak. I figured only the feeble got addicted to such reckless habits, thinking self-destruction to be a way for the human species to purge infirm genetic dispositions. But there I was, an addict of consumption.

Pouting always made me hungry so I went to my kitchenette to search the cupboards for food. The only thing there was an empty box of raisin bran. In the fridge all I found was Coca-Cola, Starbucks Frappuccino and Double Shots, iced tea, some nonfat salad dressing that had barely been touched because it was disgusting, and a bag of wilted brown romaine lettuce. I cursed my hunger as I was craving chunky chicken noodle soup, something I did not own because I was a devout vegetarian. As I took one last look in the refrigerator I made a stunning correlation between all the drinks: they were all liquid caffeine and they all had a purpose in my life. The espresso was for waking up in the morning, the iced tea for an afternoon jolt, and the Coke my preferred dinner pairing. If I'd been getting any sleep this liquid diet would have been harmless, but since I'd moved to Manhattan a full night's sleep was something I had yet to enjoy. Every day seemed to drag in to the next and the ambitions I held for projects around AndersPlace seemed to grow faster than I could accomplish them. The drinks in the refrigerator had become a substitute for genuine strength and stamina.

Realizing the harm the drinks could be doing me, I watched my hand reach out and throw them away. Just as my hand was about to grasp a box of Double Shots something stopped me. A section of my mind was refusing to let the drinks go. This sudden, irrational refusal was a definite sign of caffeine addiction. Another telltale sign of the addiction appeared on my Visa card statement. The word Starbucks was listed on it 91 times within a 30 day period. The cafe accounted for over $400 in spending that single month. Not only was my caffeine drinking out of control, so was my spending. I could have switched to cocaine to save money.

Upon discovering my caffeine vice, I would observe just how in vogue it was amongst my social circle. The image conscious used caffeine excessively, as if cigarettes were being replaced by it. To people like me, caffeine was a miracle substance. Its laxative-like properties kept me regular and in excess would allow me lose weight. It was also an appetite suppressant so the first meal of the day for me was often dinner. Caffeine was in no short supply and came in every flavor imaginable. To escape it was almost impossible.

As glorious as caffeine seemed, the fact remained that no substance was perfect. I'd lost six pounds since relocating to New York and a total of 20 pounds since the beginning of the year, which brought my weight to 140. For a 6-foot 2-inch male, that was remarkably thin. My arms had turned to bones and I noticed that when I got out of bed in the morning it sounded like the Fourth of July there were so many pops and crackles. All the carbonation I was drinking was killing my bones and joints.

In an impulse I tossed all the caffeinated drinks in my apartment in a trash bin in the alley filled with food waste from nearby pho restaurant. This way I couldn't possibly retrieve them. I skipped off to the market and bought gallons of bottled water and a commercial-grade juice machine for making healthy fruit fusions. A day later I got a headache from caffeine depravation. The headaches continued for a week but when they ceased and my caffeine addiction was no more, I figured kicking the shopping habit couldn't be much harder. Once the caffeine was out of my system I found I was more alert than I'd ever been on the liquid dope. The idea that caffeine had somehow enhanced my ability to stay awake was suddenly proven false. Waking up in the morning was easier and falling asleep was no longer a chore, but something I did when I chose to. I had taken a step closer to a more balanced life. This little victory made me consider there were even larger things I could accomplish.

* * *

I was home alone on a Friday night (the story of my life) as Loren decided she wanted to attend *All That Jizz*, a fan-fictional stage production of Elton John's early years in music, playing at a theater/strip club way-off-Broadway up in the Barrio. I couldn't remember why I told Loren I preferred to stay home and began to feel lonely when I became determined to entertain myself, somehow.

That night I discovered in my email inbox a letter from my college friend Simon, an actor and all-around performance artist. The message informed me he and several friends were opening a new show that night and that I was "required by law" to attend.

Simon Sky (born Simon Goldenstein) was the only person I still knew from college and the first openly gay person I'd ever met. I had come across Simon performing at a gay bar called The Rod on Seattle's Capitol Hill. It was there he began dazzling audiences as a ghetto fabulous drag queen named Suckresha, an act that was now making him fairly well known in New York's drag scene. Ever since bumping in to one another at Grand Central three weeks prior we'd kept in touch by email, sporadically exchanging messages about how marvelous city life was, or wasn't, depending on the day. I jumped at the chance to see Simon Sky's new cabaret show titled *My Sistahs & Me,* playing at Plush in Chelsea, the pinnacle of all gay clubs. Plush was the gay world's Carnegie Hall and I couldn't have been more proud of Simon for having a show there. The club was more of a circus than just a dancehall and bar. It occupied an old warehouse and reminded me of an airport or department store it was so big. Giant portraits of the gay goddesses, Liza, Judy, and Barbara flanked the entrance. The club was separated into several environs: a restaurant, auditorium, theatre, and dance floor, with a few different bars tucked in to rooms in between each section. It was the biggest club of any variety I'd been to. Crowds of all types flooded the place. From transvestites to Wall Street executives and tourists from Iowa, every end of the spectrum was there. It was the pop gay club of New York. Plush was the place you went if you wanted to be entertained, outraged and enchanted, all simultaneously.

In the lobby of the club where a Marilyn Monroe drag artist checked coats, I found a reader board listing all the club's events. Next to the wrestling promo for "BATTLE OF THE DIVAS: CHER VS. MADONNA – TONIGHT!" I found "MY SISTAHS & ME – Starring Suckresha, Analia Cumins, and Carmen Blows." The show was about to begin and I quickly scurried in to the theater to find a seat, not wanting to miss a moment. The auditorium was crowded and rollicking with laughter as the opening act, a set of almost nude tranny contortionists, performed their fire eating show. I hunted for an empty seat at one of the dining room tables, eventually finding a seat next to three spike-haired lesbians wearing dog collars.

For all its tacky qualities, the club managed to reaffirm a sense of glamour. The food served at the dinner theatre was of French origin and I must admit I've never had better sparkling wine than that which was served at Plush. But any form of sophistication and urbane refinement was quickly removed as a the contortionist's act ended and an array of flashing lights, beating drums and trumpeting fanfare announced the brilliant arrival of the three queens of Manhattan.

Analia, a towering blonde dressed in the tiniest white skirt took to the stage, first welcoming the crowd and then blowing kisses to the more attractive men in the audience. I received two blown kisses and a wink!

"Oh, may Jesus bless all you mother fuckers," she heralded as a bouquet of roses landed at her feet. As she leaned over to retrieve the flowers a dark brunette galloped on to the stage wearing a sequined Bob Mackie knock off. This monolith of bright sparkles and big hair was Suckresha. She snatched the roses from Analia and smelled them animatedly.

"They're just the most precious things I ever did see," Suckresha thanked in her trademark southern accent. A farce as she was certainly no southern belle. Analia scowled with hands on her hips. As Suckresha began to wave to the audience Analia snagged the roses from her in a ferocious snap. Rose petals went everywhere.

"Those are my roses bitch!" Analia clawed.

"Why I never," Suckresha jeered with dainty offense. "Fine take them. Cheap roses for a cheap whore."

"How dare you! These roses aren't cheap!" Analia lashed out as a scuffle erupted onstage, the two drag queens wrestling over the roses that would become stage mulch beneath their stilettos. Just as the wigs began to fly, Carmen Blows made her way onstage to break up the fracas. Carmen was an older gal wearing a flashy Debbie Reynolds inspired number.

"Ladies, we are not here to fight, we are here to entertain," Carmen cooed, separating the two brawlers. At this time a second bouquet of roses, this one much more elaborate than the first, was hurled into the arms of Carmen. "Besides, everyone knows any flowers thrown on this stage could only be for one lady." The crowd roared with laughter and applause. This kind of tantrum was exactly the kind of thing people had come to see.

The trio of drag queens launched into their first musical number, a disco style rendition of Carole King's "I Feel the Earth Move." They continued their show with similar versions of songs made famous by Linda Ronstadt, Dolly Parton, and Carly Simon. Their most hilarious interpretation would be when the girls went old-school hip-hop for the Beastie Boys' "Brass Monkey," their profane hip thrusts and hand movements giving the song's lyrics a multitude of new meanings. Not just a simple song and dance, *My Sistahs & Me* had elaborate sets, a league of dancers and some of the best lighting I'd seen in a show. I was impressed on every level.

It wasn't uncommon for me to feel insecure whenever I witnessed someone my own age succeeding. I know I felt jealous seeing Joey Hunter and his business associates. Yet seeing Simon Sky dressed as the fabulous Suckresha and belting out some of the best tunes the 1970's had to offer, only made me feel proud of him. It was the first time I hadn't felt jealous of someone successful my own age. Simon was doing what he loved and he was considerably good at it. Love for him poured from the audience. I admired him for his ability to entertain in the only way he knew how. I would have assumed the majority of the room, who appeared straight, as most men were seated with women, wouldn't get the queer humor, but everybody did, or pretended to by laughing along with the rest of the audience. Somehow on stage this young man dressed as a woman and singing songs everyone was familiar with was doing more for the gay movement than any protest or rally could. Entertainment was such a powerful form of propaganda. And Suckresha was harnessing it to put every straight guy at ease in the company of drag queens, trannies, queers, and dykes.

Suckresha, Carmen, and Analia finished their set with an uproarious "Son of a Preacher Man" and had an encore with Streisand's "Don't Rain on my Parade." The crowd roared as they gave their final bow and sashayed offstage. After the show I wanted to go backstage to congratulate Simon on the magnificent performance. However, to my jaw-dropping surprise, even drag queens had groupies. A line of glossy clean-cut West Village boys had lined themselves up to meet the *Sistahs*. I decided to head to the bar and have a drink, maybe hit on a guy and then head home. But it was at the bar I had another jaw dropping surprise: Loren Anders with her gaggle of model friends, all accompanied by their gay boyfriends. Loren was noticeable without hers.

"Jimmy," she beckoned, waving me over with both hands flapping.

"Hi Loren," I greeted, saying quick hello to her eight acquaintances.

"I'm so glad you came, you must've have got my voicemail," Loren purred. I took a seat next to Loren, prepared to share a drink with the group and brag of how I knew Suckresha from way back. But just then Loren issued me orders. "I need you to run up to the house and get the *People* magazine from two weeks ago. You know the one with the First Lady on the cover. I think it's in my nightstand. Nobody believes there's an article on me in it."

Loren's request was humiliating. Just as I was about to chum it up and socialize, she began treating me like one of her employees. Sure, I *was* one of her employees but it was still rude for her treat me like one, especially in a bar at that time of night in such a friendly circumstance. To receive orders to retrieve something as insignificant as a magazine seemed like a waste of my time. I was used to issuing those sorts of orders, not receiving them.

"Ok," I said as I stood up, my shoulders slumping, my breathing protracted. Every gay guy within sight knew what my body language meant: "Get it yourself bitch." Just then, further instructions were issued.

"And can you bring me a jacket or something," she added. "Maybe that red Chanel sailor-type thing on the couch in my room? This is officially the coldest July on record!" She dismissed me with a flagrant little wave her hand. I had never been treated like a butler by Loren before. Her behavior made me feel degraded and alarmed. Within a fraction of a moment my seat at the table was filled by some swishy queen Loren was dazzled to see at the club. Apparently he had worked as a stylist on a photo shoot she was in the week prior and Loren had invited him to the club with her that night. Witnessing this made my status as her one-and-only gay boyfriend seem threatened. Had I the nerve or tact I might have made a statement or told my replacement to find another seat. But I didn't. I was too polite, and fearful that the hand that fed me might take away everything I thought I loved. I turned and left in retreat, defeated by my own perception of what was going on. As I walked outside to hail a cab I wondered if I had done something to upset her. I contemplated if our friendship had simply run its course and I was being resigned to nothing more than staff in her eyes.

A moment later a cab dropped me at AndersPlace. In Loren's bedroom I found the magazine and began to consider how I would express my rebellion. I could return to the club and give her the magazine, but knowing Loren she'd likely already left Plush and gone to some other hotspot. I put the magazine back in the nightstand, left AndersPlace and walked over to my apartment. I turned off my phone, took off my shoes, and went to bed in my clothes. Before I fell asleep I damned Loren for having ruined my fabulous night. Like so many nights I'd started it alone and ended it alone.

* * *

The morning after my Plush night I woke up sober and glum. I wanted to treat myself to a nice breakfast so I bought a take-out sun dried tomato and goat cheese omelet from the deli on my block. As I returned with my hot breakfast I found Loren outside my apartment ringing the bell.

"Good morning," she said with a disproportionate cheer. Despite her visible glee, I feared she'd come to fire me for deserting her. That thought evaporated when I recalled that Loren never fired anyone herself. She had people who did that for her.

"Hi," I said flatly, my frustration exhibited on my face.

I opened the door to the building and began walking up the stairs. Loren followed me and remained silent until we got to my apartment.

"This place is nice," she offered after taking a comprehensive walk-through of all four rooms.

"It's alright." I unloaded my gourmet omelet on to a plate and opened the window to my kitchen and stepped out.

"JIMMY!" Loren shrilled, not knowing I had a Manhattan balcony, also known as a fire escape.

"What?" I asked, standing with my omelet and a glass of orange juice. From her vantage it appeared as if I were floating outside the window. She rushed to the fire escape to make sure I wasn't doing anything serious.

"I thought you…"

"I know what you thought," I said as I sat down on the terrace. Loren crawled out the window and sat next to me. We watched as cars drove by on First Avenue.

"It's not working," Loren voiced, I thought she might have spotted a broken down vehicle down on the street.

"What's not working?"

"You working for me," Loren admitted. "It's not right that I pay you. Either you're my friend or you're my employee, it never works when someone is both."

"Am I fired?" I asked, suddenly fearful.

"NO! You're not fired," she said. "You're the best goddamn personal assistant I've ever had." I was about to thank her but she continued, "you're also… and this may sound pathetic… the only *real* friend I've ever had. And I think it's more important that I have a really good friend than a really good personal assistant."

"I would agree," I said. She stared at me tenderly. Her eyes signaled regret and fear, and in that moment I forgave Loren for the night before. I had overreacted and should have taken her the magazine. It was the least I could have done on the salary she was paying me.

That morning on the terrace Loren offered to employee me part-time with the same rate of pay until I found a new job. I couldn't have been happier. Being Loren's personal assistant was easy and came very natural to me but lacked one major facet: fulfillment. The unending days of supervising her staff, who had the most repetitive and mundane tasks, had become monotonous. Surely I could train someone to perform many of the duties I was responsible for.

What an opportunity I had! Blessed Loren had scooped me up, brought me to Manhattan, given me thousands of dollars to mind her house and now said "enough, now you need to find one of the fantastic jobs just waiting to be filled out there in this great city." The dreams I'd had back in Seattle of a life exactly like the one I was now living no longer seemed like unreachable fantasies – they were now prophecies effortlessly fulfilling themselves.

For the rest of the day Loren and I were just friends. We fooled about my messy apartment for hours, redecorating the sparse walls while listening to a record player I'd bought at a flea market just for the sake of novelty. We stupidly danced to vintage country music songs by Loretta Lynn and Tammy Wynette, and would spark again the dramatic and ridiculous friendship we both found to be so intoxicating. That night was just like the first I had shared with Loren. We were back where we started and it felt so wonderful to begin anew.

AUGUST

The people of Manhattan are constantly obsessed with fads. The latest craze in emotional maintenance was the Astropist, which was a non-licensed therapist who wove astrology and other mythical ideas into their advice. My AstroPist was named Kiki LaRouche. She lived in a factory loft conversion over by the Chelsea piers. I met her while shopping for tarot cards (for decoration) in Times Square. She casually asked me if I was interested in the great unknown. I told her I was and she handed me her business card. I was intrigued by her occupation and decided on a whim to give the thing a whirl. Turns out we humans can't get enough of other people telling us what's going to happen in our lives.

A therapist-psychic wasn't the only hybrid sweeping the chic societies of Manhattan. A hybrid of any sort seemed to prompt a rage in popularity. Among them were palm reading manicurists (a pedicure was an extra $40), housekeeping escorts (they cleaned up afterwards), and the most popular: the spa/salad bar. This is where people would eat a custom array of greens as they got their back and neck rubbed. These little lunchtime havens popped up on six different blocks in midtown, only to evaporate by end of the year. I guess people didn't feel like being touched while chomping on a Caesar.

Whenever I felt down and reluctant about the future I always went to Kiki LaRouche. There was one week I wanted Kiki to explain to me how someone like myself, with so much love to give, had never found someone to love. I knew I could easily travel to one of those bars where men met each other and went home to share a night of pleasure. But I wanted a date, a game of courting, a real romance. I found no appeal in having sex with someone the same day I met them, no matter how much I wanted to. The last thing I wanted sex to become was something devoid of intimacy. To expect Kiki to be able to explain to me what I was doing wrong in attracting a man was a tall order to fill, but I was desperate. And I also knew she was brilliant and could answer any question, no matter how personal.

Kiki had rightly predicted that I would become bored with my newly riotous, exciting, and always changing lifestyle. She foresaw that I would become uninterested with staying up all night celebrating the opening of art exhibits or the vast array of independent films I'd been seeing. Kiki envisioned I'd be drawn in to a world of flourishing creativity and design where I'd play a direct hand in the outcome of projects. She said she saw flashing lights and beautiful people. I just hoped she wasn't looking backward at my trip to Europe. "And somewhere in there," she crooned, "a man awaits." The statement could've have been more exciting, if not equally vague, but it gave me hope.

I did have to take heed in that Kiki's prediction was not all that groundbreaking. Prior to ever visiting Kiki, I myself recognized I was bored socializing within Manhattan's upper-crust. One must realize that even though every night is a *new* party, a *new* launch, or a *new* show, the events are patronized by the *same* fabulous people, catered with the *same* blimey food, all with the *same* outcome: tipsy boredom. I could literally meet someone at a magazine launch on a Tuesday and start up a conversation with them, only to see this same person Wednesday at a perfume launch, Thursday at a Broadway preview after-party, and again on Friday at a hot new restaurant. The whole time continuing the conversation we'd started on Tuesday. I would wonder how with 21 million people living in the metropolis of New York, I would see the same 200 people every night.

During my last visit with Kiki where she predicted I would soon meet my beaux, she asked if I wanted to pre-pay for my next ten visits. She was offering a buy nine get the tenth visit free promotion.

"You really think I need ten more visits?" I asked, forgetting she had no ethical standards. She wasn't a psychiatrist, just a capitalist. To put it bluntly, calling her an AstroPist was more polite than calling her what she really was, a gypsy.

Kiki told me the bearish economy was treating her poorly and that business had dried up. She needed her clients to pre-pay for their next few visits or else she wouldn't be around much longer. It sounded to me like she needed airfare back to Bulgaria. When I asked what her cards said about the financial situation, she told me they didn't understand macroeconomics and that she was starving. That's when I tried to offer some advice to Kiki. I guess that's one of my flaws. Even if I don't know what I'm talking about I'll act like I do.

"You should start a hotline. Sell your services over the phone," I said. "There's got to be lots of money in that."

"I don't know," she mused as she lit candles around the room, "I've never really been into phone sex."

"Not phone sex," I stammered, "the psychic thing."

"I'm not a psychic. I simply interpret the relation between the planets, sun, and moon and the effect it has on humans." She shuffled her deck of tarot cards as I contemplated how I would phrase my question.

"What'll it be this week?" Kiki asked.

"I'm thinking."

"That's sweet of you to stop by without a question. Usually you're full of them. I'm always charging you extra." To hear Kiki compliment me was new. On prior visits she had acted like I was wasting her time.

"I have a question. I just don't know how to ask it." This is where Kiki's therapy skills came into play.

"Tell me the situation and I'll tell you how to ask the tarot."

"Well," I paused, trying to weave the many questions in my mind together in to something cohesive she could address. "I fear that no matter what level of success I achieve, and no matter how much money I make, I'll always be lonely, and that I'll never fall in love."

"What does success and money have to do with love?" Kiki asked. She didn't even need to look at the cards to figure out the answer to this.

"I don't know," I squealed defensively.

"Then why do you correlate the two?" Kiki stunned me with this question. She'd picked up on something I'd failed to. I'd always figured that when I had a career I loved and money in the bank a horde of men would pursue me. I would be a catch. I would be desired, at last. No more unrequited love. No more seeking the unattainable. Hard work in the realm of career would result in love in my personal life. Why I'd drawn these two together was something Kiki couldn't understand.

"Maybe I just believe that when I'm rich and successful it will be easier to snag a man," I attempted to explain.

"So it's self-esteem?" she speculated.

"Partially."

"What's the rest?"

"Right now I'm much more interested in pursuing a career than a man."

"What's more important?" she snapped. I was offending Kiki and didn't even know it.

"What do you mean what's more important?"

"Love or money?" The face she even had to ask this was embarrassing. Did I really sound so shallow?

"Love." When I said this she nodded and smiled. I knew the correct answer, I just didn't feel it.

"Is it possible your priorities are misaligned?" Her eyebrows bent and she pursued her lip. It was clear Kiki knew more about life's priorities than I did. In less than a minute she was able to detect why my life wasn't headed in the direction I wanted.

"My priorities are misaligned." I admitted.

"And what are you going to do about it?" Kiki asked.

"I don't know."

"And what do we do when we don't know *what* to do?"

"We consult the tarot!" I cheered.

Kiki distributed an array of cards on the table. I selected four of them and put them in front of me. These four cards would represent mind, body, soul, and destiny. Kiki flipped the mind card over to reveal The Monkey.

"The Monkey represents mischievous thoughts," Kiki said as she flipped over the body card revealing The Dragon. "Dragon symbolizes resilience and determination." She then flipped soul over, uncovering The Clematis. "Pretentious and showy." Finally, Destiny was turned over to expose The Partition.

"What the hell does that mean?" I said seeing the card of Partition, the illustration being a long winding stone wall separating two seas, one stormy, the other calm.

"It's a barrier, something has to be overcome before you can reach your destiny. I think it's pretty clear what that is."

"What do you mean by that?" I asked, baffled by her suggestion.

"Jimmy dear, lose the fragility, be the resilient young man you want to be. So what if someone turns you down for a date. They'll never get to know the wonderful person you are. Put yourself out there, gay, straight, bi, tri, we all have to do it. You've let your insecurities dictate your life. Get over it. Get out there. Have some. Get some cock. The reward is too great to even waver."

Kiki LaRouche, Astropist and soon-to-be part-time phone sex actress, was precise in her analysis. I did have some sort of negativity towards myself when it came to men. It was almost as if I was scared of them. Men were gorgeous, charismatic, wonderful creatures that I worshipped. To be afraid of them in general or by default made no sense. It was as if their opinions towards me were so powerful I feared them outright. Fear was one of the most powerful emotions steering human development. I had to find a way to override mine or else I'd never be happy.

I paid Kiki and wandered about the streets of Chelsea for a while questioning where I was to go from there. Having an epiphany was one thing, acting on it was another. I decided to make a B line and take the subway to Central Park. At the park I sat on those giant boulders near the center of Central Park South and ate a slice of pizza. It was an attempt to relax and lose myself. The sky was filled with summer storm clouds and had apparently scared everyone from the park. Taking advantage of the low park population, I rented one of those little boats at the lake and took the murder horror-romance novel (another hybrid) I was reading for an afternoon cruise. I was going to let the boat float aimlessly as I read, but once I got out on the lake I became too distracted to continue reading. I kept thinking of what Kiki had said about the psychological barrier I'd put between myself and the men I'd been attracted to. My warped perception on career and love was the reason I was single. I couldn't blame anything else any longer.

* * *

Once upon a quiet Tuesday night I got an unexpected call from Chelsea Hudson. I was enthralled to hear she'd moved to Los Angeles after an editorial shakeup at *The Sound*. It was in LA that she and her girlfriend, along with a large group of friends, had begun publishing *HLYWDBLVD*, an ultra-hip news and lifestyle guide for those trying to make it in the entertainment industry.

Even more exciting than hearing from Chelsea was the reason for her call. Apparently a friend of hers from college was helming *Rag* magazine and wanted to meet with me. *Rag* was the anti-*Vanity Fair*; a social digest of the New York City's avant-garde and underground culture. Its monthly circulation was extremely limited and if you were lucky enough to ever find a current issue you could certainly scalp it on EBay with a handsome markup above its newsstand price. To be offered an interview at such a hot title was not just alluring, but flattering.

"Their financiers were purchased by a bank that was consolidated into the old *Time* magazine corporation that falls under the Warner consortium. It's really quite simple," Chelsea tried to explain to me.

"But the magazine's original owners optioned their shares and now the magazine has broken off from the corporation." The only thing I took away from Chelsea's summation was that *Rag* magazine was going mainstream in order to pay the bills. They were recruiting new talent for the transition and were actively seeking new voices and new lenses. Unlike most magazines, which were being folded into giant media conglomerates, *Rag* was breaking free into journalistic independence. It was like 1776 all over again, but for a magazine. I leaped at the chance to be part of a revolution.

Two days later I traveled out to a part of Brooklyn known as Williamsburg for a meeting with Chelsea's friend, Josephine Sinclair. This would be my first time out to Brooklyn and I'll admit I was a little scared at first, knowing Brooklyn's vicious reputation of hardcore ghetto treachery spread across an industrial landscape of scorched earth. When I got out to the hip hood of Williamsburg, no further than a hope across the East River, I found the place to be a delight. Unlike Manhattan, Brooklyn had a lot more trees and vegetation along sidewalks and around buildings. There was graffiti on every surface but it was its own place with its own identity, and I respected that. For the first time in my New York experience I could see children playing outside, although their playground was fenced off and fortified like a military bunker. There was a slower pace to everything in Brooklyn but it still maintained a tinge of the New York pulse. The lack of tall buildings provided more light on the street. I found Williamsburg charming, its rundown industrial buildings teeming with potential opportunities. The vast abandoned spaces were not a blight but a facet of urban life. Someday this neighborhood would rebound and I would have the joy of knowing when it did that it had achieved something. Every prejudice or opinion I'd previously held of Brooklyn was erased from my mind. Just like so many locales, the reputation it had was one greatly distorted and misinformed.

When Chelsea told me she'd set up a meeting with a lady named Josephine I expected an elderly Puerto Rican lady. Instead I got a young whippersnapper fresh off the boat from Santa Monica, California. Josey, as she's known around the *Rag* office, was a skinny blond with a dark spray tan. Chelsea told me that Josey was formerly the Managing Editor of *The Santa Monican*, an under-39 weekly currently the journalistic rage in youth-worshipping Los Angeles. In a sudden career move, Josey had relocated to trendy Williamsburg with a couple of friends in order to establish *Rag*. They viewed their endeavor as an attempt to start the next great American culture periodical. Josey's *Rag* staff, made up mostly of Columbia University graduates, all happened to be sons and daughters of millionaires. Their first issue was said to be entirely funded by trust fund annuities. Just by picking up the six pound tomb it was apparent they spared no expense in producing their inaugural issue. Hundreds of pages were dedicated to art and fashion, supposedly at great cost as advertisements in the magazine were sparse and simple. Enormous essays on culture theory filled dozens of pages, written by the top minds of the day. When *Rag*, issue one, landed on the newsstands it created an instant sensation. Every copy of the magazine sold within a day, a novel feat for a $40 magazine.

I found the *Rag* offices in a former fire station on a block unlike the rest of Williamsburg, as it was devoid of any shops or lofts. I was initially concerned I'd found the wrong abandoned fire station until I saw a group of three sharply dressed young journalists exiting the building. They were sassy and joking about what a douche bag the Vice-President was.

"Is this *Rag*?" I asked one of the writers who smoked a Pall Mall trying desperately to look neurotic.

"It be," he replied.

Inside the fire station I found a large garage filled with mismatched desks all covered with loose papers. Computer networking cables were strung across hanging lights and a team of young editors gathered around a used poker table near the rear of the building. Everyone wore blocky vintage glasses in an attempt to be eccentric, if not unintentionally uniform.

"Can we help you," one of them asked.

"I'm looking for Josey Sinclair," I said, "I have a two o'clock with her."

"She's right through there." The girl pointed me into the one private office in the whole building. I entered and found Josey seated at a folding table stacked with photos and drafts of copy.

"Tell me you're Jimmy!" she nearly screamed as I entered the office.

"I'm Jimmy," I sang.

"Chelsea described you perfectly," she stood up to hug me. "You remind me of my little brother."

We began a casual conversation about various nothings. I learned Josey was Australian-born and thoroughly astute in the ways of America. She looked athletic and I was pleased to see the office dress code was liberal enough to allow one to wear a Lacoste polo shirt, shorts, and expensive looking heels.

"I don't want to waste your time," Josey said with a giant ceramic white smile, "so let's get down to business." We had a seat at a tiny little boardroom table at the far end of her office. "What made you decide to seek a job here?

"I've always dreamed of working at a magazine, let alone…" I paused, I forgot the name of the magazine for what seemed like twelve minutes but Josey didn't notice. Rather, she was staring at my mid-section. I pretended to cough, hoping it would break her stare, but it didn't. Her long gaze at my crotch was not just annoying it was drawing odd glances. Even the receptionist ten feet outside the office noticed her ogling my package.

"I see you brought your portfolio," she said, her eyes moving to the package in my hand. I handed her my collection of photos, articles, and even short-fiction. The majority of the content was unpublished and leftover from college.

"I really like your stuff," she exclaimed. She flipped through the book so rapidly there was no way she could have made an honest assessment of my work.

"Yes, I really am quite proud of it," I said hastily. It sounded rehearsed.

"So what's your goal in life," she sought, a question which always annoyed me for two reasons: First, the answer was so long and complex I usually had to lie to think of something that didn't bore people or take up an entire afternoon, and second, I wasn't entirely sure what my goal in life was.

"To be rich and famous, of course," I said simply, it being the most concise of summaries I could think of.

"I used to want to be famous," she brooded, spinning around in her chair like a hyper-active toddler, "I don't know what happened." I had hit on some sort of insecurity in her. I figured it harmless to see if I could get anything more out of her.

"What did you want to be?" I dug.

"A rock star," Josey replied. I thought she was joking at first and paused for her to give the first sign of a chuckle. But she was serious.

Josephine Sinclair and I discussed foolish and childish premonitions of fame and fortune over cappuccino in the building's editorial bullpen. It was there Josey told me that she thought I would be better to fill the position of Lifestyle Editor rather than the freelance position that Chelsea had recommended me for. Who knew you could just walk in and become an editor. But then again, everyone was some sort of editor at the magazine. Even the girl who ordered the office supplies had some sort of editor-type job title, something along the lines of Administrative Editor.

"You know, I've been published very little," I warned.

"I know, but you come on the highest recommendation from Chelsea Hudson. I really do cherish her opinion. And it's not like I can't fire you. One fuck up and you're out of here, got it?"

"Yes," I trembled.

"But that won't happen. Chelsea is such a smart woman. She wouldn't have recommended you work here if you weren't qualified." What she said about Chelsea was ironic on so many levels. For starters, I didn't really know Chelsea, and what I did know of her, I didn't really like. Back in Seattle she always acted the like sourest of beings. How she had taken a liking to me was not just absurd, it was suspicious. Josey was treating me like I was Bruce Weber or Graydon Carter. I couldn't have been a bigger nobody in the magazine world, yet I was having my ass kissed by the editor-in-chief of *Rag*. As much as I wanted to confess to Josey my reluctance to take on a job I wasn't sure I could perform, the lure of working for such a captivating publication became too great. I decided to play along in what felt like a total charade. Where it led could only be an adventure.

"You know, Chelsea and I go back a long ways," Josey blurted.

"Were you lovers?" I asked, trying to be provocative.

"Oh god no!" Josey gasped. "We went to school together."

"Really?" I said, trying to sound fascinated. In truth I didn't give a fuck. I just wanted to be shown to my desk and start working.

"Yes, we went to Exeter together. And Columbia. Graduated the same year and all."

"So you're practically sisters!" I gushed like a whore.

Josey Sinclair and I hit it off that afternoon. To thank her for hiring me I took her to my favorite restaurant in SoHo called The Corner. After several cocktails Josey got the gusto to ask me about my infamous friendship with a certain heiress.

"So what's Loren like?" she asked delicately.

"That old hag?" I joked. "How do you know I know Loren Anders?"

"She's only in every gossip column in this town. It's no goddamn secret you're her right-hand...man." Josey had no boundaries when she was trashed. "It's like you said... Chelsea and I are like sisters, and sisters talk!"

"Everything they say about her is true," I began. "She's fabulous, she has it all. She doesn't take no for an answer and we're the best of friends. I owe her my life." I indulged without limit and it felt great. Josey was such an affable joke I could have told her Loren Anders was an alien from space and she would've believed me.

"Is she ever a bitch?" she asked. Everyone wanted to know this.

"The biggest," I lied. It was so cliché, and misogynistic, to think that a woman in power was either a diva or a bitch. I only played along with it because I didn't have the energy to explain how intelligent and warm Loren really was.

"How can you work for someone like that?"

"She's not a bitch to me!" I clarified.

"So why's she so nice to you?"

"I'm her best friend. I am loyal. She is my lifeline."

"You mean your paycheck?"

"That too. But we were friends before she hired me as her Personal Assistant."

"Don't you find it a little queer that she would hire a friend to be her assistant?" Josey asked as she put her hand on my thigh. I wasn't afraid of affection with women, I enjoyed it. In fact Loren and I kissed on the lips all the time. Most of Loren's friends assumed I was straight because of the way I liked to touch her. Sometimes we'd get drunk and make out. It didn't mean anything. That's just what people did when they got bored.

"It's not queer at all," I responded. "She needs someone she can trust. Who better than a good friend?"

"So when Loren Anders comes calling are you going to abandon the magazine?"

"Nothing can keep me from my dream of being a great journalist," I fibbed. I valued Loren's friendship more than anything, more than any job or belonging. If she were to tell me to kiss *Rag* goodbye then it would've been done. After all, I remained on Loren's payroll and anything that could've jeopardized that would have been dealt with seriously. I was a kept boy; there was no two ways around it.

From the restaurant Josey and I took a cab back to *Rag* headquarters. I spent the first of many late nights working at the magazine, learning how each issue came together and who responsible for producing each section of the magazine. My nerves pulsated with excitement and vigor. It was sublime to have got a job, a desk, and my very own assistant. Notwithstanding my complete lack of qualifications, I was determined to be a success at *Rag*, no matter how much work, sweat, tears, blood, semen, stool, or charm it took.

◦ ◦ ◦

A few days into my job at *Rag* I found myself obsessed. Editing text and photos was like composing a symphony, this one made of prose and image. At the same time I radiated energy, the other editors acted morose for having to work at such a high-brow, low circulation magazine. They all talked (dreamed) of how they planned to get jobs at publication like *Rolling Stone* or *People*. I had no idea why. Those magazines were so contrived and repetitive, always filled with ads for perfume and cigarettes, featuring the same celebrity PR articles each issue. Not an issue of *Rag* went by without full frontal male and female nudity, along with enough profanity to fill a rock star's autobiography. But the other editors at *Rag* didn't want to be creative liberty, they wanted notoriety and glory. All they cared about was circulation. To them, the larger the distribution the greater the cachet. I deplored them and hoped they would leave *Rag*, if only to open up their position so someone like myself could fill it. It was the only way the magazine would ever really flourish.

One can't live off cocoa lattes and celery salad alone, so I invited Loren out to the magazines headquarters late one night. We were going to eat dinner while I showed her around the empty magazine headquarters. It goes without saying that there were constant difficulties in feeding a vegetarian fashion model, especially one who was accustomed to the finest food in the world. Among her many culinary requirements were that it be ethically obtained, low-fat, and unprocessed. You can imagine my befuddlement when she showed up with a pizza from Guido's just down the block. I hadn't ever seen her eat anything out of a box. When the smell of the pizza hit my olfactory senses I began salivating. I just hoped this wasn't some test of hers to see if I had kept my vow to remain vegetarian.

I wanted Loren to see *Rag* for what a poor excuse of a magazine it was – in a way to show her that I was pursuing what I believed in and not just some job was handed to me. We didn't have fancy offices or editors with exorbitant expense accounts who were rarely in the office. If I wanted that I probably could have got Loren to pull some strings and implant me at a position somewhere in the Conde Nast realm of superb publications. As lackluster as *Rag*'s infrastructure was, their magazine made up for it in cutting edge writing and fashion pictorials. When she saw *Rag*, Loren was surprisingly upbeat, saying she wanted me to find some way to get out of her orbit and develop my own network of friends and colleagues. But all serious talk that night would be postponed until we had our customary banter of world politics, gossip, and sex.

"I feel fat and ugly," Loren said looking for some ego therapy. I wasn't in the mood to give her any. Being a career man suddenly meant I was beyond squabbling about weight and vanity.

"You are fat and ugly," I replied. Her jaw fell open and she feigned shock. "Models can be so annoying!"

"Sorry." This was the first time I'd ever heard her apologize to me. At last she was treating me like a person and not an employee.

Having Loren at the old fire house that night was great. The two of us hadn't been alone together in weeks and our friendship needed a bit of maintenance. And although I was working while she visited, she wasn't in the least bit a distraction from the work. Loren helped me sort through a thousand photos I had to arrange for our fashion roundup section. Loren was actually captured in several of the pictures prancing down the runways of Dior and Chanel.

"You know, I've always wanted to own a magazine," Loren confessed.

"Don't even think about it!" I scoffed. She was always jealous of what I had, no matter how small or insignificant. "Please remember that the desire to own a mass media empire has been the downfall of several famous capitalists once as rich as yourself."

"You're right!" she clenched her forehead. "There's no money in magazines." To further her sentiment she looked around the room at the shoddy office furniture and cold fluorescent lighting.

As I chomped on my tasty pizza, which unfortunately was without of meat, I began to think of a dirty secret I was keeping from Loren. She, the girl with so many other more fabulous friends than I, who she could flutter off to and be with at that moment, deserved to know I hadn't been absolutely loyal to a pact she and I had made when we met.

"Loren, you love me, right," I asked her.

"More than anything!" she moaned.

"More than life itself?"

"More than *anything!*" she blurted defiantly and gave me a sloppy hug.

"I've been eating chicken and turkey."

Absolute silence. Only the faint sound of the clapping heels of a prostitute walking the sidewalk outside the fire station could be heard. It was rare for Loren to be without words.

"Do you still love me?" I asked, my voice quivering.

"You mother fucker!" Loren exploded in a shouting rage. "YOU MADE A FUCKING PROMISE TO NEVER... EVER... EVER EAT ANOTHER GODDAMN ANIMAL IN YOUR..." My face was frozen in horror. How could she be so furious? I'd never seen her so enraged, not even the time I broke one of her vases from the Ming Dynasty. She wasn't even this upset when Apple Computers sued AndersGroup (and won) for the patent to the mouse pad.

"Loren I'm sorry!" I began to weep.

"Dude!" Loren switched personas and put her arms around me again. "Chill out. It's just meat. Everybody eats it sometime."

I wheezed and shook my head. She had really fooled me and I felt like an idiot.

"I have a confession too," Loren lamented. "A couple weeks ago I was in Amsterdam for a photo shoot. Me and some models went out on the town one night and somehow we got separated and I was all alone. It was late and I was starving and I didn't speak the language so I went to the only restaurant whose menu I was familiar with."

"Don't tell me..." I closed my eyes assuming the worst.

"McDonalds!" she laughed with a cackle. She described how she'd fallen in love with their grilled chicken burger and had consumed "flocks" of them since she'd returned from Europe. "I was going to tell you that I'd fallen off the wagon but I didn't want to disappoint you. You're the only person in my life who takes the vegetarian thing seriously. Everyone else treats it like a fad diet or an allergy that has to be accommodated. You understand just how cruel it is to kill animals."

"I do."

"And you also understand how fucking delicious they are!"

. . .

As a new member of the editorial staff of *Rag* I was obligated to have my portrait taken for the 'contributors' section of the magazine. I wanted to take what is usually the most boring set of photos in the magazine do something really unique, like emulate a famous photo by Horst. Josey thought the idea was great and sent me to *Rag*'s Photo Editor, Ari Schroeder. A veteran of war coverage and the Israeli-Palestinian conflict, Ari Schroeder was a decorated photographer whose credentials provided great influence and inspiration for the young staff of *Rag*. Like many of today's standouts in journalism, I'd casually followed his career since I was in college, witnessing his gruesome shots for *Time* and *Newsweek*. Ari had in recent years made a startling move from documenting the desperation of third-world peoples for *National Geographic*, to documenting the tragic lives, loves, and heartaches of celebrities for magazines such as *Vanity Fair* and *W*. His position as Photo Editor of *Rag* would have him embedded in the brutal world of street culture and guerilla fashion. Surely the streets of Kabul and Manhattan weren't all that different.

When I met Ari Schroeder in his photo studio/loft, also in Williamsburg, I was alarmed by how good looking he was. I was taller than most men, yet Ari towered over me. There was always something so intimidating about tall men. It wasn't just his height that made him seem so large. Everything about Ari was bigger. His shoulders were wide, his arms as thick as light poles. He was a walking brick wall. Watching him operate his tiny camera with his giant fingers was an amusement in itself. Of course he was not flawless. What man is? His dark black hair, shorn to a quarter-inch in length, was receding a bit in the front and I detected what might be the softening of the six-pack abs he'd likely had throughout his twenties. Despite those very minor flaws, for a 34 year-old, Ari Schroeder appeared to be the most daunting man I'd met in New York. His size was threatening and I immediately lusted for him. His wardrobe, a pair of worn jeans and a black and grey striped Henley was the perfect look for him. It subtly said "artist" and "thinking man." I found him so appealing because he had the body of a brute and the mind of an intellectual. His portfolio of work was unrivaled. He was so handsome and accomplished I caught myself shivering with anxiety any time he was around. The masculinity he radiated made him all the more enchanting. No matter how many times I tried to convince myself that he wasn't worth pursuing I couldn't help but imagine what it must have been like to be his girlfriend. He was everything I wanted in a man and couldn't have because he was straight.

When I introduced myself to Ari he didn't smile or say anything, just shook my hand briefly and led me to the studio section of his loft. His place was a converted ceramics factory sparsely decorated with paintings and minimalist furniture. It looked like he had just moved in.

"Nice place you have here," my voice quivered as Ari tried out various camera lenses.

"Thanks," he said with little enthusiasm. Everyone who came to his home probably said the same thing. Immediately I began to feel like Ari didn't like me. Or maybe, I thought, he was just very busy, which was likely. He was *Rag*'s only full-time photographer besides being the photo editor. He had more physical labor to do than anyone else on the staff. A single issue of the magazine could contain 200 of his photos.

For my portrait in *Rag* I wanted something original and compelling, something which said "he is the star of the editorial staff!" I told this to Ari and he laughed.

"Are you kidding?" he asked bluntly.

"No," I said as my face turned red. "Think Cecil Beaton,"

"Ok," he said, stroking his chin with two fingers as he thought for a moment. A second later he laid out a copy of *The New York Times* covering the entire floor.

"Lay down on the papers," Ari instructed.

"Oh, great idea," I said. Newspapers with their contents spewed about were a recurring theme in Beaton's work. So was partial nudity.

"Should I take off my shirt?" I asked. Ari didn't respond, so I explained, "I think my skin against the texture of the paper would be great, as if I were borne from the news." Ari, cutely, raised an eyebrow at my idea.

"If that's what you want," he said. "I just push the button."

"Oh god," I exclaimed, "I'm sorry. You're the artist and I'm telling you what to do."

"No, it's alright. I'm used to it."

"It's just that I'm nervous," I confessed. "And a control freak. If I'm not a very good subject it's because I've never done this before."

"Done what before?"

"Posed for pictures."

"Never?" he asked like I was telling him the sky was green.

"Nope, never. My only request is you don't make me look like a moron. I don't want to come off as a pretentious douche bag, you know, like one of those guys who just pretends they're fabulous when really they're as boring as the next guy."

"Don't worry. It's just a picture. A tiny little picture in a tiny little magazine in a section nobody looks at anyway." He turned the camera on and motioned for me to lay on the papers.

"You're pretty bold," he said as I was slipping my T-shirt off. "None of the other editors have gone topless in their photos. Not even Josey."

I laid down face up on the pile of *The New York Times* while Ari set a crushed can of Coca-Cola next to my head. He waded up some loose papers from the recycling and set them around me. I had no idea what he was doing, the whole thing seemed bizarre.

"You know, I usually wouldn't let a guy do this to me unless…" I began to make a joke but was rebuffed.

"Ssshh," he quieted me as he examined the scene through his lens, snapping pictures here and there. "Close your eyes," he insisted, so I did. I heard the camera click a couple times and he said "there, we're done, I got it."

I was a bit frightened at what he might have captured with his camera. I put my shirt back as Ari downloaded the pictures to his computer. A moment later on the screen was the most glamorous young man I'd ever seen. He was a young flawless idol in a portrait of pop-culture juxtaposition. The crushed can and the papers made it look like I was sleeping on the sidewalk. The colorful ads in the paper next to my pale skin were a stunning contrast. I looked like a naked adolescent lost in a world of hyper-consumerism. It was glorious and I couldn't wait for it to appear in *Rag*.

As Ari sat as his computer and I stood behind him, I noticed with alarm that I'd set my hand on his shoulder while we looked at the pictures. I'm not usually a touchy person, but this man, who'd I found so intimidating at first, had somehow made me feel so at ease and comfortable. I didn't even hesitate to casually touch him. And from what I could discern he didn't mind the contact.

As I scrutinized the photos I noticed Ari did not take pictures of my chest or anything below my neck, just my face and head next to the papers and bottle. The wanton partial nudity I'd demanded now seemed gratuitous. I was embarrassed.

The pictures excited Ari. Our unlikely collaboration had turned fruitful and now he wanted to try more. I was the only muse around so he made me continue to pose for him. When he showed me to the roof of his building we came upon the most stunning sunset. I had arrived at the photo studio not long after lunch. How it was near the end of the day was beyond me. The past few hours had evaporated. Being in the presence of such a delightful man, and masterful artist at that, made the perception of time indiscernible. From atop the roof I could see the Williamsburg Bridge stretching over into the sparkling East Village. The Empire State Building's spire poked out from the top of the Midtown skyline. The sun setting behind the skyscrapers created a luminous silhouette, like that of a jagged saw which was lacerating the horizon. My figure in full color and light posed in front of this backdrop proved another of Ari's wondrous photographic visions. As he instructed me on how to stand I noticed Ari had a bit of a southern accent that had been weathered by his many years working abroad. He retained only the remnants of a drawl. I asked him where he was from and he said Birmingham, Alabama. Then he asked me where I was from.

"Why? Do I have an accent?" I wondered.

"I know you're not from New York," he contended.

"Seattle."

"Oh!" he said, his vacant expression turning to one of charm. "I love it there." He snapped a couple more of my dreary poses. "Why'd you leave?"

"I don't know," I deflected, "I wanted to see the world."

"I know what that's like," he said, snapping away. "I'm starting to tire of New York."

"How long have you lived here?"

"Two months," he said. I laughed and he returned a smile.

"Not liking the Big Apple?" I tried to empathize.

"No," he shrugged, "the Big Apple isn't liking me."

What he said sounded ridiculous. I would have changed lives with him in a heartbeat.

"You're employed," I said, "you've got a great apartment. What could possibly be the matter?"

"It's lonely here," he confessed. His camera began to beep in repetition, which indicated its memory was full. "The New York dating scene is a blood bath." We went downstairs back to his studio.

"I've always heard it was a meat market," I said, failing at trying to be funny.

"Same thing, maybe it's both, I don't know." He fumbled with his camera for a moment and then set it down on his work table. Something was obviously on his mind.

"I don't understand," I said. "Women should be falling all over you. You've got that whole eccentric artist thing going on. It's very *now* you know. And I should know, after all I am Lifestyle Editor for Williamsburg's most read magazine." My attempt to humor him failed spectacularly. Instead of laughing or smiling he just looked at me like I was speaking Dutch. I began to wonder if I'd misunderstood what he had said.

"The women do fall all over me," he replied after a pause, "that's the problem."

"Oh, I get it," I said. "You're overbooked! Too many to sift through before making a sincere decision?"

He didn't respond to this. I suddenly felt like I'd overstayed my welcome at his place and decided to leave.

"Thanks for the great shoot," I said, picking up my jacket off his sofa. "I'm really impressed with the photos you took. I wasn't sure how this would go."

"You're going?" he nearly shouted.

"Yes," I looked at my watch. "I've been here for almost five hours. You probably have a thousand photos of me." As I went to leave Ari followed me to the door like I'd just stolen something.

"See you Monday at work," I said as I opened the door.

"Dinner!" he suddenly burst.

"What?" I said as I turned to face him. He paused for a moment searching for what to say next.

"We're co-workers. It's tradition that after every shoot I take the model out to dinner," he said, I suspected when he started the sentence he hadn't formed the end of it, giving him the most vulnerable pitch to his voice.

"Good," I said, "I'm starving."

"Let me grab my keys," he barked excitedly. He must have been famished.

Williamsburg was buzzing with the young and trendy in search of sex and dinner. For a moment I thought we'd stepped through some magic portal and been transported to SoHo. The streets were packed with expensive cars and beautiful women looking for men. It was strange going to dinner on a Friday night with a guy I was deeply engrossed by, yet couldn't flirt with. As we walked and I saw all the other beautiful couples flirting and laughing, I couldn't help but fantasize that I was on a date with Ari. In my head we were boyfriends. In reality we were just two dudes in search of some grub. There was some likelihood he had no idea I was gay and I didn't want to do anything to tip him off. When we stood next each other waiting for the crosswalk light to change I caught myself wanting to reach down and hold his hand. I had to keep telling myself "he likes women, he likes women…" but it did no good. I wanted so badly to take his hand in mine.

"The choices are Italian, Thai, French, Mexican or Japanese," Ari said. As he spoke I dreamed of what it'd be like to kiss him right there, to feel the scruff of his face on mine, to feel his soft warm lips, to feel his tongue in my mouth. In thinking these things I forgot what it was he had asked me.

"Too many choices?" he asked, as if that was the reason I offered no response, only a bemused gape.

"Yes," I covered, "I have this thing about eating out. My belief is the person who pays for dinner chooses what's for dinner."

"Alright," he said "Mexican it is."

"Good choice," I bolstered.

Ari lead me to Cancun on Metropolitan Avenue where we sat outside. The moment we sat down he ordered us a round of blended margaritas. We munched on chips and salsa and looked at the menu, neither of us talking. I tried to think of anything to say but couldn't.

"I have to admit that I'm a big fan of yours," I eventually murmured.

"Really?" Ari asked, doubting my sincerity.

"Yes. I remember seeing your piece in *National Geographic* about the women of Kabul and how they hadn't changed after the fall of the Taliban. How even years later they feared persecution."

"That was two years ago," he said, as if it were ancient history.

"I know. It was an unforgettable piece."

"How old are you?" I was curious to know why he asked this.

"I'm twenty-two." When I said this he just winced and looked down at his menu. Our margaritas arrived just after that. We both sipped ours quickly but even liquored up Ari seemed distant. Silently he kept on looking at his menu. A few minutes passed without either of us saying anything. This upset me. I didn't want our dinner, the closest thing to a date I'd been on in years, spoiled by his aloofness.

"So where'd you go to college?" I quizzed, trying to stifle the silence.

"I didn't," he uttered, decorating a chip with guacamole.

"Oh, so you're a natural talent," I flattered.

"Where'd you go?"

"The University of Washington… but I dropped out."

"Good idea. College is for pricks," Ari said and then devoured a few more chips.

A moment passed, then another. We ordered our meals and said very little to each other as we ate. It was typical for me to be silent in the company of a good looking man, but Ari was just as quiet. I wondered what the point of him taking me out to dinner was if he was just going to ignore me.

"I don't want to sound like a jerk or anything," I said to Ari as he scanned the room, probably looking for the closest exit, "you seem kind of angry."

"I'm sorry," Ari said with a look of regret, almost embarrassment. "I've been getting very little sleep lately. I'm just tired."

"Oh." I felt like an ass for pointing it out.

"I'm sorry," he apologized again, "if you want to leave that's fine."

"No!" I recoiled. Even if he didn't talk to me the rest of the evening I was entertained just by examining Ari's stone face and body, one seated so close to my own I wondered what it would have been like to put my hand on his leg, or more interestingly, to have permission to do so. What it must be like for the women, the hordes of them, who lined up to do such things to him.

"In this city a free dinner doesn't come along very often," I explained, "so I'll stick around." When I said this I detected the slightest grin on his face. "I'm sure you have some very fascinating stories to tell about photography. You've been everywhere."

When our food arrived along with our second round of margaritas he explained how the wilds of the Amazon and the treachery of Sudan paled in comparison to the massacre that was backstage at New York Fashion Week.

"The models are like athletes," Ari dazzled. I could tell he was as much enchanted by fashion as I was. "The men and the women both. They train and train, it's crazy, as if modeling is a competition. But don't get me wrong, it is. These people make hundreds of dollars a minute sometimes… and all they do is stand there and pose! They have to nail it every time. If they don't there's fifty other anorexics waiting in line to take their place."

The rest of dinner was boring as hell and I'd become eager to go home, regardless of Ari's good looks. After dinner was paid and we found ourselves standing outside the restaurant I casually thanked the photographer for dinner and asked if he knew where the closest subway stop was.

"It'd probably be easier and quicker to take a cab at this time of night," he said.

"Okay, thanks." I stepped out in the street to look for any cabs. There were none. I expected for him to say goodbye and start walking home, but he didn't.

"Hey, are you going into the office tomorrow?" he asked.

"Of course. Why?"

"If you want I could give you a disc with your pictures on it. I'm not going to be back to the office until Wednesday and that way it's sure to get in this next issue."

At that point I didn't want to go back to Ari's place. The margaritas had made me drowsy and I dreaded the long, tipsy walk. But I weakened, thinking of how proud I'd be having my glamorous face in *Rag* a month early. I followed him back to his loft, all the while daring myself to grasp his hand. When we got to his apartment Ari suddenly livened up, throwing his jacket across the room to snag a coat rack. He began whistling an old Sinatra tune and went into his bathroom to pee, leaving the door partially opened. I curiously took a peek through the crack in the door to see nothing more than a bathrobe hanging in the reflection of the mirror. As I listened to him whistle I took a seat in his living room. I stared at his many bookcases, each stocked with those giant photo books from masters like Avedon, Ritts, and Weber.

"Want something to drink?" Ari offered as he emerged from the bathroom. I stood up and shook my head. He went to the refrigerator to poke around. He didn't see my response until he had two Corona beers in his hand. I could tell he was disappointed when I told him "no thanks."

"Are you sure?" he asked softly. "I have lime wedges," he appealed desperately.

"I better get home," I said. "I can barely keep my eyes open."

Ari's demeanor changed again, his liveliness vanishing as he retrieved the disc with my headshot on it. When he returned with the disc and I reached to take it he took my wrist in his arm and pulled me close to him until his body was against mine. Immediately his lips were on mine and I was overwhelmed, I'd never experienced such pleasure and shock simultaneously.

"What are you doing?" I lambasted, lurching back from his kiss fearing maybe in my drunkenness it was me kissing him. "You're supposed to be straight," I added.

"I'm not," he said. Everything that had happened that afternoon and evening began to take on a new meaning. His behavior was not of aloofness, it was that of lust and fear. I stood there looking at Ari, the most beautiful man I'd ever seen, his eyes searching mine for acceptance.

"Oh shit!" he blasted.

"What?"

"You're gay, aren't you?" he worriedly asked. "If you're not I'm sorry. I assumed you were because I asked some girls in the office and they said you were." Ari turned away from me while grasping his head in thought. "This is why I should leave New York. Everything I do is a disaster."

"Ari!" I cried walking after him, "I'm as gay as they get. I just had no idea you were and I was playing it straight. When you kissed me I… I don't know, I wasn't expecting it."

"I'm sorry," he moaned. He walked out on his balcony and set down on the step. "I guess I've had a bit too much to drink tonight. I can't believe I kissed you."

"Don't be sorry," I said sitting next to him, "just do it again!" I softly put my hands on his neck and guided his lips back on to mine, this time our embrace gentle and lingering. As we held each other I felt the release of a thousand pent sensations. The feeling of his body against mine the greatest thing I'd felt. I laid back against the doorway as he kissed me again and again, each time I would recline further until I was laying down on the floor of the terrace, his body now hovering over mine.

"Thanks again for dinner," I joked between deep kisses.

"Anytime," he said quickly before kissing me again.

I had to pull away from him to say, "Do you treat all the models like this?"

"Just the cute ones."

I was going to make some stupid/witty comment about how all models, by definition, were cute. But I didn't. All I wanted to do was kiss him. With our bodies rubbing together as we kissed something else began to take shape in both our trousers. Before the passion could consume us further he laid next to me as our speeding pulses and erections subsided.

"You're intense," he laughed in my ear.

"That's intense?" I mocked, "You don't date much."

"Is it obvious?"

"Yes," I babbled, pecking kisses on his stubbly neck.

"I have an excuse," he whispered, his tongue massaging my ear lobe.

"What's that?" I giggled.

"I'm painfully shy."

"There's no excuse for trying to find love," I sermonized, as if lonely me had any knowledge of dating and relationships.

"How many boyfriends have you had?" Ari asked openly, unaware a question like that was taboo on a first date.

"Honestly?" I delayed, not wanting to reveal the truth. He nodded wanting to know, so I said "zero." His mouth gaped in reaction. "You're not supposed to ask a guy that. The answer is never good."

"You've never had a boyfriend?" He asked in disbelief.

"No," I pouted, feeling pathetic. My reaction prompted Ari to wrap his arms around me.

"Why not?"

"Boys don't like me. They think I'm too complex. And I'm not a whore. It's not like I troll the clubs looking for a suck-and-fuck."

"That's a good thing," he encouraged. "I've only had two."

"Two suck and fucks?" I joked.

"No! Two boyfriends," he iterated.

"Let's not talk boyfriends," I said.

Ari sat up and I followed.

"If this is just going to be a one night thing I'm not interested," I explained, my margarita having worn off suddenly. "I can't work with someone I've had a fling with."

"Fine," Ari whispered, pecked a kiss on my cheek and stood up. I was shocked. He handed me the photo disc and smiled at me. For a moment I thought he was dismissing me because I wasn't in to casual sex.

"How's tomorrow night?" Ari asked.

"What's tomorrow night?" I was still confused.

"I'm hoping to take you on a real date. That way there's no chance you'll construe my interest in you as a one-night sort of thing."

I gleamed, hugging him so tightly I never wanted to let go. Before I could catch the words, I said "I love you." My entire body wobbled in disbelief when I heard myself say this.

"You can't honestly love me already!" he chuckled with amusement.

I didn't want to back off from the statement. If played correctly, I could have made the statement just a facet of my sense of humor. "I do. I loved you before you kissed me. Back when you were straight. Back when you had cilantro in your teeth at the restaurant."

"I had cilantro in my teeth? Why didn't you tell me?"

"It was cute."

"Wait until you know me to love me. You might not want to."

I dropped the disc on the floor and pushed Ari on to his couch. I straddled his body and lifted off my shirt. He took of his to reveal his tanned, southern skin. His chest was covered in a sexy sheath of soft hair. I loosened both my belt and his as he sat back in glee witnessing me unbutton his pants. As I rubbed my hand on his crotch I began to consider the implications of going any further.

"I'm not sure I should…" I said. I looked at him to see him smirk.

"It's okay if you don't want to." Ari sat up and instinctively hugged me, our two naked torsos feeling so good together. In my fervor to display my interest in him I'd overcompensated by taking things too far, sexually.

"I should go," I stated, quickly putting my shirt back on.

"Okay. Can I have your phone number?"

I gave Ari my number and email and he gave me a goodnight kiss on the cheek. When I got back to my apartment twenty minutes later I found an email on my computer from him. It read:

SUBJECT: 2night

Hey Jimbo, tonight was hot. I had a great time. When Josey told me I had to take your picture I got a little nervous because I've seen you at the office and thought you were really cute. It's unreal to think that you like me. I guess I was afraid I wouldn't be your type (I'm a few year older than you are, haha). Are you free tomorrow night? Call me.

Sleep well, ARI ☺

I found his email hilarious. *Not his type?* He was *so* my type, I thought, and detailed how "my type" he was in a cute little reply. In my response I suggested we have dinner in Manhattan for our first "real" date. Ari's reply to my reply arrived approximately seven minutes later. He accepted my offer for dinner, proclaiming it was my turn to choose the restaurant and that he would pick me up.

I woke up early Saturday morning. After a cup of tea and a shower I arrived at AndersPlace. It was the day I was to meet and begin sorting through the tower of resumes for Loren's new personal assistant. Jacques, the butler, greeted me with a scone at the door. He was the friendliest French butler in all of Manhattan.

"Good morning Jacques," I tattled, kissing the butler on both cheeks. This was something I'd been doing to every French person I'd met since June when I'd cavorted around Paris.

"Bonjour Jimmy."

"Where's Loren?"

"She is in her room. Packing."

"Packing?" I asked. It sounded absurd to hear Loren was doing any sort of physical labor.

"Yes," he scowled. "Very bad news from Seattle."

"What bad news?"

"I don't know the specifics. I just know it's bad news. She got a call this morning from Hubert. She's been upset since. She told me to fuck my fucking scones in my fuck hole. Whatever that means."

I went upstairs immediately to find Loren and her three maids packing several giant Louis Vuitton cases full of couture. When she saw me she didn't say anything.

"Loren, what's going on?" I prodded.

"Oh Jimmy, thank god you're here. I have to go back to Seattle."

"Why, what's wrong?" I helped one of the maids fold a long gown in to a case.

"Pick up an issue of the *Wall Street Journal*!" she burst.

"I'm sorry, I've been so busy at the magazine," I cried. "What's happening?" The maids were just packing Loren some suitcases for a business trip. They were emptying her entire closet in to boxes.

"The AndersGroup stock has really tumbled in the last month. It's gone from forty-five dollars to…" she winced in pain, "nineteen."

I felt dizzy when she said it, instantly recalling the time she told me she owned fifty million shares of the company. If shares went below twenty dollars it meant she was no longer a billionaire. In terms of stock, Loren was now just a mere millionaire 950 times over.

"Last month we reported earnings," she began to explain.

"What was wrong with the earnings?" I asked.

"There weren't any."

"Oh."

Loren supervised the maids as they rolled the cases down to the foyer and into a waiting truck that would haul them out to the airport.

"Do you think I should grab some stuff from my place?" I asked. After all, anywhere Loren went I seemed to follow.

"Jimmy, no. You have to stay here and take care of the house," she urged. Any pain I was feeling for Loren was immediately anesthetized, realizing I'd have AndersPlace to myself, probably for weeks. "I shouldn't be in Seattle long, just to get things working again. I'll call you when I get there. I left a couple dollars for you in the cookie jar in case things get drastic."

I held Loren tightly and we kissed each other. She hadn't even left and I already missed her. She waved goodbye as her motorcade pulled away and I went back inside giddy, thinking how wonderful it would be to entertain my new friend Ari Schroeder in Loren's manse.

Upon Loren's departure I made a full inspection of AndersPlace, discovering it was in pristine enough order to let some of the staff take a holiday. I asked Jacques the butler to take some paid time off. He delightfully agreed and I arranged for him to vacation at the Anders's villa on Moorea until I summoned his return. Two of the three maids I sent on vacation too, keeping my favorite maid, Greta, and the part-time chef Helen on staff.

Recalling Loren's reference to cash in the cookie jar, I opened it to find thirty-thousand dollars. She really had no grasp on what ordinary people needed in order to get by.

During my inspection of the house I found the article from the *Wall Street Journal* that she referred to:

ANDERS RE-GROUPING? STOCK HITS 5-YEAR LOW

Seattle — Global diversified financial services company AndersGroup, once touted as loss-proof, reported zero profits in their second quarter last month with operating expenditures 15% greater than any previous quarter. Company CFO, Grant Parks, cited bad timing, outlining that several of the company's liquidations were halted due to economic instability and costs associated with restructuring their European operations. A day prior to posting earnings, Merrill Lynch downgraded AndersGroup stock from hold to sell, something investors have been doing ever since. The stock closed at $18.79 on Thursday, down over 60% since its high in July of $47.18 and its all-time high of $88.92 in October of last year.

Loren Anders, the company's acting President and largest stockholder, with 17.5% of outstanding shares, released a statement on Wednesday asserting she would be much more involved in the company's future operations. Anders has had to deflect growing criticism from both investors and gossip columnists since her successful foray into fashion and modeling. Since April when she first appeared in the pages of Vogue *magazine, the young billionaire has been leading a celebrity life, showing up at Hollywood parties and mingling with the jet set.*

In her memo to shareholders, Anders asked that they not "let psychological unreason justify selling AndersGroup stock" or lead them to believe anything has changed at the company. Many see this assurance as too little, too late. Anders very publicly relocated to New York City, away from AndersGroup headquarters in Seattle, and has spent many weeks in Europe, not supervising the restructuring but strutting down runways.

Peter Murdoch, Senior Financial Advisor for Moody's in Manhattan and self-proclaimed fan of the "Anders Soap-Opera," has described Loren's new career as model, and her virtual disassociation with the company that made her a billionaire, as merely an illusion.

"No matter what she does, she is AndersGroup," Murdoch believes. "A very large number of investors in AndersGroup are online traders who've seen Loren become a matriarch since the death of her father. She had a very large role in transforming the company from a mid-size holdings firm into the global finance player it is now. For her to tell everyone nothing has changed is important. The

public has always believed her to be running the show and they question how good a job she can do when she hasn't shown up for work at company headquarters in nearly two months."

The article completely embodied the same concerns I'd been having about Loren and her relationship with AndersGroup. I knew very well she'd been keeping in touch with headquarters, but the public did not. She appeared so many times in the tabloid media, with paparazzi shots of her dining with friends or romancing male models, that the perception of her as a hard working business woman had been erased. All the world ever saw of her was the ad campaigns she appeared in and the gossip pages she had become a fixture of. She had kept her involvement at AndersGroup completely private and investors in the company had been convinced she was no longer playing a role. Furthermore, her relocation to New York removed her from the Anders corporate culture in Seattle. Thousands of people each day reported to work at AndersCenter. Her departure had left them without their corporate mascot and figurehead of glamour and prestige. Many of her employees likely felt abandoned by her. The impact on company morale had to have been tremendous.

After reading the article I did what any smart investor would do: I went online and purchased as many shares of AndersGroup as I could.

* * *

It was the night of my first real date with Ari Schroeder. For two hours I'd spent doing the pre-date ritual of the shower, the shave, and the endless search for something to wear. As I groomed myself and anticipated Ari's arrival at AndersPlace, I began to think of what a relationship with him could mean. He was very much a man, an independent artist, and I was unbelievably attracted to him. I started to worry that maybe he was better looking than me and feared if people on the street saw us together they'd ask what that ugly kid was doing with such a handsome hunk of a man. As I nervously roamed the halls of the mansion attempting to kill time, I reassured myself that I was good enough for Ari. I had charm, I had wit, and I had ambition. What more could a guy want?

As I continued to wait for Ari, I began to analyze my greatest insecurities. My most common was the fear of becoming feminine.

When most people meet me they tend to assume I prefer vagina to penis. It's been a shock and a disappointment for many ladies to learn of my love for men. But I was becoming curious as to whether or not I'd become flamboyant. This concern extended from an unprecedented amount of men coming on to me in recent weeks. This wave of flirtatiousness was initiated by a cute young male grocery clerk who gave me *that* look... the one where their mouth is saying "paper or plastic?" but their mind is saying "latex or bare back?" Maybe it's only the more attractive array of men (like myself) that experience this. I don't mean to be narcissistic but I take care of my looks. I work out. On a scale of 1 to 10 I was at *least* a 7, and probably a 9 in certain parts of the country.

Okay, I know I'm vane as hell so I'll just admit it: I think I'm hot. In fact just last Tuesday I was outside Bergdorf Goodman window shopping when I looked up to see the cutest guy... then I realized it was my own reflection. It's one thing to have someone tell you you're cute but to actually believe it is a lot more gratifying. One of the many great things about being gay is being able to check yourself out and enjoy it!

Just as my mind began to wander on to topics as to how flattering it was being hit on by every sales girl at the cologne counter, the chiming door bells of AndersPlace rang, heralding the arrival of the magnificent Ari Schroeder.

I galloped down the marble steps of AndersPlace in my new Cole Haan's that clicked with echoing madness as I scurried to the door. I opened it to behold Ari dressed in black slacks with matching jacket and white shirt. *Elegant. Masculine. Perfect.*

"Holy shit!" I praised and threw my arms around him.

"You like the suit?" Ari inquired with anxiety.

"It's fancy with a capital F. I thought you were hot last night in your frayed jeans, but damn, you shine up like new penny," I said with my stock southern accent. "C'mon in." I pulled Ari's hand to take him into the great entrance hall of the mansion.

"What is this place?" Ari asked with dazzle in his eyes.

"It's a house. It used to be the French embassy and before that it was a hotel, but now it's just a house. I borrowed it from a friend."

"It's humble," he quipped as we walked past the largest mosaic tile in North America.

I gave Ari the grand tour of the Anders house and was sure to introduce him to Loren's two pets, Cartier and Pucci. The black lab

Pucci, the most affectionate and lovely animal ever created, responded to Ari by gleefully wagging his tail and licking him. There were sparks between the two boys immediately.

"Finally, someone with a real dog," Ari exclaimed upon seeing the Labrador.

"Of course he's *real*," I defended, not understanding Ari's premise.

"I think Manhattan has the highest population of poodles and cocker spaniels on earth. They happen to be the two dumbest breeds on the planet," Ari said, kneeling down to Pucci to pet him. He didn't even back away when Pucci began to lick his face. "This is what a dog is supposed to be. How old is he?"

"He just celebrated his first birthday last week. His name is Pucci. He's very well behaved. The nicest dog I've ever met."

"I had a dog just like him when I was a kid. His name was Tom the Dog. He was the best. We bought him from this old guy who used to take him bird hunting." Seeing Pucci had made Ari seem more youthful and lively. This 34-year-old Manhattan photographer had suddenly turned back into a 13-year-old Alabaman. It was marvelous to watch him connect with the dog. He even hugged Pucci. It was the most affection the dog had seen in its entire life.

"Are you hungry?" I asked as Ari tried to persuade Pucci to roll over.

"Very. I had a shoot in Southampton this morning. I don't think I've eaten all day."

"Good. How does a picnic sound?"

"A picnic?" he asked. "But it's nighttime."

"Night picnics are the most romantic," I appealed. "Follow me, I've got something to show you."

If there is one Manhattan urban legend that every New Yorker knows, it is the alleged dangers that lurk in Central Park at night. Sure, people get raped and slaughtered in the park all the time, but so what? Thousands... no, millions of people use the park, therefore stories, myths and rumors are sure to abound from such a popular locale. Considering the dangers of the park after dusk I took Fernando, one of the armed AndersPlace guards to watch over Ari, Pucci, and myself as we set out on our evening picnic in the park. Knowing the park would be desolate, I arranged for a large picnic blanket circled with hurricane lanterns to be set up in the center of the Great Lawn. As we made our way into the huge space - a giant refuge of nature in the middle of the tremulous city - it appeared we'd entered paradise in the midst of chaos. When Ari took notice of the scene he gasped; Pucci, having sensed the romance had a similar reaction and would brush his nose against my hand as if to say "gee sir, that's so romantic."

"It's amazing," Ari said, hugging me with one arm as he carried our picnic basket.

"It's the perfect setting for dinner," I said. "We have just enough light and the park to ourselves. Loren's chef made us a wonderful dinner."

"I can't believe this. Nobody ever..." he began to say, pausing timidly.

"What?"

He hesitated sparingly then admitted, "Nobody's ever done this sort of thing for me before."

"That's a shame."

Ari and I unloaded our picnic basket as Fernando and Pucci stood guard several yards away in the darkness. The basket was filled with tiny finger sandwiches, fresh baked crackers topped with extravagant sauces and garnishes, and of course, a bottle of Bordeaux.

Dinner started with a conversation about Alabama and how Ari missed it. I knew nothing of the state, only its stereotypes, and listening to his description of his home made me want to visit it, someday. He talked of his family, his broken home, his father's suicide, his mother's alcoholism and eventually the one family member he still kept in contact with, his sister.

"Not having a proper home can really drive a person..." he stumbled with his word.

"Crazy?"

"No. Towards things that don't matter. Like a career. I think what drove me into photography so young was it was the one thing I enjoyed, and it didn't involve my family." He yanked the cork out of the wine and poured us both a glass.

"Do they know you're gay?" I delicately asked.

"I don't know. I haven't seen my mom in... probably five years. I've told my sister, she knows, she's fine with it. Are you out?"

"No." My face took on the color of the wine. "I've been thinking about telling my mom. After she has a heart attack I'm sure she'll ask if I have a boyfriend and I'll have to say no and it will just seem so pathetic.

Kind of like what's the point of telling your mom you're gay if you don't have a boyfriend?"

"But you have had…" he insinuated sex.

"Not exactly. Everything but… butt." We laughed at my accidental pun.

After I made this confession to Ari he relaxed a bit. It was warm so we took off our jackets and shoes. There's just something about a lush green lawn that begs for bare feet. The wine was doing its job well and we kissed several times. Moments later as we were laying on the picnic blanket looking up at the starless, pink city sky.

"Back home," I said, "on a cloudless night, you can see the entire universe from the front yard."

"The city sucks. We can't see one goddamn star," cursed Ari.

As he looked up at the sky I turned on my side to face him. I put my head next to his and looked into his eyes as we spoke. Out of the corner of my eye I could see Fernando squirming and trying not to look our way. Maybe he was trying to offer us a moment of privacy. Surely it couldn't have been the first time he saw two guys kissing on a blanket in the park.

"Ari, what's your favorite color?"

He contemplated for a moment. "Burnt orange. What's yours?"

"I don't know. Why are you asking me?"

"Because you asked me!" he recoiled. He turned on his side to face me directly. "You're kind of nuts, you know that," he teased adoringly.

"Yeah, I know that."

On a picnic blanket at night in Central Park I would ask Ari every question I could think of and he would answer every one. It was my attempt to learn who he was in full. I discovered he preferred painting to photography, lost his virginity to a woman when he was 16 and to a man when he was 25. He told me his greatest fears, accomplishments, and heartaches. Ari Schroeder revealed to me everything I asked, willingly and without discretion. It was the first time I'd ever had access to someone without limitation. His heart, his body, and his mind were all my playground.

SEPTEMBER

Having been new to love and affection, I became eager to drown myself in a prospective relationship with Ari Schroeder. I'd naively believed courting someone included dating them frequently. I found that idea to be obsolete. For whatever reason, couples no longer went on formal dates. Romantic evenings spent in restaurants dining on gourmet food while talking aspirant nonsense were rituals of an all too formal past. Such wooing was more often a television writer's idea of what modern dating was all about. In this contemporary era, dating meant spending time with the person you wished to be entangled. You could "date" while reupholstering a sofa or sharing the Sunday newspaper. The formality of dinner and a movie was dead. Being with the one you desired in a comfortable setting was found to be more rewarding than time spent in a restaurant or theater could ever be. With comfort you found the quirks that made your lover unique. For someone like me, with nothing to hide and a preference for revealing my flaws immediately in order to determine if the person I was dating would accept them, this modern method was precise, straightforward, and efficient.

Having formerly worked the grueling nine-to-five office schedule, my body was still programmed to wake not long after sunrise. Ari, however, was a nocturnal creature who'd sleep until approximately noon and would often stay up all night and only go to bed when the sun began to emerge. These polar schedules of ours were not bothersome in the least as we always had the afternoon and evenings together. Any more time together would likely have been asphyxiating. Never did I tire of waking up next to such a divine creature, knowing that if I had any worry or concern, or just felt lonely, I could wake him up and he would console me.

Often when I woke up next to Ari I would crawl around him, perversely examining his entire body - this fascinatingly flawless man was lying next to me and I felt so proud. Ari's skin was dark, like the color of caramel. I suspected Italian or Spanish blood in him, maybe even Israeli. He was undoubtedly Mediterranean and worldly. He kept his black hair trimmed short, as if he were in the military. One of his more precious features was his cute sideburns, down to his earlobes. I was jealous of these as I had yet to be able to grow a supple set of sideburns. I figured a beard, or even scruff that wasn't patchy, was still a decade off for me.

When Ari was awake it was my pleasure to be probed by his dazzling eyes. His green eyes blazed in even the faintest of light. I'd felt nothing more erotic in public than when he would look at me in a way that just spoke to me so sexually it'd become disturbing. *How could a man be so sexy that just by his gaze I'd become aroused?* Affection was so new to me that I was just becoming privy to the hidden language of glances and stares that lovers spoke.

One morning and I didn't expect Ari to wake for several hours. In my AndersPlace bedroom I lay there with my head on his chest staring at his chin, feeling him breath, grateful for this man in my life. How unpredictably fortunate I felt. Not just for having him, but to have a fledgling career at *Rag* and a triple-booked social calendar. So many aspirations that once seemed unfeasible were absolutely within reach.

I wanted to lie with Ari there all day and just consume his warmth. We were like two kings in our enormous palace - just the two of us and a couple of unaware security guards downstairs protecting the place. I dreaded having to get up, shower, dress and head out to Williamsburg that day. But I considered if I wanted to have it all and keep it all, I would still have to report to work.

It's always been said that New York City is at the forefront of underground culture. To work at a magazine that documented and celebrated such meant continually searching for the undiscovered. Imagine the perplexities I faced when I discovered everything "new" and "subversive" was in disappointing truth, passé. As Lifestyle Editor of Rag, it was my duty to find, capture, package, print and exploit whatever it was that had been deemed the Next Big Thing. I would find by visiting contemporary art galleries around SoHo and Chelsea that most of the city's more popular rising art stars were imports, often from Europe or the West Coast. I had yet to meet an artist actually *from* New York.

At the weekly *Rag* meeting that balmy Monday morning at the old firehouse in Williamsburg, I brought up my frustrations of New York's defunct and absent avant-garde.

"It's such a letdown," I pouted to the group of nine editors. "I thought coming here would be a mind boggling discovery of contemporary and futurist ideas. Where are those ideas?"

"Just this weekend I was thinking the same thing," chimed Arthur Bosch, the Performing Arts Editor. "I had the sudden realization that everything playing right now on Broadway is either a revival, a revue, or based on previously published works. And two of the biggest shows are based on films!"

The group became uproarious. It was like I'd cracked open a tomb full of rants, everyone genuine in how New York, supposedly America's (and the world's) capital city when it came to art and culture, was somehow so corporate and filtered it was now at once devoid of anything truly new. Things didn't come from New York, they were brought to New York.

Valentina Harper, one of the managing editors and likely the oldest staff member, immediately began: "We can't kick every artist out of SoHo and the Village and expect to produce art. The era of New York as a hub of art died when their housing was obliterated."

"The city is in a tailspin," the fashion editor would comment. "Economically, socially, artistically. We're just in a period of tremendous fluctuation."

"We've been in fluctuation since the millennium," screamed the Visual Arts Editor. "It's time something happened! We haven't had a genuine art movement since Warhol!"

"Valentina's right. I think it says a lot that this magazine, a righteous hotbed representative of what the New York arts scene produces, is located in *Brooklyn*," the film and television editor would offer. It was an opinion we all shared.

"The real artists don't come to New York anymore, there's no need for it," another editor would opine. "They stay right where they are. Just last week San Antonio or Austin, I can never remember which is which, won an award for having America's finest new modern art museum. With America becoming more astute to contemporary art, the whole society that once surrounded it and nurtured it here in New York has been decentralized."

Our discussion was anticipatorily fierce. Editor-in-Chief, Josephine Sinclair, was charmed we'd come up with something so relevant and would quickly announce that the December issue of *Rag* would be coined the "What's Really New" issue. Her new agenda would send each editor and their staff scouring every inch of every New York borough, sniffing out something entirely fresh. If we were to find that nothing really was new, we planned on printing a tribute to the glowering subculture of the late 1950s.

Because of an impulsive theory I'd had, *Rag* was now headed in a sudden new editorial direction. The entire staff's current projects were halted and new ones dispersed. I got a pat on the back from Josey for the idea but was left with the same quandary at the end of the meeting. *What's really new?*

The rest of my day at *Rag* was spent proofing the final stories for the November issue, which we were putting to bed. As I sat there attempting to concentrate on the text before me, my effort was thwarted as thoughts of running home and sleeping next to Ari saturated my mind. Feeling unproductive, I doubled my determination to get my work completed when the phone rang.

"Hello," I drearily answered.

"You fucking whore," Loren jollied, "what is this in your bed?"

"Where are you?" I asked, stunned. She wasn't due back from Seattle for two more days.

"In your bedroom... at *my* house. I just got in." Her voice had the tone of an accusation.

"I'm guessing you're referring to the man. He's my... *friend*."

"It's about goddamn time," she said, laughing relentlessly. "Oh shit, he just turned over, I think I know him." I heard her scoff. "He has a huge hard on."

"What?" I panicked. "Leave him alone, he doesn't get up until around one."

"He's waking up I think," she said, then I heard some giggling and Ari's brusque voice in the background.

"Loren, are you there?" I asked in to the sudden silence.

"Jimmy!" she wailed, "how do you know Ari Schroeder?"

"He works at *Rag* with me. How do *you* know him?"

"He shot me about two months ago for Chanel... or was it Dior? I can never remember. We also worked together for a piece we did with *Allure*."

I could hear her telling him something but couldn't make out the words. She must have been covering the phone with her hand as she spoke.

"This might sound really insecure," I prefaced, "but did you sleep with him?" Loren had a habit of sleeping with photographers.

"No," she sobbed, "but I wanted to. When do you get off work?"

"Soon, I'm almost done. I should be home around three."

"While you're at work I'm going to play with your friend," she laughed childishly. "He looks like marvelous fun," she said using the accent of a 1960s European cinema ingénue she often channeled in photos.

I didn't get back to Loren's house until around five o'clock. At that time I found Loren had ordered Chinese take-out and was eating it with Ari in her movie theater.

"What's going on here?" I asked sitting down between the two. I kissed Ari hello and hugged Loren. Not having seen her in two weeks, to have her back in my life was a comfort I didn't know I needed.

"Just having some chow Jimbo," Ari said with his mouth full of Szechwan noodles. Loren giggled at his accent and the reference to me as "Jimbo."

"Everything swell back in the Emerald City?" I asked Loren. I was curious of how my former metropolis was fairing without me.

"Yep. It's the same old gem we left. It didn't rain a single day I was there."

That night Ari and Loren played pinochle while I called around to her AndersPlace staff members, asking that they return to work the next day. The only person who didn't take my call was Jacques, who was in Moorea. If I was him I wouldn't have answered the phone either.

"What are you doing tomorrow?" I asked Loren. We hadn't spent a full day together in months.

"Are you joking?" she winced, displaying a sardonic scowl.

"It's only the start of the most important week of the year tomorrow!"

"What?" I asked. As someone employed to know these sorts of things it was a tremendous embarrassment not to know the answer.

"Fashion week!" Ari and Loren cheered in tandem.

o o o

New York halts for seemingly none.

Diplomats, prime ministers, kings, terrorists, and celebrities continuously fail in bringing the city to a disorderly pause. But there is one event that always seems to cause gleeful pandemonium all about Midtown: Fashion Week.

In just seven short chaotic days, the fashion world and glitterati descended on Manhattan in order to view what was new on the runway. With my connections to Loren, the biggest supermodel of the season, and Ari, one of the most respected photographers of his generation, I had unprecedented access to the event. I hardly even needed the press pass *Rag* had given me as Lifestyle Editor. With this access and perspective, I was determined to find a story for the magazine that was unlike anything printed before.

My favorite American design house, Uthia (a young SoHo standout that had three years ago launched its New York showing) decided to ditch the tents of Bryant Park for the ballrooms of the Waldorf=Astoria. The design house presented both its men's and women's shows on the same runway simultaneously, something almost no other designer did. New thinking and a general audacity made the label a standout amongst the younger design houses. In the last six months its pieces began showing up at high-end department stores around the world. Its latest collection would determine if its early and uncommon success would continue.

Ari Schroeder was assigned to shoot backstage at Donna Karan, a show scheduled at the same time as Uthia. Loren was appearing in three shows later that afternoon and was attending meticulous fittings all day in preparation for them. I arrived alone at the Waldorf an hour before the Uthia show was set to begin. Being in the hotel made me recall the first day I'd landed in New York. I'd learned so much about the city in just a few months yet still felt strangely distant to the place. The hotel was bustling like always and entering the ballroom was to discover a dominion that had existed all along but I was unfamiliar with. That was just how New York was. This infinite city crammed and compacted on to a tiny island could never be completely explored. Its relentless evolution and progression could never be met. From the sky to the subterranean, Manhattan's internal organs were continually producing new environs. Layer upon layer it grew within itself, building new and refurbishing old. How the immensity was sustained nobody knew.

Most fashion show goers arrive later than requested, as was the case at this show. If it weren't for the hotel's regular patrons the place would have been empty. In the hotel's smaller ballroom, for the sake of preventing boredom, The House of Uthia had organized a museum-style exhibit of all their new accessories. I ogled at each watch, wallet, and pair of sunglasses, dreaming I knew someone-who-knew-someone at the house capable of furnishing me with a piece. At these shows it didn't matter how much money you brought with you, all the designers cared about was clout. If I'd been from venerable *Vogue* and not raggedy *Rag* I surely could have made off with a briefcase full of enviable accessories.

After I cased the small ballroom I took my assigned seat in the larger ballroom where the runway was setup. On my chair I found the obligatory goody bag stuffed with Uthia fragrances, look book, skincare sampler, and coupon for 10% off my purchase at the Uthia boutique on Madison. A moment later people began filling the room, each one more flamboyant and eccentric looking, so many of them dressed in monochrome I thought I'd gone color blind. They all laughed and giggled and kissed each other. I don't think I saw anyone introduce themselves to anyone, they all just seemed to know each other. It made me feel lonely sitting there clinging to my free goods. While I was thankful to have received a gift, those dressed in monochrome shoved the bags off their chairs as if it were garbage littering a seat on the subway.

Right on cue, the room crowded up into a frenzy moments before the house lights dimmed, the stage lights gleamed and resounding techno music pulsated throughout the Waldorf. On stage walked the lankiest models in the most sci-fi costumes I'd seen all season. The model's faces painted white, their bodies sheathed in metallic colors. This presentation was not clothing, it was costuming, something I hated in fashion. As the exhibition progressed I started to bemoan the presentation. Each new item to trot on to the catwalk was a more abstract version of the last, all of it an apocalyptic fashion graveyard. The women's dresses appeared to be cut from foam packing material while the men's ties had the appearance of having been sliced from radioactive shag carpeting. The texturing and concept was brilliant, but these pieces belonged somewhere else. *Did these designers really expect someone to wear this shit on the street?*

The next day every paper in town had a boner for the Uthia show. It killed me to read the unearned merriment. The disappointment launched me into a tailspin of disappointment, something I didn't know fashion could do to a person. I considered if it was possible that I'd lost my usually respectable taste or had lost touch with youth culture. I spent the rest of the weekend at my apartment alone, reading popular fiction from the 1920s. Ari was so busy covering the events he didn't call me, neither did Loren who was busy being the event. On her first runway show of the week Loren was capable of causing a major news scandal when she took to the Oscar de la Renta catwalk wearing a head to toe black burkha. The crowd gasped when she appeared but cheered and clapped when the concealing garment was blown up and off her (Marilyn Monroe style) to reveal only a diamond encrusted bra and panties. The theatrics were immediately noted as fashion history. And for a few days, there was no one more famous or talked about than Loren Anders. The incident was one of those media sensations that took on a life of its own when it caused a cultural debate on the depiction (and derision) of Muslim traditions in the western world.

My letdown at the Uthia show had very little to do with the high-concept clothing but more to do with my own vast expectations. The label was a virtual unknown to the mainstream media outside New York and I was hoping to capitalize on it by exploiting them for the 'What's Really New' section of December's *Rag*. However, the designers at Uthia had suddenly done something fairly tired: a concept presentation. Every designer in the The Big Four (London, Milan, Paris, New York) does this, typically every five years or so. They present a show that is completely un-wearable, un-sellable, and unforgettably genius, and function's only to reestablish the designer as an uncompromising artist after some moderate commercial success. It's not unlike a car company producing a car no can could afford to buy. The purpose was to put vision before practicality and lift the brand to a new artistic apex.

"Fuck fashion," I said to myself as I lounged on my fire escape, watching the sun go down over Manhattan. That evening I trashed the Uthia sampler I'd been given as well as the daily newspapers which heralded the show. Suddenly, I was on a rampage. The expensive fashion magazines I'd bought over the last several months went hurtling down the garbage shaft, then all the New York society papers. Once all the hype was out of my apartment I felt sanitary - cleansed of the endless hype and drama of fashion. "It's all just bullshit," I laughed, watching those glossy pages slide down the trash chute, the beautiful model's faces landing in the most disgusting of rubbish. It was an exquisitely beautiful juxtaposition.

It was too early to go to bed so I sat on my couch drinking white wine and dreading having to go to work at *Rag* the next day. How could I document what was new if I hated everything coupled with such a moniker? The only thing new to me was that fashion no longer mattered. Fashion was unfashionable.

"Fashion is dead," I huffed. The comment would echo. When I said the phrase I laughed, but it began to stir something in my mind. What if a fashion oriented magazine like *Rag* were to print such a phrase on its giant year-end cover? The idea prompted me to imagine what it'd be like for a magazine to scold society for embracing the cliché, retro, recycled shit every design house was feeding to art-starved consumers worldwide. I went to my desk and began brainstorming how I could translate my irritation with fashion into magazine copy. I drew the phrase FASHION IS DEAD across several pages of paper, making a mock cover of *Rag* with the words spread across it. I started a list of everything I hated about fashion in general. In an intense panic I found therapy in itemizing all of my disgust.

Reading the list back was upsetting and revealing. I hadn't described the fashion industry, but Loren Anders. At that time I knew not what to make of my list, knowing if anyone was to read it they'd think of me as ungrateful. For all the generosity Loren had paid me in the months we'd known one another, how could I resent her so fully? But I was obsessed. I was envious of her. She had everything I wanted and the opportunity to have more. Loren had skyscrapers with her name emblazoned across the top of them. She had unlimited fluctuating wealth and enough cash to buy a country. She dazzled me endlessly, reinvented the miserable creature I was into a divinely happy, medicated, louse living in the world's most dramatic of places, New York City.

As if I was crazed, and I don't doubt I was, I began writing the story of Loren Anders, and not just the public profile everyone was familiar with but complete with all the tantalizing truths that would drive sales of her autobiography to the top of the charts if she'd ever finish it. Afraid that one of her legal cronies might stumble upon it I was sure to leave her name out of the story altogether. Instead, I let ambiguity of work its enchantment, while also saving myself the risk of being sued for libel.

I began the story like so:

> When daddy died, he left her the largest inheritance ever. Billions of dollars in cash, and even more billions in assets. With this kind of money it's easy to get what you want. And she has. "Money can't buy happiness," poor people always say. They're poor because they're naïve.

You've seen her on the cover of every fashion magazine known to woman. When she broke up with her last boyfriend you likely saw her in the pages of every tabloid recognized in the gossip crowd. However, it's how she landed on the covers and in the pages of the world's most read publications that might intrigue you the most.

There's no question as to who I am talking about. She is everywhere. If you're at the market you'll probably see her staring back at you in the soft-drink aisle. If you're at the liquor store she's likely offering you up some gin. She's a cover girl, pitchwoman and tycoon. If you're not careful she might just be Senator, Governor, or President someday, as Americans often get their celebrities and politicians muddled.

Her rise to fame and unfathomable fortune is not undocumented. But it is her stealthy alignment of corporate clout that makes her sudden notoriety questionable. With unrivaled influence she changes thousands of lives. Layoffs, acquisitions, mergers, liquidations: it's all in a days work for her.

The story continued in length detailing curious acquisitions the AndersGroup (renamed Xgroup for the article) made during Loren's tenure. Each of the companies acquired had gained major profits after mundane changes of legislation in Olympia or Washington, DC. The article questioned whether Loren was somehow connected to lawmaker's campaign finances and voting records. It was the most scathing, speculative piece of tripe I'd ever written. Exciting, lurid, dangerous — it was all those things. At most it was inflated tabloid entertainment. My pulse raced faster and faster as I continued writing. Everything I loathed about Loren went on the page, whether or not it was truth, speculation, or pure resentment. On paper I was taking a bat to the only person who ever cared about me, and it felt good.

* * *

Fleeing Manhattan for *Rag* in Brooklyn was a pleasant distraction on Thursday. I'd proofed my piece on the "billionaire model" and was ready to hand it over to Josey Sinclair for her approval and insight. I didn't get to my desk until around ten o'clock because I'd spent the first part of the morning making some last minute revisions. When I got to headquarters I stopped by the espresso machine, gossiped with my assistant and ranted to the Fashion Editor about the subsequent duplicity that was Fashion Week.

On my desk I found a note that read: Got plans tonight??? Call me. ~ARI~

Attached to the note I found one of those electronic medallions that unlocked doors without contact. I'd seen Ari use one at his apartment and was so excited to see he had loaned me one. I assumed he'd meant for me to meet him at his loft after I got off work. All day I contemplated over what kind of night I was going to have with him. I wanted to cook for him and pamper him when he got home from work. It was funny how paternal I'd become of him. It was like I was suddenly his domesticated husband wanting to anticipate his every need. As unlike me as it was, it sure felt good knowing someone was looking forward to seeing me. Compared to my job, either for *Rag* or Loren, none of it meant anything compared to my relationship. Not until that moment when Ari displayed his anticipation in meeting me after work did I feel my day had any true purpose.

My feelings for Ari reminded me of the blind adoration my mother had for my father. When I was a toddler she had adopted the role of the archetypical 1950s housewife, even though she was not of that generation. The women's liberation movement had somehow forgotten my mother, and I was glad. How lucky I felt to come from a home with parents who were still married. There was nothing greater than having a mother who was home all the time and whose sole function seemed to be to appease her child. If I got sick at school she had nothing else to do but to come pick me up. If I was scared of something she was there to comfort me. Her adult life had been forsaken to raise me. I felt adored; she likely felt worthless. My mother eventually got a job in a hospital when I was eleven. As tortured as those housewives of another era were, I couldn't help but covet them. How happy it would have made me to able to spend all day at home and have the man I worshipped at work, making a living for us. To tend to his needs, iron his shirts, and make him dinner. Such a role made my mind salivate with envy and idyllic thought. *What could have been so horrible about domesticity that triggered women to burn their bras?*

As much as I wanted for us to replicate the typical American family as best we could, the reality was that I was just a gay guy lusting after his boyfriend. We couldn't marry and in some states we wouldn't even be allowed to adopt children. Any shard of semblance we could have with a straight family was either minute or illusion. We couldn't have what my parents did, but we could try.

OCTOBER

October was my favorite month of the year. Not just because my birthday occurred right at the beginning of it but because the changing seasons were so fierce. It's the time of year where the wheels fall off any remnant of summer remaining and the indications of autumn's arrival are ubiquitous. Afraid that living in a city as dense as Manhattan had made me oblivious of the season's change, one look at browning Central Park convinced me that I had not missed a moment of the earth's revolution.

As I often do when I'm feeling lonely, aged, or just bored, I hauled out my memoirs dating back to when I was seven years of age. If there is one thing I've done in my wearisome life consistently, it's been to keep track of every dull moment of it via scrapbooks, journals and photography.

When I was 14 I wrote a piece for the *La Conner Dispatch* titled "When I grow up...," a recurrent column of stories by students on what they thought they'd be when they reached the era of adulthood. My article read:

> As Hollywood's richest young screenwriter I often can't believe how lucky I am to work with my best friends: Steven Spielberg and George Lukas. I sometimes find they are jealous of my success, having recently won the Oscar for my epic World War 3 film "America The Brave" and having also signed a $1-billion contract to write five films for Warner Brothers.
> And to think I'm a billionaire at age 23...
> Dreams really do come true!

Reading the article as a 22 year-old that would turn 23 later in the month, I was shocked. *Did I really believe I'd have a career at 23?* The article wound up distressing me. There in my hands I had proof of not living up to my own expectations. It didn't occur to me that I had been a wildly imaginative 14 year-old. My only thought was that I was a failed 22 year-old.

* * *

I'm often shocked by ordinary events, such as that moment when you're wiping your ass after taking a giant greasy dump and for some illogical reason your finger pokes through the toilet paper and you finger bang your own asshole (after which you smell your finger in disbelief of what you've just done). In a similar fashion something so shocking happened to me that I really had to consider whether I was conscious.

It began in the kitchen of AndersPlace. I was discussing a work related injury one of the prep cooks had sustained in order to file their claim with worker's compensation. Loren came into the kitchen wearing her pajamas, which wasn't out of the ordinary because it was early Sunday morning.

"Isn't your birthday on Wednesday Jimmy?" Loren pondered with a yawn, opening the refrigerator and exhuming a pitcher of orange juice.

"Yes it is," I said flatly, not wanting to give the slightest hint I was excitedly speculating what she might buy me for the occasion.

"Birthdays are so silly," she said dismissively. I began to worry she might suddenly abolish the practice of celebrating one's life until she continued. "I mean a person goes 364 days and they only get *one* day to commemorate their birth? Their entire existence is worth but only one day?"

"It's how it's been for centuries," I said.

"Fuck centuries," Loren spouted, "and fuck this town."

"What's wrong?" I pleaded, her temper rising as she poured herself a glass of juice. She furiously swallowed an array of supplements that had been laid out by her nutritionist who came by the house twice a week.

"Did you know the other day I found a poem on the street?" she asked so angrily I considered she was opposed to poetry in general.

"Poems are nice," I said, attempting to pacify. "You sound upset."

Loren marched out of the kitchen and returned several minutes later with a tattered shred of paper that read:

When I was a zygote,
My mommy said to me,
"Honey, I'd give birth to you,
but I don't have the money."

I never had a mother,

I never had a dad,
When I got incinerated at the abortion clinic,
It really made me sad.

"That's bizarre," I said stoically. I wanted to laugh at the poem but it didn't seem right to do so, given the subject matter and how upset she was by it.

"Yeah, it's bizarre," she vented, "It's also disgusting."

In the past several days Loren had come down with a nasty cold. She only had herself to blame, having foolishly shared a cigarette with a trampy Finish model while at Paris fashion week the previous Wednesday. Loren would confine herself to her master suite, only emerging randomly for meal requests. At these times her mood was tense and flippant. I had prepared to spend the day quietly doing my typical house duties of conversing with her staff on the state of the household and minding all the tiny details. But suddenly she insisted we fly to Miami Beach.

"Let me call my property manager," she said. "I think I have a house in Miami Beach. I'm not sure. But it doesn't matter… it's in Florida. Birthdays should be celebrated in the sun. Not this bleakness."

My jaw figuratively dropped to my toes as Loren retreated to her study to make some calls.

"All I got for my birthday was ten grand, cash," the prep cook mocked as I put Loren's orange juice back in the refrigerator. "You get a week in Miami?"

"There's a hierarchy here."

"Obviously," he assessed.

Loren did indeed own not just a home but an estate on the island of Miami Beach. Not six hours after she suggested we flee grim New York for beaming Miami, we were there, sipping cocktails on the palazzo of her Ocean Drive villa. As a special birthday wish I asked Loren if Ari could come with. She responded, "I'll murder you if you don't bring him along. For god's sake, you can't be the only person I talk to my entire life."

For some reason I'd always thought of Miami as a Los Angeles on the other coast. But after a quick limousine tour of South Beach and the Deco District my preconception was radically changed. Miami was a town with strong Latin and Caribbean flair, of fervent tropical characteristics and its own mamboing pulse you felt the moment you landed at the airport. I loved Miami immediately. It felt foreign, exotic, a little too hot, crowded and disorienting. It was everything a vacation should be.

"How many houses do you own?" Ari asked Loren as we bathed in the dimming sun. I was embarrassed by his pedestrian question, though I wondered the very same thing.

"I don't know!" Loren giggled at her own ridiculousness. "Property is just such a good investment, especially in America. It's foolish to ever liquidate it. My dad collected houses. I think he had one in every state that touches an ocean. Except Louisiana. He hated Louisiana."

"What's wrong with Louisiana?" Ari asked. As a former Alabamian he happened to love the state, especially New Orleans.

"I don't know. He was a *crazy* man," Loren testified. "Crazy-brilliant you know. Like those rocket scientists who can design a probe to mars but can't manage to comb their hair. That kind of brilliant. He had all sorts of prejudices, especially against certain companies. He wouldn't drink Florida orange juice and refused to drive or ride in a General Motors vehicle."

The sun sank behind our heads and the air temperature began to drop quickly. Inside Loren showed us the villa's great atrium where we sat to have drinks before going out to dinner.

"Jimmy, why haven't I ever met your parents?" Loren asked. I was stunned by her sudden interest in my family.

"They're farm people," I said, shrugging. "They don't get out much."

"I keep forgetting you have parents. I guess I've become so used to not having a mom and dad I just assume most people are without them," Loren said. "I want to meet them. Fly them to New York, we can all meet there!"

"They won't come to New York," I laughed. "They don't care for airplanes. Or cities."

"Then Seattle," she squeaked undetermined. "We'll meet them in Seattle."

"They won't go there either. They're not like us, they have lives."

"Farm lives?" Loren brooded over what a simple agricultural life spent harvesting the land would entail. "How peculiar."

"Do you know you're gay?" she asked. She had to have already known the answer to this.

"No. They don't," I said infirmly.

"Why not?" Loren asked with alarm.

"I'm discreet," I offered.

"They're your parents. Shouldn't they know?" Ari appealed.

"No, I understand it," Loren permitted. "It's really nobody's business. I don't go around telling people I like it up the ass. So why should he?"

"Actually, he doesn't," Ari said. This caused Loren to erupt in laughter. I was humiliated listening to my two closest friends assess, however briefly, my sexual inclinations.

"If I had parents I wouldn't ignore them," Loren put in.

"I don't ignore them!" I retaliated.

Ari, always mitigating, changed the subject. "Loren. Is it true your parents were assassinated?"

"Not officially," Loren explained, "but everyone and their grandma knows they were. Helicopters like theirs don't just explode and fall out of the sky."

"The uncertainty must really both you," Ari proceeded. He dared to ask her things I never could.

"Yes. But I have to live a life. And besides, if my parents were alive I'd probably be stuck in some miserable Ivy League school studying Latin or economics. Instead I'm having the time of my life being a fag hag in South Beach!"

• • •

On Monday Loren met some of her model friends for an all day party on her Atlantic Ocean yacht, the *William Anders*. Ari and I tagged along to ride jet skis, following the yacht as it travelled south to make a loop around Key Biscayne. I'd never ridden a jet ski before and would never have imagined they were so much fun. Like riding a motorcycle on water, the little watercrafts were as enjoyable as a rollercoaster. It was like no other October afternoon I'd experienced before, bouncing along the warm water off Miami Beach in tropical bliss.

Tuesday, the day before my birthday, Loren arranged for her helicopter to be flown from Manhattan to Miami in order for us to take an aerial tour of the Florida Keys. Upon our return in the afternoon, we met a prominent Parisian fashion designer in Coral Gables at the Biltmore Hotel for lunch. Loren and the designer were discussing a possible acquisition of his fashion empire into the sprawling AndersGroup. Far from a formal presentation, Loren made promises of corporate autonomy and full artistic control, something any creative business person ensures whenever they're being electively gobbled up by a massive bureaucracy. No matter where she went, Loren was always on business.

That afternoon was spent on Loren's yacht playing cards while we sailed out to North Bimini, one of the islands of the Bahamas. There we ate dinner and headed back to Miami Beach late in the evening. The following day, my birthday, we lounged around the pool at her house and went out to dinner downtown. It was low-key, private, and special, just as I had requested.

Thursday I got up early before either Loren or Ari and snuck out of the house. I wanted to see Miami on my own, secretly despising the filter of Loren's luxurious environment. My hopeful frolic around Miami Beach was tainted by one event: rain. A small tropical cloud had burst above the city and sent concentrated showers down upon stunned early morning beach goers and myself. Knowing the rain would soon pass I stood underneath a booze billboard propped up along the beachfront.

The drizzle sent everyone running indoors. Unafraid of the rain, I enjoyed the desolation it had created. The sudden change was so charming I left the cover provided by the billboard and strolled down the beach, soaking up the hot downpour. In so many ways it resembled a steam shower. The rain on the surface of the beach and pavement created a scent both floral and mineral. It was unlike anything I ever smelled and can still remember. I would always be able to recall that smell.

I'd been walking for several minutes and began to crave a cup of espresso. Looking around for a place to get some, I noticed I was not alone on the beach. A peculiar young man, my age and height with the same slim build, was walking my way down the stone beachfront path. He carried with him an umbrella and wore the most eccentric attire I'd seen in months. His pants were black dress slacks, like those of a man's suit, cropped to just below his knees so they looked like long shorts. Beneath those he wore tall cross diamond socks that stretched up past his knees with sporty black loafers. His shirt was a dark sleeveless pinstripe, accented with black neck tie with a dove silhouette near the tip. The oddest accessory, his belt, appeared to be constructed from woven coaxial cable. On his head sat an audacious bowler hat, his eyes covered by enormous rectangular sunglasses. His ensemble was so out of the ordinary I would have taken his picture had I a camera on me.

I stopped walking down the beach just to marvel at this boy's garb. So fresh and inspiring I actually caught myself taking mental notes of the outfit in order to reproduce it for a *Rag* photo shoot. As the boy passed me I wondered who he was and what he was doing, for most men around these parts wore only swimming trunks, maybe sandals. I figured he surely had to be someone of distinction, like a designer or artist of some kind. I should have stopped him, but I didn't. I just let the oddity pass when I should have told him just how well he'd put himself together.

The peculiar boy was gone before I could ask him anything, probably for the best. I ran back to Loren's villa and began making sketches of the boy's dress. The glasses, the belt, the hat, the stripes on the pants and shirt... it was a masterful bundling. As I sketched in the guest bedroom where Ari slept, I could hear the hissing of the espresso machine in the kitchen. After a few moments of cementing my visions in pencil I raced downstairs to find Loren, peacefully mixing a cappuccino and reading the *Miami Herald*. (The scene shocked me initially; I didn't know Loren Anders could make her own coffee).

"Hey kid," she greeted me between yawns.

"I just had the greatest inspiration," I spouted.

"With Ari?" She laughed at her own crude joke.

"No," I growled. "I went for a walk, alone, and saw this guy walking down the beach. He was wearing all black, some pinstripe, it was *so* minimalist. When I get back to *Rag* I'm going to ask to set up my own photo shoot. "

"Minimalist," she said, "like Prada?"

"No. It was very American. But not in the stark Calvin Klein way. Maybe *edited* or *tailored* are better words to describe it."

"Hmm," she tried to envision such a thing. I showed her my drawings and she, the maven of Fifth Avenue, granted the look as "innovative."

"When are we going back to New York?" I asked with anticipation. As great as Miami was, I wanted to get to work in capturing my vision in the pages of *Rag* immediately.

"Saturday," she said as if she had randomly picked a day off the calendar.

"Oh."

"But if you want to go back right now we can," she said with a yawn.

"Okay!"

"Oh thank god," Loren cheered. "Since Tuesday I've been dreading how bad this week long birthday idea was! I'm not as generous as I thought I could be."

I raced upstairs and packed all of Ari's and my things. I gently roused Ari, dressed him (he was much too hung-over and tired to do it himself) and put him in the car. I took one last gander at Loren's villa and the beautiful surroundings of Miami Beach, feeling grateful in a way to the town. She was, for the most part, a warm and tropical oasis who'd reenergized my creative soul. I'd found what was really new… in Miami. This realization furthered my opinion that great things were taken to new York and rarely originated from there. It was by every measure an imperial city.

. . .

By the time we touched down in New York I'd crafted a collection of 30 drawings for my new fashion concept of stark simplicity molded from outdated business attire and obsolete technological peripherals. I gave the concept the name of Apocalysm (a melding of "apocalypse" and "minimalism") and drew figures of women clothed in dresses made of mouse pads and cell phones; men's suits stitched from the cloth of woven printer cables; hats for both sexes made from emptied computer terminals.

Loren and Ari took her limo to Manhattan but I was so excited by my potential fashion find I took a cab directly to the *Rag* headquarters in Brooklyn. Inside the old firehouse I found towering piles of packing boxes on every desk. I immediately assumed we were finally moving to an adequate office in Manhattan. I looked around for the Fashion Editor but couldn't find her. In fact I couldn't find any of the editorial staff, only some of their assistants. I wandered into Josey Sinclair's office to find her on the phone, sullen, discussing "the new magazine." I assumed she was referring to a new upstart threatening to take all of *Rag*'s readers. This was a recurring fear of hers that we'd all heard before. She was the most insecure woman I'd ever met.

On Josey's blank desk I arranged my drawings.

"*This* is what's new!" I declared as she hung up her phone.

"How was Miami?" she asked, avoiding my drawings.

"Marvelous. Look at these, it's pure craziness, it's wonderful, I saw this boy walking down…"

"Jimmy," she interrupted, "the magazine is done."

"You finished the December issue already?" I asked. She shook her head.

"No. *Done*, as in bankrupt."

"How?" I begged. Hearing the word 'bankrupt' immediately made the veins behind my knees itch and my stomach pull at me. It was a feeling of sudden weakness I can only liken to an intense, sudden hunger. I appealed, "Why? It sells. We have more advertisers than ever!" I shrieked.

"At the beginning of the year our financiers told us we had twelve issues to prove we could stand on our own. Circulation is stagnant, any extra money we had was used to fend off a lawsuit, and our advertisers don't like the fact we openly bash their products in our copy."

What Josey was saying didn't exactly surprise me as much as disappoint me. The magazine was making waves, it was controversial and a lot of people believed it to be too forward-thinking for a mass audience to understand. This was a fatal problem for a publication that relied solely on mainstream advertising for revenue. It now appeared the waves it had caused were making it capsize.

"But it's popular!" I appealed, "Everyone is talking about this magazine."

"Everyone in New York is talking about it," she conceded.

"I know! So how can we be bankrupt?"

"The rest of America is not reading *Rag*, they're reading *People* and *Us*. We don't have celebrities in our magazine."

"That's what makes it so great," I said.

"The whole of the country doesn't give a shit about what New Yorkers read. As a matter-of-fact, marketing studies show that many Americans avoid magazines that emphasize New York culture."

"They're idiots!" I raged.

"No, we call them 'consumers' Jimmy." Her traditional business thinking was infuriating. To try and appeal to everyone meant appealing to no one.

"What about the December issue?" I asked.

"It's now our farewell issue. About half the editors quit upon hearing the news. The other half called in sick today. I have no doubt they're at job interviews right now."

Rag had folded. Not because it was a bad magazine, but because it couldn't find readers. The bookkeeping disarray caused by its break from a giant media network had sealed its fate. The little magazine I loved had gone in to cardiac arrest, the office of disarray and moving boxes its corpse. Its fearful editorial staff fled immediately in search of new work, many clamoring to the same media giant the magazine was a former property of. With only one department editor remaining, myself, I was provided the largest and most influential opportunity in my lifetime.

Josey loved the article I'd written on Loren, calling it foreboding and daring. She agreed to place it in the magazine's "Journal" section. The rest of the December issue was embryonic in its development. Prior to their departure the staff failed to turn in any articles for the News, Entertainment, and Media sections. I suggested to Josey, who was busy looking for a new job herself, that we do a retrospective issue, to which she said with little anxiety "fine, whatever." In seeing how unconcerned she was with the direction the magazine went for its curtain call, I knew then the final issue of *Rag* magazine would be my primary responsibility. Within the day I summoned all the assistants into the tiny boardroom and discussed the direction of the final issue. Unlike the whiney editors they worked under, this piece of the staff listened, took notes, and understood my direction. At the end of the business day *Rag* magazine had its final issue, if only in concept.

On Friday the staff of *Rag* was given formal written notice of the magazine's undoing. The letter we all received stated there'd be one more week of paid labor and everything after that was voluntary. Without the bureaucracy of running a staff partitioned into nine departments, everyone at the magazine was reporting directly to me. This new, scaled-down team had created the final (and finest) issue in just four days. This leaner staff meant I had much greater editorial power as no one in the room became a voice of dissent. Within a grateful whim, I would erase the story which proposed to fictionally expose Loren Anders as a ruthless tycoon lining the pockets of famished politicians. Some things, like friendships, did not seem to be worth risking for the sake of avant-garde journalism. When the story was gone from the magazine I couldn't believe how close to recklessly ending my friendship with Loren. I was on the brink of ruining the only thing that had any continuity in my life.

The cover of the December *Rag* was a portrait of a dark, wistful looking forest made not of trees, but skyscrapers. In the center of this photograph a young, faceless, idyllic couple, wearing the wardrobe I'd envisioned on the way back from Miami. They held hands as they walked, incredulously examining the treacherous landscape which enveloped them. In giant-bold letters across the bottom half of the cover read the phrase: WHERE IS THE NEW?

NOVEMBER

The most frustrating aspect of falling *out* of love with someone is when neither party intends for it to happen. Both people can strive to find the spark that once made their romance so intoxicating, but eventually must recognize that much of the relationship's original lure to be its random, unforeseen happening. Ari Schroeder and I found ourselves in just such a happenstance. No longer were we lovers but close friends who cuddled and occasionally had sex. After the fall of *Rag* he too was forced to find a new job, a task which took up much more of his time than either of us would have estimated. Despite being a photographer who'd experienced a lot of success, and even a bit of notoriety, Ari found his talents to be in greater supply than they were demand. Sadly, such artists were abundant in Manhattan. Just like *Rag*, most magazines were scaling back their budgets due to a reduction in print advertising. For someone as expensive as Ari, a man who didn't have to work to pay the bills, this resulted in a sabbatical for him. He was averse to taking any sort of pay cut just to land a job. He had a certain worth, whether or not someone was actually willing to pay him what he wanted. If nobody did, he would do what any artist did in lean times: compile a book of past work.

Ari's growing resentment toward the city and all urban confluences erupted after he was turned down for a job at *The New York Times Magazine*. His frustration materialized in the form of him screaming at me for not making reservations in time to snag a table at Carmela, a new Italian restaurant he'd been talking about for weeks. Rejection is a fact of life for every artist. But for Ari, who hadn't heard the word "no" in ten years, he dealt with a string of rejections poorly. He became artistically frustrated and lost his ability to visualize what it was he wanted to shoot. When he came up with the idea to leave New York I was supportive, even though it pained me to think of him leaving.

On his last day in Brooklyn, I arrived just after dawn at his loft to help him cram a cab full of the nominal essentials he was taking back to Alabama (clothes, photo equipment, mementos, and artwork). The entire time we spent disassembling his already stark apartment I fought off a torrent of unexpected sentiment. There I was, aiding in the departure of a man I almost certainly loved, helping him return home to a place that for me had no allure. I couldn't help but think what could have become of our relationship if *Rag* hadn't collapsed, if I hadn't been beholden to Loren's every need, and if he weren't in the city he despised. Certainly we could have found a common ground and a way to make our relationship work.

"You must really love your family," I told Ari, "to move all the way back to Alabama for them." I couldn't comprehend doing the same. Yet for a moment as I thought about it, the farmlands of my youth, quiet, still, unchanging, and always serene were at once a remote and tranquil escape from New York. I longed to return home, if only for a moment to absorb the serenity and flee the moment it was captured.

"I don't know," he observed, "I think a break from the city will be nice."

"What about your career?"

"There are plenty of things to photograph in Alabama."

"Trailer parks," I said. This was probably the meanest thing I could have said.

"See! That's why you should come to Alabama. You don't know anything about it," he replied, making me feel like a child.

If I'd been older and in search of settling down I suppose I could have thrown myself into a relationship with Ari and moved to Alabama with him. It may have been divine living together and starting lives as one. But what we shared, even from the very beginning, always felt temporary. When we began seeing each other I didn't know where the passion could take me, but never held the idea of spending a great amount of time together. Maybe it was my self-doubt, the feeling he was too good for me, or it was just that I knew, somewhere inside me, our relationship would deteriorate.

Ari Schroeder returned to the only place he'd ever known as a real home, Birmingham, and became a father figure to his niece and nephew. The two of us would keep in touch by email and occasionally talk on the phone. I never resented his decision to leave New York. He was a gentleman, a fragile soul, a gifted artist and the first friend I'd made in New York City.

. . .

We Americans are a strange bunch of people.

On an ordinary fall Tuesday afternoon the federal government raised its national terrorism threat level to the second highest on the rainbow colored chart of potential danger. By that evening, in the face of fundamentalism and fear, New Yorkers from Staten Island to The Bronx made it a point to celebrate their liberty and ability to throw a party for almost anything. Young, beautiful, delighted creatures would frolic with great drunken hysteria about the shining cityscape in search of the flashiest locale they could unearth. Their faces, marbled in glee, as if never knowing of heartache, would sing and joke as their accompanying bodies would dance and move, ostensibly never ceasing. This unabashed carousing was fear driven, but any New Yorker would argue they were only praising their freedom. The only sexuality present was one of heightened disregard of social mores. Everyone danced with everyone, regardless of sex or stature. "This is Freedom!" a drunken teenager would shout at a homeless man just before puking in the gutter he was sleeping in.

Loren Anders was celebrating something extraordinary herself. She'd purchased what was being considered this century's greatest new painting by America's only prized young painter whose name was on everybody's lips. Titled *Generation Why*, the painting was seven feet high and nineteen feet wide; the size of a Times Square billboard. Sold to Loren by Sotheby's four days early at the cost of $11.7 million dollars, she honorably battled buyers from the Pompidou, Tate, MOMA and Guggenheim for its title, gloating in her victory by taking all the buyers from the museums to her new restaurant, L'Anders NYC, on the Westside.

"It's like being swept up into an urban storm," Loren dallied as we stood before the painting in her new gallery wing. "I feel like I'm inside it, being thrown about the city." Loren's depiction of the work was acutely precise: a battlefield of skyscrapers, flames, heavens, sky, pedestrians, cars, river water, subway trains and masses of debris tumbled about without gravitation, as if they were inside a giant Earth-sized laundry dryer.

"I think you've described it perfectly," I said. Every additional moment I examined the painting I found something new, a tiny little detail that would alter the veiled meaning of the piece. The piece was so detailed you could even make out the headlines on the newspaper a tiny woman read as her subway car split in two.

"Look at the time!" Loren flailed as I remained immersed in the canvas. "We have to go."

In Loren Anders's armored limousine we sailed with police escort to the Financial District to her secretive Billionaire's Society meeting inside the basement of the New York Stock Exchange. The limousine was directed into the garage of the building where we were lead on foot through a labyrinth of tunnels until we arrived at the discreet entrance of the society's own swanky club, The Platinum Room.

"I apologize in advance if this is a little…" Loren began to spiel.

"Mysterious?" I interjected.

"'Sedate' is the word I was going to use. These people can be a smidge conservative," she explained. I detected satire in her voice.

"You're clear," a security guard declared. We were lead by a concierge through a set of double doors into the most thunderous and lavish ballroom I'd ever witnessed. Before me lay an arena of round tables sheathed in glittery silken linens where Wall Street's power players dined, uproariously bickering and amused, entertaining their wives, husbands, life-partners, mistresses, escorts and other discreetly sexy playthings. The entire room was awash in silver and light. They called it the Platinum Room because every fixture, wall covering, and ceiling ornament sparkled with a glossy metallic sheen.

As Loren lead me to her table, the only empty one in the joint, I noticed this strange club had a large stage flanking one end which was sheltered beneath black curtains bejeweled with crystals. Just as we were seated a triumphant orchestra burst into play, the curtains began to rise, and an army of a hundred bejeweled chorines danced across the stage. A radiant, intoxicating tingling ascended my spine as I watched the lights, the girls, the orchestra and the dazzled spectators. It was a scene of much desired distraction.

"Jimmy, I believe we've entered a new era," Loren whimpered in my ear.

"In style?" I asked.

The dancers on stage galloped in intricate formation about the stage. Their costumes, glittering silver ensembles, looked as if they'd been inspired by a 1920s vaudeville vision of the 21st century.

"No. A dangerous new era," she said, her voice sounding ominous. "Look around us. None of these people have any reason to be celebrating. We're in a time where the actual and real is not observed, only the desired. People only acknowledge what they want or like. This is the era of illusion."

"Loren," I eased, "that's how it's always been. People are fools. Get used to it."

"You may be right, but I don't want to be a part of it."

Loren's statement was cold, but laudable. We were in the middle of an occasion without reason. It was a dinner without companionship. Our circle of friends had just two ends, Loren and myself. The table that seated twelve had but two diners and it was lonely. Despite the solitude, we enjoyed the jolly show. The dancing ladies were themselves of a different age – one of shining glamour and infinite optimism. We all needed a little optimism. But not all was at peace with my closest friend. Loren was suspicious, as if she'd taken a wrong turn somewhere and was now contemplating how she'd arrived in such a queer neighborhood. After one drink she excused herself and I would watch her approach the restrooms but then exit through the same way we entered. I tossed a wad of cash on the table and chased after her. Outside I could see her running down Wall Street towards Broadway. I was now running as fast as I could after her as she scuttled up the Canyon of Heroes.

"Loren, what's wrong!" I bellowed, slowly catching up to her just as we came to City Hall Park. As I put my hand on her shoulder to try and calm her she collapsed in my arms, crying and laughing in concert.

"I don't know what's wrong with me Jimmy. I don't know what I'm doing. I just feel so..." she had no more words.

"Trapped?" I said bluntly. Prior to this I'd never known Loren to be depressed or unstable. To witness her crumbling was like learning of an outrageous falsehood.

"More than you know," she confessed.

"I know you do," I said. I held her for several minutes as she cried. We sat down on one of the benches next to the gates of the park. "It's can't be easy."

"No. You're wrong," she countered. "It's too easy and I've cracked. I have it so much easier than ANYONE!" she shouted with livid anger. Loren was castigating herself for becoming the rich party girl, the cliché out-of-control debutante. "I'm an alcoholic. I'm on every anti-depressant they make... and it's not a good combination. Just ask my twelve doctors," she laughed pathetically at her joke, attempting to cover the anguish.

The next morning, Loren Anders, the face of a thousand brands, would retire from modeling by firing her agent and dispatching her assembly of lawyers to the various companies in which she had contracts with in order to negotiate her escape. For the following ten days she would isolate herself inside her Fifth Avenue mansion with a nurse, visited occasionally by her one remaining physician. Her ever vacillating staff of aides would be put on leave. I, her only companion, waited with great impatience at my apartment, ready at a moment's notice to run on foot over to her house the moment her rehabilitation would be complete.

In an effort to empathize with Loren, I concealed myself to my own apartment during those ten days. In the tight quarters I would deliberate with great introspection as to how I'd casually permitted my friend to nearly over-indulge herself. I was amused watching her drunkenly cavort about her glamorous world, never recognizing my heroine as a mortal. She must have blamed me, I thought, having encouraged her in many instances to heighten the hedonism. I'd been both her coach and cheerleader in our indulgences.

In the isolation of my apartment I reflected on how we'd both stumbled. As a great philosopher once proclaimed in song "…we are living in a material world." I could not agree with her more. Whenever I hear someone complain about these modern times as being too violent or depressing I really must laugh. The other night I caught myself watching *The Seven Year Itch* on my computer in bed while eating ice cream between sips of a butterscotch macchiato. We live in such absurdly luxurious times that for someone to complain about it is entirely foolhardy. American life is so easy. Everything is insured and assured. We have so many options, securities and conveniences that many people have become devastatingly complacent. Today may carry the moniker of The Information Age, but it often seems no one pays any attention to truth, solely drama. As we've cautiously penetrated the 21st Century, the "material world" philosophy has changed. No longer are we living in a materially obsessed world but a society obsessed with cachet, where the only thing that matters is not the consummation of excess goods but the appearance of being prosperous. It doesn't matter if you're rich, only that you *look* rich. Truth is irrelevant, perception matters most. Misperceptions are as valid as reality.

During the days I waited for Loren to rid her body of the numbing substances she'd become addicted to, the capacity to enjoy relaxation and intense meditation would become mine. Everyday I'd wake moments prior to dawn, stumble to the door, and get the newspaper. For someone like myself who worshiped technology and every advancement in communication America and Japan could wheedle, finding I enjoyed the process of digging through the gangly, oversized pages of black text seemed a setback. The newspaper, so old and ill-innovated became my favorite and only connection to the outside world. Groceries and anything else I needed from the outside world were delivered. And for ten November days I was a recluse who no longer indulged himself on booze and good times, but the intoxicating, if slightly dated, words of Hemingway and Fitzgerald, discovering these giddy and hyped times of extreme ambition and anesthesia nothing but a replication of the Jazz Age.

. . .

On an unusually dewy Monday morning at the site of the AndersPlaza on Manhattan's east Midtown, river water found its way through the site's cement barriers in one explosive surge. Eight of the building's lower levels were submerged entirely. The building's inner scaffolding would collapse entirely, drowning six workers and injuring over 100. After a media debacle and enormous public quarreling, the AndersPlaza project was altered from a lustrous 1,000-foot glass phallus into a dirt-filled hole covered with topsoil and shrubbery. It would later be renamed AndersPark. The event would completely alter the way the public viewed the AndersGroup Corporation, especially on the East Coast. The company would within days decide to cancel its eastward realignment from Seattle to New York. In the aftermath of the disaster, the Board of Directors would hastily oust Hubert Redding from the position of Chief Executive Officer. For days cable TV news would foment scandal over leaked internal email in which Redding berated the City of New York, specifically its process of ensuring work safety at construction sites. Strung together they provided a narrative that the AndersGroup CEO was willing to sacrifice worker safety in order to complete a project on time. Highly reactive to bad press, the board of directors met in a midnight session to address the uproar. Within a few hours of deliberation they voted to replace Hubert Redding with Loren Anders. Yet at the time Loren was unaware of the disaster, as she was in the midst of rehab treatment. Four days post-catastrophe, Loren emerged from her isolation to face the gruesome news, tranquilly attending all six funerals and tirelessly visiting the scores of workers hospitalized. She would console the families, widows and fatherless children, offering her sincerest and heartfelt commiseration. Like all moneyed employers who face the adverse death of their workers, Loren began writing bereavement checks to the families of the workers who'd been killed before any litigation could start. Beyond money, she provided personal comfort to the families affected by the disaster. She spent hours meeting and consoling them and helping them move past the disaster in every way she knew how. Her experience in losing her parents seemed to help her bond with those she reached out to. Mourning the loss of those killed in the AndersPlaza disaster inadvertently became Loren's first act as CEO. Her second was to cancel the project outright.

Considering she was a former party girl, the media was considerably fair to Loren, never once insinuating her to be uncaring for the victims of the AndersPlaza disaster. Her well-timed secret detox made it appear as though she was so distraught over the calamity it took her four days of grieving to publicly accept the loss.

After hearing of the corporate uproar at AndersGroup headquarters in Seattle, I knew Loren's departure from New York City was imminent. What I did not anticipate was her excitement of being elected as CEO. Never before in the history of the company had the shareholders shown their confidence in such an overwhelming manner for Loren. But as shareholders often do, they voted with their pocketbooks, not on a vision or principle. AndersGroup, for reasons much more psychological than factual, had seen its stock plummet and then ascend from $42, to $16, then back again to $38, all within the past year. Investors were weary and demanded a steady hand at the helm of the company. No matter what ex-CEO Hubert Redding did, it was the opinion of most shareholders he was only keeping guard while Ms. Anders was primed for the seat of Chief. Now with the status of celebrity and the ability to raise the price of shares every time she made an appearance at an AndersGroup function, Loren was not simply a figurative leader but one in absolute terms.

The media coverage surrounding the AndersPlaza construction accident would only heighten Loren's image as an emblematic capitalist. A report began circulating that Loren sold six-hundred million dollars worth of her personal property during the AndersGroup stock slump in early August to raise the funds needed to purchase nearly 33-million shares of company stock. The purchase increased her share of all stock to 83 million shares, or 29% of all shares outstanding. This was during the same time CEO Hubert Redding was selling off, decreasing his share in the company to less than a half-percent. This widely read account of Loren's maneuvers during a time of great stress for the company resulted in a wave of good hope toward her within the company. Hundreds of cheering employees would greet her arrival at AndersTower the day she reported for work as CEO.

• • •

Before Loren left New York for Seattle to assume her role as CEO of her father's company, she invited me over for a feast on Thanksgiving Day. The city was preparing for its first snow storm of the season. Not a single flake had fallen on Manhattan yet snow plows and ice melting equipment could be seen accumulating in the park and along busy avenues. The excitement of living in The Center of the World had somewhat dissipated and I'd dreamt of taking some vacation from my eternal job as Loren's personal assistant. I dreamed of going to Paris again, or anywhere in Western Europe. There remained so much left to be discovered on that great continent I couldn't wait to arrange some time off to explore it.

After her detox, Loren began acting much more congenial toward her employees, including me. She was having me work only 20 hours a week, instead of 80, and insisted I attempt to find work at a magazine like *Rag*, declaring that I'd never appeared happier than when I was employed in the field of journalism. As the year's end began its approach I began an internal monologue, one screaming of determination to forge a truly independent life. I'd freed myself from caffeine and wanted to do the same with anything else that was doing me harm. This would mean no more free rides from generous billionaires, no matter how glamorous and amusing they were.

The Upper East Side was cold and desolate as I treaded across East 90th and up Fifth Avenue carrying a homemade cheesecake. The moments in Manhattan when everyone was seemingly inside sleeping or out-of-town were some of the most cherished times I'd experienced there. To have New York City to one's self is incredibly empowering in so many ways. AndersPlace was equally barren. The guards had the day off and after passing through the automated security gates and entering the mansion I'd thought possibly Loren had already left town. I wandered about the endless quantity of rooms as I'd done so many times, sadly examining all the items which had been either packed up, shipped to storage, or sold at auction. Sadly, the mansion was no longer to be a private residence. Beginning in February the building was slated to be converted into six floors of AndersGroup offices with a multi-level penthouse for Loren on the top three floors. The ultimate New York townhouse would be no more. Her era of exorbitance was over. In the economic downturn the futility of AndersPlace would with sudden befuddlement be realized.

The sound of a whirring electric mixer startled me as I moseyed through the defunct art gallery; the giant *Generation Why* mural conspicuously absent, likely leased to the Louvre. Following the sound of the mixer, I found Loren in the kitchen mixing the batter for cranberry muffins, all the while preparing, by hand, our Thanksgiving dinner. Always one to wear the right attire, Loren donned a red and white swirl hostess gown beneath her chic black chef's apron.

"Jim!" she welcomed, wiping her hands on a cloth before hugging me. I couldn't remember the last time she called me anything other than 'Jimmy.'

"You're cooking," I proclaimed.

"Yes," Loren sang, "I love to cook."

"Since when?"

"Since I discovered it was fun. You brought a cake."

"Made it myself," I replied. "When in the world did you find time to start cooking?" The moment I said it I felt moronic. Loren, reading my shriveled expression, only smirked at the ill statement.

"If you'd like you can set the table," she offered. Loren pointed to sets of silver and china stacked at the end of the kitchen's center counter. I took the plates and went into the former solarium just off the kitchen, now a small dining room emptied of its foliage.

"There are seven settings!" I shouted back into the kitchen.

"I know," she returned. "We're having guests."

Five guests? Five *mysterious* guests? Why didn't she tell me we were having guests?

"Who?" I inquired

Loren came into the solarium as I distributed the elaborate sets of silver.

"It's a surprise," she said, batting one eye.

Great! She'd gone and invited the five Seattle eccentrics, the young and opportunistic who'd clung to Loren for career opportunities. Didn't she know they sought her for this reason? I figured now that she was headed back to Seattle she probably started attending their inept dinners again. Not a very good idea for a recovering alcoholic.

"A surprise?" I lamented.

"Yes. You'll never believe who's coming to dinner," she gushed.

I followed Loren back into the kitchen after finishing the table arrangement. I watched as she pulled a giant turkey from the oven, gave a stir to her two variations of gravy, decorated a vegetable tray with garnishes and cut my cheesecake up and placed the pieces on individual dessert plates.

"Turkey?" I moaned.

"Yes. I shouldn't deprive our guests. And if I'm giving up alcohol then I'm eating meat."

"Sounds fair to me."

The doorbell chimed. Our eyes met at once.

"Did you want to get that?" Loren asked.

I grimaced dreading the presence of the inevitable reunion.

"Not really," I said.

Loren glared at me with disappointment. I followed Loren to the foyer. Cheerful murmurs came through the doorway. Whoever it was at the door sounded awfully excited.

"Here we go," I said to myself, preparing for the onslaught of vane, narcissistic personalities. She opened the door and there was silence. Then I heard Loren introduce herself.

"Nice to meet you," I heard her say without seeing who it was she greeted. Inquisitive, I approached the doorway to find five strangers, all of them either teens or early twenty-somethings, dressed rather feebly, their faces inscribed with such eagerness on I suspected they were performing some sort of prank or singing carols.

"Everyone, this is my friend Jimmy," Loren introduced me. "He'll be having dinner with us."

With uncertainty I peered at Loren, unknowing of what she'd arranged.

"Jimmy, this is Brian, Andy, Jenny, Erica and Anthony," Loren cautiously recited their names as if just learning them herself. Intent on remembering their names I carefully looked at all five of them, repeating their names in my head. The five seemed amused when I shook each of their hands. What unexpected formality they probably thought, coming from someone their own age.

Hostess Loren led the six of us into the kitchen after taking everyone's coats. Giggling emanated from the five as they witnessed the scale and grandeur of the house. Perpetually insecure, I initially believed they were chuckling at me.

"Would anyone like something to drink?" Loren tendered. Their reaction to her offer was unsure. I could tell they all wanted something but did not know how to decipher between what would be considered common or outlandish.

"I'd like some sparking apple cider," I said.

"Okay," Loren said. "Anyone else?"

The five strangers approved of my beverage suggestion. As Loren fetched the drinks I took the guests into the garden lounge, a sitting room off the solarium decorated in excessively floral wallpaper and paintings of extravagant flower arrangements.

"This is so beautiful," Jenny gushed. I affably suggested the five of them sit down and they did. Their manners were precisely restrained, like they were afraid of breaking something. Other than Jenny's comment none of them spoke and I found the time waiting for Loren's return with the sparkling cider overwrought.

"I'm curious," I ventured, "how is it the five of you know Loren?"

They all looked at each other with bashful uncertainty. Loren entered with champagne glasses filled with cider and I continued to await reaction.

"Loren," I reiterated, "I was just asking our friends here how you met."

Loren smiled graciously but paused before responding. Serving the glasses, she replied "at the 72nd street youth hostel. I was there last week, volunteering, and I thought how wonderful it would be to have some company for dinner. You know, even company as amusing as yours can be a bit tiresome Jimmy."

The guests laughed anxiously at her joke.

"What is a hostel?" I asked.

"An inexpensive hotel," Loren replied.

"Not exactly," said Brian, the ashen lank with a shaved head. "It's a homeless shelter."

"A homeless shelter?" I foolishly pondered.

"Yes. We are all homeless… for the time being."

"But you're so young," I mulled. My verbal alarm did not embarrass me as much as it did Loren. I had to question how five rather attractive yet unkempt young adults who showed no sign of mental illness could be without a home. "I apologize if I sound uninformed, but how did you become homeless?"

"Jimmy!" blasted Loren. "That's so rude to ask."

"I'm sorry," I retreated. "I'm just stunned."

"No, it's fine," insisted Anthony.

With eloquent brevity, each of the five enigmatic guests described the unfortunate and erratically malicious events which led to their homelessness. With surprise and fascination I would listen as they recounted, without pity or blame, the events. Brian, a New Jersey runaway told of how his parents had become irate after finding he'd smoked marijuana with a school friend and how their strict religious views had been a catalyst for his leaving home. Andy, a Californian who'd traveled to New York City to be an actor, revealed he'd been in foster homes throughout his life and was struggling to make it on his own. Jenny, a Yale dropout, confessed of her own irrepressible mania and depression which she cited for her self-emancipation. Erica, a goth chick from Idaho with a tattoo of barbwire encircling her neck, angrily illustrated the guilt and frustration she felt while growing up a closeted lesbian. And Anthony, a young man with such polish and beauty it was a tragedy no one had found him and loved him, chronicled his life as a simple mistake. His mother, a teenager with strict Catholic parents, would give life to him and abandon him at a convent in The Bronx. He would drift from one home to the next, continually forgotten by each of the families who'd housed him, until the age of 16 when he decided to no longer allow a family to let him fall in love with them and then find some excuse to return him to the state's custody. By the time I heard all their stories I couldn't help but feel like the most fortunate person in the room.

Loren served the perfect Thanksgiving dinner. It was lavish but homey and I questioned if she'd secretly had it catered and staged the whole scene of her mixing and baking things. For two hours the seven of us would feast, laughing over the silliest topics of conversation. To my fascination I'd listen to Andy as he theorized the cause of the many misconceptions of America in Europe and the rest of the world. Jenny and Erica took an interest in Loren's haute couture while Anthony and

Brian played billiards in Loren's game room. The night was a splendid and gratifying affair. I was so proud of Loren for inviting these wondrous kids to dinner. How real and unique they were, so genuine in their speech, free from the overtly elaborate tales most Manhattanites spiel incessantly on with. These five new friends knew not of Chanel or Cristal, they cared only of survival and a greater wellbeing and to be offered equality and a chance to succeed. I was greatly intrigued as they described with downright joyful, almost nostalgic words, their follies on the streets. How hard it was to eat and remain clothed. Behind every bush and down every alley lurked a predator. They were animals in an inhumane cityscape fending for themselves, their survival the result of clever thinking and luck. Yet it was not heartbreaking for them, it had become a merit, a conquering. Detecting their wistful remembrance made me aware these five homeless stragglers were most likely homeless no longer. After a long chat over my lauded cheesecake, the guests would leave and I would ask Loren of her offerings to them.

"I'm going to give them jobs at the company," Loren prided. "I'm taking them back to Seattle with me."

"I can tell they're excited," I confirmed.

"They are. It's the first time anyone's treated them fairly. No one has ever told them they are worth something."

Loren scooped up the dessert plates from around the table as I collected the silver (I counted each piece, making sure none of the visitors had made off with any of the invaluable French tableware). In the kitchen we loaded the dishwasher and I began to prod the motives of Loren's rapid transformation from hedonistic supermodel to the personage of humanitarian.

"How exactly did you meet them?" I asked. "I've never heard you mention your visits to homeless shelters."

"A couple days ago I was feeling real down. Like I had no purpose in life. So I went shopping, because shopping usually cheers me up. I was over at Gucci, looking at heels and handbags. I probably spent more than most people make in a year or decade, and it did nothing to lift my mood. When I left the store I was completely breaking down, like never before. I began thinking I might have something psychologically wrong. But outside the store there was this boy asking for change. Gucci was having a sale and I probably saved three hundred dollars. So I gave the boy the three hundred dollars and he just about had a heart attack. He was so joyous. So thankful. He hugged me even. And for the first time in… I don't know how long, I felt good about something I'd done with my money."

"So what happened after that?"

"I asked the boy his name and he said it was Brian. The same Brian you met tonight. I told him to come with me and that I was going to help him. And he told me he couldn't, that he would lose his bed at the shelter if he wasn't in by six o'clock. So I had him take me to this shelter. It was a real sewer of a place. He introduced me to his friends, who were the other four we dined with tonight. He kept raving about how generous I was to them and they thought I was a goddess or something. I became so spellbound by them I arranged to have them excused from the shelter in order to have dinner with us tonight."

"They could have been sociopaths!" I cautioned.

"No, I made sure of it. I met with the shelter manager before arranging the dinner. They're the finest you could ever meet."

"I see… only the best transients for Loren Anders will do!"

She laughed and we retired to the living room to finish off the cheesecake.

"Can you imagine what it must be like to be orphaned at birth?" Loren proposed, "To never know your parents is like never being able to look in the mirror. To never be able to see what you're made of."

"You were orphaned. You should have some idea," I noted.

"Yes, but I was practically a grown woman when they died. I blossomed early. Their deaths were premature but in a way, a very slight way, I'd prepared myself for my parent's mortality."

Imagining what it must have been like to be an orphan didn't interest me. But Loren seemed transfixed by the topic, almost as if she wanted to confront me with such a disposition.

"Jimmy," she began her confession, "I've been keeping something from you and it's about time you found out."

"What?" I barked, terrified at what it might be.

"I've been calling your mother regularly, updating her on your status," Loren said. "I don't appreciate being lied to! She says you never call, you never email her. I've never been as close to someone as I've been with you, yet felt betrayed by them at the same time."

A haze of disbelief began to envelope my conscience as I listened to Loren and her revelation. I wasn't sure if I was betrayed or relieved. I was mad at Loren for her secrecy but also mitigated in my worry for my parents. If she'd communicated to them the status of my wellbeing then it was one less thing I had to apologize for when I saw them again.

"Loren…" I began to protest but then lost my words. I was going to apologize but I had nothing to feel sorry for. "You don't know my parents."

"I know they love you," she rallied. "I know you're punishing them for something they didn't do."

"I'm not punishing anyone! I just need to be myself. When I'm around them I feel like a child. How can a boy become a man if he's constantly reminded of his childhood?"

"How can a boy become a man if he's oblivious to his collective life?"

The hostile atmosphere began to suffocate me. I left Loren and made my way out on to the solarium's terrace which hung above Fifth Avenue and Central Park. The park at night was a giant rectangle filled with lit ribbons of paths, unoccupied by humans, as if the wilds oppressed by day overtook the park nocturnally.

"How could someone leave this?" I asked myself, looking at the skyline of the Upper West Side across the vastness. To my left a few miles down the avenue Midtown stood frozen like a giant tsunami of stone and glass, threatening to crash down on the asylum of the park's greenery.

I heard Loren's footsteps on the terrace behind me.

"What's wrong?" she asked.

"Just thinking," I said. "I needed some air."

Loren put her arm around mine and we both stared out at the park. It was so quiet. The holiday had managed to drain the streets of inhabitants. It was a momentary pause in activity as shoppers ready for their traditional American shopping gorge would certainly choke the city's shops and thoroughfares within twelve hours. Emptiness followed immediately by abundance. This was a city, and country, which celebrated such polarity.

"I can't believe you're leaving New York," I said to Loren. Saying it out loud made it a reality for the both of us. My face began to warm and the tear ducts of my eyes began to tickle.

"I know," she replied, "I feel like I just stepped off the jet. Just last month I finally got my New York State driver's license. I was just starting to settle in. And now I have to pick up and move again."

"Don't you ever get sick of it? Do you know what it's like to love a city? To fester in it… to not leave its confines for months?"

"How boring," Loren snapped. "A city is just a city. There are hundreds of them. And the more I travel the more they all look the same."

"You can't be serious. There isn't a city in the world that even closely resembles New York."

Loren sighed tiresomely. "So I suppose you'll miss it?"

"Miss what?" I professed.

"New York," she stated. Her face began to change as she contemplated my response.

"Loren, I'm not leaving New York," I said. She stood there staring at me without expression, digesting my statement. "You could stay here. You don't have to go back to Seattle," I pestered.

"I have responsibilities!" she snarled.

"No you don't!" I countered, "You're one of the very few people in the world who has absolutely no responsibility. You don't have to do anything you don't want to. Nobody ever told you to become a model and you were a success at that."

"No I wasn't. Modeling was a huge mistake!"

"No it wasn't!" I redeemed, "your drunken exploits made you a household name. Ten times as many people know you than knew of your father."

She contemplated my statement, its truth irrevocable. Even delusional Loren could not deny she'd managed to ascend to the top of the jet set hierarchy. As she thought for a moment her body changed. She went from poised elegance to inebriated slouch. I had worn her down.

"It'll be perfectly fine," Loren granted. "You can be my East Coast society arbiter. My man in Manhattan!"

"You're not upset?" I asked sensing she was obscuring her disappointment.

"I can't blame you for wanting to stay in New York. This place can corrupt a person. Don't you feel like when you're in New York City there is no world outside? That the whole entire planet has converged on this island?"

"Yes," I rooted, "I feel exactly that. It's why I don't want to leave."

"I'd stay here if I could, but I can't," she said. "No matter what you say, I have responsibilities."

"I know," I contended, "I'm sorry. I shouldn't have said that you don't."

"Honey, if you're not going back to Seattle with me then you can stay here at the house. I've had nightmares about that apartment of yours."

"What!" I entreated in disbelief.

"The permits and all the planning for the renovation won't be done until after the New Year," Loren explained. "I'd have to hire someone to keep the place up anyway. If you're going to be in town and on the payroll it must be you. You know the place better than anyone."

My jaw dangled from the top of my mouth as I processed what Loren was proposing. For me to live in her house, if only for a month, became the most salacious idea conceivable.

"Are you serious?" I gasped.

"Yes. It just seems wasteful not to use a place like this," she replied. This comment was really facile as the woman had a dozen villas, mansions, and castles strewn about the globe going unused.

Just after dawn on Friday, the woman who'd transformed my life beyond my ability to comprehend, ascended from the territory of New York and returned to the place she'd found me. Watching her jet take off and vanish into the wintry gray sky stirred an unwelcome feeling of reprieve and nervousness. I identified this emotion as abandonment.

December

With my best friend Loren Anders removed from the glitterati scene of New York, and Ari Schroeder, my first love, back in Birmingham, I discovered myself completely alone in the city. With nothing to distract me from making it on my own, and a multitude of opportunities now available, I decided to start a new version of existence.

The place I rented on First Avenue had been a rare find and a great first Manhattan apartment. But no matter how charming or homey I thought it felt, the truth was that the place was a dive. The clunky faucets and other fixture were all older than I was, the patchwork of parquet needed to be refinished, the drafty windows may as well have been made of paper, and the walk to the subway, a mere ten blocks, suddenly seemed too far to tolerate. I longed for both modernity and classicism; a place that embodied both traditionalism and newness. Curious to see if I had the monetary wherewithal to exit my lease, I collected from all the pockets in which I'd stored my Anders payroll cash. After 40 minutes of recalling where I'd stashed all my funds and another 13 minutes of counting all the bills, I amassed within the boundaries of my unassuming apartment $33,640.71. Anxiety overwhelmed me as I shoved the outrageous gob of cash into a used Saks bag and made my way for the bank. It was stupid, I knew, to have stashed so much money in my apartment. The place could have burned down or ransacked by hooligans. As I tried to covertly walk down the street without looking as though my Saks sack were stuffed with currency, my awareness of everyone on the street who happened to glance at me became suddenly heightened. Anyone could be a mugger, I considered, staring down haughty dog-walkers, nannies pushing strollers and the various street vendors. Even little children, dressed in formal school uniforms, I considered a threat.

The bank teller did not give me a second glance as I propped the bag of money on her counter. After looking at my bank receipt and balance, which read $51,070.98, I rejoiced. Ever skeptical of dramatic events and realizations, I attempted to calculate how it was I'd saved so much money. With my salary from Loren I deemed I'd made about $90,000 since being hired in the spring. With my panic of being pursued by the IRS, I'd stashed about half of all my earnings until I learned through Loren's accountant that my taxes had already been withheld from my generous salary, so when she said she'd pay me $3,000 a week she was talking take home *after* taxes. But my short-term memory loss would reactivate itself and I'd continue pinching pennies. Then there was my *Rag* salary, which I'd spent none of. I'd kept the magazine's money sealed away in the fear they'd find I was not a journalist, just a boy posing as one, and demand their money back.

After paying my last month's rent and the fee for breaking my lease, I began to visualize how I'd pack up all my belongings. I owned nothing of great, irreplaceable value. The truth was I'd become tired of moving and thought how brilliant and eccentric it would be to simply stuff everything down the trash chute (except the sofa). And how can one call it "starting over" if he retains all the items he had in his former life? So I sent all my glassware, flatware, pillows, music, movies, and even couture, down the chute. I did not experience the anxiety of loss or severance, but of release. Those items, I thought, belonged to someone else, a Jimmy Minor who no longer existed: a frivolous, boyish, insecure and careless youth who drifted around in the indecisive winds of other beings. He was no more. I was now a lone adult. Independent. Eager. And ready to leap on any opportunity that presented itself.

A pungent sense of emptiness stimulated me as I left my apartment building having thrown every material belonging away. I marveled at how quickly my material life had been disposed of. It was as if I'd died and someone, a stranger, hired by my family or the city, had come to cleanup my unit so some other drifter fresh off a bus or plane could rent it. A wave of contradiction and contemplation struck me as I began to discern fulfillment from having nothing of permanence. Literally, I'd just thrown my life away. How could something so apparently major be so easy?

Walking the streets of Manhattan was therapy in itself. The random, hectic streets somehow provided so much distracting madness that thought and introspection was inevitable and cyclical. I was so filled with contemplation when I arrived at AndersPlace that I didn't go in. I continued down Fifth Avenue with my thoughts and when I arrived at Washington Square Park four miles away, and what seemed a fraction of a moment later, I felt I was in a meaningless and vacant realm. Nothing in my life meant anything. Nothing was happening. At that moment there was pause and reflection only. No decisions were due to be made.

No tasks waited fulfillment. It was an interlude, like that of a Broadway show, where the curtain and lights were down but the audience is fully aware of the dozens of people backstage assembling sets and changing costumes. It was the midst of one of life's intermissions and the bell which summoned the second act could only be anticipated.

• • •

As I began my stay there, AndersPlace became haunted with the chill of barrenness and sting of recollection. I could feel its prestige had somehow dithered as The Lady of the house was no longer in residence. The brushed nickel moniker that read 'AndersPlace' was removed from the entryway the same day Loren left. To imagine her lush quarters being stripped and converted into banal offices made the manor seem perishable. To enjoy such luxury, knowing its existence was in peril, made staying at the home not a chore, but a responsibility. The beautiful marbles, tiles and ornaments all had their executions before them. To not enjoy their final days would have been a criminal act.

Considering that I only owned the clothes that I had on, I walked to the nearest department store and restocked my wardrobe with minimalist pieces of blank T-shirts, classic sport trousers, black shoes, and a black wool coat. The whole look cost less than a thousand dollars, a priding achievement as I'd committed myself to curtailing my wild spending. I wanted to live for as long as I possibly could on what I had. Every instance where I spent less money than I could have was an affirmation to a modest, sustainable lifestyle.

The moment after I stocked the fridge of the mansion, the Tri-state region was struck with a blizzard (something the news was calling a "Nor'easter"). I'd never seen as much snow as that which fell on Manhattan that first week of December. I questioned how a city so close to the wide-open Atlantic could muster such a cruel winter. The snowstorm would last for three days, shutting much of New York down. Because four feet of snow buried the tracks of many above ground rail lines, it caused many trains to remain underground in Manhattan. Rail service to the boroughs was discontinued and many employees were unable to commute to work. The thick white sheath did not deter me from exploring my island, and as anyone would do, I headed straight to Times Square. There I found absolute desolation. Plows had carved a path for cars on Broadway and sacrificed Seventh

Avenue as a dumping ground for the masses of snow. Snow melting machines, which looked like heated trash dumpsters, lined most of 43rd Street but were completely unable to keep up with the snow. It fell faster than they could melt it. The thick, wind-swept powder had clung to almost everything, even the kinetic billboards and towers. But one billboard eerily lay naked from the snow: that of Loren Anders wearing a tiny red dress, holding a giant bottle of Coca-Cola. What a fool she was, dressed so skimpily for the blizzard. I thought of calling her and telling her how ridiculous the billboard made her look, but then considered it was only five o'clock in the morning in Seattle. Instead I snapped a picture of the billboard and sent it to her.

I walked up Broadway, across Central Park South and up Fifth Avenue until I arrived back at AndersPlace. Before going inside I crossed over to Madison Avenue to one of the resilient street vendors and bought the latest issue of *Architectural Digest*, *Vogue*, *Vanity Fair*, *Elle Décor*, *Harper's Bazaar*, *Vogue Hommes International*, *The New York Post*, *The New York Times* and my baby, *Rag*, in her lustrous final print. For the next day-and-a-half I sat alone in my temporary mansion and scrutinized every word of these publications, worshipping design, beauty, and style. I began to feel isolated and broke free from my haven and began a touristy romp through a Manhattan still buried and decelerated. I spent a day at the Metropolitan Museum of Art, then a day taking in the Empire State building and Statue of Liberty, then a third day patronizing the Guggenheim, Whitney, and Museum of Modern Art. A second blast of snow hit Manhattan and the folks who ran the Broadway shows began liquidating tickets. Continuously opportunistic, in a matter of two days I'd catch three shows and win tickets to the Holiday show at Radio City.

After completing my sightseer's tour of New York City, I returned to AndersPlace for a day of relaxation and had one of the masseur's from the Bliss spa visit me for two hours of profound cosseting. When I went to bed that night I couldn't decide what I would do the next day. Shopping had no appeal and neither did spending the day alone watching movies and reading magazines. After putting on my robe over my pajamas and my wool coat with sneakers, I went to the roof of AndersPlace. From the top of the mansion I could see into the prewar apartment building next-door as well as the entire length of Central Park. The night was cold and my original impulse was to go back inside. But I decided I would stay out on the roof until it was too cold to function. This was a perch I'd recall the view from for the rest of my life. And so for over an hour I dangled my legs off the side of the steeply pitched cast iron roof of the landmark. Then it began to snow again and I watched as the white flakes slowly glided on to the ground, the buildings, and me. How vulnerable those little things were, so much like myself. I found it captivating to watch as these elaborate little structures crashed furiously into giants, melting and seeping into them, becoming whatever it was they hit.

I was like a snowflake, melting in to whatever I came in contact with.

Back inside I lay in bed questioning the direction in which I was descending. Why it was I'd thrown all my things down the trash chute. Why I was alone. And why aloneness was becoming my inevitability. But it was not loneliness I desired, but loneliness that I was accustomed to. My reclusion was an attempt at normalcy, not satisfaction. Rarely did I choose isolation over socialization out of preference, but because of familiarity. I did not know my parents as well as I would have liked, nor did I understand Loren and the manner in which she determined her actions. Baffling me most was why I'd let others determine my trajectory. It was my parents who sent me to college, thus my forlorn lifestyle in Seattle. It was Loren who'd harvested my ambition to become the ultimate personal assistant living in New York City. And there I still was, clinging to the life which I'd loathed and rejected. This had to have been a process of mourning unavoidable change.

Sleep was now obtainable. And the next day the snow that had once stressed the city's affairs was suddenly gone. Unsure of what to do with myself, I filled my time with meaningless errands like running out for the newspaper, buying different varieties of herbal teas, and patronizing the independently run galleries of Chelsea. It was a dull existence I would maintain for almost two weeks until I deemed it too tedious to continue. Now too frugal to buy a good time with my hard-earned stash of cash, I took to looking for employment. In the ads of the *Village Voice* I found a listing for "Artistic Photographer Wanted!" After calling the number on the ad and discussing with the elderly and progressive Upper Westsiders who'd placed it, when they listed "artistic" they actually meant "adult." This did not faze me. I'd done plenty of racy stuff during my tenure at *Rag*. So what if my new work had a couple wrinkles?

Wilbur and Prudence, the couple who hired me for their explicit photo session, had no idea how much to pay a photographer for erotic work. After some careful bargaining and me showcasing my fresh, avant-garde portfolio, the three of us settled on a fee of $3,000. I would snap portraits of innocent societal upheaval: Wilbur fucking Prude on their dining room table, Prude blowing Wilbur on their balcony overlooking Riverside Drive, and my favorite, Prude wearing a nurse's outfit as she gave Wilbur (wearing half his genuine antique military uniform) a sponge bath and a hand job. In the 21st Century this kind of kink wasn't anything to blush over. I was just relieved no shit was involved.

With a new wad of spending cash I hit the town, dining at every restaurant the *New Yorker* was recommending and taking in every Broadway show, no matter the ticket price. The money was gone before the weekend arrived and I went back to AndersPlace with a familiarly glum temperament. For three days I would raid the annals of the video store on Lexington, refreshing my fondness for some old classics while discovering some contemporary sensations I'd somehow missed in the last couple of years. It was in-between one of my dashes to the video store that something dreadful occurred. After returning to AndersPlace from having just picked up a restored edition of *A Streetcar Named Desire*, I came across a squadron of carpenters measuring and inspecting the interiors of the mansion. An AndersGroup property manager had let them in to the place without informing me beforehand. These men were polite in the least, making all sorts of racket as they dragged their ladders and chattered ignorantly at full volume. When I introduced myself as the house sitter they assumed I was just another hired-hand who could be put to work. One of the men, a loutish Turk with sun damage who I assumed was the boss of the group, told me to roll up all the "fu fu" rugs around the house citing the potential slipping danger to the workers. After rolling up only four of the carpets I quietly made my way upstairs to the bedroom I'd been staying in where I began feverishly packing up my clothes and other few belongings. With two suitcases in tow, I went down to the service stairwell and out on to the street. After catching a cab on Madison I told the driver to take me to the Waldorf. At the hotel I checked into a suite and unpacked, all of this occurring less than twenty minutes after being told to roll up the rugs.

Having checked in under the name Paul Varjak for the sake of a thrill, I felt like a felon or adulterer in my superfluous hotel room. I unpacked my clothes and brushed my teeth, then put on my tennis shoes for a stroll around the city. As I walked down Fifth Avenue in front of

Rockefeller Center I was fortunate enough to witness a squatting woman piss in front of the Atlas statue, her urine running the width of the sidewalk so each passerby would have to leap over it. The brownish-yellow stream created an impressive curtain of steam that rose from the sidewalk as it traveled. A headache set in from there and at once the traffic, crowds, and the blatant attitude from every facet of the city became offensive.

I continued walking southward toward the Empire State Building and on my way would come across the New York Public Library and Bryant Park. Opposite the park on the exterior window of a skyscraper's lobby was a giant mural, on it rows and rows of beautiful flowers. There in front of me were hundreds of acres of infant and blooming tulips splayed out before a rustic barn. Behind the barn were the ragged edges of a giant mountain range. "I know those mountains," I said aloud, standing in a crowd of busy New Yorkers who must have figured I was just another crazy bastard of the street, that is if they noticed me at all. I wondered how many of them had ever seen a mountain in real life. It felt good to see real mountains. The only ones in New York were made of glass, steel, and concrete.

Standing in front of the monolithic fresco brought a torrent of familiar and calming ambiance to the moment. I'd seen this work somewhere before, though I'd never been to this building prior. I knew everything in this picture, and as I stared at the tattered barn I realized it was my dad's barn - those rows and rows of tulips were my family's flowers. This giant picture in the middle of Manhattan was of my parent's bulb farm. This was not just my parent's home, but *my* home. In the crowded city of New York the home I grew up in stood as a representation of something peaceful, a sanctuary. This giant mural announced to everyone who walked by it "This is tranquility! This is the goal, this is why you're working your ass off every day. Dream of this, it will motivate you!"

I left Bryant Park taking comfort, knowing with one phone call and a short airplane ride I could easily have something, evidently, New Yorkers envied. I had been born in to a world that others coveted.

Oddly curious, I found in my wallet a card which could be redeemed for a flight to New York City from Seattle. I received the card after I asked for a refund on the airline tickets I'd purchased with my credit card. I took a cab out to the airport to see if they'd let me redeem it for a trip to Seattle. The nice lady at the counter said she could "work something out," and then asked me when I wanted to fly out. I told her "ASAP" and within two hours I was onboard the last flight of the day to Seattle. The clerk at check-in was suspicious why I didn't have any luggage. I told him another airline had lost it. I had left all my belongings somewhere on a curb in New York, where they belonged.

Over Colorado or Wyoming, somewhere, I realized New York City now epitomized a failed aspiration. The place I considered to be my promise land, the urban paradise I dreamed of inhabiting and living was just a myth; another lie I'd created to make myself feel more glamorous and elite. It seemed for everything New York City had going in its favor it had something else lacking, making it just another bland locale I'd grown tired of. To grow tired of New York felt treacherous.

It was night, but I couldn't sleep on the plane. We had yet to land but I could already feel a sordid wave of humiliation overtake me. This was failure. I had failed and I was running home. I could just imagine what all my hick relatives were thinking to themselves. What a stupid little faggot I was to them. My dad would always say, "You can take the boy out of the farm, but you can never take the farm out of the boy." I really hated the saying because it could be manipulated to any circumstance and was entirely hackneyed. Another reason I loathed the statement was because it was true.

As I recall, the entire flight I worried about what people would think and whether or not my parents would hate me, as I was certain they would. I never even told them I dropped out of college, fled Seattle, became damn-near bankrupt, and then met a girl who changed my life but not in the way they'd assume or hope. But it did feel good to be back in my hometown. When we landed I could smell Seattle. Not that she's rank, she just has a scent about her. She was the smell of home. You don't realize it has a smell until you take a vacation and you come back and it smells like home. It was a fresh smell. I guess the constant showers kept her smelling fresh, even a bit piney.

As I exited the aircraft in a procession of tired travelers I would watch in amusement as two old hillbillies (the man in a Members Only jacket and tattered slacks; the woman in a polyester dress she'd bought at J.C. Penny circa 1986 for an Easter Sunday celebration) would literally pounce upon me as I exited the terminal. They were my parents. My mother cried and my father hugged me so hard I felt my ribs crack. The entire flight home I'd swore they'd disown me and blame me for emancipating myself. I feared they assumed that I had shunned them and their lifestyle. There in the middle of a crowded airport I never felt so loved in my life. And even though they had no interest in New York City — or any large city for that matter — they were still interested in my adventure. My father asked "did you have fun ruining your life?" It was callous but the three of us got a laugh out of it.

When we got to the parking garage I saw my dad's aged pickup truck waiting for us. This truck, an old Ford farming rig, was as old as I was. I considered making a joke about the truck but decided against it. Saying, "I have pairs of pants that cost more than that thing," didn't seem right to say, even though it was true. Being snide was no longer my style.

On the way home we passed right through the heart of downtown Seattle. I anticipated having spent so much time in colossal Manhattan it would make Seattle seem insignificant, but it didn't. Seattle still felt luminous, rising, and thriving, a city with boundless objectives. It had no permanence to it like Manhattan. And even though my parents didn't say it to me, Seattle did seem to whisper "welcome home." The town's sparkle seemed to be furthered as I saw so much under construction. Tower cranes lined the avenues of downtown and it reminded me of my childhood when my father would take me to the Washington State Farmers Convention, back when Seattle was still making a name for itself. Before me was not a "boomtown in flux" like I'd read in the *New York Times*, this was a thriving city that'd determine its own fate.

As our old pickup truck continued up the freeway and past the downtown core, I could see over the skyline to the radiant Space Needle shimmering in its array of spotlights. I then grasped, for the first time, the reason I loved the Needle so much. It was not the tallest or most famous landmark in the world, but it was the most motivating to me. It was a monument to the future whose elegance was not impeded by giant steel girders attempting to break a world record; it was a stirring vision of objectives, not a patronizing declaration of superiority (i.e. the 1,889-foot-tall AndersTower twelve blocks south of the needle). The Space Needle was reserved and timelessly stylish. For a moment I felt it represented me perfectly.

Through the rambling suburbs we drove for nearly two hours. Few words were spoken during our drive out to the farmlands of my hometown. I'd forgotten how dark the night can be in the country and how dazzling the stars could shine on a clear night. How alive the desolate landscape can make a person feel, even one as perpetually lonesome as myself. Early in the morning, hours before the winter sunrise, we arrived home. In the living room our Christmas tree stood. It was puny and decorated with ornaments whose worth was far more sentimental than aesthetic. As sorry as the tree looked, it was the most beautiful one I'd ever seen. It was the same fake tree that had been present in our living room during the holidays since I was a baby. It's metal and plastic branches shimmered with a cheap glint and I wouldn't have changed a single about it.

"Where's Shadow?" I asked. I was expecting my dog to leap out of some corner at any moment wiggling her tale and slathering me in kisses. She would have been just as happy to see me as my parents were.

"She passed Jimmy," my dad muttered. "Just before Thanksgiving." I could see a palpable ache in both my parents' eyes. For them to watch our beloved Labrador pass away without her being able to say goodbye to the only person she cherished, me, must have been difficult. To hear that my childhood companion, and our only pet, had left this earth while I was busy chasing whatever it was I pursued in the city only cemented the idea that I had made a mistake in not keeping in contact with my parents. Nearly a year had passed since I'd seen or spoken to them and it was all my doing. Out of selfishness and a yearning to be my own man, I had walled myself off from those who raised me. I must have expected I could return to the place I was raised and nothing would change. In returning home I found that everything had changed, only the appearance of things had remained constant.

My parents went straight to bed but I remained awake, sitting on my bed in my perfectly preserved bedroom examining all my old belongings. I'd always thought it demeaning to return to the formidable cradle of my upbringing and adolescence. Being in the room, so intact and representative of the day I left, made me feel as though I'd traveled through time. Almost as if the Jimmy of four years ago would burst into the room at any time and find the Jimmy of the future inspecting his belongings.

The walls of my room were densely covered in movie posters and magazine clippings of musicians I'd idolized in high school. Those same musicians were anonymous today. Between the splattering of posters were postcards I'd collected over a decade of romances with big cities. These postcards heralded the skyline of New York, the architecture of Paris, and even the not too distant allure of Seattle's subterranean and famous happenings. So strange it was looking at these postcards, knowing that when I hung them on my wall I was audacious enough to forecast my voyage to these exotic places.

As I examined the cards I found myself removing one of them: New York City. I placed the postcard in the trash, not wanting to be reminded of the city. To me, New York was now a wasteland of disposable trends and incessant hype. It was also a lover who'd broken my heart, a place who'd discarded me. I would return to New York triumphant someday, but in the meantime didn't want to be reminded of it. The postcards of Rome, London and Paris remained as I felt I'd never visited them. My stay in Rome was less than eight hours and my transitory memories of Paris were indistinguishable from those of London. For a foolish and temporary moment I could not separate my memories of Trafalgar Square from those of the Place de la Concorde. I would need to return to those cities if only to reconcile my memories of them.

I turned off my bedroom light, took my clothes off and laid down on my bed. I closed my eyes and struggled to drift off. As I attempted to doze I heard a strange, repetitive sound. It was my breath, slowly inhaling and exhaling, making a slight noise. It was an insignificant wheeze, nothing unhealthy, just the sound of the air going through my nose. I wondered if this was new but grasped "no, this is just the noise you make when you breathe." I thought it was funny, living in the city with the constant noise of something, be it a raucous neighbor, sirens, traffic, garbage trucks, subway trains or just the hum of all things in motion. All the urban noises had made me forget I made a tiny little sound when I inhaled. In a way living in the city had made me feel a little less human.

I found in the passing days, when normalcy and calm returned to my life, I no longer felt humiliated for returning home. I credit this new outlook to my parents who, to my surprise, told me how proud they were of me for coming back home, saying I made the right decision when things became emotionally difficult. My father even said, "It sure took some pretty big balls to move to New York by yourself." I didn't tell my parents about Loren Anders. They had no idea that the Loren that would occasionally call and email them about me was the famous billionaire from Seattle. They assumed the reason I returned home had something to do with my finances. I didn't tell them of the money I'd earned, only mentioning I could pay them rent because I'd brought a little "New York money" back home with me. They liked that.

Being home again was a relief in so many ways. Everything was familiar, nothing was rushed, and there was very little to do. I'd never been so happy just sitting around being bored. I found it strange that in the crowded city I felt so alone but now out in the country I felt there was a new companion with me – an almost metaphysical one. It wasn't a multiple personality, imaginary friend or anything partially psychotic, it was self-awareness. I had failed miserably in my rebellion and at age 23 was moving back home with my folks, again. This was humility. Everything I thought I knew turned out to be either a delusion or a farce. The ambitions I once had now seemed so distant, so imprudent. Suddenly starting over made it seem like it would take a lifetime to conjure up new dreams of success. But what else can one do out in the countryside surrounded by nothing but fields of gorgeous tulips?

What helped me the most in returning home took place that first night back. As I was lying in bed, my mind became too active contemplating feelings of regret and humiliation to sleep. I turned on the bedroom light and sat up in bed. I looked at the wall covered in postcards from cities and countries worldwide. I noticed one from my Aunt Suzanne that she'd sent me when I was in ninth grade. It proclaimed "Greetings from the top of the Sears Tower in Chicago!" Knowing there remained an abundance of remarkable places I'd yet to discover was comforting. But being in the heart of the center of nowhere – home - suited me best just then.

I closed my eyes and laughed at myself. The City had embodied acceptance and prosperity, the two accomplishments I desired most in life. But my journey, proving ineffective, could now be regarded as a cowardly jaunt. I'd been running from my parents for so long it then appeared bizarre how welcome and acknowledged I felt being back in my old bedroom.

Whenever a dream of mine is broken I do not scoop up the pieces and attempt to hastily reassemble what I can. Instead, I leave the pieces there, broken and scattered for future travelers to witness and take heed upon. Fortitude and determination are worthless without the knowledge of when to retreat. The journey toward contentment is not one steady leap but a series of conflicts and victories. Despite my regrettable pitfalls, this journey was a success in so many ways.

THEREAFTER

The death of Loren Anders was a shock, not just to me, but the entire world. As a woman who exemplified modern glamour and American capitalism, it was almost unreal to think that someone so untouchable was mortal. Until her death I did not know how many people she was beloved by. Crowds would gather in front of AndersGroup buildings from Sao Paulo to Shanghai to pay their respects. Having seen crowds protest AndersGroup construction projects in Manhattan and elsewhere, it was odd to see the world mourn the loss of somebody they seemed to revile, not adore. In death it was exposed that far more people appreciated Loren than deplored her. So many people, more than I had ever recognized, viewed Loren as a friend they didn't actually know. The world's fondness for her, something that only became apparent to me after her death, was one I didn't understand at first. But as time passed I came to understand that people identified with her not because they saw themselves in her, but because they saw who they wanted to be in her. Something Loren often said, and something I would ridicule and roll my eyes at, was the anecdote "extraordinary people live extraordinary lives." As extraordinary as her life was, her death was probably the most spectacular.

Only a few weeks had passed since I'd returned home from my follies in New York. During those weeks I got the chance to celebrate Christmas and New Years with my parents and family. I was actively looking for a job but in no rush to find one. In early January Loren and I exchanged emails. We arranged to meet up for lunch in Seattle but never got around to actually setting a day and time. I would learn of her death just like everyone else: the television. During dinner one night a friend of my mother's called and told us to turn on the TV because a small plane had crashed in to a skyscraper in Seattle. Even before my mother had the chance to turn the TV on something inside me had already explained the demise of Loren Anders. When we saw the news it was disturbing and all too reminiscent of the September 11th attacks on New York and Washington, DC. We learned that a stolen private jet had crashed in to the top floors of the AndersTower, which was where Loren's office was. The crash occurred just after 7 PM so, thankfully, nearly all of the tower's 19,000 employees were no longer in the building. Initially news reporters speculated about the incident, insisting it was a terrorist attack, possibly the work of Al Qaeda. I knew it was nothing of the sort. Loren had met the same fate that befell her parents. Since their ascendance, the Anders Family had been embroiled in a secretive, corporate war that would end up destroying them. It was a war fought in the shadows, without media scrutiny or government intervention. It was a global race for market supremacy, the modern form of colonialism. Battles were fought between allied corporations who sought resource and labor monopolies in developing nations. The Anders had worked hard to spread a movement of organized labor through South America and Asia. It was their counter punch to having to compete with corporations that exploited labor in Third World countries. The AndersGroup, unwilling to reduce their ethical standards by outsourcing their labor to countries without worker's rights, did what no other corporation had ever done. They went on the offensive and became political in foreign affairs, not through lobbying governments but by rallying and supporting social movements that would bring impoverished regions and nations in to the modern world. Their most heated battle, and the one that is speculated to have ended in the death of Loren Anders, didn't involve oil, gold or some other unsustainably rare commodity. It was silicone that killed the Anders.

The "Silicon Conflict" (or "Semiconductor Crisis") began in 1985, a year before Loren Anders was born. It started like so many skirmishes in that its origins revolved around an insignificant dispute that escalated in to something much larger. In 1985 a group of Indonesian and Malaysian microchip manufacturers formed a cartel to protect themselves from the broadly expanding industry that at the time was still widely based in the United States and Japan. This cartel, while not officially recognized by any government, acted like an organized crime circuit in that it prevented any unsanctioned microchip manufacturer from establishing manufacturing facilities in the two countries. For nearly ten years the cartel lured semiconductor manufacturers from all over the world to Southeast Asia. By 1998 when personal computers and cellular phones couldn't be manufactured quickly enough, nearly half of all the world's microchips for mobile devices were manufactured in Malaysia. If the price the cartel wanted for its chips wasn't paid they made it a point to harm any company that crossed it by aligning itself with the company's competitors. The cartel began exercising its power by starving various computer and phone makers of desperately needed technology while supplying their competitors with inexpensive microchips. AndersGroup had acquired a small South Korean microchip maker in 1996 with the hopes of expanding its fledgling operation with factories in Malaysia. When efforts to do so were successfully blocked by the cartel, AndersGroup began developing a strategy to deal with the cartel. As they watched their market share shrink while the industry boomed, a desperate plan was hatched. Throwing money at the problem, AndersGroup acquired one of the microchip makers that were allied with the cartel only to watch its factory shut down days within gaining control of the company. Knowing that no amount of money could get them a toehold in manufacturing, AndersGroup began lobbying both the U.S. State Department and World Trade Organization for a breakup of the cartel. Their complaints went without response as both the State Department and WTO proclaimed that no such cartel existed. Defeat seemed at hand, something William Anders had never seen or felt before.

At the turn of the millennium AndersGroup's foray in to microchip manufacturing was being portrayed as the company's first big debacle. Billions had been sunk in to an endeavor that had yet to make a single dollar. For a company that up until that point was venerable in its ability to acquire a deteriorating company and make it a major player, the idea that it could fail at anything began to take hold. That was until William Anders visited a microchip manufacturing facility in Indonesia. There he found working conditions abysmal. The running water was far from potable and bathroom breaks were restricted to one per ten hour shift. Factories were nothing but sweat shops for computer parts. He was horrified to learn that peripherals manufactured for the company's own operations were being produced in such conditions. William Anders made a personal appeal to every CEO of every American, Japanese, and European microchip manufacturer to visit the factories in Southeast Asia. He insisted they clean up their production facilities or else he would alert the media of the poor working conditions. Few of the CEOs followed his advice and William Anders fulfilled his promise to take American news reporters to the factory where he'd witnessed such inhumane treatment of workers. But the media turned its back. A war was looming in the Middle East and not an inch of newspaper or moment of television was dedicated to laborers in Southeast Asia. AndersGroup was facing its second defeat in the Silicon War, one that could have been trouble for the company had it not been profiting from its finance and real estate ventures.

In 2003 William Anders founded AndersCare, a humanitarian and political organization. His goal was to expose corruption in developing countries, especially those in Southeast Asia, and to bring the concept of organized labor to a hemisphere where it was still foreign. Within two years great inroads would be made by unionizing the labor forces of many of the companies that supplied the cartel's microchip manufacturers. Suddenly AndersCare was influencing the cartel's actions and watched the pact's power wane steadily until William and Cathryn Anders's helicopter exploded over Seattle and crashed in Lake Washington. To this day the crash is blamed on mechanical failure, but in circles more keenly aware of the battle the AndersGroup had been engaged, their deaths are viewed as the result of something more sinister. The few people who've investigated their deaths and the potential link it has to the Silicone Crisis have described it as an act of blowback, or unforeseeable retaliation from a group of rich thugs trying to control one of the world's fasted growing industries. Murderers exist in all societies, even global commerce. It would be naïve to presume that a company executive, aligned with a manufacturing cartel in a distant realm of the world that already mistreated its workers and deprived them of their dignity, wouldn't hire a saboteur to carry out an assassination.

Enter the family heir, Loren Anders. Suspecting her parent's death to be the result of the secret "war" they were fighting, Loren strategized for months on how to fight back. Her plan, one she crafted while getting her hair done, was one that stunned the Board of Directors at AndersGroup. Her proposal was to have AndersCare funnel money to the political campaigns of elected officials who promised to break the cartel. The plan was massively complex and met with great skepticism at AndersGroup. Corporate lawyers warned of the illegality of the effort and the project was cancelled in favor of the further promotion of organized labor. To unionize the microchip maker's labor, and not just their suppliers, would mean doing something that many human rights organizations, large and small, had advocated but failed at. Loren was warned that organized labor could result in higher semiconductor prices for the entire industry, including their own subsidiaries. But Loren didn't waiver. She figured it was only a matter of time, maybe 20 years, before the organized labor movement swept the developing world that was getting rich off high-tech. AndersGroup could either ride the wave or drive the wave of fair labor practices. Loren advocated standing on the side of human rights, not profit. Their plan was secretive but vast, employing hundreds of professional trade union experts to rally employees in cities from Kuala Lumpur to Jakarta to form labor unions with legal representation and vast financial backing. Having assumed they'd turned the tide in the war in which they were embroiled, complacency set in and the idea of a counter attack became remote. When an airplane crashed in to Loren's office it was clear the war was not over.

According to the media, the man who stole a corporate jet and flew it in to the top of the AndersTower was a mentally ill pilot longing to become famous. He had been fired by an airline after failing a random blood alcohol test – alcohol characterized as just one of his many addictions. This just a year after his wife had left him. Yet his act was carried out all too precisely. Loren Anders, as hard of a worker as she was, spent less than two hours a day actually in her office. Most of her work day was spent in meetings on lower floors or in other buildings altogether. Usually she only went up to her ceremonial office to use the bathroom, prepare for meetings or just admire the view. I'm certain the pilot who crashed the jet in to her office had to have other contacts, ones who alerted him of Loren's whereabouts. Having examined Loren's schedule from the day she was killed, I calculated she spent no more than 17 minutes in the top floor office that day. I can't help but think the whole thing was orchestrated.

The crash did not destroy AndersTower. The building withstood the collision so well that almost all employees were allowed to return to their offices the day after the crash. Of course there was substantial damage to the top of the building. The distinctive Anders arrowhead "A," formed by the sloping top floors was now missing its tip. Six other people, other than Loren and the pilot of the jet, were killed when he crashed in to the building. The fact that more people were not killed either in the building or on the street from the debris that fell from so far up was an absolute miracle. Given the accuracy of the impact and the precise timing at which the "accident" took place, I remain convinced Loren Anders was assassinated.

When a billionaire is killed lawyers are rallied. In the case of Loren Anders, a detailed and choreographed legal mechanism was put in to place the moment it was determined she was dead. Her attorneys, all 39 of them, elected one of their own to read, confirm and certify the name of her heir. In a vault far beneath the surface streets of Seattle, before the fire was fully extinguished in AndersTower, the name of the heir was read. The media had speculated she would donate her vast fortune to a long list of charities or distribute it amongst her only remaining family members – distant cousins she abhorred. Instead, she left it to one of her friends; someone the world didn't know of, someone who wasn't a member of the jet set and who wasn't already wealthy. It would all be left to someone who didn't care much for the spotlight. When Loren's lead attorney read the benefactor's name, James Leroy Minor, his reaction was visceral. "Who the fuck is James Minor?" he asked his assistant. She replied "Her friend Jimmy." The lawyer still had no recollection. She added, "You know, the gay guy who spent all that goddamn money redecorating the house in Manhattan." From what I'm told the lawyer just sighed, maybe out of disappointment or envy, I don't know. After the will was read they boarded a helicopter and flew out to my parent's home where I was staying. When they landed on the front lawn my parents assumed it was some sort of military operation taking place. Instead, five lawyers approached me, informed me of my fate and explained it was in my best interest to come with them. I refused.

It remains unclear to me why I rejected everything those lawyers were telling me. Maybe it was because I had just come to terms with living away and alone from Loren Anders. She had such great strength, so much drive and charm. I learned so many things from her. Seeing her lawyers on our front lawn made her death real and not just something on the television. The lawyers would continue to explain that my life would be in danger and my parent's house besieged by the media once my identity as the sole heir to Loren's fortune became known. I relented, told my parents to come with me, and we all got in the helicopter.

Just because I inherited Loren's wealth, didn't mean I inherited her position at AndersGroup, a company whose subsidiaries and assets have since been disassembled and sold off to companies ranging from General Electric and Boeing, to Dannon and Cadbury. Not that I cared. I had no desire to ever hold any sort of position at the corporation. I had no ambition to prove myself in the business world. I considered myself an artist, not a tycoon. I knew nothing of finance or of the global corporate power structure. Because I inherited nearly a third of all shares in AndersGroup I could have appointed a Chairman who'd appoint me as President, like Loren did, but chose not to. I left in place everything Loren had done, and began a 5 year process of liquidating all my holdings in the company. By the time I finished selling all my stock, AndersGroup had changed its name, been purchased by an investment bank, sold to a media conglomerate, and ultimately broken apart by the U.S. government in an anti-trust case that would wind up in the lap of Supreme Court justices. These proceedings were the last days of the battle the company had been engaged in – a sort of peace treaty and resolution. The Anders corporate war machine had been dissolved and obliterated and whoever it was fighting against it no longer felt threatened. After all this, I deemed it my wisest decision not to get involved in the dealings of Loren's former empire.

The Anders Family Trust, the actual thing I inherited from Loren, was a holding company with 13 employees whose sole purpose was to monitor all the family's investments, property and legal interests. They also outlined and enforced the fiduciary responsibilities the family had at AndersGroup. With $8-billion in assets, the trust made me just another one of America's growing number of billionaires. During the months of paperwork it took to place all the assets of Loren in my name, I learned of the great number of threats that had been made to her while we were friends. The security force that protected Loren, which operated just like a private Secret Service, gave me a lengthy welcome to the family when they briefed me in detail of all the threats to Loren's life they had interrupted over the years. I was disturbed to learn of a man who'd been apprehended trying to board a ferry to Shaw Island, where Loren and I were staying, when Loren's security detail, along with the Washington State patrol, found a sniper's riffle in the trunk of the man's car. Even more ominous, they told me of a van they found parked outside AndersPlace in New York City that contained enough explosives to bring down the entire residence. These two events startled Loren who demanded to be told of all threats to her, maybe to her detriment. It explained why we left Shaw Island so abruptly after committing to a long spa weekend, and why she rarely stayed at AndersPlace in Manhattan. Surely she felt she put everyone she knew in danger just by being around them.

Far from any such threat, today I live in the secluded palace William and Cathryn Anders built on Cypress Island in the San Juan Islands of Washington State. The mountainous island of 5,500 acres is remote and accessible only by private boat or seaplane. It is dense with forest and rocky bluffs, private beaches, few roads, and even fewer inhabitants. Most of the island is owned by the forest service. The few hundred remaining acres are owned by the Anders Trust. In no way is it a deserted island, thank god. There are approximately 40 other residents on Cypress Island. At last count, 19 of them were employed by the trust. It really is quite a stunning realization that so many people are involved in taking care of me. I like to think that I take care of them too, in my way. After all, it's not as if I live some lavish life of endless parties, travel, and shopping. It's mostly the house that requires so much minding. I believe most of my employees are needed for the exterior of the home. The collection of formal gardens and fountains that surround Anders House (my clever name for the home) and which I absolutely cherish, require round-the-clock maintenance. I've spent days just wondering around the intricate, ever-expanding grounds. It is pure heaven. I thank Loren everyday for leaving me this immense home. I have everything because of her. Something I've never been able to understand is why she neglected to ever visit this place. After her parents died she never once, that I know of, visited Anders House or Cypress Island, something I find strange as it was considered their primary family home. They had a city home in Seattle near AndersGroup headquarters, but this, their most stately home, was where they unwound as a family, playing softball with friends and riding horses. It was at Anders House they hosted regal events, sometimes with prime ministers and heads of state. There is even a series of photographs depicting both the Reagan and Clinton families staying at the home. From age 9 to 19 Loren lived nearly full-time on Cypress Island, away from the spotlight of the city and the liabilities that came with being rich near those who may wish to do them harm. Even when we took our little day trip to Shaw Island she failed to mention Cypress, despite it being clearly visible from the ferry.

I've tried to preserve the house just as William and Cathryn envisioned. While that takes a lot of manpower, I can't help but think what kind of impact would be made on the local economy if I were to just let nature take over the house and grounds. Upon taking up residence at Anders House, I found there was no good reason to ever leave home. If someone had told me when I was 22 that I'd live out my life on a secluded island I would have ridiculed them with something like, "Jimmy Minor loves culture and the crush of people and cars and foods found only in the modern metropolis!" I would have followed the statement with an eccentric cackle. I thought I loved the city because it was there that rich people flaunted their wealth. It was in the city I was able to observe a world I did not belong to. This was a symptom of insecurity. Now I am able to acquire anything for my own personal amusement, be it a painting or a person. The allure of living in the city has eroded. Sure, I'll travel to Seattle or New York on a whim. After all, there's something creepy about absolutely *never* leaving home. But the excitement of exploring a new or foreign city is lost on me. Sadly, they are all starting to look the same. I can't tell Baltimore from Frankfurt; Shanghai from Toronto. The only thing left to explore is myself, and having recently undergone an evaluation by a psychiatrist, I can say there is a lot of inner territory for me yet to discover, or maybe just acknowledge.

Nowadays I spend my time expanding my mind and senses. I have a chef but he is more of an instructor than a laborer. He teaches me how to cook, an art I've come to treasure, mostly because it nourishes in a way no other art form does. The meals we cook are great and vast. I insist on eating dinner with my closest employees, all 19 of them. Most nights only about 6 of them show up. The other 13 are usually busy in their personal lives, or in their job, such as my security staff. Despite that, those who do make it always have a great time. Most reliable is my personal physician, Jeffrey, who is always talking about airplanes and NASA. He's an old geezer but he's great. He's almost like a grandfather figure and besides being my doctor, he cuts my hair too. He served in the military and cutting hair was his specialty. Now his specialty is general medicine. And then there's my personal assistant, Elizabeth. She is really annoying and vain, a former publicist from Los Angeles, but she does her job exquisitely and everyone enjoys talking about her and exchanging quotes of the latest insane thing she's said. Being away from Hollywood has done her a lot of good and I've been able to watch as her life on Cypress has steadily improved. My chef Andrew is always present for dinner, as is his wife Gretchen who buys my clothes. There is an ongoing joke amongst the staff that she is my "stylist," which is actually an insult to her because, according to them, I have no style. I consider that the result of not having been to Fashion Week in so many years. Also one to never miss dinner is Carmela, my personal trainer who also makes sure my five dogs get all the exercise they need. There's also one more person who never misses dinner, and that's my personal photographer, Ari Schroeder. Ok, he's not my personal photographer. He's my husband. After Loren's death he was the first person to call and make sure I wasn't one of the casualties. During that time he was the only person I felt I could confide in. That's the thing about money. Once you have a lot of it you can't really trust anyone who didn't know you before you had it. Or, like Loren did with me, you can only befriend those who don't know about your money – at least initially.

Isolation is something most people cannot or will not appreciate. I am not one of those people. I have always cherished my independence from all things. The highlight of my existence is going to the farmer's market. Just this morning I went to the one in Anacortes, located no more than a five minute helicopter ride from the house. There I found the most magnificent little Brussels sprouts. They're a bit smaller than I prefer but a surprise for this time of season and will surely cook to perfection. Because I purchased so much from him, the man at the vegetable stand I tend to frequent gave me some carrots to try for free. Resembling arthritic toddler fingers, these little carrots are filled with more flavor than an entire bag of the steroid carrots they sell at your average supermarket. Shopping for vegetables, seeking out quality, and enjoying all forms of beauty, something I was always too rushed to do when I lived in the city, is all I need to sustain my existence.

I can't imagine still having to work. Those days, spent doing meaningless tasks, including those months spent as Loren Anders's assistant, are now so apparently wasted. Sure, our country and planet would be nothing without the working class, but I couldn't tolerate being one of them again. I know I sound so elitist saying that. But from this vantage of privilege and wealth, the only luxury I spoil myself with is the will not to work. Life is too short to spend it doing other people's business. There is so much joy to be derived from appreciating the beautiful world we are blessed with. Kayaking around the waters of the San Juan Islands, collecting paintings by Caravaggio and Hockney, learning to play piano and enjoying and noting the differences between appellations of wine, are all things I could not do fully and with as much passion as I have if I were forced to work. I often evade thinking about my life having taken another path.

There are days I feel out of touch with who I really am and become convinced that wealth has corrupted me. I get swept up in materialism and pride, wishing to destroy those who might ridicule me in the press. I counter these feelings with a trip to my former life. Not the one so expertly preserved at my parent's house, but the one in Seattle. When I became Loren's assistant my apartment in downtown Seattle was left as is. A snafu of some sort had voided my lease but not allowed the unit to be re-rented. As the heir to the Anders Trust I now own that building. From time to time I return there and become instantly humbled. The scale of that apartment is so breathtakingly small. It is a cage. One I'm so pleased to be freed from. Sometimes I'll amuse myself and pretend I still live there. That is until I start to feel I'm suffocating and run and jump in my waiting helicopter on the roof.

When I first met Loren Anders I was convinced we were the same person, aside from me being a man and she a woman, me being gay and she straight, her being rich beyond all imagination and my finances consisting of nothing but credit card debt. It is now in her shoes, so to speak, that I can say I am nothing like her. Whereas she sought glamour and a status of not just fame, but iconography, I seek anonymity. I may enjoy the tremendous monetary privilege she has bestowed upon me, but I live as modestly as one can in my position. I don't seek the things that destroyed Loren. I don't crave notoriety, I don't long to be feared, and the idea of being a celebrity, however minor, repulses me. Because I don't seek such tumultuous things, I will never have to endure Loren's excruciating bliss.

ACKNOWLEDGEMENTS

This book could not have been written without the many people who contributed to its creation, whether they realize it or not.

I want to thank my parents for instilling early in me the belief that there is a place in the world for dreamers and that dreams can only be realized by those willing to work hard. Thanks are also given to my big sister Amy, my childhood hero, who wasn't afraid to beat up any schoolyard bully who called me a fag. My fascination with strong female characters is surely the result of having had one as a hero so early on. Kim, thanks for being my first fan. Thank you New York City for kicking my ass. I needed it. Thank you Janae for showing me that someone can get everything they want without compromising. Many thanks are due to Joe and Kelli for taking a chance on a guy who had little experience and letting me wear all those different hats. Many thanks to Jennifer, Marissa, and Jason - my first readers - your words of encouragement kept me going on a journey I thought might never end.

Lastly, thank you Ian for encouraging me to take a path in life I didn't think was possible. You made me realize the world has changed and I can't cling to ideals that could never materialize. You've changed everything for the better.

www.ingramcontent.com/pod-product-compliance
Lightning Source LLC
Chambersburg PA
CBHW052025020726
47501CB00004B/1241